SEAL Team Seven Books 1-3
Connor
Logan
Zak
By
Jordan Silver

SEAL Team Seven
CONNOR
BY
Jordan Silver
Copyright© 2014 Alison Jordan

Table of Contents

SEAL Team Seven
Logan
By
Jordan Silver

Table Of Contents

SEAL Team Seven
Zak
By
Jordan Silver

Table of Contents

SEAL Team Seven
CONNOR
BY

Jordan Silver
Copyright© 2014 Alison Jordan
All Rights Reserved

Table of Contents

Chapter 1

CONNOR

"I'm here to fuck you."
She watched me from the bed as I approached her; eyes wide not with fear as much as with uncertainty. After all I hadn't given her any indication in all the months of her teasing and flirtations that I was the least bit interested. I kept my feelings well hidden from her and everyone else around me. "If you're attached to whatever that is that you're wearing I suggest you take it off because it's going to be in shreds in a second."

She made some sort of noise in her throat that was cut off when my mouth came down hard on hers. She was sweet and soft, just the way I knew she would be. Which is why I'd avoided her thus far. A woman like her has no call being with a man like me. She's sweet tea and pecan pie on a southern porch on a hot summer day I'm pizza and beer. She's cashmere and pearls in the back of a chauffeur driven limo and I'm leathers and jeans on the back of a chopper. I tried for her sake to leave her alone. No matter how much I wanted to go there I did not want to fuck up her life.

There was no way the people in her circle would ever accept me but she didn't seem to care. From the first time we'd laid eyes on each other she's let it be known through coy smiles and flirtatious laughs that she wanted to be under me. After three long months, hard as fuck months of denying myself and jacking my shit to visions of her first thing in the morning and the last thing at night, I was here to collect.

I didn't give her time to remove the lacy bits of scrap she wore instead I tore it from her body. "Oh…"
"It's okay don't be afraid I promise to take very good care of you. I'm going to turn on this light." I switched on the light next to her bed as she watched my every move. I wanted to see her, all of her.

She had tormented me since the first day I saw her. Her laugh, her smile and her sweet scent have been following me into my dreams. I looked down at her as she rested on her elbow looking at me with hungry eyes. Cool it Connor, if you go at her like you want to you'll scare her half to death, better take it nice and easy this first time. No

point in scaring her off before you even got
started.

"How did you get in here?" Her sweet
southern drawl like something out of an
antebellum flick danced over my nerve
endings.
"I picked your lock. We have to do
something about your door it's for shit.
We'll deal with that later." Or there was the
other alternative but we'll see how things
go. I laid over her on the bed pressing her
back into the mattress. I didn't want any
more words, tonight was for fucking,
branding. There'll be time enough for
talking later.
Her breasts were a dream; high and round
with pale pink tips that my tongue couldn't
wait to taste.

"Umm, fuck I knew you were gonna
be sweet." I teased her nipple with soft licks
sucking hard one minute, biting down the
next. Her body was on fire beneath me and I
could feel the softness of her thighs as they
opened to accept my weight between them. I
was still wearing my jeans and the Henley
having only kicked off my boots.

"Undress me." I pushed my hard cock
into her soft folds through my jeans as I
lifted off far enough for her to pull my shirt

over my head. I took her lips again as her hands fumbled with my zipper. Her warm hand wrapped around my length and she sighed around my tongue. I stroked into her hand once, twice. "Too soon." My cock was as hard as it had ever been and I knew that wanting her the way I did, it wouldn't take much for him to blast. I wanted inside of her sweet warmth in the worst way.

Pulling out of her hand I worked my way down her body to her heat. I inhaled her sweet scent first before lapping up her already escaping juices. I fucking knew it. Sweet fucking pussy, her taste went right through me.

What the fuck was I getting myself into here? I was way over my head. This was no one-night stand, not that I ever believed it would be. I'd come here tonight knowing she was going to rope me in, knowing that this one woman was going to be the one. I'd fought it for as long and as hard as I could but in the end it was fate.

"Connor…"She tried pulling my head away. "It's too much." Her body already started to tremble under my tongue. Fuck if she reacted this strongly to my mouth I can't wait to impale her on my cock.

"Ssh, let me have you." I gentled her with my touch, like a stallion with a mare. Licking deep inside her folds and teasing her plump clit between my fingers.

I ate her pussy until my jaw locked up on me. My cock was hard and throbbing as I climbed back up her body. Pushing my jeans all the way off with my feet I kissed her lips hungrily. Her soft skin felt amazing under my hands as they ran all over her. Opening her legs wider I fingered her sweetness plunging my fingers deep as she rode my hand to her third climax of the night. I meant to bring her off as often as I could tonight.

We'd both waited a long time for this and I didn't want to rush it when I finally got inside her. I wanted it to last I needed to brand her. The need was like a living thing inside me. Something I'd never felt before in my life, never wanted to. I sank into her as I looked into her eyes, my hands caught roughly in her hair. She made a small sound of distress as I stretched her with my thickness.

"This is what you wanted take it." I pushed into her sweet as fuck tightness until she'd swallowed all of me. Her pussy was tight, tighter than any I'd ever felt. I had to take a breath and still my movements. The lure of her was almost too much, just as I knew it would be. I stroked into her again and again because I couldn't help it. I had no defenses against her. She'd smashed down my walls. I knew what this meant, what the feelings running through me as I fucked her meant for me, for us. So be it.

"This changes everything Danielle. Do you understand?" She nodded her head yes as she bit her lip, her eyes closed, her pussy locked tight around my cock. I stopped all movement and pulled her head back farther.
"Open your eyes...I need to hear you say you understand me. This changes everything I'm not asking you I'm telling you. You wanted me, I'm here this..." I thrust hard and deep once to get her full attention. "Says you now belong to me, heart body and soul; you fuck up it's going to be your ass. Do...you...understand?"

"Yes Connor." Her eyes were wide on my face with just a hint of fear this time. I had no doubt I looked like a crazy man on top of her. I could feel the skin drawn tight against my cheekbones the way it did when I went into warrior stance. And this was the hottest battle I'd ever fought in my career.
"I'll give you time to adjust to having a man like me in your life, but heed my

warning. The you that you were when you woke up this morning no longer exist. There's no more Danielle. It's now Connor and Danielle. I'll teach you what it means to belong to me later right now I just want to fuck. Are you with me so far?"

"Yes Connor please." She curled her pussy up trying to get more of my cock inside her.

That sweet Georgia peach voice of hers is going to get her drilled into the fucking bed time and again. I lifted her legs and spread her so I could fuck her deeper and harder. There was no way I could play the gallant lover, not this first time. Maybe the next round or the one after that but this time was all about me putting my stamp on what I'd finally decided to own. I looked down at where we were joined and her eyes followed mine. She had lost all control of her body.

Gone was the prim and proper southern belle. Beneath me was a woman full of heat and passion. Her nails scored down my back as she fucked up at me trying to get my cock as deep inside her as possible. I gave her what she wanted with a hard pounding thrust that made the bed shake and bang into the wall. Her soft cries were buried in my chest as she licked and bit me there, too far gone to know what she was doing.

That's just the way I wanted her. Her ass moved wildly as her pussy milked my cock. Fuck yeah.
"I love the way you move beneath me, fuck, I always knew you were gonna be trouble. Fuck me."

We tore the sheets from the bed as we rolled over it together. Me on top her on top, me behind her. I fucked sweet Danielle until I had nothing left. It had been a while since I'd fucked. In fact not since the first time I laid eyes on her. Somehow giving what I wanted to give her to someone else seemed wrong. Even when I had no intentions on pursuing her she was all that I'd wanted, all that I'd thought about.

She lay in my arms exhausted from the rigorous fucking. Her skin was red in places where I'd been too rough but she didn't complain. "Sleep sweet Danielle I think I've ridden you enough for one night." She blushed and hid her face in my neck before settling down again. I held her close as her breathing evened out in sleep, and relaxed as I felt my freedom slipping away.

There was no way after having her that anything less than forever would be enough. I'd despaired of ever finding this with anyone. Never gave it much thought after I joined up, but one look at her and the feelings she stirred up inside me were all consuming.

She made me think of happily ever after and family. All the things I'd once sworn would never be for me. I'm just happy that I'd found her now that my life was settled. So that I would never have to leave her behind while I went into battle. I turned our bodies so I could spoon with her for the rest of the night. Until I slipped from her bed at the crack of dawn tired but energized. A night spent in the saddle like that will do that to ya.

"When will I see you again?" She wasn't in much better shape than I was as she laid back against the pillows her body still flushed from that last round of vigorous fucking. I'd grabbed a quick shower in her bathroom to wash away the heavy smell of sex but I still carried her scent on me.

"I have to go to work I'll see you after that. Do you have a lease on this place?" I kept talking as I got dressed to leave. It felt like I was leaving a limb behind or some shit. It's gonna take a while for the newness to wear off I guess. But right now I think I

needed at least a year in sweet Danielle before I would be comfortable leaving.
"No it belongs to my dad why?" Her soft voice brought me back.
"I just wanted to know how long it would be before you could move."
"Move?"

"Yeah I want you with me. That's a deal breaker. If we do this you're with me" I spoke over her as she was about to say something that I'm sure I didn't want to hear. I'd made up my mind somewhere around the third or fourth time I was fucking her.

We'd crossed the point of no return no point in fucking around now. I've seen enough to know life is too fucking short not to grab it by the balls. And when everything you ever wanted and didn't know you needed fell into your lap you'd be a dumb son of a bitch not to hold on tight. I've been many things in my life dumb has never been one of them.

"But…"
"No buts babe, I asked you if you understood and you said yes. There's no more discussion. Get your shit together I'll be back around six to get you. Stay sweet baby." She knelt in the bed with the sheet wrapped loosely around her as she reached

up for my mouth with hers. Rumpled and well fucked that's what she looked like.

"Fuck." I was out of my clothes and between her legs before she knew what hit her. "This is going to be hard and quick baby hold on." I spread her beneath me and with a cursory thrust with my fingers to make sure she wasn't too dry to take me I entered her hard. Her body bucked beneath mine as her legs came up to cradle me. Burying my face in her neck I pounded into her like I hadn't just spent the whole night inside her.

The tight grip of her pussy around my cock had me gritting my teeth against the onslaught of emotions raging through my chest. "How fucking long?" I threw the question out there as it burned through my mind. Her hands clutched at my ass pulling me harder into her heat. I wanted to fuck her all day and never stop, wanted to stay locked inside her until we were both too tired and too spent to draw our next breath.

I found her mouth with mine and ravaged it, biting into her lip as lust threatened to consume me from the inside out. "Never this fucking good." I took her ass in my hands forcing our bodies closer together. I seemed to be trying to draw her into me. To mold us together or some fuck but I couldn't stop myself.

I'd lost all control. All that mattered was this moment and the woman beneath me. The woman I was fucking so hard the bed shook and banged into the wall over and over again. I didn't care as long as she was right there with me and her wild cries coupled with her fingernails digging into my ass told me that she was. "Cum for me Danielle." I latched onto her neck and bit down hard before sucking her skin into my mouth. She screamed and I felt her warm juices flood my cock, that's all I needed to go off inside her hard and long.

We were both out of breath, both panting for air and I couldn't move. She'd done me in, sucked everything out of me. "I knew it, I fucking knew it." I rolled off of her but kept her in my arms. I couldn't even bring myself to let her go, not yet. "Are you mad that we made love again?" I looked down at her question. She seemed a bit confused, as she very well should be. I didn't even know what the fuck was going on and I'd thought I had it all figured out.

"That wasn't love making babe, that was a branding." The question is who the fuck branded who? I pulled her out of bed and headed for the shower. We washed each other in between kisses. Had I ever done this before? Why did she make me want to do sappy shit? What was it about her that made me want to be everything she'd ever wanted? This is bullshit.

"Connor what did you mean…before when we were you know?" She shrugged her shoulders and kept her head down. I pulled her head back with a tight grip in her hair so I could see into her eyes. "Fucking?" She nodded as her face heated up. Fuck me I got myself a shy girl. "Which time?" She fortified herself to look me square in the face as she answered. I could tell it was hard for her, guess she doesn't do too many morning after conversations, which is fucking A ok with yours truly.

"When you growled how long?" Fuck I hadn't even meant to say that shit out loud. "I meant how long will your pussy own me?" I reached down and pushed two fingers inside the pussy in question making her climb to her toes as her eyes closed. "Fuck Danielle, I can't fuck you all morning I've got shit to do." She bit her lip and nodded but I knew she wasn't hearing me her hips were already moving against my hand.

"Turn and face the wall." I sucked her pussy off my fingers and looked down at my cock, which seemed to have a mind of its own. I've never fucked anyone this much in my life we had to be going for the Guinness book or some shit on this one. "Cock that ass for me baby." I ran my hand down her back to her ass and then switched up. "Change of plans." I knelt behind her and lifted one of her legs for better access. I swiped my tongue the length of her pussy and she twitched. Ooh yeah. I fucked her with my tongue for a good ten minutes from behind with her leg cocked in the air while stroking my hard leaking cock.

I couldn't get enough of her pussy's taste in my mouth and she juiced a lot for her man. When my cock threatened to revolt I stood up and slid into her from behind. Wrapping my arms around her I fucked in and out of her at an easy pace. Work is gonna to have to wait.

This time was sweet and slow, no rush. My cock already knew her inside so I could take my time. The branding was over ownership had been claimed it was now bonding time. "When I get you home I think I'll fuck you for a week solid. I'll let you out of bed long enough to eat but that's it. You think your tight pussy can handle that?" I squeezed her nipples and bit into my new sweet spot on her neck. She was too far-gone to answer but I didn't need one. It is what it is and I plan to fuck her as hard and as often as I could for the next little while.

"Sometimes it will be hard, rough, sweaty and dirty as fuck. Then I'll take you like this. Nice and slow so you know your man can give you both. Now lean over and grab the wall baby." As soon as she was in place my cock went to work, plunging in and out of her like a battering ram. "Fuck yeah, you hear that?"

The slapping sound of our hips meeting was loud and the sweet sound of her pussy juice slipping and sliding all over my dick was the sweetest fucking thing I'd ever heard. Reaching around I pinched her nipples and her ass picked up speed fucking back at me hard and fast. "Connor?"

"Yeah sweetheart right here it's okay, let go I've got you." She flung her head back onto my shoulder and came on my cock with a loud groan. I wasn't too far behind her. Her pussy brought me up to my toes as I tried to dig as deep into her as it was possible to go while emptying my balls inside her with a roar.

We needed another shower and then I really had to go, my brothers were probably wondering where the fuck I was. "Don't make me wait Danielle, be ready when I come for you tonight. Now come kiss your man goodbye and try not to put too much sweet in it I need to get the fuck gone." She walked over to me holding her towel together.

I took her in my arms and kissed her cute as fuck nose. "Stay sweet baby I'll see you later." I didn't dare risk kissing her the way I wanted to again, who knows when the fuck I'd come up for air. I kissed her quick but she turned her face up for more. "I'm not sure that's a good idea babe." She pouted at me. "So fucking cute." I gave her what she wanted and then with a finger trailed down her cheek I left.

Chapter 2

CONNOR

Back at the compound where I lived with the men I considered my brothers I got ready for the day. I was getting a bit of a late start which none of the nosy fucks let me forget as they tried sticking their noses in my business as soon as I caught up with them. I was prepared for their shit, which I knew would be forthcoming. I'm the one always saying this relationship shit wasn't for me. I wasn't against it for others but it just wasn't for me.

Now I would be the first to take the plunge. I wonder if I should let them in on just what the fuck was in store for them when their time came? This all-consuming obsession that fucking ties you up in knots and owns your ass. I think I've become part bitch overnight or some shit. What the fuck am I thinking?

"Fuck Connor you smell like a bitch." "Fuck you Zak." I smacked him behind the head as I went by on my way to the coffee. The other five assholes were all staring at me like I was some sort of anomaly.

"Fuck bro I know that scent." Logan sniffed the air around me. He better not know that fucking scent.

"What the fuck! you assholes don't have anything better to do? We suddenly cleaned up the streets and we're having an off day?"
"Whose scent is it Logan?"
"I can't put my finger on it Quinn but I know it." He looked like he was really giving it some serious thought. If anyone could sniff out what's going on it would be my brothers in arms. Seven ex SEALs who'd spent the last ten years together both on duty and off. We were closer than most brothers of blood. Just this once though I wish they would mind their own damn business. I wasn't quite ready to share yet. I wanted to savor the newness of it first before life intruded. I sound like a bitch.

"If you're through sniffing my ass maybe you girls want to fill me in on how things went last night?" Anything to get the meddling fucks off the scent.
Everyone grew serious because what was going on in our little burgh was no laughing matter. Some fuck was using our backyard to traffic drugs and what we suspected might be worse or so it seemed. So far we haven't

been able to find anything but suspicions were high.

Our little town in Georgia was a perfect little out of the way haven. Its close proximity to the water and underground caves along with some other shit that we had yet to explore made it the perfect venue for criminals of a certain ilk. We knew from experience that these were the perfect breeding grounds for some serious shit. Out of the way, not really on anyone's radar. It was the ideal spot to carry out all manner of criminal activities.

We'd scoped out the area first thing to make sure we had our flanks covered from all angles. Yeah it was a bit over the top bordering on paranoid but we believed in better safe than sorry. There hadn't been any red flags but that had been almost two and a half years ago. Though we'd seen the potential for some shit if someone was of the mind to go that route.

It would appear some enterprising soul had reached that same conclusion and was now making good on it. What they didn't know was that there were now seven ex SEALs taking up residence here who were not about to let that shit happen. We've only been here less than a year. None of us had ever lived in this town before so we were new to the area. No one knew who the fuck we were and of course seven grown men descending on them out of nowhere must've been food for the fodder.

There were whispers and speculation of course but since we never answered any questions other than our names the town's people had learned not to ask. What conclusions they'd drawn on their own was anyone's guess, but we weren't really interested in that shit either. We just wanted to get settled in and do our thing while being left the fuck alone.

Bikes and tats put fear in people but if someone wanted to pass judgment without having all the facts that was on them. So far no one had approached us with any bullshit and we hoped to keep it that way. The way I see it, we didn't go around asking people who the fuck they were so they should give us the same courtesy. This was home now, one we planned to make ours and we'll fit in in our own way the way we always did.

We'd all grown up in different parts of the country but our old commander had been from right here born and raised. When he'd died three years ago. For some fucked up reason he'd left this land and all his earthly possessions to the seven of us. It had made our decision when the time came for early retirement that much easier. As members of the same team we'd each put in a few more years of service, but we'd all known from day one that we were going to not only keep the land, but we were also going to make this town our home.

Not really having any ties to any one place it was easy for us to make that decision. After years of eating, sleeping and fighting together we knew each other inside and out and trusted one another to have each other's backs. So it only made sense that we would stay close to each other when we came back to civilian life.

Two years ago we'd drawn up plans for what we wanted to do. The one thing we all knew for certain was that we wanted to stay together. There was more than enough land for the houses we wanted to build. The first thing we'd done was build up a high wall around the perimeter so no one knew what was going on inside.

The town's people thought it was some new development going up but we'd cordoned it off to start construction on the homes we were going to have built; and since we were still on active duty then we didn't want to leave the place unprotected. Not the most trusting motherfuckers I know but we trusted no one except each other.

Construction had been started six months later with each of us getting two acres. We situated our homes in such a way that they were literally right next door to each other. The land was in the back and to the front but. Off a ways from the houses we'd built our office. It's where we were planning to run our construction firm.

We'd decided a long time ago even before our commander had been so generous, that when we left the service this is what we would most likely be interested in. We could easily have gone into security or something of the like but after years spent securing land air and sea we pretty much wanted out.

The houses were done in a year and a half. We couldn't do everything ourselves because of our duties but we'd worked on each other's places when we had down time and that had sped up the process quite a bit. Six months after we'd settled in and hung out our shingle so to speak, we'd caught wind of the shit that was going on around us.

There's no way in hell we're going to let shit like that take root in our backyard. After years of fighting and danger the name of the game was peace and quiet. Now for me that shit had been amped up a notch. I have a woman to protect. I don't want this shit anywhere near her so the sooner we got to the bottom of whatever this was the better.

The town's people after realizing that we weren't here to start shit had pretty much accepted us with open arms. Well most of them had anyway and as far as they knew we were navy men. No one knew what faction we'd been working for as that shit tended to be top secret for good reason. Most of them probably still thought we were a biker gang, which we weren't. We just loved to ride. I could understand how seven rough looking fuckers all over six feet tall with tats might give them that idea but we were on some other shit.

Though we were in the midst of a recession. With our connections and the Commander's which he'd hooked us up with through papers he'd left behind, we already had some sweet jobs lined up to do construction on government buildings among other things. If things kept up and the government didn't fuck up the economy anymore than it already had we stood to stay in the black for a long time to come.

These days we did a whole other kind of demolition and I don't think any of us missed the other. War is hell. Now with this new development we were spending our nights doing recon and shit. I guess old habits died hard.

Whoever was behind it was proving to be a wily fuck though because so far we had nothing. It wasn't easy for seven men on bikes riding the streets at night to be conspicuous, especially in a town where the biggest action was bingo night at the lodge. Everyone wanted to know everything all the time.

Those who'd accepted us were mostly part of the older crowd who'd known the commander and they mostly wanted to talk about our navy days. Which was usually a short conversation unless we made shit up. We couldn't share the shit we'd done with anyone, but the old guys still liked hanging around us. We'd started hanging out at the local bar to keep our ears and eyes open but so far we hadn't seen any unknowns coming and going which led us to believe it was a local doing this shit.

"So did we find anything last night or not?"
"We think we're closing in on a few hot spots but right now the fuckers are proving to be a little slippery." Logan passed me a plate of eggs and bacon. For now since there were no women in our mix we all tended to gather at one house for meals. Today was Logan's turn for breakfast duty.

I guess to some it might seem strange for seven grown men to be this close. We pretty much did everything together. But after spending so many years together in some of the most fucked up situations imaginable we were comfortable with each other. We ate meals together we hung out together; it was very rare to find one of us alone without the others. We'll never outgrow that pack mentality I guess. I don't think any of us would know how to be any

other way at this late stage in the game. We
were in it for life.

This whole business with the trafficking thing was a bother that none of us wanted to deal with. We were all just looking to settle down and enjoy the fruits of our labor away from the fuckery. The old guy who'd first come to us with his suspicions didn't have too much information but he had enough to peak our interest. An old pal of the commander's, he knew a little more about who we were than the rest of the town so he knew we would want to know about that kind of action in our own backyard.

We'd cautioned him to stay quiet about the things he'd shared with us because we had no idea who or what we were dealing with yet. These characters didn't take too kindly to folks sticking their nose in their shit. And in our experience you could never be too careful. Sometimes the least likely suspect turned out to be the guilty party.

Him and a few of his friends who hung out down at the lodge swears there's some kind of gang activity afoot. Strange men in and out of town in the last few months and lots of foot action down on the old boardwalk after dark. He'd reported some type of vessel coming and going at strange hours every few weeks or so. It all spelt trouble to us but we tried to play it down so as not to scare the old guys half to death.

They all fashioned themselves as PIs or some shit. So to keep them from getting caught up in something that might get them hurt or worse we'd promised to look into things. I'm not sure they'd heed us about keeping their noses out of it though. These men were die-hard patriots who had lots of pride in their little burgh where most of them had spent their entire lives.

I could see why they loved the place so much. It was quaint and still full of old world charm. The old homes here were as old as the city; those old antebellum structures that conjured up visions of lawn parties and ladies in period dress. That's how I see Danielle. That old world genteel beauty and grace seemed ingrained in her.

"Huh, the old guy said he thought they were using the old boardwalk; anything show up there yet?"
"Nope, we checked over every part of that place and there was nothing. We do have that list though and we're still working down the line we'll get something. So you wanna tell your brothers why you smell like

roses?" Logan grinned as the others chimed in.

"Connor you got laid?" Zak is such an ass; my glare didn't keep his big mouth shut. They all kept trying to figure it out. "You fucks wanna mind your own damn business?" Damn it's like we were in a hole in the desert playing the waiting game. Waiting to blow some fuck's head off his body for being stupid and there was nothing to do but talk shit to and about each other to kill time. I sniffed myself to see just how strong her scent was on me. Fuck.

"Danielle Dupre." Logan snapped the front legs of the chair he'd been leaning back in back into place with a thud. "Fuck Logan." I gave him a hard glare. How the fuck did he sniff that shit out? I calmed a little when I remembered that that's how she'd first caught me. It was her scent that had brought her under my radar. After that it hadn't been hard for the rest of her to reel my ass in.

"Thought you weren't gonna go there brother?" "Is there a problem Ty?" "Nope, just saying. We had this long drawn out conversation where I told you to go for it and I distinctly remember you giving me a laundry list of reasons why that wasn't such a good idea."

"Yeah well shit changed."

"Congratulations man. So when are you bringing her home?" Logan was grinning like a proud papa the ass.

"Tonight."

"You need help with the move?"

"Nah my place is already furnished if she wants to change shit she can just buy what she needs."

"She knows she's moving in here?" Quinn asked while refilling my coffee, nosy fuck.

"Yep." That got a good laugh out of all of them but I just gave them the finger. They pretty much knew that I'd most likely ordered her as opposed to asking her.

"Let's go slackers that building isn't gonna erect itself." I pushed back from the table and got to my feet.

"We were waiting for you lover boy. You sure you got enough strength left for this?"

"Piss off Quinn." We headed out for work some in trucks some on bikes. I had to leave my bike home since I would be picking up my woman and her shit after work. My woman, fuck that felt good.

Chapter 3

We each had our part to play when it came to the business. As equal partners in a business this size and being who we are. Men who don't trust anyone outside our core, we had to handle everything ourselves. We had a secretary to field phone calls because none of us wanted to do that shit but everything else we handled ourselves.

No accountants no lawyers none of that shit. Everything was done as a team, all decisions had to be approved by all or it was a no go. So far we hadn't had any problems and weren't expecting any. We'd protected each other in some of the worst the world had to throw at us I saw no reason we couldn't do this just as well. That's what comes from having each other's best interest at heart. I never thought I'd feel that way about anyone else but my brothers. Never thought I could let anyone else get that close. Fucking Dani had done it with ease.

I didn't even mourn my freedom. I didn't feel constricted the way I always thought I would. Quite the opposite, I actually felt freer somehow. Weird fucking feeling to be looking forward to losing your freedom, this falling in love shit is a racket and women are slick as shit. All sweet smiles and come and get it looks. Leading you around by your dick. That wasn't so bad I guess, but when they wrapped themselves around your heart that's when your ass was in trouble. Shit.

We each agreed that the reason the commander had left his earthly goods to us was because he'd overheard us on plenty occasions talking about what we wanted to do when we got out. The one thing we wanted was to stay together. There was no question of that and we had two choices of what kind of business we wanted to have, security or construction.

To a man we chose construction. After living a life of uncertainty it was good when things just fell into place like they have been since we came back stateside. And our new home wasn't too shabby either. It was a far cry from what any of us had known before.

The town had about twelve thousand residents most of whom had lived her their whole lives. Not exactly a metropolis but Savannah wasn't too far away maybe forty-five minutes if we felt the need for a big city getaway. Business was looking good so far and we were slated for jobs as far away as Atlanta and even into the Carolinas.

We weren't strapped for cash. The SEALs paid pretty well and it was a good living. Especially for men who didn't have families and knew from early on what they wanted to do with their lives when they got out. The commander had also hooked us up with a good money guy after he started taking an interest in us outside of navy life.

Coming from money himself, he knew a lot of the ins and outs of that world. A world seven young guys who at the time of their meeting were from some of the worse neighborhoods in the country knew fuck all about.

He'd handpicked us right out of combat training to form the special team. We were like a force within a force, not even the navy knew what the fuck we were doing half the time. Not only had he overseen our Ops, but he'd also taken a personal interest and that's how we ended up where we are now.

It was hugely due to him and his talks that we had found ourselves on the paths we'd taken in life. I guess you can say the old man had molded us into the men we are today. Men who could be proud not only of their service to their nation, but also of who they were inside as men.

I knew for myself I'd come a long way from the hell that had been my beginnings. I didn't even want to think about that shit today. I wanted nothing to blacken my day. I'd just made a monumental change in my life. She was the best part of me, the best thing to ever come into my soiled world. Fucking amazing.

We rode through town to the jobsite no doubt looking like a caravan of thugs. I'm pretty sure this town had never been overrun by the noise of six Harleys at top speed. I never really gave two fucks what anyone thought of me, or my brothers before; but I'm guessing shacking up with Dani might change that. I played around with the thought in my head for a hot minute. Nah, not gonna happen. I still don't give a fuck. She knew what I was when she started making eyes at me. She'll deal.

We pulled into the lot where the rest of our crew was already hard at work. Our present project is an office complex that if done right would take us at least half a year from start to finish to complete and we planned on doing it right. We charged top dollar for anything we signed on for because we had other men and women to support.

Men and women that the government had fucked over after they'd lost part of themselves fighting a war not of their making. We already had a waiting list a mile long of more of our brothers and sisters looking for work. This little town was gonna be overrun with old seadogs by the time we were through because we didn't plan on leaving anyone behind.

"Hey Rosie you sure you wanna get all sweaty and shit? Might take away your girl's scent brother."

"Fuck off Quinn. They all had a god laugh at that before we got ready to do our thing.

We put aside all the bullshit as we got to work. The foundation had already been laid and the outer walls built up with reinforced steel. Logan had made the call to go back to the old way of doing things. It cost a lot more but once we explained things to the owners they were more than willing to fork over the money.

This area was prone to hurricanes and a rogue tornado or two over the last decade. When other matchstick buildings would blow in the wind we were building this one to last. We were building the first thing to be erected in Briarwood since the fifties or some shit so there was a lot of interest from the town's folk.

There was a new business whose headquarters were in Atlanta but it was cheaper for them to have offices here since Real Estate prices were insane these days.

The head guy is some type of oil tycoon or some shit with offices all over the south and Midwest. He's already making noises about hiring us to do some other jobs for him because he likes our shit. At this rate we'll be in the black for a while yet, which for a new business is always a good thing. But for the shit we want to do it's excellent.

I thought of her pretty much every other minute throughout the day. Which was fucked because I could seriously lose a limb if I wasn't paying attention. I can't believe she's mine, fuck. It's like my birthday and Xmas rolled into one. I felt like smiling all the damn time for no fucking reason whatsoever. The fuck?

The first time I ever laid eyes on Dani she was with our office manager Candy. The two women were good friends though Candy was from the complete other end of the spectrum from my girl. Dani is old southern money. Her family owns half of the fucking state while Candy's ancestors were coal miners. That's another thing I like about my girl, she doesn't put on ears like some of the other fucks around here.

We'd thrown a little party for Candy's birthday and Dani had been one of her guests. One look and I'd felt my heart hurt. That alone had convinced me to stay the fuck out of her way. I didn't like that feeling of lost control, or the way my eyes couldn't seem to help seeking her out throughout the night. Everything about this fucking woman had teased my senses. Her walk her laugh; every little thing she did. Even the way she flung her hair over her shoulders to get it out of the way.

I'd noticed her noticing me too and that hadn't made shit any easier. My dick was hard for damn near three hours that first night. And when some guy at the bar had hit on her I'd wanted to plant my fist in his face. I've never reacted that way to any woman before in my life.

Living the lifestyle I'd lived in the service I never thought it was fair to subject a woman to that shit. Never know when you might be called up or some shit. Plus I'd heard horror stories of affairs and shit and knowing me I'd probably end up doing twenty five to life so I'd steered clear. Was lucky enough to keep myself protected. I fucked when I needed to but I kept my heart out of the fucking equation.

But that night she'd followed me with her eyes as much as I was trying to pretend that I wasn't doing the same. She stood out like a jewel in a tarnished crown in her designer blouse and her silk skirt with those heels that made her legs look like sin. It had been hard as fuck ignoring the invitation in her eyes. The hunger that I saw there, but I'd done it.

I'd done it every other time our paths had crossed too; until yesterday when she'd walked by me on the sidewalk and acted like she didn't see me. I guess she'd grown tired of me ignoring her and decided to give me a taste of my own medicine. But that shit hadn't sat well with me at all. I guess you can say that was my wake up call. She'd let it be known in little ways that she was interested but I'd avoided her. Until last night!

Now she's mine and there's no going back. That shit scares the fuck out of me. I'm not the settling down type, never wanted to be. I know what I come from, the legacy the two fucks that had spawned me had passed down, and I never wanted to continue that cycle. But now here she was and everything she is forced me to put aside my prejudices against anything domestic and just go full tilt.

My brothers always joked that it would take a very special kind of woman to bring me to my knees. I guess they were right after all. Everything about her just does it for me. From her sweet as honey voice that just makes me want to fuck her into the wall every time I hear it. Her laugh that reminds me of tinkling bells, and the sweetest smile.

And I haven't even started on her kickass body; not too tall at about five foot four, she's a good foot shorter than my six four frame, small and petite. She's the beauty to my beast. She has dark hair and green eyes to my blonde and blue and everything about her just sings to the man in me.

There's still a lot I didn't know about her though, things we'll have to talk about. I had no doubt that she will catch hell from family and friends for her choice in a mate but that was too fucking bad. I'd made a promise when I was buried deep in her last night into the morning, a promise that I aim to keep.

I hope she was ready for what she'd unleashed. There were things I wanted from her that I'm not sure a girl like her would even know about. My body hardened just thinking about all the ways I wanted to love her and be loved by her. I know with a woman like that I'll have to be on top of my game.

Thankfully I'm in a position to keep her in the style she was accustomed to. But even had I not been she would've had to learn to deal. What I wanted from her was a forever kind of deal. One man one woman for all time. She's the only one to ever bring that out of me, and I'm pretty sure lightning doesn't strike twice so this was it. For both of us.

Chapter 4

My day couldn't end fast enough. I was in a hurry to get back to her, to move her out of her place and into mine. To have her where I can protect her. To some it may seem like I'm moving fast, well except my brothers. They'd understand the need for me to do things this way. And I didn't really give a fuck what others thought, especially not when it comes to my woman.

I have one way of doing this shit. All the way or not at all, and after being buried in Danielle's sweet pussy all night I knew it was going to be all the way. In fact from the first glide of my dick inside her I knew she owned my ass. So there's only one thing left to do. Tie that shit down quick.

I'd put my stamp on her last night, having her set up in my home will just seal the deal. I'll spend the next few weeks getting to know her and letting her get to know the man she'll be spending the rest of her life with. I think that's only fair since I plan on consuming her life completely from now on and there was still a lot we didn't know about each other.

I know she works running a charity with her mom but that's about all I know about her work. I know she dresses like she's walking off the pages of a fashion magazine and she smells like heaven. I also know she makes me hard just thinking about her and there's no way I'm ever going to let her go especially not after having her.

She was in my blood now, I hope like fuck she could deal with my shit. She'd made a good start last night. No matter what I threw at her she'd taken me and I'd had a lot of fucking to do. After weeks of wanting and denying myself I'd made a meal out of the poor girl. I have no doubt she'd be sore today but maybe tonight I can eat her little pussy and make it all better. Fuck there goes my dick.

"Bro you've got the biggest fucking grin on your face." Logan's voice carried across the construction yard to me so of course the other ladies heard and had to give their two cents. "Maybe we should give him the day off, he's been staring at that two by four for the last ten minutes like he's forgotten what it's for." Ty went back to spackling the wall he was working on and I ignored his ass. "I thought he was gonna kiss it there for a minute he was staring at it all lustful like." I gave Cord the finger and went back to what I'd been doing. They were right though I'd gotten lost in my head.

Shit if she was gonna affect me like this I'm gonna have to figure something out. Maybe after a couple weeks of constant fucking I can get back to normal and she wouldn't consume my every thought as she was now. I knew it would be like this, knew she'd take over my fucking life, a little bitty thing like her making a grown man sweat.

She was waiting for me when I got there later that evening. I'd barely given myself enough time to get cleaned up at the site before going to get her. I couldn't wait to bring her home with me, to have her where I can get to her at will. Not only to fuck her, but to protect her too.

Always foremost in my mind was keeping her safe. For a man like me having seen the shit the world has to offer, finding something like this, so rare to begin with. It makes you crazy thinking of ways to protect and shield. More than any nation or any high profile dignitary that needed protection, she was now my number one concern. Any fucker that even looked at her wrong was in danger.

"You ready?" I could tell that she was a little nervous but she nodded all the same and started picking up her bags.
"Leave them I'll get them." She smiled shyly at me as I walked over and wrapped her up in my arms kissing her long and hard.
"Umm, I needed that. You missed me?"
"Like crazy." She cuddled into my chest where my heart was beating out of control. It does that whenever she's anywhere near; that and my dick gets iron hard. I wanted to fuck but I wanted her home even more so I had to calm my dick the fuck down.

"You scared?"
"A little, I've never done this before."
"There's nothing to be afraid of. I told you I'd take care of you didn't I?" I looked down at her inhaling the sight of her. All I wanted to do was drag her over to the bed and fuck her into forever. But I wanted her in my bed in my home under me the next time I took her, that shit was important to me.

"Yes but shouldn't we date each other first?" She laughed shyly up at me and I couldn't resist kissing her cute little nose and her brows.

"Isn't that what we've been doing the last few months? All that flirting and those coy looks of yours? I thought that was our mating dance. It doesn't matter we're beyond that shit now let's go."

I took her stuff down in four trips. My girl had lots of clothes as was to be expected; but damn how much shit do women collect? It's a good thing I had room in the truck and a rack on top.

"Did you want to take any of this furniture with you?" If she did we'd have to rent a truck or some shit over the weekend.

"Maybe my writing table." She pointed out a piece of furniture that looked like something you'd see in a museum.

"How old is that thing?"

"It was my great great grandmother's, late seventeen hundreds I think."

Damn shit was probably worth more than my house.

"Let me help you that's heavy."

"No way Dani out of the way."

I got her settled in my truck with the desk strapped to the top and we headed for the compound, where I'd had to threaten the guys to stay hidden at least for tonight. They were all chomping at the bit to meet her officially. She would be their first sister in law so I had no worries that they would all be welcoming. I just didn't want her to be overwhelmed her first night in her new home and nothing is more overwhelming than a team of nosy as fuck ex SEALs.

She seemed to relax as we drove and I learned a little something about her; my girl is the touchy feely type. She held my hand while I drove and fuck if I didn't like that shit. Her hand was so soft and small in mine that I felt my heart clutch. Please let me do this shit right.

One of the reasons that I'd fought the attraction so hard was that I never wanted to see sadness on her beautiful face. It would kill me to fuck up her life in anyway. I just didn't see how someone like her could ever be with someone like me. Now after the night we'd shared, I cant see it any other way.

"You ever been on the back of a bike baby?" I kissed her knuckles because shit, I couldn't help myself. Even in jeans and a soft T-shirt she was hot as fuck. Her tits pushed against the material making two indentations and I knew she was turned on because her nipples were hard. It took all my concentration to stay the course and not pull over and take them into my mouth. I moved her hand to my dick, which was now trying to tear through my jeans it was so fucking hard. She blushed of course but kept it there.

"No I've never been on one before. It's looks fun but scary at the same time. I do love to watch you guys when you're riding out together though, I think it's sexy." "You do do you? What would you say if I told you you would be the first woman to ever get on one of those bikes?"

"Really? Wow, why is that?" I doubt she realized her fingers were squeezing my cock and then rubbing it out. I couldn't help pushing into her hand for more. Should I let her in on just how much power she now had over me?

There was a reason for us not letting just anyone on the back of our bikes. Like our homes that shit was sacred, yeah we're fucked up like that. There had been a great many who'd wanted the privilege but had been shot down. A fuck was a fuck but the keeper was a whole different story. A man's bike was for his keeper.

"Only a man's true mate should ever be on the back of his bike. I think our rapping brothers call it a ride or die bitch."
"Um, I'm not hip what exactly does that mean?"
"It means that if shit gets real I trust you to be there with me one hundred percent. It means through thick and thin. All the things marriage used to mean but have since fallen the fuck off. You getting this?"

"I think so but…"
"Don't sweat it right now babe. We'll go over all that shit at a later date. Just know for now that you're the only one I've ever even considered having there and that means a lot to me. It also means a huge change for you. You do realize that I'm never letting you go ever right?"

I didn't bother looking over at her to see if she accepted my dictate or not. That ship had fucking sailed when she wrapped that sweet as fuck pussy around me and sucked my life essence the fuck out of me. A man knows when he's cumming just to break one off and when he's planting seeds in a garden he wants to grow. Little Danielle's gonna find herself bred before the fucking year was out. I have no doubt. Fucking game changer.

Chapter 5

The boys were nowhere to be seen when we pulled in but I was sure the nosy fucks had us within their sights. She looked around in surprise, which was understandable. Not too many people knew what existed behind these walls. We'd built them that way purposely; our own little haven away from everything and everyone else. It just made people more curious but that was easier to deal with than being out in the open feeling exposed.

It was going to be fun to see how I did living with someone else. Pretty sure it was gonna take some getting used to. She wasn't anything like my brothers I might have to brush up on my etiquette and shit. I got out and helped her out of the truck before getting started on her million and one bags.

"Welcome home Danielle." I hugged her loosely around her middle and stole a kiss before setting her aside. Nosy fuckers were probably snickering behind windows and shit. If any of them came out here I'll flatten the fucker.

"This is beautiful Connor, Candy told me a little about the place but not much. I

think she signed a privacy clause or something." She laughed a tad uneasily. "Close enough." I lifted a couple of her bags from the truck and headed for the house before I realized that she wasn't falling in step next to me. I looked over my shoulder to find her just standing there. She looked at me in surprise. "I was kidding."
"I wasn't come on let's go before they come out here."

She searched my eyes to see if I was playing around but the truth is that her friend had had to sign something that we'd come up with to protect our privacy; we took that shit very seriously.

We've all been in some situations before that if certain people were to ever discover our identities there could be trouble. That's one of the reasons for us sticking together like this, the reason we all knew we will be spending the rest of our lives together. It had been a stroke of luck that the commander had left us this land. We would've found another place somewhere else no doubt, but this was as good as any. Plus it had saved us a fuck load of money.

"Connor I really was kidding you…"
"I know; did you eat?" I didn't want her getting scared so I needed her to drop it. The

truth is we're a clannish secretive bunch and she was now part of that shit. She'll get used to it eventually.

"No I wasn't sure what you wanted to do." She was so fucking quiet and reserved. What the hell did she see in me anyway? Fuck if I know.

"You want to go out to eat or you want to make something here?" We were finally inside and I only had a few more bags and her desk to grab.

"I'd love to make something here."

"Sounds good let me grab the rest of your stuff and I'll show you around okay sweetheart?" I couldn't resist stealing another kiss on my way out the door. So fucking sweet.

I showed her around the house after dropping her stuff off in our room. Our room, yeah I like the sound of that.

"This is all very beautiful Connor." We were standing in the middle of the sunken living room with the fireplace that was almost as tall as she was. I'd put a lot of effort into this place. At the time I had no idea someone like her would be gracing it with their presence. I'm glad now that I'd gone the extra mile.

"Yeah well it's home now so you can feel free to change anything you want. I'll set up an account for you for anything you want to do with the house. Tomorrow we'll go down to the bank and get your name on my accounts..."

"Connor don't you think that's a bit much? I'm sure you know I have money of my own I don't need to take your money."

I studied her for a long time without saying anything. How can I put this so she doesn't run out the door screaming before she'd even got settled in? And what the fuck had happened to men that women thought they had to take care of themselves even after they were under a man? A real man was supposed to take care of that shit. If she was a feminist I was about to fuck her whole program up royally because I don't play that shit. My woman's my fucking responsibility and fuck anyone who doesn't agree. The fuck!

"I take care of you from now on Danielle no debate on that. I don't care what you do with your money but anything to do with the house is on me. Your clothes and shit are on me, though you may put me in the poor house." I tried to lighten the mood because I didn't want this to turn into a thing and from what little I'd seen so far she could be a little stubborn. I didn't want that to change. She could be as stubborn as she wants with others but when it came to this, to us. I rule this shit no question.

"I don't know about that Connor." "Don't argue with me Danielle it won't work, just do as I say and we'll be fine. Let's go find something to eat." The sooner she learned that I'm not the arguing kind the better. I grew up with that shit and I'd be fucked if I'm gonna have that in my life. As far as I'm concerned there's only one way for a relationship to work. As the man it's my responsibility to love, cherish and protect. Anything that stands in the way of that is dead. It's also my place as her man to take care of her in all things and the moment she accepted me into her body for the first time she gave me that right.

She followed me into the large open-air kitchen where we scrounged around for something to cook.

"We have the makings for pasta Alfredo, salmon filets; we can fire up the grill but I'm afraid that might be a red flag to my brothers to haul ass over here."

"I don't mind." She looked over my bent shoulder into the refrigerator as I tried to find something good for our first meal together.

"I do, I want you all to myself for tonight. So what's it gonna be? I forgot to ask you're not like a vegetarian or anything are you? I never once saw you eating."

"I eat pretty much anything as long as it's dead."

"Are there live things you can eat?"

We joked and teased each other as we prepared a light meal of pasta with garlic bread and a salad. We moved smoothly together, like a well-coordinated dance routine. Every once in a while I stole a kiss or copped a feel. But I liked it best when she was the one stealing kisses and touches of her own with no prompting from me.

It felt right having her here, sitting across from her having a light conversation over a dinner that we'd prepared together, our first of many. She was my fucking reward. After a life of bullshit this amazing creature was my prize. I could do that shit all over again if I knew it would lead to this.

Fuck she owns me. How the fuck did that happen, and so effortlessly too? Just a look and a smile and she'd hooked me. Shit was more dangerous than flying mortar. I have to admit that even though I've been in some tight spots before where my life was threatened. I don't think any of them scared me as much as sitting here at this table looking at everything I always wanted and never knew I did; and praying not to fuck it up.

After dinner we cleaned up together and then had coffee. There was something plaguing me as we sat there. Something that I'd never asked another woman in my life. Never cared truth be known but with her I needed to know.

"We need to talk but we're not doing it in here, let's step outside."
She followed me out the door to the backyard. Standing in front of her it hit home just how small she really was compared to me. Last night when I'd been fucking her, her small stature had been the last thing on my mind.

Now looking down at her so tiny and fragile looking it hit home for the first time what it really meant to have a woman that you wanted for your own. How much more vulnerable she seemed. How can I protect her always? Did all men have these questions? I'll have to take that out and look at it later. There was no point in asking one of the others because they'd never been here before either, I'm the first to wade into these waters.

"Who had you?"

"What?" She took a step back. I could see that my question had thrown her but I wasn't about to let up. I needed to know.

"Last night when I took you, you weren't a virgin. Not that I expected it of a twenty five year old woman but I need to know." Just saying that shit fucked with my head. It was completely irrational but I didn't give half a fuck I needed to know.

"It was um, Robert, my ex fiancé." I could sense her discomfort and for the life of me I couldn't figure out why this shit should matter but it just did.

"How ex is ex?"

"Um, I broke up with him the day after we first met." That went right through me. That was sweet as fuck and said a lot but I'll have to come back to that later.

"Why?" I took a step closer to her taking her chin in my hand.

"Why?"

"Yes; why did you break up with him the day after you first met me?"

"You now why." Her face started to blush but I pushed on.

"Tell me." I held her eyes with mine reading the truth of her words there.

"Um because I knew I wasn't in love with him and that it wouldn't be fair."

"Good girl."

"Why did we have to come out here to talk?"

"Because I don't want talk of another man in my house, scratch that in our home. You don't have any dealings with him ever again."

"Connor."

"That's dead, not up for discussion he had you I don't want to ever hear his name pass your lips again; we clear?"

She swallowed hard and stared at me like I'd lost my mind. I very well might have but that's what's inside of me. The thought of that fucker whoever he is even breathing the same air as her fucked with my head. There's no way I'd ever believe that he wouldn't always want her.

The fact that she'd been the one to break things off told me that he probably wasn't completely out of the picture. I wouldn't believe that he wouldn't want her back. Knowing what I do now, how sweet she is, how she feels under me, around me, no fucking way. I wanted to know everything about their relationship. How long it had lasted, who'd approached who? But I didn't want to freak her out any more than I probably already had with my dominating ways, she'd find out soon enough.

"Were there any others?" The fuck Connor what's with you? She's a grown woman she wasn't sitting on a shelf somewhere waiting for your ass to come along. Doesn't matter I need to know.
"No." She turned bright red and looked at the ground.

I wasn't sure if that was worst or not. I took it in and decided to drop it for now. This shit would drive me nuts if I dwelt on it too much tonight. We were too new, still at that learning stage and I'm sure there were going to be many things from her past that I'd try to erase.

I'm territorial like that so the fuck what? I know my thinking was off, I wasn't a virgin last night either and I can't remember ever feeling this possessive of a woman before. But with her it was as if something inside me, something that had been hidden there had reared its head. The need to own her, to completely take her over in every way was strong. I look at her and all I think is 'mine' all fucking mine.
"Let's go on inside it's getting chilly out here."

Chapter 6

With my arm thrown around her shoulders I led her back inside the house and to the den. Honestly all I really wanted was to drag her off to bed. But I didn't want her thinking that that was all she meant to me, women can be strange that way. So I forced myself to sit through a movie while sitting on the couch with my arms around her, my cock hard as fuck and wondering when he was gonna get to play with her again.

"Do you mind if I ask you something Connor?" She broke the silence halfway through the film that I'd been having trouble following because her scent was getting to me.
"You can ask me anything love." I squeezed her shoulders.
"In that case I have lots of questions."

She turned that beautiful face up to me, eyes wide and bright and so beautiful she made my heart ache. I couldn't resist running my finger down her cheek and touching her lips softly with mine. "Shoot."
"Okay first, why do you all live here like this?"

"We're brothers, we made the decision a long time ago that when the time came we would do something like this. We didn't know where in the country we would've done it. We hadn't settled on any one place yet but we knew this is what we wanted. Then our commander died and left us this land so here we are." I didn't bother asking if she had a problem with the arrangement because nothing was going to change. I'll always live with my brothers and she'll always be with me. There was no point in debating it.

"Okay I think the town thinks you guys are some sort of gang or something. I mean they know you're ex military but what with the bikes and the fact that you guys are always together I think there's a little fear that you might be some kind of biker gang."
"Do you have that fear?"
"No, I like the fact that you guys are so close, it feels like you made your own family you know."

"That's exactly right baby we did and that's what makes it special, we had the choice and we chose each other. What's your next question?" She seemed to need some time to put this one into words so I squeezed her shoulder gently.

"Spit it out sweetheart it can't be that bad."
She bit her lip and bowed her head a little.

"Why did you not want to be with
me?" Her voice was barely above a whisper
and I had to bend to hear her.
"Is that what you thought, that I didn't want
you?" I had to look at her to gauge her
sincerity; I can't believe she'd been that off.
"Nothing could be farther from the truth
sweetheart, I was trying to protect you."

"Protect me? Protect me from what?"
"Me." I lifted her face to mine so she could
read the seriousness on my face. This was
probably one of the most important
conversations we'll ever have and I needed
her to understand where I was coming from.

"I don't understand. Why would I
need protection from you?"
"Because I'm not like most men baby. I live
by my own set of rules I'm never going to
be anyone's ideal of the perfect man. I don't
believe in towing the line and falling in with
everyone else. None of us do, our women
are going to have to be strong to put up with
our shit. I didn't think you were going to be
able to deal with me."

"I still don't understand."
"I'm an all or nothing kind of guy babe. If
you're with me you're with me all the way

no half stepping no looking back. There might come a time when you fuck up and I can't promise things will be easy. I'm going to expect things from you that you might not be ready to give. I'll try to be patient but you're gonna have to learn real fast because last night we crossed the point of no return."

"What does that mean?"
"It means that I now own you, that you're mine one hundred percent. It means you do what I say when I say no questions." Her body tensed beneath my arm and I tried to soothe her.
"I'm not going to abuse you baby, it's not like that; it's just that I've seen enough shit in the world that I've learned to be careful. I don't want you to ever be in danger so if I tell you not to do something and you do it anyway it might set me off."

"And what happens then?"
Oh I could see I was scaring her now. It couldn't be helped though she needed to know the truth of what she was getting herself into.
"Then you get your little ass spanked for disobeying me and for putting yourself in danger. I might overlook some things but that one's a no no."

She didn't seem to believe me so I nodded at her to let her know I was dead serious. She took a deep breath and just looked at me. She'd probably never been spanked a day in her life but I know me. I would have no problem taking a belt to her ass if she fucked up and put herself in danger. Hopefully we never got to that point ever because that's one thing I wasn't looking forward to.

"Don't worry about it baby just don't fuck up and you'll be fine."
"But how will I know?" She seemed really concerned about that so I set about trying to ease her fears.
"It's simple, no other men ever that's a given. You're free to do whatever you want to this isn't about that. But you will not go anywhere that I tell you not to. I'll need to know where you are at all times that one's not up for debate. It's more about your safety than my needing to control you though make no mistake about it Danielle I will control you. It's the only way I can do this."

"You're scaring me."
"No need to be scared I'm here to protect you and take care of you. These are just some of the things you're gonna have to get used to being with me. I gave you plenty of chances to move on Danielle, you chose to stay. Don't think I missed all those signals

babe, I didn't miss them and oh yeah. That little stunt you pulled the other day, don't do that shit again."

"What stunt was that?" Yeah like she didn't know. She yanked my chain to bring me to heal and she damn well knew it too. I can't fault her for going after what she wanted. "That day you walked right by me and pretended you didn't see me. You do some shit like that again it's gonna go very badly for you. I cant say as I liked the feeling too much so consider yourself warned. Now back to your safety. Try your best to never disobey me on that score and your ass should be safe from my belt but Danielle, the first time you break that rule will be the last you get me?"

She blushed and planted her face in my chest so I brushed her hair back soothingly. I had no doubt I was scaring the shit out of her but like I'd told her. I've seen some shit that would make the average man padlock himself in a house and never set foot among humanity ever again. There are some sick fuckers in the world and a lot of the time women find themselves at the wrong end of that evil shit. I don't know that she would ever be in that type of danger here in this little burgh but I wasn't willing to take the chance.

"Would you ever like, fold your fists and hit me?" I felt my heart clutch at her question as memories threatened to intrude, memories of the one who was supposed to protect becoming the monster. I've always believed that has to be a woman's worst nightmare. Something I could never find myself doing, I'd die first before I ever did that to her. It would kill me if I ever saw that fear and degradation in her eyes.

"No baby that's fucked, there're grown men who couldn't take one of my punches I could never come at you like that. But if you pissed me off and did something I didn't like I might tan your hide."
"Wow, I didn't know people actually did that."

" Fuck if I know what people do, but that's me. Like I said it's nothing for you to worry about just don't fuck up. There're only two things that might get me to that point. If you put yourself in danger or you fucked with another man. Outside of that your ass should be safe from my belt. As for me folding my fists and knocking you around, not only would I never do such a thing but my brothers would have my ass if I even thought of doing something like that."

"Okay, I feel better I don't think I'll be getting any beatings because I don't like putting myself in danger and I don't want anyone else but you." She turned her face up for my kiss and I took her lips willing myself to leave it at just one kiss and not jump her right then and there. The kiss heated up a little so I eased off and just held her close to me and we went back to watching the show.

It felt right sitting here with her like this too. l felt settled for the first time in my life, like everything had finally come together. As soon as the credits started rolling I turned the TV off though, my cock was about ready to rip out of my pants it was so hard.

"Time for bed." I was about to burst, it had been hours since I had her and I couldn't wait a second longer.
"I'm going to have you now." I started stripping her on the way up the stairs my hands going straight to her ass. I knelt behind her for a better look.

"I love your ass it's so fucking perfect, sweet." I bit her on her cheek and she squealed and ran before turning back to me halfway up the stairs.

"I love everything about your body, it's so strong." She was off and running again, her face red. I caught up with her in the bedroom where we started hurriedly taking off the rest of our clothes. She ran her hands over my chest and arms with her head on my chest, as she seemed to be drawing in my scent. I pulled her in close and rubbed my naked cock against the softness of her stomach.

I was hard and hurting to get inside her. There wouldn't be any foreplay tonight. One finger inside her pussy told me she was wet enough to take my length without too much trouble. I'll take care of her after, but this first time I couldn't hold off.

"Hop up here." I pulled her up in my arms with her long legs wrapped around me her pussy right over my cock, her folds cradling me. Her hips started to move slowly up and down as she masturbated my cock against her clit and back down to her slit. Taking my cock in hand I lifted her enough to reach her opening and pulled her down on me filling her.

"Yeah right there baby, you're so fucking tight." I fucked her standing up lifting and dropping her on my cock as she moaned and clenched, her juices running down my thighs.

"Give me your mouth."

Making love to her felt like nothing I'd ever felt before, she fit me like a glove. Hot, wet and tight as I stood in the middle of the room with her impaled on my cock. I held onto her ass as I fucked up into her but pretty soon that wasn't enough. I needed to be deeper inside her. The mating hadn't been fulfilled yet it was going to take a while for me to feel like I'd staked my claim, almost like imprinting myself on her in her.

"Baby I want to do you from behind." Pulling her off my cock I turned her around and propped her over the bed. I ran my cock from her clit back to her ass before she reached back and opened herself with both hands inviting me into her pink sweetness. Fuck, my mouth watered at the sight and I wanted to suck on her pussy but not as much as I wanted to fuck her. I watched as my cock forced its way inside her going deep on the first plunge.

At her screech of ahh I held still until she grew accustomed to having me in her like this. I could feel how deep I was inside her as the tip of my cock butted against the rubbery flesh of her cervix before pulling back out. I had to close my eyes against the feelings that threatened to over power me. Fuck, being inside her felt like I'd found my place, like there was nowhere else I wanted to be. This was it for me she was it for me.

"Grab the sheets babe." She fisted the sheets and I started up again. Slow and steady getting her used to having me so deep inside her. Slow and steady, that's how we made love until the need became too much and I had to fuck.

With fistfuls of her ass cheeks in my hands I fucked my little southern belle the way I'd been wanting to ever since the moment I first laid eyes on her. I needed to stake my claim here and now to own her pussy, own her. Wrapping my hand around her throat I pulled her head back so I could tongue fuck her mouth. I wanted to do things to this girl that I've never done to anyone before but was she ready for it? There was only one way to find out.

"You're driving me crazy Danielle, what the fuck did you do to me?"

She didn't have a chance to answer because my hand was cutting off her circulation as I fucked into her wildly from behind. Her fingers dragged across the bed as her body shook with the force of my hips slamming into hers.

I kissed her again my tongue buried deep in her mouth as she sucked and fought for air her pussy clenching sweetly around me as her body struggled. I was totally out of control, couldn't get deep enough inside her hot little pussy. I wanted to brand her somehow; the need to completely control was overwhelming. This is why the debutante and the ex SEAL was a bad idea the shit I needed from her sexually would probably scare her half to death.

"I need to get deeper inside you fuck…I can't…I can't…fuck…" I went out of my head as her pussy tightened and she pushed back telling me without words that she was with me all the way. Thank fuck. I pulled her hair hard pulling her head back making a deeper arch in her back. The only place we touched other than my hand in her hair was my cock in her pussy and my other hand cupping her so I could force my fingers in there with my cock.

My long pole going in and out of her looked like I was sawing her in two when I finally looked down at where we were connected. She spread her legs wider trying to ease the pressure and I released her hair and smacked her ass hard.

"Close them." She fucking came from having her ass smacked fuck yeah. My sweet innocent girl liked to play rough. We'll see.

I pulled her hands behind her back bent my knees and dipped deeper into her.

"Have you ever been fucked in the ass sweetheart?"

"No unghh." I couldn't believe how well she was taking my pounding. There was no whining about me being too rough; in fact she seemed to revel in it as she moved her ass around and around on my cock changing up her movements. I know when I finally cum it's going to be a fucking tsunami.

"I need you to cum baby I'm there, cum for me."

I touched her clit and went deep one last time as she trembled and shook in orgasm. I caught her scream in my mouth pulling her head back roughly as I emptied my nuts deep inside her womb.

Chapter 7

After cleaning up and heading to bed I was finally able to relax for the first time that day. I hadn't realized that I'd been holding my breath waiting for something to go wrong to keep her from me. But she was here now and there was nothing that could take her away, I won't let it.

"Does your parents know you're here?"

"Um, yeah I told my mom."

"And what did she say?"

"She wasn't too happy about us living together without um, marriage but she respects the fact that I'm an adult."

"That's it? That's her only issue with us that we're not married?"

"Yeah."

"Well then she won't have to worry for too long because as soon as you can arrange it we'll tie the knot."

Her head flew up off my chest where she'd been busy at work drawing patterns with her fingers and making my dick twitch. "You're going to marry me?" Why was she so fucking surprised?

"Uh yeah, what did you think we were doing here Danielle? I brought you home with me baby that should've told you something."

She ran her hand through her hair before gliding over my body to lie on my chest her face in mine.
"I don't know, I just never thought you would want to."
"So you were willing to live with me even if I wasn't offering marriage?"
"In case you haven't noticed Mr. Connor Malone I'm silly in love with you."

Now I'm the one damn near blushing. A woman like that tells you so effortlessly that she loves you can do things to a man. I suspected of course but to hear her say it in her sweet voice, no words.
"I know baby, I'm in love with you too…don't cry come 'ere." I turned her to my side and rolled so I could hold her the way I wanted to. My leg thrown over her hip my arms wrapped securely around her sheltering her from the world.

Damn how did I get so lucky? First I met my brothers all those years ago and we all just bonded for life. Then the commander who'd been the salt of the earth had pretty much taken us under his wing all those years and later leaving us this place. Now this, the most beautiful woman in the world was in love with me. It was almost too good to be true. After the childhood I'd had this was like a fairytale, something you only saw in the movies.

When I was living in hell all those years ago did I ever wish for this? Did I ever dream it was possible? I don't know but I do know I'm holding on with both arms and I'll fight to the death to keep my little piece of heaven. I pulled her in even closer inhaling her scent, running my hands over her body reveling in the fact that this was all mine.

"So it's settled we'll get married as soon as possible, there's just one thing. It's just my brothers and I none of us really have any family to speak of other than each other. My parents are long gone, well my mom is anyway I never met my dad he died before I was born. Logan's mom lives out West somewhere; she's a nice lady she kinda sees the rest of us as hers too since we're all pretty much orphans so I hope you won't be too embarrassed that my side of the church will be damn near empty."

"I don't care about that, I don't even care if we just go down to the courthouse and get it done I just want to be your wife." "No, no courthouse. I'm sure you're one of those types who dreamt of her wedding day since she was knee high to a grasshopper. Probably have your dream dress picked out and everything so no. You'll have your dream wedding, just give me a figure and I'll get you a check."

"No Connor…"
"Babe I know the people around here think we're poor soldiers but we're not hurting for cash. One of the things the commander did when we were younger was teach us how to manage our money very well. He taught us how to play the market among other things to safeguard our funds. Now Quinn is better at that shit than the rest of us so he handles that, but trust me none of us are hurting and the business as young as it is is doing pretty good. We have enough contracts to see us through a good couple years so I don't want you to worry okay."

"Okay, but you do know the bride's family is supposed to pay for the wedding right? It's tradition."
Fuck I know about weddings and shit? "If it's tradition and they want to then by all means I won't stand in their way, but I want to contribute as well. Now lets get some sleep we both have work tomorrow.

"Connor?"
"Yeah sweetie?" I squeezed her shoulders.

"Would you like to meet my mom and dad?"
"I'd love to meet your parents." Shit I've
never met anyone's parents before. I'd
joined the service straight out of high school
and the girls I'd messed around with back
then weren't the sort that you had to meet
their parents. The poor boy from the wrong
part of town didn't exactly mix with the
higher ups. Now look where I'd landed; with
the cream of the fucking crop.

She likes to take care of me. That's the first thing I noticed the next morning when I went downstairs after my shower. I'd had her up against the wall in the shower stall as the water poured down on us. Her legs wrapped around my waist as I went in and out of her stroking nice and easy. I could get used to this shit, having her pussy first thing in the morning. The only reason I hadn't had her again during the night is because I knew she had to be sore. Hard fucking two nights in a row would do that to you.

So I'd behaved like the perfect gentleman all through the night only allowing myself to cup her pussy as I slept behind her. A few finger thrusts while I rubbed my leaky cock against her fine ass was all I allowed myself but as soon as morning came I was in that pussy again. I hope she didn't get tired of me fucking her anytime soon because I seriously didn't see any let up in sight anytime in the near future. And as sweet as her pussy was shit, morning evening noon and night is what I'm thinking.

In the kitchen she was making me breakfast, already dressed in her silk blouse and linen skirt and high heels that made her calves look amazing. She wore pearls around her neck and that damn perfume that made me hard as a fucking rock. She was busy making me bacon and eggs with toast and potatoes and all I could do was shake my head. She couldn't be real, the whole fucking package and she'd just dropped right into my fucking lap.

"Hey honey I'm making you breakfast, a nice southern spread. You didn't have any grits in the cupboard so I'll pick some up later." She turned to me over her shoulder with that smile of hers.
"Not sure about the grits sweetheart."

"You'll love my cheesy grits honey I promise." That sugar sweet voice of hers. I was looking forward to listening to that for the rest of my life. She had to scratch her leg or something and as she lifted the edge of her skirt I caught sight of the top of thigh highs with a garter belt.

"That's it turn off the stove."

"Huh?" She didn't have time for anything else because my mouth came down on hers and I consumed her with a kiss before turning her around in front of the sink. I lifted her skirt pushed the seat of her panties aside and wrestled with my zipper freeing my cock and slamming into her.

She squealed and her body shook. "Fuck baby did I hurt you?"
"No keep going I like it, I like the way you lose control." She was already out of breath and her pussy was doing its thing sucking my cock in.

"You drive me fucking crazy, your pussy is so good baby. I'll try to be quick and not mess up your clothes." I wasn't sure about her skirt though because my hands were rough as I pushed it up higher around her waist. The sight of those damn garters made me ravenous.

"From now on you have to always wear garters under your skirts and dresses." I pounded into her pushing her body into the edge of the sink with each thrust. I wanted to go slow but fuck I couldn't it was as if my dick had a mind of its own. He was on some seek and conquer mission or some shit. Or it could just be that her pussy owned us.

"Fuck baby why can't I ever get deep enough inside you?" It was true, no matter how far inside her I went I wanted to get deeper. The picture we made was highly erotic. Like an old fashioned story the lady of the manor and the stable boy. We were so completely opposite to each other in every way.

The sight of my large work roughened hands on her peaches and cream skin made me even harder inside her. This is why I was sure it was going to take some time before I got enough of her. Why I was pretty sure I was going to be in her as often as I could get my cock up. That contrast, the way she fulfilled every dream I never even knew I had. I bit into her neck too overcome to do anything else before I growled like a wild beast and emptied inside her. When I finally pulled out after her body settled, she was a limp mess.

"Oh shoot I'm leaking."
She cupped her pussy as she ran to the downstairs bath to clean up. She was such a funny sight toddling on her heels skirt tucked up around her waist as she tried to catch my sperm as it ran out of her…oh fuck. I sat down hard in the chair. I hadn't worn a condom. Again. It seems like I was always forgetting. Or was I subconsciously

trying to tie her down? I've never ridden bareback with anyone else before, not once in thirty-four years. How could I not have remembered? But she felt so fucking good. I knew it was gonna happen. Knew I was gonna work towards that eventually but we hadn't talked about it. Fuck. I was at least going to give her a few months to get settled in here before planting my kid in her.

"What's wrong Connor why aren't you eating?" She went to get me coffee when she reentered the room.
"Sweetie are you on birth control?" She stopped short and looked at me like Bambi caught in the headlights.
"No, I'm allergic so the few times I uh, ahem…we used a condom."

"What do you mean the few times wasn't it a regular thing?"
"Um no, you see…you sure you want to bring that up in here?"
"You're right let's head out back." She brought her coffee and I took mine. You'll never guess that she was just bent over the

kitchen sink getting drilled hard. She was all put together not a hair out of place.

"Okay so tell me."

"Robert and I dated in high school that's when we uh, you know. Then I went away to school and so did he and we kind of grew apart until a year ago when we met again and hit it off."

" Don't say his name...go on you went away to school, and..." I wasn't too jazzed about hearing about this shit first thing in the morning and especially not after having just fucked my woman but I guess she had a point to make.

"Well, I wasn't in a rush to hop back into bed with him, maybe that should've told me something." She mumbled that last part to herself but I heard her loud and clear. "Anyway I decided I wanted to wait until after the wedding. It's one thing to experiment when you're a teenager with hormones making you crazy and quite another as a grown woman who wants to do things right."

"Uh babe I fucked you on our first date, in fact that wasn't even a date."
"Yeah but I didn't have a choice you just took me over."
"Any regrets?"
"Nope I wouldn't change a thing."

"So he had you when you were eighteen, fine I can live with that that brings us back to the birth control thing."
"I'm sorry I forgot."
"Not your fault sweetheart we'll deal with it as it comes."
"Would you be terribly upset if I was?"

I had to think about that seriously for a minute, fatherhood. It wasn't something I'd ever given much thought to that's for sure. Until her, I could see us raising a couple kids together very happily. Before I could answer though I saw six strapping men heading our way.

"Shit brace yourself here comes my nosy ass brothers."
She shifted her body closer to mine as the men drew near and I felt it in the gut. She'd done that shit subconsciously, just gravitated to me. I liked the fuck out of that shit. My arm went around her shoulders as they stopped in front of us.

"Unhand the beauty brother it's our turn. Hello Danielle we're the brothers, I'm

Logan, this is Zak, Tyler, Quinn, Cord and Devon." Each guy came forward to give her a hug. I was watching to make sure she didn't become too overwhelmed by the hulks but she seemed to be holding her own. She'd met them before of course the night of the party but this was different, now she was being greeted as the new little sister.

"Welcome to the family lil sister."
"Why thank you Zak that's mighty nice of you."
"Do you cook?"

"Geez Tyler, she just got here don't run her off with your appetite already." Cord punched him in the arm. Ty is a greedy fuck. Next to combat, eating is his favorite thing; it's a running joke among us. Tyler just shrugged off Cord's ribbing as per usual that boy made no bones about his eating habits.

"As a matter of fact I do. Why don't you boys come on over to our house for dinner tonight around seven? That'll give me plenty of time to put together something nice."
Our house, like the sound of that too.

Their mouths were all hanging open in shock and I have to say I was a little

dumbstruck myself. Not that I'd expected her to snub them or anything. It's just I have these ideas in my head of a southern debutante which she was to the bottom of her tiny little feet. But she's been smashing them left and right. Full of surprises my little Danielle.

"What is it, what are y'all staring at?"
"You're gonna cook for us, all of us?"

"Why yes Quinn I am. Now are there any allergies or any dislikes I should know about?"
"Turnips I hate fu…uh freaking turnips."

"That's alright Devon you can swear I hate turnips myself nasty things."
I was pretty proud of my girl as my brothers beamed at her and her generosity. "Alright clear out I have to get my girl to work I'll see you lot in a little bit." I led her back inside while the others went about their business. Breakfast was cold by now but I still wolfed mine down while she picked at hers. "You ready to head out babe?" I took the dishes to the sink and rinsed before putting them in the machine. "Come on you'll be late."

"Connor you don't have to take me it's no trouble for the car to come pick me

up here." She stood to get her brief case and purse before following me out the door.

"No way baby I'm going to be away from you all day let me enjoy these last few minutes."

I got a kiss for that before helping her into the truck; I stole another one when I belted her into her seat. Can't stay away from her, it's going to be hell being away from her all day. Maybe the guys were right

and I needed to take some time off and just spend it inside her until this gnawing need was at least under control.

"So what is it that you do anyway?"
"My family runs a charity and I'm the new vice president under mom."
"Yeah? What kind of things do you do I'm not too familiar with this stuff?" I held her hand in mine as I maneuvered in and out of traffic.

"We raise funds for different causes like the new wing at the hospital that's so badly needed, that's our latest project. Um sometimes I have to attend state dinners and

throw parties but we usually use the estate for that."
"You like it?"

"I love it, it's very fulfilling being able to help others who're in need."

We talked about our jobs and shared some childhood stories, which I steered more towards hers than mine. My childhood was fucked and not something I was in too much of a hurry to share.

Hers sounded like something out of a fairy tale, which is what I kind of expected. She'd grown up with the American dream. Cheerleader, junior pageants, which she seemed a bit embarrassed about and family vacations. That was great at least one of us will have something like that to pass on to our kids.

"It sounds perfect babe. Makes me wonder why you'd ever want to get tangled up with the likes of me; don't answer that it's too late now. I've had a taste of you now and you're stuck." She blushed and hid her head in my shoulder, which meant I had to kiss her hair.

I dropped her off at the front of her office building and watched her walk in before turning around and heading to the site. Fucking unreal. I'm in jeans and work boots and my woman wears silk and pearls. I had a big stupid ass grin on my face as I pulled onto the lot though.

Logan the unofficial head of our little family came to meet me as I climbed out of the truck.

"You did good brother she's a keeper."

"Yeah it's unbelievable. Who knows maybe there's hope for you and your girl."

"Nah I don't think it's in the cards for me brother but I'm happy for you though."

Hardheaded fuck. I decided to leave it alone for now but I knew that if I could find my perfect girl there was nothing stopping my brothers from doing the same. A week ago I would've been singing a different tune but now shit, my Danielle is starting to make me believe in miracles.

Chapter 8

I got caught up in measurements and fittings as the morning progressed. The first floor of the structure was almost complete we had six more floors to go. Pretty soon we were going to have to hire more hands because the work was pouring in but we needed to find the best. We'd already discussed it, with the recession in full swing there were plenty of people looking for work but we had to take our time and sift through until we found the perfect fit. We'd all decided our first choice were vets we knew better than most how much they needed it. But that's another story for another time.

"Who's making the lunch run?" Shit time had flown, I'd been so caught up in my head I hadn't realized it was that time already. Just a few more hours and she'll be back in my arms. Geez Malone when did you become a bitch? I shook my head at my inner musings I've been doing that a lot lately, talking to myself.

"I think it's lover boy's turn." I threw a piece of wood at Tyler, which he ducked.

"Fine I'll go what do you animals want?" I pulled off my work gloves and took a swig from my water bottle.

"Turkey club for me extra mayo."

"Yes Logan we know you have the same damn thing everyday."

I took their orders and headed off to the center of town where the only decent restaurant was located. I called in the order on the way so it would be ready for pickup when I got there. This way I could just park out front and run in; a quick in and out.

I walked right up to the counter where the middle-aged waitress Anita was getting my stuff together and got an idea. Pulling my phone I called her.

"Hey sweetie did you have lunch?"

"Not yet I'm swamped, I think maybe I'll grab something a little later."

"How do I get to you?"

"Just ask at the front desk."

She sounded excited which made me feel like I'd made the right call. I ordered her the salad she asked for and added a sandwich. I don't think salad was a substantial enough meal for lunch. I exchanged small talk with Anita while I waited for them to fill the new order before heading out.

At the front desk they were expecting me and I headed up to her office. She was all smiles when she saw me and got up from her desk to greet me.

"Hi."

"Hi." I couldn't help kissing her so I did just that. I pulled her in close and kissed her, her taste going straight to my dick.

"Well now Danielle I sure hope that's your Connor."

She pulled away red in the face. "Momma shh."

There was an older woman maybe in her forties standing in the doorway smiling at us. She was tiny like her daughter but that's where the similarities ended. Where my Dani was dark she was light. I guess she must look like her dad, which would make him one beautiful man.

"I can see the questions Mr. Connor. She takes after her great great grandmother on her father's side she got none of me or her daddy."

"Momma this is Connor, Connor this is my mom Catherine."

"Pleased to meet you ma'am."

"The pleasure's all mine son now my girl has been buzzing all day about a wedding. I know you're just here to bring her lunch but maybe one evening soon you two can come up to the house and we can go over some things. Her daddy might need some working on. He's very fond of his little girl he isn't going to take too kindly to her living in sin, so I'm thinking we'd better get this wedding business squared away right quick."

"Yes ma'am how about Friday night? We already have plans for this evening." "That'll be just fine gives me time to soften him up a bit, Jeremiah's bark is worse than his bite not to worry." She patted my shoulder before leaving us again.

"So I guess I'll see you later, you need to pick up anything for tonight?" "Yes I do so maybe I can leave a little earlier. It's no problem for me to get a ride to the store and back to your place except…"

"Except what?" I pushed the hair back from her face as she bit her lip looking embarrassed again.

"I don't have a key."

"Shit how could I be so stupid?" I took my house key off the chain and passed it off to her with some cash.

"I'll see you around five then I guess, you call me if you need anything."

"I will thanks honey."

Damn. I stole one more kiss before leaving her.

"What took you so long bro?"

"Shut up Ty, come and get it boys." I passed out their food and ignored the looks.

"You went to see her didn't you?"

"Not that it's any of your business Zak but yes, I took my girl some lunch. Anything else you nosy asses want to know?"

"Yes does she have a sister, any friends?"

"No find your own woman brother; I met the mother, we're having dinner with her folks Friday night."

"How was the mother?" That was Logan for you get right to the heart of the matter.

"She was actually pretty cool, nothing at all like I expected." I gave Logan a pointed look, which he ignored.

They went about their lunch asking me a million and one questions like they'd never had a woman before. Granted she was the first of the sisters, we all knew that whatever women we brought into our midst had to fit in. And since she'd won them over this morning and was cooking for them tonight she was already off to a good start. They seemed almost as excited as I was to have her with us. Poor thing I hope she could keep up with this bunch.

That evening when I got to the house the smells hit me at the door. She was in the kitchen wearing soft worn jeans and a t-shirt. This time she had diamond studs in her ears and her hair was up in a sexy ponytail high on her head. She looked like a high school cheerleader. All soft and pink and fresh like she'd just left the shower. I walked over and wrapped her in my arms from behind, dirty work clothes and all.

"Hey you."
That smile she turned up to me always hits me in the heart. I wonder how long it'll take me to get used to the idea of her, of us. It still seems so unreal, like I'm going to wake up any moment to find it was all just a dream.

"I love you Danielle Susannah."
There I'd said it first and nothing blew the fuck up. Somehow saying it first felt different to just saying I love you too. That's probably why my gut felt like it was tied in knots bigger than my fist. I never thought I'd be saying that shit to anyone. But I'm a man who believes in facing shit head on.

I'm in love with her all the way, totally and completely gone.

"I love you more." She nibbled on my lip as she turned in my arms.
"I doubt it but it's good you think so. I'm gonna go clean up and come help you, I expect those animals will be here soon."
"That's no problem I've got it under control. I got some beer and stuff for you guys, I wasn't sure what you liked so I got a mix."
"Damn are you sure you're real? What are you making anyway?"

"Chicken fried chicken with peppered gravy, skillet cornbread, fried okra and baked macaroni."
"Geez baby that shit sounds like a lot of work. You sure you don't need me to do anything?"
" Nope I've got it all taken care of I like doing this stuff don't worry. You go get yourself together and come keep me company."
"You're the best." I stole one more kiss before heading upstairs for my shower.

The guys were showing up when I came back downstairs. Ty of course was one of the first. I could sense the melancholy in him. He was probably thinking about his own Georgia peach. The little filly has been giving him the eye since we got here but like me he was playing it safe.

Feeling the way I feel today I have no idea why I fought it so hard. Hopefully he wouldn't wait too long to come to his senses. I didn't even try to bring that shit up though because he'll just shoot me down. My brothers are very good at sticking their noses in but when it comes to getting them to take their own advice it's like pulling teeth.

Pretty soon the kitchen was full of people as us guys stood around with beers in hand shooting the breeze. The atmosphere was light, the air sweet with her scent and the food she was making. She'd set the dining room table with these fancy dishes that I guess she brought over with her.

"You didn't need to break out the good china for this bunch babe, they would've been fine with paper plates."
"They're our first guests Connor be civil."
She bumped me out of the way with her hip.

"He's two minutes out the cave little sister don't pay him no mind." Cord grinned at the left hook I halfheartedly threw his way.

We headed out back while she finished doing her thing. The talk had turned to the trouble that was brewing in the town and since she wasn't going to be touched by that shit ever we headed out of hearing distance. That's sort of an unspoken rule among the men.

Our women, no matter who they maybe are to be sheltered from the fuckery of the world. It's a bit archaic but who gives a fuck? It's who we are and any woman we ended up with will have to understand. Danielle with her soft sweet as pie ass did not need to be dealing with drug trafficking and criminal bullshit. As my woman her biggest worry in life from now on should be what the fuck to wear, that's it and I don't give a fuck who agrees.

They still hadn't been able to find anything that would help us get to the bottom of what was going on. There was evidence of activity down on the pier but the few nights the guys had staked out the place without me they hadn't found anything suspicious.

"So what's our next move?"

"Fuck if I know but we have to do something soon before those old guys decide to take things into their own hands, that won't be good." Logan swigged his beer as the rest of us sat around my back patio overlooking the pool. It gave me ideas about late night skinny-dipping with my girl. I'll have to gag her though if we were going to be doing anything more than swimming because she can get loud when shit gets hot. And Danielle naked in a pool beneath the stars, shit will definitely get hot fast.

I tuned back into the conversation when my body started responding to the shit in my head.
"Well we definitely know something's going on there but what? Is it drugs, human trafficking, what? There isn't anyone here that sends up a red flag and we've looked into the towns around us. There's some potential there but nothing we can pin down. I say we set up some sort of surveillance out there and see what we get."

"I like that idea Ty, I don't want anything fucking up our little paradise here." Devon was the youngest by a year. Of all of us he must've had the best childhood until he was fourteen and his parents got killed in a car crash. Then shit went to hell fast when he ended up with a drunken uncle who liked talking with his fists. He was the only who had grown up with a family and if not stellar surroundings at least they were better than the rest of us had. I thought for sure he would be the first to settle down because it's all he's ever wanted. To get out and find a nice woman and set up shop in a nice place, a place like this.

"Maybe we should've called the cops let them handle it, we're civilians now remember?"
"We'll never be just civilians Cord and besides we don't have anything to take to the cops except rumors that we ourselves have yet to substantiate. No I think Ty has the right idea, we just have to find the best way to do that shit. I hear your woman coming bro." Logan turned to the door just as she appeared. Ears like a fucking hawk. "Food's ready boys."

There was a stampede into the house where she had a spread set out family style in the never before used dining room. I think we all stood around for a good minute after she was seated, just taking it in before grabbing our own seats. She'd gone out of her way to make it nice. The table was set and there were flower petals of all things strewn across the top of it. She'd even put little tea candles in glass jars with marbles or some shit in the bottoms in the middle of it. I felt like a proud husband every time my brothers complimented her on her efforts.

"Man Danielle, are you hung up on this guy? Because I'm just as good looking as he is."
"Shut up Ty, hands off my girl."
"Can't blame a guy for trying."
"Thanks for the compliment Ty that's very sweet."
"So what's for dessert?"
"You're a pig bro."
"What? I know this nice southern girl wouldn't serve us dinner without dessert."
"And you will be right, I made a nice pecan pie, we'll have it with some vanilla bean ice cream."
"Sweet."
"You guys have KP." I warned the greedy fucks as they cleaned their plates.
"For a meal like this I'll even mop the floor." Devon was forking food into his mouth like it was his last meal.

Chapter 9

Later that night after all was quiet again I had her on her hands and knees on the bathroom floor. It was wild and deep and out of control. She'd taken a shower and was putting moisturizer on her face when I came in and got a look at her, with just a towel wrapped around her.

I'd only meant to nibble on her neck and cop a feel. But the towel slipped and I got a feel of her flesh and that's all it took for me to take her down. I ate her pussy while she leaned over the vanity counter, until she leaked into my mouth. Her hand reached back pulling my face into her as I tongued her clit before burying my tongue deep inside her.

When she begged me in her sweet voice to fuck her I'd almost lost it and that's how she ended up in this predicament. I had no doubt her knees were hurting on the hard marble floor as I pounded into her without let up.

"Hold on baby this is gonna be short and sweet." Her ass bounced with each plunge of my cock, and when she leaned her shoulders closer to the floor I went deeper. I could see the pink of her pussy as my cock pulled out.

"I want to fuck your ass so bad baby, fuck." Just the thought of my cock slicing through her sweet ass brought me to the brink. I guess she liked the idea as well because she screamed. Her pussy locked me inside and I felt the hot rush of her pussy's sweetness as she came and came while I kept plowing away unit my cock was dry heaving into her.

We were both breathless and limp but I had enough strength left to pick her up and take her to bed.
"I don't want you to wash my scent off of you. I want to hold you all night with my cum inside you."
She cooed and buried her face in my neck.

Life was damn near perfect for the next few days as we got into the groove of living together. We moved around each other like we'd been doing it for a long time. We fucked more than we did anything else in that first week. Our dinner at her parents' place had been postponed because her dad had to go out of town for a business matter and her mom apparently always traveled with him. It was a family tradition she said she wanted us to keep as well. Never spending the night away from each other. I could get with that no problem.

She had all these cute little quirks that I just fell in love with the more time we spent together. Like the way she twitched her nose when she watched TV. Or the way she held her tongue between her teeth when she was concentrating really hard on something. I found myself touching her all the time for no reason other than that I could. I especially love the way she curls herself around me in bed when it's time to sleep. It's getting so I can hardly remember not having her there with me. She'd worked herself completely into my life in just a short space of time.

My brothers too treated her like she'd always been a part of our family. They spent the evenings regaling her with tales of my wayward past until I kicked them all out. She'd cooked for them three evenings out of the last six she was here and I was ready to tell them to quit, until she let me know she really enjoyed it. Seems my girl likes trying out her culinary skills on her new brothers. And they were only too happy to let her.

So that's where we were a week after the big move. She was settling in, I was learning how to live with someone female. Which was easier than I'd thought it would be. I loved seeing her makeup bottles and perfume and what not scattered around the bathroom counter. Or seeing her clothes hanging next to mine.

I guess it was a good thing I'd learned to be tidy in the Navy because my baby was not into tidying up. She was use to having maids and shit to do that for her so it was taking her a while to get into the habit of picking up behind herself. She had no shame in admitting that though she loved to cook she hated everything else that had to do with housekeeping. Laundry was her worst nightmare. She was so cute as she tried to figure out the washing machine while I stood in the door of the laundry room watching her.

When she gets flustered and frustrated she cusses, but not your average cuss words. No my woman's too well bred for that. She says things like bugger and drat and frak. Cute as hell.

"Baby I'm going to be gone for a little bit tonight okay. You'll be fine here by

yourself. Unless you want to call Candy over for company."
"I just might do that I haven't seen her since I moved in. She comes to the office after I've gone and leaves before I get home in the evenings."
"Good then you should call her up."
"Will do."

She didn't bother asking me where I was headed because I'd told her that sometimes the guys and I had to go out in the evenings. I'd only told her a little of what we were doing, there was no sense in scaring her. And besides like I said I'm of the mindset that there're just some things a woman doesn't need to worry about.

My brothers and I have been patrolling the boardwalk for the past few nights but still we hadn't seen anything that we could use. There was definitely more foot traffic there after sunset but nothing to give us reason to believe there was anything illegal going down. Still the old man who had come to us didn't strike me as a flake so we didn't want to give up too soon. Could be someone had gotten wind of our presence and was watching and waiting. If that was the case then we were going to have to change shit up.

We took our bikes down to the pier.
The boardwalk had been fixed up sometime
in the last two years and there was talk of
putting up rides and shit for the kids. But for
now there were just a few benches here and
there along the rail that overlooked the water
and a few flowerpots. Someone was making
noise about building a little ice cream shop
down here, which wouldn't hurt. There was
room for a lot of development but I'm not
sure what if anything was going to happen.
Right now our only interest is in keeping the
riffraff out.

Briarwood was a quiet little town. The
history wasn't as rich as some of its
neighbors but it had seen its colorful days.
The coast had once been a haven for pirates
who made it this far down from the keys and
as legend has it, there had been plenty of
smuggling going on back then too.

Like most southern towns it had the
taint of slavery attached to its history but
today it was a diverse place with the
descendants of both parties still in existence
if old man Connelly was to be believed. He
was something of the town historian. He and
his crew of four hung around at the lodge or
the local restaurant telling tall tales. These

days they were more concerned with the goings on down here by the water.

"I see tracks over here but that could be anybody, maybe high school kids fooling around out here."
We'd spread out over the grassy area above the water's edge. The pier went out about fifty feet, not long by any means but this little inlet didn't need much more than that.

Leading off to the sides were grassy areas that could do with cutting. At the end was a little wooden building that had been closed since the repairs. There was space underneath where you could walk on the sand if the water wasn't too high and that's where we concentrated our efforts next.

If anyone was meeting out here for illegal purposes this would be the best place for them to hide. It was out of sight of anyone coming in either direction and with the absence of any lights it was more than suitable for a meet. Old man Connelly had said he was sure this is where they were meeting whoever they were. But so far we had yet to see any evidence of that in the few weeks we'd been on the lookout. There was never anything left behind to say that someone had been here.

"We've got cigarette butts."
Devon was crouched down with a penlight pointed towards the ground. We'd left our bikes and walked in on the off chance that tonight would be our lucky night and we'd actually catch the culprits in the act. It wouldn't do to show our hand too soon. Seven men showing up on bikes might tip them off.

We all gathered around the place where Dev indicated.
"That could be anyone bro, high school kids smoke too you know."
"Yes Quinn I know but I don't think they're hiding under piers in the dark to do it. These weren't here the last time we were out here. I say we bag them and see what we see."

"Do it." Logan passed him a napkin to wrap the three butts in and we searched the area for anything else that might've been left behind that we could possibly use. It was a far cry from our assignments in the service. At least there was no threat of imminent danger. Not yet anyway, piece of cake.

"We get a brand off those butts Dev?" Devon studied one of the butts he'd picked up with tweezers and studied it under the penlight.

"Shit this is no kid bro. These are Dunhill Blue. Imports and a little too expensive for your average high school punk." Well shit. I was hoping against hope that there was nothing here. Even with everything I've seen in life I was really hoping not to have to deal with fuckery for at least the next little while, and especially not in my own backyard. But there could be no valid reason for anyone to be in this particular spot unless they were up to no good.

"So they were here since the last time we were; fuck. Looks like we've got something here after all guys maybe we should look a little more see what else we come up with." We spent a good hour scouring the brush with no luck before Logan called a halt. I was ready to get back to my woman anyway.

"I still say we figure out how to set up surveillance out here the sooner the

better. I have a bad feeling about this even though we haven't seen anything so far. In fact that in itself bothers the fuck outta me. If whoever this is is good enough to hide from us then this is no small town outfit. This could be serious shit." Tyler looked around at the quiet around us where darkness had fallen hard in the last hour or so that we'd been out here.

"I'm with you brother something's going on. I just can't quite put my finger on it yet. But right now I just want to get home to my woman doesn't look like anything is going down here tonight."
"That's right brother rub it in."

There was a lot of ribbing and bullshitting around as we headed back to our bikes and headed for home. I knew the guys were just teasing but I couldn't help feeling a little sad that they hadn't found what I had. Not for lack of the local female population trying. My brothers have never had a problem attracting the ladies, none of us have. But like me they were all set in their ways and the women who caught them were going to have to be something special; like my Danielle. Damn it felt good knowing I was heading home to her.

"Baby where are you?" I called out for her as soon as I entered the house. After years of living alone it sure felt good to have someone to come home to. The fact that she was the sexiest thing on two legs was just the icing on the cake. I dropped my jacket over a chair in the kitchen as I walked through the house. There were no lights on downstairs except for a little side lamp that she'd no doubt left on for me.

Damn I don't remember anyone doing something so simply thoughtful for me except for my brothers, in a long time if ever. My mother sure never had. But I wasn't about to let thoughts of her and any of the bullshit from my past intrude here. All I wanted was my girl.

She was in the bedroom on the bed surrounded by a ton of papers.
"What's up baby what're you doing?"
"It's for work I have to send a proposal and they want all this information before they will even consider supporting the project."
I leaned over her to take her mouth, felt like I hadn't kissed her in way too long.

"Find anything?"
"Not gonna answer that babe, I told you before I left the only reason I told you where

I was going is because you need to know your man is not out there doing you wrong, but you don't get involved in this no way no how."

"But maybe I can help I do know the area better than you guys."

I looked at her long enough that she could get the seriousness of what I was about to say to her.

"You don't ever get involved in this do you understand me? It's not exactly Baghdad; if my brothers and I can handle that shit then we can certainly handle whatever is going on here. Now that's the last time we're gonna discuss it and Danielle, don't question me again. I told you before if I tell you not to do something it's for your own good."

She didn't look too pleased but she backed down, good girl. I don't want her anywhere near anything that could be potentially dangerous, that's what she has me for to stand between her and danger. There was no give in me on that.

Having seen the shit I've seen over the years I know how important it is to protect what's mine. Someone like her who I'm sure have been sheltered her whole life wouldn't understand but in time hopefully she will. "I'm hopping in the shower be right back." One long hot kiss and I was gone.

I took my shower while she finished up her paperwork before bed. I didn't even bother with pajamas just came into the bedroom with my dick swinging. She was lying there waiting for me. I took a moment to study her as she reclined against the pillows.

Her hair spread out in a wild untamed mess and her long legs looking sexy as sin beneath the tail of my oversized shirt. She must've felt my stare because she turned to me, a smile breaking out across her magnificently beautiful face. My heart gave a little tug as I grinned back at her. I can't believe she's mine. If I'd ever wished for anything I could've never imagined her.

"Lose the shirt baby." I walked towards the bed purposefully, her eyes following my every move. I saw the flush of heat as she pulled the shirt off over her head, exposing her beautiful breasts and her newly waxed pussy. I'm going to be a real pig tonight because the sight of her made me iron hard and my mouth water. "Open your legs for me."

She spread herself open for me to climb between her thighs. I started at her smooth pussy lips licking her with my tongue. She tasted sweet and spicy as I slipped it farther inside. Lifting her ass in my hands I ate her as she lost all control and fucked my tongue hard. My cock was more than ready for some action so I made my way up her body. I teased her navel with my cock tip before grabbing my swollen cock and straddling her chest so she could suck me off.

Her mouth opened and she swallowed my cock head licking the pre cum. She took me in and sucked me deeper into her throat. I wanted so badly to fuck her face but she wasn't ready for that shit yet so I eased off. There was cock juice and spit running down her chin onto her chest as I fucked back and forth into her mouth slowly. My hands held her head in place for my thrusts; her cheeks were puffed out her throat working overtime.

"That's good baby." I eased out of her mouth and kissed my way down her chest nibbling on her nipples and fingering her pussy until I was in position between her thighs. I felt around for her pussy opening with my cock head before pushing in.

"You okay baby?" She made this hurt noise when I pushed into her like maybe I'd gone too deep too fast so I held still. "Give me your mouth." She lifted her head so I could take her lips as I started moving. "Open your legs wider."

She pulled her legs open and held them up with her arms as I dug deeper into her. "Your fucking pussy babe, what the fuck?" I didn't know a pussy could feel this good, like I never wanted to leave the sweet haven of her body. The cute little noises she made only made me want to pound her harder, faster. I slammed into her with each thrust her pussy's grip tight. Her eyes held mine, and her mouth was opened in amazement as she fucked back at me.

"Hold up your tit for me babe." She lifted her breast up for my mouth to explore. I sucked on her plump nipple and my cock grew even longer and harder inside her. I ground into her trying to bury my cock in the end of her. Her nails down my back, and her heels digging into my ass trying to get me even deeper inside her was just adding fuel to the fire.

"I'm cumming Connor, ahhh." She tightened around me just before I felt her release around me.

"Again, I want you to cum again." One hand went to her clit to help her along. Her body was flush with heat as she sought release.

"I'm glad you're not on birth control, I want to plant a kid in you. I'm going to plant a kid in you." The thought of breeding her made me fuck her harder. Lifting her ass in my hands I pulled her tighter to me as I buried my face in her neck and sucked. She scratched my back hard as I pulled the flesh of her neck between my teeth.

"Yeah baby that's right cum for me." She came with a loud cry and I emptied inside her. Once again I didn't let her go clean up but pulled her into my side to sleep.

Chapter 10

We went through what was fast becoming our morning routine the next day. Except this morning there was a knock on the door and Ty came in. My girl didn't miss a beat just stepped over to the fridge and got more eggs. I was about to give him the stink eye to get him out. He was messing with my morning kitchen sex. But he was soon joined by the others so there was no point. These fuckers have no shame. They each pulled up a chair after grabbing a cup of coffee as if they were invited.

"Morning folks, sorry but this bunch smelt cinnamon rolls and there was no stopping them, I tried bro."
"Yeah thanks Logan I'm sure you tried really hard." Cock blocking fucks.
"Dude homemade cinnamon rolls that's almost worth breaking the bro code. They smell amazing Danielle."
"Thanks Logan there's more than enough I made plenty." She seemed happy enough to have them all here waiting to be fed as she opened the oven and removed the savory offerings. I thought Ty would snatch the plate from her hand with his greedy impatient ass.

They fell on them like starving wolves and pretty soon the plate of twenty or more was clean. She made a mountain of eggs and rashes of bacon while I made another pot of coffee.

"You freaks better not make this a habit."

"No deal bro, this shit is too good. Don't mean to sound sexist Danielle but as the only lil sister around here looks like you're going to be having cook duty." Ty was busy stuffing his face as usual the pig.
"The hell she is, go get your own woman to cook for you."
"Selfish bro, that's just plain selfish and mean."
"Whatever."

We cleaned up the kitchen when we were done and I headed out behind them to take her to work. We held hands the whole drive over as we talked about what she wanted to do that evening. I had yet to take my woman on a date but she seemed content to just stay in for now. Fine by me, I'm not the out and about type but I'm sure she was accustomed to that shit.

"I'll see you later baby." She leaned over for her kiss and I tried not to suck her face off.
"Later."

I watched her walk in and then headed to work feeling lighter than I ever have in my life.

There was no time for mooning over my girl the rest of the morning I had shit to do. I volunteered to make the lunch run even though it wasn't my turn, which opened a shit storm of bullshit.

"Okay lover boy just don't forget to bring back lunch."
"Fuck off Zak."
"Say hello to our girl bro."
"What makes you guys so sure that I'm going to see her?"
"Uh, you volunteered to make a lunch run dude, dead give away."
"Whatever I'll be back."

I called ahead as usual and placed my order with a little something extra for my girl. I jumped out of my truck out front full of excitement like I hadn't just seen her hours ago. I had to smile to myself at how much I felt like a kid again.

Not that I ever really felt like a kid before. But I imagine this is how they felt on Xmas morning or in the summer when school was out. I headed for the counter where my order was being packaged but was brought up short in the middle of the room when my body reacted.

What the fuck? I only felt that tingle in my body when Dani was close and she was at work on the other side of town. I got my shit and was about to call her to make sure she was okay. Couldn't think of any other reason for my sensing her this strong when she wasn't here. A quick scan of the room didn't turn up anything but it was as I was leaving that I heard her voice. She sounded...upset?

I walked around the huge potted plant that blocked a part of the room from view and my heart stopped. She was sitting at a table with some stuff shirt who seemed to be playing tug of war with her hand. My first instinct was to fuck everybody's shit up. I couldn't see through the red haze that covered my eyes as I set my body in fighter stance. But it was her next words that pulled me back from the brink just a little.

"Quit it Robert I thought you said you needed to talk."
"Get your fucking hands off her asshole."
She almost jumped out of her chair when she heard my voice.
"Connor..."

"I'll deal with you later. You, hands, now."
The little fuck released her hand and
glowered at me when I stepped closer.
"Who is this person Danielle?" She looked
at me as she stood and came over to my
side.
"This is Connor Robert."

"Him? That's who you think you're
going to marry? Your father will never
allow you to marry this…this person."
Twenty five to life that's all I thought when
I looked at him so I tamped down on the
anger and ignored his dumb ass. As long as
he wasn't touching her anymore the fucker
could live. "I'll watch where I put my hands
next time boy. I'm not too jazzed about
motherfuckers touching what's mine. This is
your one and only warning."

"Say goodbye Danielle." I didn't give
her time as I pulled her out of the restaurant
behind me.
"Connor I can explain."
"Don't talk to me right now you fucked up."
"I'm sorry I was just…"
"Shut your fucking mouth, I warned you."
I put her in the truck and belted her in. I was
so furious it took me two tries to get that shit
right.

"Connor…" She tried again but I was
in no mood to hear her.

For the first time in my life I came very close to striking a woman. Something I would never have imagined myself capable of.

"I told you to shut your fucking mouth." I dropped my hand quickly from her jaw; what the fuck was I doing? I didn't even realize I'd grabbed her face hard enough to leave impressions in her skin. I needed to calm the fuck down and quick. People were already looking as they passed by on the street.

No way was I going to be that fucking person. The asshole came to the doorway of the restaurant but had the good sense not to say a fucking word. I'm not sure I would've been able to walk away a second time. I gave him a look that had him taking a quick step back and had to be satisfied with that for now. I knew this fucker wasn't completely out of the picture. I hope he understood that today was his one and only shot though. Next time there will be blood. I hopped into the driver's seat and sped off back to the site. She didn't say anything else but she was scared; good she needs to be.

I dropped the sacks of food on the table where my brothers usually gathered to have lunch when I got back to the site.

"I have something to take care of I won't be back for the rest of the day." Logan hawk eyed me as I turned to leave.

"Hold it, what's going on?"
"It's personal." I was barely holding onto my sanity by a thread here and I needed to be the fuck gone.
"Yeah and we're your family we don't hide shit from each other." The others sensing something was up stood around us.

"Is that Danielle in the truck?" Tyler looked in the direction of the truck and the others followed suit.

"What's going on Connor? Something happen to her?" Logan came to stand in front of me.
"Just let me deal with this shit I'll talk to you guys later."

"Connor you move from here we're gonna have problems. I know you brother I can read you like a book so I can see the fumes coming off you. Talk to me, we've been in tighter spots than this before and pulled through. Now what the fuck happened in the last half an hour to turn you into Killer?"

I don't think my brothers have ever called me that shit off the battlefield. It's the name they'd given me years ago because according to them when we were in the field my whole persona changed and I went into some other place in my head. They might not be too far off the mark with this one.

I wanted to commit murder. I can't believe she met this guy after I told her not to.

"What did she do bro?" Quinn watched me like he was ready to jump if I made the wrong move.

Fuck, I really didn't want to do this here and now. I just wanted to get her alone so I could deal with whatever the fuck that was. But I know these men. If they think I'm a danger to her they'll never stand the fuck down. "I caught her with her ex Quinn that's what the fuck she did."

"No way bro, she's in love with you anyone can see that shit."

"Well I saw them with my own two eyes Dev."

"Could you have misunderstood the situation?"

I made to head back to the truck but Logan got in my way again. "That's what I'm going to find out."

"Not like this you're not, you need to calm the fuck down before you do something we'll all regret."
"I'm cool."
"Zak get her out of there."

"Zak don't go near her; I said I'm fine, now either you trust me or you don't." I had to stare down each of my brothers to get them to back off. If I was freaking them out this much I can only imagine what she was feeling.

It took them a minute but eventually they stood down.
"Just stay cool brother we're here if you need us."
I nodded my head at Logan in understanding though I wasn't sure how cool I was gonna be dealing with this fucked up situation.

I walked away before they changed their minds. I knew that each of them had grown fond of her in a short space of time. They all knew what finding the one meant. We all knew this about each other.

It's not like we'd sat around and discussed the shit like a bunch of women. But we each knew how important it was. What it meant for one of us to bring a woman home. They'd all seen me struggle with whether or not to pursue her when she kept sending out signals. She was one of us now, but she'd fucked up. Now I have to go see just how much.

Back in the truck I didn't say anything to her as I started it and drove off. I didn't talk to her the whole way home, just concentrated on driving and trying to get a handle on the anger that was burning in my gut. I could see that she was nervous as I drove through the gates of home but I didn't care. I didn't try to reassure her when she looked at me with pleading eyes. A deal's a deal. With me there was no room for screw-ups. Two things, I'd asked her for two fucking things and we weren't even in a month yet and she pulls this shit.

"Get inside." She jumped out of the truck and ran to the house. I wasn't quite sure what I intended to do to her, I just knew that she'd been warned. The memory of his hands on her burned into my brain as I got out and followed her. She stood in the middle of the kitchen wringing her hands nervously as I walked in. I just stood there and looked at her for what felt like hours as I tried to calm myself down.

"Come here." She did the wrong thing then when she shook her head and backed away from me.

"Don't fucking run from me Danielle I said come here."
"No Connor please you're scaring me."
"Come...here."

She still didn't move towards me and that just pissed me off farther. Before I could think better of it I was removing my belt and she took off running. "Don't make me come after you baby." I followed her retreating form out of the kitchen, anger burning in my gut. My woman fucking ran from me.

"Connor quit it I didn't do anything." She was crying and pleading as she tried to escape me. I caught up with her on the stairs and grabbed her arm, pulling her around. I don't think I've ever been that mad in my fucking life. She'd run from me like I was some kind of fucking monster. This on top of what I'd just seen was almost too much for me to take.

"Where in the fuck are you going?" She kept her eyes on the leather belt in my hand.
"What did I tell you about seeing him?" I pulled her forward and glared into her face. I didn't care that her eyes were filled with terror. In that moment I didn't give a fuck about anything but getting the picture of the two of them together out of my head.

"I wasn't seeing him he called and said he wanted to talk I felt, I felt..."

"You felt what Danielle, what the fuck did you feel?" I shook her when she didn't say anything more.

"I just wanted to keep the peace. I felt I owed him an explanation after the way I'd just broken things off. Someone told him about us. I was just trying to keep things calm."

"That's all bullshit. I told you to stay away from that fuck and you let him put his hands on you?"

"He didn't..."

"I saw him with his fucking hands on you don't lie to me."

"Please I didn't mean anything by it."

"I've never hit a woman in my life but right now I could smack the shit out of you. I don't know what the fuck to do with this."

"You don't have to do anything because nothing happened." Her body was trembling in my hands and I found myself in the precarious position of wanting to reassure her and tan her ass at the same time. I looked at her and some of her fear finally penetrated. I'd never wanted to see that look on her face. Never wanted to be the one to put it on any woman's face. And especially not the one I was supposed to love above all others.

"This is fucked. Do you know how close I came to hitting you? I refuse to let you destroy me. I've spent my whole life trying not to be this person and in one day look at what the fuck you brought me to. Was it worth it to see him huh?"
She didn't answer me just hung her head and cried. "Connor I'm sorry I didn't think...please."

"Look I'm the fuck out of here, I think I need to get the fuck away from you right now."
"No Connor, please I'm sorry it won't happen again I'm sorry." She grabbed onto me as I turned to head back down the stairs.

My brothers were right I needed to calm the fuck down before I did something I'd regret. With this much anger and heat I'd only end up doing more damage than good anyway. I felt empty as fuck. Disappointed, disillusioned, all the things I've been trying to avoid my whole fucking life when it came to this relationship bullshit.

"Get off of me, I don't know what to believe right now. You told me you understood you fucking lied; you do not want to fuck with me on this shit."

My head was too hot; I knew that was a dangerous thing for her. Knew that in the next few minutes I could start down a road that might taint our relationship forever. I was so fucking pissed right then though that it almost didn't matter. This is the reason I'd made her swear that she understood. The memory of that asshole's hands on her kept playing over and over in my head.

She cried harder and held onto me instead of trying to get away like she had been. I looked down at her, her tearstained face was now even more afraid than before. Her eyes wide with fear, not of my belt but of me walking away. I couldn't say anything to her for the longest time, couldn't do anything but just look at her. I was trying to come to terms with what I'd almost done; the weight of the belt in my hand was almost sickening.

Looking into her eyes seeing the agony there was like a bucket of cold water in my face. I grabbed her neck and pulled her forward into my chest.

"Stop crying I'm not gonna hurt you I will never hurt you okay."
"But you're gonna leave me." She cried harder and grabbed onto me with both hands

as though she could keep me there by sheer will alone.

I hugged her closer and took a deep breath. I didn't know what the fuck I wanted to do; this was new territory for me. I've never felt the urge to fight over a woman, never wanted to slap the shit out of one either.

For all I know it could've been as innocent as she said but the fact still remained that she'd gone behind my back and did the one thing I'd asked her not to. That shit stuck in my craw, if I couldn't trust her then there was nothing. The thought fucking gutted me.

"Look at me." She turned her face up to me, and I studied her. I had to get her to understand so that this would never happen again. I never wanted to reach this point ever again in my life. I have no problem spanking her ass this is not about that. But I would be damned if I'm going to raise my hand to her when I was this angry. I knew that I could really hurt her if I did that shit. So how do I get past this? How do I work this so we never end up here again?

"You fucked up royally baby, this is not something I take lightly. I told you I didn't want you anywhere near him again. I laid my cards on the table there was no room for misunderstanding. You fucking disrespected me so you know what. Before I do something that I'll regret I think it best that I stay the fuck away from you for the next little while."

"Where are you going?" She tried running after me as I turned to walk away. "I have to get back to the job site."
"Can't you stay and talk to me?"

"No Danielle, I have nothing more to say. Why don't you figure out what you want? I'm done, what you almost caused me to do is not something I can just shove under the rug. You have to decide if you can live with what I want from you, if you can't then I'll help you move your shit when I get back."

I felt sick when I got back in my truck and headed back to work. I wanted to go hunt that fucker down and put my hand through his face after all, but this wasn't about him. She's the one who fucked up, he has no loyalty to me she's supposed to. Besides if I put my hands on that fucker he'd end up dead.

I wasn't too worried about that crack he'd made about her father. I wasn't marrying him if he couldn't accept me then fuck him too. Maybe it was a good thing that this had happened now, when we were still fresh, still new. I guess I should feel some relief that I'd been able to pull back and not go through with it. But all I felt was drained.

I had a lot of shit to think about in the next few hours before I went back to her. I wasn't ready to try to understand her reasoning, as fat as I'm concerned she had none. Fuck. If we get past this I'm going to drive this shit home once and for all because I'm never going there again.

Chapter 11

My brothers eyed me the rest of the day like a ticking time bomb about to detonate. I ignored them too and took out my frustration on hammer and nails. Each time I tried to make sense of the situation I came up empty. I was trying like hell to get a handle on my anger but I kept coming back to one thing. She'd disobeyed. It wasn't like there was room for misinterpretation. I don't want you anywhere near him again is as plain as it gets as far as I'm concerned.

I guess I wasn't doing a very good job of containing my anger because the others kept their distance though I could sense their eyes on me every once in a while. I ignored them and did my thing. I had to put it away for now to clear my head. I wasn't getting anywhere going round and round in my head. I was still pissed, nothing had changed there.

Of course Logan was the one to approach me a little while later.
"So how did it go brother?"
"We're good."

"Don't feed me that bullshit bro, talk."
"She fucked up big time Lo. I don't even know what to do with this shit. I told her to stay the fuck away from this guy and what does she do?"

"I'm sure she didn't mean anything by it. You can't make me believe that she has any interest in this guy. We've all seen her with you Connor, she lights the fuck up when you're around. And when you're not looking she fucking eats you alive with her eyes bro."

By now the others had joined us and of course I had to hear their input as well. Everyone had pretty much the same take. Dani would never cheat on me. That wasn't necessarily my problem the problem was she disobeyed.

"Guys you know what this is about, I can't have her being disobedient. What if some shit happens and she doesn't listen and gets hurt?"
"You're thinking like a SEAL bro..."
"I am a fucking SEAL Zak."
"You know what I mean. This is civilian life they don't think the way we do she doesn't see it as being disobedient she's just you know..."

"Did she tell you why she was with him?" Ty was usually the more silent of the group except when it comes to food. He especially steered away from talks about relationships. That's why it was so surprising that he'd been the one hounding me about going after Danielle. So I know out of everyone he would stand for her.

"Yeah, something about explaining things to him. Someone told him about us and I guess she never told him why she broke up with him months ago and he wanted to know."
"That seems reasonable to me, and they were in a public place bro, it's not like she met him at a hotel or some shit."

"I know that Quinn but you're all missing the point, I told her not to do it. If I tell my woman not to do something I expect her to follow orders."
"Bro do you hear yourself? This is not the battlefield."
"You think so Cord? It's the toughest one yet bro. Wait until it's your turn and we'll see how the rest of you handle your shit."

I went back to work, done with the conversation. I didn't expect anyone to understand why I felt the way I did. As close as we all were there were some things that I'd never shared with my brothers, just as I'm sure there were some things they kept close to the vest as well.

I'd grown up hard and rough in one of the toughest inner cities of the nation. Gang bangers and turf wars were an everyday thing. Going to school was like walking through a minefield most days but that was outside. It's what went on inside behind closed doors that scarred me for life. A disinterested mother and an alcoholic abusive stepfather who thought it was fun to use me as an ashtray on a good day and a football on the others.

By the time I was thirteen I'd suffered more broken bones and black eyes than a professional prizefighter but still no one stepped in. No one seemed to notice the scrawny little kid who was just drifting away right before their very eyes. Worse than the beatings and the abuse though was the way those two treated each other. Although they were my worst nightmare they were all I had and the screaming and fighting between those two made me sick with fear.

If anything happened what would happen to me? Where would I end up? I used to count down the years until it was time to get out. I'd set my sights on the service as my fastest way out; that had been my goal. But in the meantime I had to endure them; it was from them I learned my first distrust of the human race. I saw the infidelity and the beatings, the name-calling and the degradation.

I promised myself then that I would never hit a woman. That I would never find myself in a relationship with such contention. In my head I'd decided that the woman I met and fell in love with some day would be perfect, we'd never fight, never argue. As a grown man I knew that was just a pipe dream but I still didn't want any of that shit in my life. What Danielle did today took me back to a dark place that I thought I'd escaped from, a place I never wanted to revisit again in this lifetime.

By the time I reached the house that evening I still wasn't any closer to knowing what the fuck I wanted to do about the situation. She was in the kitchen when I walked in but I just walked right by her and up the stairs to the shower. I had my head buried under the water's spray when I felt arms wrap around me from behind.

I didn't turn, not even when she laid her head on my back. I'd spent the last half hour questioning whether or not I could live without this. Whether I could go the rest of my life without her in it. That's how scared this shit had made me. I would rather spend the rest of my life alone than to relive my past. But I knew I could never live without her now. I'd had her; her sweetness had seeped into me and wrapped me up tight. I'd fucking die without her.

I pulled her around in front of me pushing her hair back so I could see her face. Her red puffy eyes told me she'd spent the afternoon crying. I pulled her to me and kissed her hard holding her as close as I could before pushing her away again. We studied each other for the longest time without saying a word.

"You do this shit to me again I'll fucking kill you Danielle and be done with it. Do you understand me?" I shook her for emphasis as her eyes filled up with tears. Dragging her against me I took her mouth hard lifting her so she straddled my hips. "Put me inside you." Her hand reached between us and fed my cock into her pussy.

"Now fuck me like you're sorry." She slid up and down the length of my cock. It was then I realized how long my cock really was as she lifted herself on and off of it. When it bent for the third time I took her down to the bottom of the shower and fucked into her hard.

"This is your punishment." I pounded into her as the water washed over us. I fucked her hard and deep working off all the fucking anger that was still burning inside. When I couldn't get the friction I needed because of the hard surface beneath her I pulled her up and with her pussy still locked around my dick headed out of the shower. I barely ran a towel over us before throwing it to the floor and heading for the bed.

I didn't talk to her. There were no soft words and touches. I knew damn well I was using my dick to punish her ass and she knew that shit too. I held her eyes with mine as I plunged into her over and over again. Lifting her legs all the way up and out, I held her ankles open wide and watched as my cock sliced into her pink swollen pussy.

"Play with your clit." Her fingers came down to touch her clit as I fucked her deep. Bending over double I took her nipple into my mouth and sucked hard before biting into it hard enough to make her scream. She came all over my cock and went wild. Fuck yeah baby. I pounded even harder trying to erase the anger, trying to exorcise it inside her.

"Connor…" She tried to ease off my dick by sliding up the bed but I followed. "Stay." I pulled her back onto my cock hard as fuck. Dropping her legs I stopped moving inside her and wrapped my hand around her throat. "Look at me. Who do you belong to?"
"You Connor, please…" She started crying again but fuck that, she fucked up she wasn't getting off that fucking easy.

"That's right, this is mine." I thrust into her hard once. "You are mine, all of you. Turn over." I pulled my cock out and waited. She got up on her hands and knees and I slipped my dick back into her. Grabbing a fistful of her hair I fucked into her trying to release the anger and the pain.

I wasn't careful with her this time like I usually am. Instead I fucked her the way I've always wanted to. I bit into the skin between her neck and shoulder as I held her hair tight and pounded into her, going deep. She begged me not to hurt her pussy anymore but I didn't stop. I wanted her to feel pain, the same way she'd made me fucking bleed.

"Next time I won't hold back. Next time I will whip your ass black and blue. Give me your fucking tongue." She turned her head and fed me her tongue as I lifted her almost straight with her back to y chest. My cock pounded up into her hard and fast until I came hard and long with an animalistic growl.

She dropped onto the bed holding her hurt pussy. "That little stunt you pulled just cost you your fucking freedom." I went back to the bathroom to finish cleaning up. My head was still hot but not as fucked up as it was earlier. I now find myself in the position of having to deal with her in a way I never would've expected.

She's my little southern belle, she's soft and sweet and should be treated like the princess she is. But now there's going to be another element added. All the shit I'd held off from doing to and with her because I thought she was too soft was now on the fucking table. She'd unleashed the bastard in me, now she could deal with that shit.

She was sitting on the side of the bed looking like she'd just come through a storm. I didn't have time for that shit either, I'd be fucked if she was gonna get away with disobeying me. "Let's eat." I walked out of the room wearing my jeans and nothing else. I was fucking starved suddenly. She'd made a roast and potatoes.

I set the table and waited for her to come down. She wasn't walking too straight when she finally showed up but I didn't have time to care about that shit either. She sat and played with her food until that shit got on my nerves. "Eat." She looked up at me like I was a stranger; she better believe she'd never seen this motherfucker before. I looked at her and down at her fork until she picked that shit up and started eating. There was nothing said for a good five minutes. I was too busy slicing into my meat and imagining that fucker's face.

"Connor."
"What is it?" I didn't even bother to look at her.
"I'm sorry."
"Yeah well you should be." That was the end of that. We went back to eating in silence.

Chapter 12

We were finally getting somewhere with the fuckery that was going on in the town. It wasn't much but it was a start. The cigarette brand that we'd found was only sold in one town remotely close to Briarwood so that pinned it down. The town of Blue Fin was an affluential area with industry big wigs and those secretive motherfuckers that owned everything. The ones you never heard shit about.

We couldn't exactly go around asking questions in a place like that so we had to try piecing everything together behind the scenes. Old man Connelly didn't know of any connections between the two towns but promised to do some digging on the sly. There was no way to keep him from doing that shit so all we could do was make sure he was being careful.

We still hadn't been able to set up surveillance because there was no good time to do shit the way it would do the most good. But Logan said he was working on it. That was his shit so we left him to it. We did put ears down there though which so far hadn't picked up anything useful. Either they had a routine as to when they visited the pier or they weren't meeting in the same spot anymore. And since there hadn't been any more cigarette butts we were more inclined to believe they hadn't been back since. We'd left a few from the last time so there wouldn't be any suspicions, just in case the fuckers were that diligent. Then again if they were they wouldn't have left them in the first place.

At least the nights out got me out of the house and away from Danielle's sulking ass. She usually spent the time on the phone with her girls, probably discussing what a dick I am. I give a fuck.

For two weeks I stayed on her ass. I drove her to and from work and when it was my turn to do a lunch run I took her lunch. My brothers did it the other days. They hadn't said anything more about the situation and I didn't bring it up. What was there to say?

They still had dinner with us most nights and I'm sure they could sense the tension in the air. The only time there wasn't tension is when I was fucking her. Then there was a whole other kind of tension. I wasn't as mad at her as before but I was still pissed that she'd done that shit.

She was into walking around me like she expected me to lose my shit any second and that was beginning to wear on my nerves too. She didn't seem to understand I was just waiting for her to get what she'd fucking done wrong. She'd said sorry a million times but I still don't think she understood how serious this shit was to me. Or what the fuck it is she was supposed to be sorry for.

To her it might've been an innocent meeting to clear the air as she'd claimed. To me it was my woman disobeying me. And not just disobeying me but doing it with the fucker she'd once been engaged to, the only other man to have her. Maybe I'm wrong, maybe this shit shouldn't mean anything, but fuck it meant something to me. I didn't even want the fucker breathing farther more being in the same room as her.

We were sitting at the dinner table once more. She'd tried playing the 'I'll eat later' card a few nights ago and I'd nipped that shit in the bud. I'm sure she thinks I'm being too hard on her but she has no idea. I'm trying to avoid any future fuck ups of this magnitude because there's no guarantee I'll be able to hold back if there is a next time. She lifted her fork to her mouth and I noticed her bare hand and remembered something important that I'd forgotten to take care of.

"Tomorrow we're going shopping." She picked her head up and looked at me. She was probably wondering if all was forgiven since this was the first time I'd initiated a conversation since that bullshit happened. Like I said the only time I said anything to my woman in two weeks is when I was buried balls deep inside her. And then it was usually only to remind her who the fuck she belonged to. She's been on a steady diet of that shit.

"I promised Candy and Gabriella…" I cut her off before she went any farther. "Don't care babe. Tomorrow, you and me." I got up from the table and walked to the sink. When I turned around she was still pouting. "I guess you didn't hear me when I said your little stunt cost you your freedom. Well let me spell that shit out for you again. You don't do anything without me telling you it's okay. Nothing Danielle, and fix your fucking face."

"I can't believe you're really being this way over one stupid mistake. A mistake that wasn't even…" She cut herself off this time and kept her head down.

"Wasn't even what? A mistake? Is that what you were about to say?" I walked over and grabbed her chin lifting her face to mine. "That's where you're wrong, and that's the fucking problem. You don't see it as a mistake you don't see what you did wrong. Until you do we'll never get back to where we were." I dropped her chin and walked away. She followed behind me in a huff. "Connor we can't go on like this, this is crazy. It's been two weeks of the silent treatment and the cold shoulder. I'm not accustomed to living like this it's not fair."

"Oh I see, it's all about Danielle, forget the fact that you fucked up. I should cater to your spoilt ass because it's what you're accustomed to." She folded her arms and her little face became mutinous. She looked like she'd like nothing better than to belt me one. It was almost laughable but I wouldn't give her even that. She had to earn my smiles again fuck that.

"I just think you're taking it too far Connor. For heaven's sake you brushed off dinner with my parents because of this." She's right, I had. When her mom had finally called with arrangements for dinner I'd told her I couldn't make it but maybe her daughter could. I'd even dropped her there and picked her up. She'd been miserable as fuck but I had no intentions on playing pretend for her family. Not now not ever.

"You should've told them the truth as to why. If your mom had asked me I would've told her. And if your father is any kind of a man he'd understand where I'm coming from. On the other hand if he doesn't I don't really give a fuck about that either. You're my woman, they're my rules, learn to live with it."

I turned again and headed up the stairs, I was done with the whole fucking situation. She was never going to get this shit. How do you make your woman understand that you needed her to do the shit you say because you don't want to hurt her? Because you're afraid that if she slips up again you might lose your shit and do something that you know you shouldn't?

I heard the TV come on downstairs as I lay across the bed to read. I'll let her have her little snit before I was ready for her ass. It's probably not very nice of me to admit but I enjoyed making her body sing for mine even though she was pissed at me. No matter how mad she was as soon as we got into bed and I turned to her she had no defenses against me.

Tonight I had something new for my little wife to be. She's been fucked more in the past two weeks than all the others combined. From the time I got her in the door in the evenings I was in her. That's because I spent most of the day thinking about this shit, so by that time I needed to work it off.

At night as soon as dinner was over it was on again. She didn't have time for anything else since I was basically fucking her into submission. She hasn't complained as yet, not since that first night when she said I hurt her pussy. I guess she was getting used to it.

I think the nights we went patrolling the boardwalk were the only peaceful ones she had, until I came home and climbed into bed with her. The funny thing is though, that she always turns to me in the night. Those first few nights I tried sleeping with my back to her. Within an hour of her falling asleep she'd be pressed up to my back with her nose in my spine. Of course me being the fucking sap that I am I usually rolled over and held her. That's the only time I let my guard down and was sweet to her. When she was asleep.

I gave it another hour before calling her up the stairs. "Danielle get up here." I heard the TV turn off and not a minute later her feet on the stairs. She knew better than to make me wait, we'd already played that game. It had taken her pussy a good day to get over the pounding she'd endured over that debacle. Even if she wasn't getting what it was I needed her to get, she was learning in a roundabout way what she had to look forward to if she fucked with me.

"Come here. Lose the clothes on your way." I was already naked, reclining back against the pillows with my dick in hand. I stroked slowly up and down as I watched her get undressed. Even that was done the way I'd taught her that I liked, slow and precise. She kept her eyes on mine the whole time until she was standing there before me bare.

"Touch yourself." I heard the sharp intake of breath before she pinked up. But her hands moved to obey me. "Slowly." She touched her nipples first, pulling and twisting on them until they were pointed and swollen. Her hands moved down her stomach nice and slow until she reached her sweet snatch.

She used her middle finger to rub against her clit back and forth. "Now go inside." Two fingers went up and inside her as that one hand stayed on her nipple. "Fuck yourself on your fingers." I had to ease up on stroking my meat because what she was doing to herself was really getting to me. Her body still captivates me, still makes me want to howl at the fucking moon. Even with my mad.

"Suck your pussy from your fingers and then come here." She pulled out the two fingers pushing them into her mouth and licking them clean. When she was done she walked over to the bed where I was waiting for her. "Climb up." I helped her up and over my face sitting her pussy on my tongue.

"Ooh." She was already moving on my tongue; she did like having her pussy eaten. I feasted on her until my mouth was full of her taste. But that's not what this was about. I eased her off my face and sat her on my chest before reaching over to the night table. Holding her eyes captive I reached around behind her. "Lift up." She lifted just a little so I could reach her ass to oil it up for what was to come. After I'd oiled her up nicely I passed her the tube. "Grease my cock."

She bit her bottom lip as she squeezed some into her hand and rubbed them together. Then she massaged it into my cock nice and slow. I could see her nervousness in the erratic beat of her pulse. Pulling her lips down to mine I kissed her nice and slow letting her taste her pussy on my tongue.

"Sit up. Look at my cock." I held my cock at the base. It was long thick and angry looking. She swallowed hard as she knew that every last inch was going into her ass. Eleven inches of steel, she could barely handle me in her pussy; let's see how she does with her ass. "Hold yourself up for me." She lifted up a little and looked down between her legs at where I was rubbing my bulbous cockhead back and forth from her pussy to her ass. On each third slide I'd slip just the tip inside her wet pussy before pulling back.

"Lean over baby. Not that much. Right there." I took her nipple into my mouth and sucked as I eased my cock inside her ass slowly, inch by inch until there was about three inches inside her. I could feel her body getting ready to tense up so I held still and concentrated on her tits. Her hands gripped the headboard as I pushed another inch inside and she hissed.

"Relax because you're taking all of me. Mouth." She leaned down and fed me her tongue as I slipped farther inside her ass and started to thrust. I used short strokes at first until she was seated completely on my cock. I fingered her clit with my thumb making it nice and wet before finger fucking her with it.

"Ride." She had one of those hurt so good looks on her face as she learned the ins and outs of having a stiff cock in her ass for the first time. I helped her out with a hand on her hip guiding her up and down until she got the hang of it and took over.

She was soon riding my cock and grinding down on the thumb in her pussy. "Feels good?" She nodded her head yes as she picked up speed. "Uh huh." Her tits bounced as she rode me easier and easier. I pulled my thumb out and sat up so I could tongue and suck her nipples, first one then the other.

When they were nice and plump I grabbed two fistfuls of her hair and brought her mouth to mine. "Kiss me." Our mouths fought for dominance until I nipped her lip and won the war. Taking her to her back I drove into her harder and deeper testing the waters so to speak. She didn't cry out for pain or at least the little peep she made wasn't cause for concern so I kept going. With her legs over my arms I straightened my legs, and planting my toes into the mattress fucked into her ass straight. She bucked and hissed as my groin rubbed against her clit with each forward stroke.

"I'm cumming Connor." I took her mouth again licking her lips before pushing my tongue inside. She sucked me into her ass and mouth simultaneously as her pussy juices gushed onto my lower stomach. I wasn't too far behind as the contractions of her ass soon had me spewing inside her.

I came with a loud harsh groan before pulling out and back, diving into her pussy with my tongue. I licked up all her spilt sweetness until there was none left. "Stay where you are, just as you are." Her legs were still up and open leaving her pussy well exposed.

I made fast work of cleaning my cock in the bathroom before going back to her, my cock hard and throbbing. The greedy fuck never gets enough of his girl. She watched me as I came towards the bed stroking my hardness. Climbing up between her thighs I teased her pussy with my cock.

Up, down, and back again until she writhed and begged me for it. "Please

Connor." She was hot and panting for my dick, just the way I like her. "Please what Danielle?" I tapped her clit with my heavy pre cum covered cockhead. "Oooh…make love to me please." Not good enough. I went back to teasing her only this time I fed her two inches on each downward slide before pulling out again. "You want me to make love to you, or fuck the shit out of you?"

She pinked up and bit her lip but when I slipped my tip inside she arched and gave me what I wanted. "Fuck me, please Connor, just fuck me." I pulled back and slammed home hard making her scream. Laying my body flat against hers with her hands clasped in mine over her head I ground my cock into her at an angle.

I searched for and found that little patch inside her that makes her sing and rubbed my cockhead against it. She creamed my cock and bucked beneath me, her head raised so she could sink her teeth into my neck. I never stopped fucking into her even when her pussy clamped down and pulsed around me. "Fuck yeah take my cock baby."

"Too much Connor, it's too much…" I attacked her nipple with my teeth as her over sensitive skin heated up beneath me. I used my whole body to tease her. Rubbing my groin into her clit, my arm brushed against her other nipple. There wasn't a part of her that wasn't on fire.

Now I want her mind. "You loved getting your ass fucked didn't you Danielle? My sweet little Georgia peach, tell me." I reared up and looked down at her as I stroked into her slower this time, giving her room to talk. She was too far-gone, her body wild and uninhibited beneath the onslaught of my cock. I jabbed her with my cock hard to get her attention.

"Answer me or I'll stop." She turned glazed eyes up to me as her fingers tightened around mine. "You want me to stop?" "No no don't stop…YES I loved having you there." I'll let her get away with that one for now. I lifted her legs high and wide for deeper penetration then bent over her so I could whisper in her ear. "I've changed my mind about waiting. Since you want to be disobedient we'll get started on my son now." I pulled back to catch the look of surprise on her face. "I will fuck you everyday until I know he's in you. Then and only then Danielle will I stop being this fucking pissed. Tell me you want my son." "I do…I…Connor." I guess she did like the idea because she came hard as fuck on my cock.

Chapter 13

The next day we got up and dressed to go on our little shopping trip. She had no idea where we were off to and I didn't answer her any of the ten times she asked over breakfast. Things were a little less tense between us today. After I'd made up in my mind to fuck my son into her my mind had finally found peace. The idea made me hard just thinking about it. She wasn't going anywhere no matter what so there was no point in prolonging the issue. Also with my kind in her, that should send the message to other assholes to back the fuck off.

I didn't even know where Robert the fuck lived. I've never seen him around and I thought it best not to get that information less I lose my shit in the middle of the night and go off his ass for being stupid. "Come here baby." I pushed back my chair so she could come sit in my lap. She had the biggest fucking smile on her face as she put her arm around my neck.

I missed this shit, missed the easiness between us. If she didn't get it by now she never would. But somehow I'm sure she won't ever be making that mistake again anytime soon if ever. She didn't wait for me to ask for her mouth, she took the initiative and planted one on me.

I had her straddling me with her jeans undone in five seconds flat. "Take these off." I helped her wrestle out her jeans and threw them to the floor before unzipping and releasing my cock. She sat back in my lap and I pushed her shirt and bra up and out of the way.

The guys knew not to show their faces over here on a weekend morning until much later but I'd told them last night I had to make a run this morning so they had to scrounge for breakfast themselves. There was a lot of grumbling and complaining especially from Ty but whatever.

I sucked her nipple into my mouth and rubbed my cock on her clit, clit fucking her with just the swollen head. She made those little hissing noises she makes when her pussy needs me so I didn't make her wait too long before lifting her far enough to seat her on my cock and pull her down all the way until her ass was touching my thighs.

"Tongue." She gave me her mouth as she rode up and down on my cock with my hands on her ass moving her just how I wanted her. "Squeeze my cock babe." She did the flexing exercises I'd taught her and I almost bit off her tongue. Getting to my feet I laid her back across the table pushing the dishes and shit to the side so I could fuck into her the way I needed to.

Spreading her open I looked down between us where my cock was sawing into her long and deep. I thumbed her clit making it even puffier as her hot pussy sucked my cock in like she was starved for it. "Cum baby." I took her nipple again and ground into her hitting her sweet spot until she screamed into my mouth.

I emptied inside her before pulling out and retaking my seat. "Clean me off babe." She dropped to her knees and took my cock into her mouth licking her pussy juice from my cock and nuts until I was semi hard again. "You might as well finish him off now. " She got to work deep throating my shit until I came a long time later down her throat.

When we were done fucking around I took her back upstairs and cleaned us both up before going about the shit I had to do. I had her on the back of bike as we headed out of town, what I was looking for wasn't going to be here I'm sure. We talked and laughed on the way and I felt the stress ease with each mile that went by. She held me a little tighter around the middle as we sped along and rested her head on my back. Every once in a while she'd squeeze me and I'd smile behind the screen of my helmet. I know what that shit was about. She'd been fucked hard, she'd been introduced to new kink and she liked that shit.

Her mouth opened wide when we got off the bike in the parking lot of one of the nation's most exclusive jeweler. "Let's go." I had to practically drag her along behind me. She was probably wondering what an ex SEAL could possibly afford in a place like this. I'm sure the asshole hadn't gotten her a ring here. Yes I had to top his shit. I'd never seen her ring come to think of it. "Who chose your last ring?" She got a very uncomfortable look on her face so I took it between my hands and looked into her eyes. "We're all good baby just answer the question."

"He did." She didn't want to have this conversation at all and neither did I but I needed to top this motherfucker in every way. I hadn't forgotten that crack he'd made about her father not allowing her to marry someone like me. Like I was some sort of fucking mutt. "How many carats?" She looked up at me as if about to argue.

Oh yeah, I'm well aware of the way the human mind works. It's how I profiled the assholes we hunted in the Navy. How I gauged their next move so I could take them the fuck out. There's never gonna be a day that she looks down at her finger and think his was bigger or better, fuck that. And since this one was never coming off her finger it had to be her favorite. "Two and a half."

"Fine, your choice, four and a half and up." She pulled back on my hand. And started to shake her head. She also looked nervous as fuck. "Don't worry Danielle, you won't break me if you buy a ring that you like. I told you before I've been investing my money for years. Never had anything to spend the shit on before. I want you to have the shit you want, something you and your girls can coo over. You got me?" She still wasn't too convinced but at least she wasn't looking like she was ready to bolt any second.

Inside the store the saleslady came over all smiles and offered her assistance. I stood back and watched the action as they went through tray after tray of rings. I read her body language, I know my woman so I knew the minute she saw THE one. I wasn't surprised when she kept going though. All I did was shake my head as I stood off to the side out of their way but I kept my eye on it for her. Two hours later she chose some bullshit ring that was about half the size of what I'd told her. She'd looked back at that damn ring sneakily of course, about every ten minutes or less.

"So you like this one?" The saleslady held up the bullshit ring and my girl looked back at me. I'm sure the shit had to be at least twenty-five grand. Harry didn't do shit for much less. I walked over to the case where the ring she'd fallen in love with sat and pointed. "We'll take this one."

"Connor..."
"Quiet." The saleslady came over and removed the tray and started spouting off specs. Something about cushion cut whatever. I had no fucking idea and could care less. It was five carats and it's the one she wanted that was good enough for me. She tried to argue with me but I just gave her a look. "This the one you like Dani? Tell

me the truth." She nodded shyly and hung her head.

"Babe what did I tell you before we came in here? See this is why you're gonna stay in trouble you don't listen for shit." I said that shit out of earshot of the others in the store. I wasn't about embarrassing my woman in public, but damn her head is hard as fuck.

"You can ring that up ma'am."
I took it out of the box as soon as the transaction was over and slid it onto her finger.
"This stays, always. It doesn't come off for any reason." She stared at that shit until I lifted her mouth and kissed her right there in the middle of the store. And that easily I felt the last of the bitterness fall away. Don't be fooled, I'm still waiting for her to get what the fuck she did wrong the only difference is now I'm willing to wait for her to get that shit. It's the only way she won't fuck up again.

We were one step closer to complete ownership. All that was left was the wedding which I'm gonna get on as soon as fucking possible. Her mom had made noises about these things taking time to plan but I'm giving them three months tops and even that was pushing it.

We walked around for a few but I could tell she was anxious to get back. Probably needed to call her girls and talk about her new haul. "Can I go show mama?" See that's a sure sign that my girl had got the right fucking ring. She couldn't wait to show that shit off and fuck yes I was pleased as shit. "We can do whatever you want babe." Her sweet smile was back in full force and I realized how much I'd missed that shit. Hopefully for the next little while there wouldn't be any fuck ups to send me off my ass again.

After we swung by her family's estate so her mom could gush over her ring and her dad could finally size me up it was back to the compound to my nosy ass brothers. Her old man hadn't been what I'd expected though. He'd asked me into his library while the women went on and on about weddings and shit. I was ready for anything he had to throw at me. After the last couple weeks there wasn't anything that was going to get in the way of me holding onto what the fuck was mine.

"Connor I have to admit that when my wife first told me about you and my daughter I had my doubts. You have to understand that little girl out there is my one and only offspring so it wouldn't have mattered who you were I would've felt the same. I'm sure you know she was engaged for a little while to someone else?" He looked at me through the cigar smoke and I stared back at him.

"Yep." He laughed at my stance before taking a seat behind the sea of wood that he called a desk.
"Stand down soldier I'm not about to start anything those two out there would have my guts for garters if I did. I just wanted to give you my blessing. My little girl is as happy as I've ever seen her and that's all that matters to me. With that said you hurt my baby and I'll skin you alive."

"She's my baby now sir so you have no worries." I relaxed my shoulders a little since it wasn't looking like he was going to start shit. We kicked around old army and navy tales killing time until the women were done doing whatever the hell they were doing and joined us. My girl came over to me and wrapped her arms around me. "Daddy you haven't been giving my guy a hard time have you?" I squeezed her shoulders and kissed her hair to let her know that it was all good.

"We have to get going my brothers will be waiting for us." I wasn't exactly uncomfortable but I didn't want to hang around. He seemed cool enough but this shit was weird. I was fucking his daughter and he knew it. Not sure I could be as cool about that shit as he seemed to be.

"We're having all boys." I told her that shit as soon as we were outside. "What? Why?" She stopped short and looked at me like I had two fucking heads. "Not up for debate babe, just make that shit happen."
"Uh Connor I'm pretty sure that's on you."

"Yeah but females be pulling a fast one and putting in a good word for what they want, kind of a Blitzkrieg move. None of that sneaky shit Danielle. If you want your man to have a peace of mind no girls." She thought that shit was funny but I was dead serious. I have no problem violating Danielle's sweet as fuck body but fuck. I can't think about this shit it will make me lose my fucking nut.

Chapter 14

After that it was back home. Where we were now, surrounded by my brothers. All in all the day had turned out just fine. My woman was happy and I no longer felt like killing a motherfucker. I couldn't wait to get her alone to seal the deal but the boys had other ideas.

"We need to go celebrate you two." Logan brought up the idea of going out for drinks and dancing later and since she seemed excited by the idea I went along with it. I'm not much for that shit but I can't keep her locked away behind stonewalls forever. She called up some of her girls at my request and we headed for the showers after the others left.

Seeing my seal of ownership on her hand did something crazy to me. She was shampooing her hair when the light caught that shit just right and my cock grew stiff. I barely let her get the soap out of her hair before I was covering her mouth with mine, backing her up to the wall. "Wrap your legs around me." She did as I asked and I just pushed my finger inside her to test her wetness. She sucked it in and pushed so I pulled it out and sank my cock inside her instead.

"I'm gonna fuck you hard and rough baby hold on." I pounded into her pinning her to the wall with my thrusts. Our mouths fused together as I fed her my tongue before taking hers into my mouth. Her pussy was tight and needy around my length as she tried her best to keep up. I wanted to fuck every inch of her. Mark her in more ways than one. The need to stake my claim completely was too much to ignore. We had a few hours before it was time to leave hopefully that would be enough.

I almost cancelled the night but she pouted, she was all excited to show off her ring and shit. I don't know how she was walking after the freaky shit I'd just done to her but she was. I could go another few hours but I guess I could hold my shit until we got home later.

"Um babe I like that shit." She had on low rider jeans and a satin halter-top that matched her green eyes and heels that were a mile high. I think she was trying to match me in height with those shits. She did some wild shit with her hair that had curls falling down her back and all I could think of was grabbing fistfuls of that shit while I hit her pussy from behind. Damn I've become a fiend.

The guys were waiting for us when we stepped outside all of us looking like we were in uniform. Jeans, Henley, and leather jackets with shit kickers. No wonder people think we're a gang.

I made sure she was fine on the back of my ride in those fuck me heels and we headed out.

The place we'd chosen was in the next town over. It was the only place within decent distance that had any kind of nightlife. Or any place I wanted my woman hanging out anyway. Her girls were there when we pulled up and the screaming started as soon as she got in the middle of them.

We herded them all inside and got the waitress to put some tables together in the back in view of the dance floor. My woman had already warned me that she planned to dance her ass off. I was cool as long as she had a good time we were good. Her girls were a rowdy bunch, nothing at all like I expected from this bunch of debutantes shit. They started doing shots right off the bat and the boys and I decided we'd better stick to beer and nurse them shits. This bunch might be trouble.

There was one in particular that I knew could set shit off with one of my brothers, then again except for Candy who we all knew I saw a few that might be trouble. We pretty much set up as security and watched them do their thing.

"I see trouble written all over this shit?" Zak tipped his beer and rocked back in his chair. There were a few unknowns checking out the girls as they danced and laughed together. Dani had invited what looked like every female from Briarwood and these chicks weren't just any run of the mill females. These were the type of women that went the extra mile, which meant they were all put together. Some of them I'd never seen before but the few I did know, huh.

We kept them supplied with drinks and kept an eye on them to make sure no assholes got stupid. The women didn't seem interested in the looks coming their way so that was our cue to step in if anything went south. If they were interested in dancing that was their business but the men seemed to think they were all spoken for so we were able to relax after an hour or so.

Shit she brought Gabriella Danforth over to introduce her. I kept my eyes on Logan when she rose up on her toes to kiss my cheek and offer congratulations. I could see him grinding his molars and his face drew tight. Damn not even his brother who was here to celebrate his engagement was safe.

"Thanks Gabby." I set her away from me to avert any shit and watched as the two girls walked away back to their friends on the dance floor. I looked around at the others to see if they'd noticed what I saw. I shouldn't have doubted, nosy fucks. I wasn't going to be the one to bring that shit up.

Logan can be a little touchy about that subject. We all know he has the hots for the little blonde but he refused to go there. Kinda like me with Danielle. If she wanted him though his ass was in deep shit. Again I won't be the one to tell him that shit.

When some dude took her hand and led her off to dance I knew there was going to be trouble. Seven chairs scraped against the hardwood floor, one louder than the others. Jackets were discarded just in case as we moved out behind Logan but stayed back to see what play he was about to make.

Logan reached them in a few short steps and without uttering a word took her hand off the guy's shoulder and pulled her away. I know it's not the time but that shit was funny as hell. His face looked like thunder as he dragged the poor girl off the dance floor.

"Hey." She mouthed off at him but he didn't say a word to her just kept going. The guy didn't say anything just shrugged his shoulders and moved onto the next dance partner who seemed willing and the rest of us headed back to the table.

Logan sat her in the chair next to his but he was still not saying anything. She turned to me as I sat to the other side of her.

"What's wrong with your brother?" I tried not to smile at this shit.
"Which one?"

"The asshole jerk." She pointed her thumb at Logan.
"Watch your damn mouth."
She turned to him and leaned in closer.
"Make me."
Oh shit. The others were glued to the action; this shit was better than the movies. Logan the lone wolf had met his fucking match.

"Watch yourself little girl before you bite off more than you can chew."
She tried getting up but he blocked her in with his leg. "Sit your ass down, you try getting up again you're in trouble."
She huffed at him but sat still shooting daggers at him with her eyes, arms folded like she was ready to blast his ass.

"Well then looks like another one bite the dust. You fuckers are falling faster than a Red Baron bomber.
"Shut the fuck up Ty." I kicked his chair and the ass just laughed at me. I eyed the rest of them trying to send them the message that maybe we should leave and let these two deal with their shit but the nosy fucks weren't budging.

I went and got my girl to dance. "You having fun baby?" I pulled her in close for a kiss with my hands on her ass.

"Yes it's the best, thanks for this, the girls are having a blast. You do know some of them have their eye on your brothers right?"

"You playing matchmaker baby?"

She grinned up at me. "I just want everyone to be as happy as we are. And Connor, I finally get it."

"What do you get baby?" I looked into her eyes as we stopped moving in the middle of the dance floor. She's so fucking gorgeous damn. I lucked the fuck out big time.

"I understand why you were so mad. I thought I was just doing something innocent, my intentions were good but you'd already warned me not to have any contact with…him so regardless I shouldn't have met with him."

"That's absolutely right baby." I kissed her again to show her that I appreciated that shit.

"But I might forget and mess up again."

"No you won't babe because next time your ass will pay the price." She gulped and put her head on my chest. Now all was right with my world.

Chapter 15

Logan caught my eye a bit later and gave the sign that he was leaving. The two of them left together hand in hand, well now. I grinned at my brothers who were all sitting at the table while I slow danced with my girl. They were starting to look a little nervous; especially Ty whose wanna be wifey was in the crowd.

We danced two more songs before she realized one of her girls was missing. "Connor I don't see Gaby anywhere." "She left with Logan." "She… I better go make sure she's okay." She tried pulling out of my arms but I held tight.

"Nope, you're not going anywhere babe they're grown." Speaking of which I felt like sneaking away myself, there was a nice little walk down to the water at the back of this place. I nodded to my boys and took her hand and headed out the door. Her girls were busy having fun and the guys were keeping an eye on them.

"Where are we going?" I didn't answer her, just led her through the balmy night with her hand held securely in mine. I made sure no one else had the same idea as I led her down the small incline and found a nice spot in a little copse of trees.

"Strip." I threw my jacket down on the sand so her ass wouldn't get all gritty and shit. And opened up my jeans while she kicked off her shoes and pulled her pants down her legs. The moonlight made her skin glow and the warm breeze carried her scent.

"That's good babe." I pulled her to me and kissed her with all the hunger I had inside for her. I pressed my already leaking cock into her middle. "Feel what you do to me." Her fingers in my hair pulled harder as we tongue fucked each other's mouths.

"I want to take you from behind out here in the open. I don't wanna fuck or make love sweetheart. Tonight I need to mate. This." I held up the hand with the ring. "This calls for a mating."

I got her down on her knees and spread her pink pussy lips open for my mouth. I drank from her before sinking my tongue inside. There was a heightened sense of intensity brought on by being out in the open like this. Just the moon and the stars for light as she knelt before me naked. I'd only shed my jacket and shirt, my jeans were unzipped and riding my hips; that too made a picture.

When she came on my tongue and her cries rang out in the night I moved around in front of her. I wanted her mouth before I took her. I wanted my cock to be at its fullest for this. She licked around my cockhead before taking me into her mouth and sucking. I wasn't too careful with her hair when I grabbed two fistfuls and pulled her head on and off my cock. when I started hitting he back of her throat I pulled out and got back in position behind her.

Sinking two fingers deep I went after her g-spot until she was fucking back hard against my hand.

"Please Connor."

"What do you need baby?"

"You, inside me. I need you." Her pussy clenched around my fingers as her juices flowed once more. I pulled them out and reached around feeding them to her as I slammed into her pussy. I kept the fingers in her mouth as she sucked hard and bit into her neck while jack hammering into her pussy. She never stopped screaming around my hand and cumming on my cock. I wanted to fuck her all night just like this. Never wanted it to end.

After that night we went back to being us, only with the added bonus of me loving my girl even more. Something about putting your ring on your woman's finger makes a man feel settled. And the way she flitted around the house all happy and shit, singing and dancing. That shit made my fucking life complete. On top of all that the sex was plentiful and hot as fuck. I hope that shit about women losing interest after marriage was a myth. The fuck am I saying? I'll never let that shit happen. I can't see not being inside her every chance I get just like I am now.

We had a new addition most nights at the house; it seems Logan had put Gabriella on lock down. She didn't seem too torn up about it. Though she seemed to be giving poor Logan a run for his money. It was fun to watch him trying to bring her to heel and her kicking and screaming all the way.

Most evenings their posse was over at the house going over wedding plans and bitching because I wanted shit done in weeks instead of months. Complaining asses. That was good though because it freed me up to do my thing with my brothers at night. It also had the added benefit of making the others run for cover. No one wanted to get too close to my house in the evenings when the women were coming over. They seemed to think falling in love was some sort of contagious disease or some shit.

"I'd rather be in the trenches than your house right now bro. Those women are like armed drones, they hone in on your ass and bam. Look at poor Logan."
"Fuck off Ty, let's get this shit moving so I can be done. Gabriella wants to go see some fucked up movie." He grumbled that last bit but we heard and laughed our asses off.

Gabriella is about my Dani's height, which means she's a little bit of a thing. Blonde and blue, she's a southern belle to the tips of her toes. Somewhere along the line she got a healthy dose of attitude and fuck if it isn't amusing to watch. I don't think Logan prayed this much on the battlefield. These days he's always searching the heavens for guidance. At least that's what we think he's doing when he's looking up to the sky and mumbling shit.

We'd finally got somewhere with the cigarette butts we'd found. A little undercover snooping garnered us the information that there was one particular guy who special ordered that brand of cigarette so that pretty much narrowed it down for us. We were being careful with it though until we knew all the players. It wouldn't do to show our hands too soon by going after this guy when we knew there had to be others involved.

Dennis Crampton didn't look like the kind of character to be caught up in this shit. On paper he reads like the poster boy for the senate. A farther dig into his background showed he had connections in very high places, which might make shit more difficult. But we weren't too worried about that shit. If he's dirty we'll take his ass down no question.

He's early forties with a wife and two kids. His business looked to be doing well and his finances were solid. It was all too neat on the surface though, which sent up red flags if you knew what you were looking for. The clean in and out of his finances were just too fucking perfect.

"Find the money Quinn. We tug on that thread who knows where it will lead."
"I'm on it Logan. Con you say Danielle knows him right?"
"Yeah his wife is on the board of the charity or something like that. I asked her that shit in a roundabout way so as not to raise any suspicions. Plus I needed to know how close she was to this asshole. She doesn't have too many dealings with him but they've attended the same functions and parties. I have to figure out how to keep her away from him until we know how much of an asshole this jerk is without tipping her nosy ass off to what we're doing here."

"Even more reason to move on this shit. We might as well look into all the moneyed men in the area. Chances are if one of them is into this shit more might be as well." Logan looked at me then. I guess he was thinking of my soon to be father in law, which would be all kinds a fucked if he was involved. But I didn't get that vibe from him any of the times we'd met. Yes Dani was now in the habit of dragging me to her parents' house for dinner at least once a week.

I've learned something in the last six weeks or so since our engagement. Even a strong man has no will against the woman he loves. As long as she was happy I found myself agreeing to shit that I never thought I'd do. I gave a fuck that my brothers laughed their asses off when she dragged me off shopping or some equally female bullshit. And don't get me started on when her and Gabriella got shit into their heads about doubling up.

It usually involved some girly shit like cake testing or some crap. Thankfully I didn't have to bear that injustice alone as Gaby insisted that Lo come with. The first time he'd asked her why the fuck he had to even be involved and she'd said it was practice for their own wedding he'd turned white as a sheet. Funny shit.

Now we're over run by women and our peace and serenity was a thing of the past. "You got Gaby's tag yet?" I'd put Danielle's in a matching bracelet I'd got for us. Hers had my initials and mine had hers. What she didn't know was that the clasp, which couldn't be opened without a jeweler's help hid a tracking device. What she didn't know wouldn't hurt her. I slept better at night knowing that shit was there.

"Yep she's all giddy with her new bracelet which she's been warned not to remove under threat of a whipping."
"Bro they can't come off, didn't you do what I told you?"
"Yes but we're talking about Gabriella here. I think you got the nice one on this deal."
"What's the matter Lo? The little woman giving you trouble? You two know you have to represent right? And not make the rest of us look like assholes."

"Speaking of which Zak you're all coming to dinner tomorrow night no excuses. The girls are cooking up a feast or some shit."
"Why it's not Thanksgiving or some shit. This another one of Dani's sneak attacks?"
"I don't know Ty all I know is that when I was leaving the house she told me to pass

that shit on." The grumbling and bullshit started but I knew they would be there. They didn't like disappointing her any more than I did.

Chapter 16

That night Quinn called when I was just about to fuck Dani for the second time. We were both panting and out of breath; she was sprawled across my chest barely moving but her scent still had me rock hard and seconds were sounding and looking good.

"What's up?" I ran my hand over her ass trying to dip low enough to get a finger inside her from this angle.
"We've got a problem bro. Meet at Logan's in ten."
What the fuck? I looked at the phone and hung up. "Gotta make a run babe be right back." I sucked her tongue long and hard, gave the pussy a little finger action while she grabbed my dick and then hopped into the shower for a quick wash-up.

Everyone was there by the time I arrived. No one was bleeding so whatever this was couldn't be too bad I hope.
Quinn threw an envelope across the table at me before I even sat down. Opening it I didn't understand what I was looking at at first until I saw one of the names on the sheet.

"What the fuck is this?" I jumped up from my seat ready to lay a motherfucker out.

"Calm down brother we know it's not what it looks like but we've got to figure it out." I paced the room back and forth like a caged animal after Logan said that shit. My mind was going in ten different directions at once but I couldn't grab hold of any one thought.

"There's no way her mom or dad did this so who the fuck could it be?"

"That's what we've got to find out and fast. Did you see the dates on that? They're expecting something in a week. Now Logan finally got eyes down there but they're not enough to cover the whole area the place just isn't set up for that kind of surveillance but at least we can see who's going and who's coming. The first thing we've got to do is get her to move it."

"What the fuck bro! Who the fuck are these people? She moves it they know she's onto them and they come after her. Only we can't protect her because we don't know who the fuck they are."

"There's one way to find out." Logan stood from his chair and cracked his knuckles. The others got up as well and I exhaled. My night had just gone to shit fast.

"We go after this guy now we may never know all who's involved." Devon pulled on his leather.

"He'll talk, if he wants to live he'll fucking talk." I pulled my phone to call her and let her know something had come up. No doubt she'd hear the bikes revving up and wonder.

"Babe something came up I'll be a little longer than I thought. Do me a favor and lock up and set the alarm."

"Connor is everything okay?"

"Everything's fine babe just go to sleep if I'm not back and I'll wake you when I get in. I love you."

"I love you too." I rolled my eyes at the assholes who were in my fucking face like we didn't have some serious shit to take care of.

Blue Fin was a fucking ghost town this time of night, then again so was Briarwood but at least we had a few street lights. This place for all its high-ticket homes seemed more rural. The homes were more widely spaced apart and there were more open spaces. We'd put in the GPS to where we were headed and stopped about a few hundred feet away to prepare.

"How're we doing this bro? It's your woman your call; the wife and kids are in there."
"We do it without the kids knowing we were even there. The wife goes to sleep, that's all you sleeper." Devon was good at dosing people so they didn't even know they'd been zapped. The shit you learn in the military.

"Con try not to kill this fuck before we get all the information we need."
"I just want to know how he got her info to set her up for the fall. I have my suspicions but if that shit is right somebody just might die tonight after all."

The security on the place was a joke, or maybe that's because we knew what the fuck we were doing. There isn't any place really that Cord the sneak can't get into. We each have our own talents. Mine aren't that

useful in the real world unless a
motherfucker needed to get dead. And since
these assholes had chosen my woman's
name and information to use for their money
laundering bullshit it looked like I might
have to go into service.

Cord split off from Zak and Quinn who went to make sure the kids were in bed where they were supposed to be. None of us were too jazzed about putting kids out. Neither did we want to scare them half to death if they woke up in the middle of the night to seven strange men in their home. Logan and Ty went to wire the place and I waited.

Cord came back with the okay and we gave it another minute before I headed up to the room to see one Dennis Crampton. I pulled the pillow out from under his head and dropped it over his face. When his struggles lessened and he was at the edge of darkness I removed it and pulled him from the bed. Now he knows I mean fucking business and won't think twice about offing his ass.

Downstairs the others were waiting for us. I dropped him in the middle of the circle and waited for him to stop gasping for air. I'm sure we made a sight. The room was in darkness but the moonlight coming through the windows was most likely catching on the combat paint beneath our eyes and the bottom half of our faces. We'd decided that this was the best way to keep our identities hidden for now until we knew what else we were dealing with.

"Tell us about your little operation Crampton."
"I don't know what you're talking about." I think he didn't realize his finger had been broken until the loud snap sounded in the room. The shock of the pain kept him from feeling it for at least a second or two. The gag stuffed into his mouth ensured that the screams wouldn't wake his kids.

"Each time you bullshit me I'll break something else, then we'll head upstairs and get started on the others your choice."

He started pleading for his life and the lives of his family but it all fell on deaf ears. Of course next was the sob story of how he got caught up in something he had no control over. He didn't know the men who'd approached him were into smuggling. He'd tried to get out when he realized but they'd threatened his family. Fucking liar. The money Quinn had found painted a different story. He got a little tight lipped when it came to names but one more finger here or there was soon enough to loosen his fucking tongue.

I was waiting for one name. I don't know how I was so sure that it was the one I

suspected. Maybe it was wishful thinking on my part. Maybe it was just me looking for any excuse to bury the fuck because he was the only one other than me to have laid hands on my woman. Don't ask my why the fuck that bothers me it just does.
Still it wasn't reason enough to off a motherfucker. This shit might be though.

"So you've been smuggling drugs in and laundering money out for the past two years and no one got wind of it."
"We were always careful I was just the go between kind of."
"Kill the bullshit, we've seen the paper trial you're up to your eyeballs in this shit. Now what we want to know is how does the Dupre foundation play into all this?"
"How do you know about that?"
"I'm asking the questions here asshole. Now talk."

"They don't, that's Rob's thing. Some chick he's fucking…" I punched him before he could get the words out of his mouth. I felt hands on me pulling me back as I swung again.

"Easy brother easy." Logan whispered in my ear and reminded my ass that if I went off because he'd mentioned Dani that it would be a dead giveaway. I shook him off and shook the blood from my eye as I went to stand over the piece a shit again.

"How did he get her information?"
"What do you mean? She gave it to him she's part of the organization. She handles the money that's her thing."
No fucking way. I didn't even stumble back from the force of his words because there was no way my Dani was involved in this shit.

"You're lying, he did it himself, stole the information or tricked her somehow. How did he do it? And don't fucking lie to me again."
"I'm not lying I swear." He cowered away from me almost in the fetal position. "Why don't you go to their condo and ask them yourselves?"
"Come again?"

"Rob and his chick Karen they have a place not too far from here." Shit I didn't even know the asshole lived here I always thought he lived in Briarwood. I looked at each of my brothers in turn. Who the fuck was Karen? I'd pretty much met all of Danielle's friends by now and I don't recall a Karen in the bunch.

"Who else is involved in this thing? Who's your boss?"

He dropped a few names that none of us knew but we could easily verify. We'd got pretty much everything we needed from him. It was time to move on to the next player.

"We'll be watching your house, you tip these guys off that we're onto them you won't draw another breath. If I find out what you're saying is a lie same goes." He clutched his maimed hand and tried to stand as we headed out the door. I wondered how he planned to explain his misfortune to his wife and kids.

Chapter 17

On a hunch I called up Dani on the way back to our bikes. She sounded like she'd already been fast asleep which just might work in my favor. She wasn't exactly with it when she first woke up. "Babe does Karen still work for you guys?"
"Connor? Yes. What, what happened?"

"Nothing happened baby just go back to sleep." She mumbled something and hung up. I shut the phone off and turned to the others. "At least that answers that question." I didn't even have to say anything else. Tyler got out his nifty little reconfigured smartphone and put in some info.

By the time we reached the bikes he had what he was looking for. "Got her. Karen Skeet twenty-eight. Huh looks like the asshole traded way the fuck down. He held up the screen to show us the bleached blonde who looked a little rough around the edges.

"What does it say Ty?" I climbed on the back of my ride and waited while the others did the same. I was already pissed way the fuck off so whatever he found out about this bitch won't make much of a difference but I liked to have as much information as possible when I was about to do a job.

I wouldn't like to find out after the fact for instance that this person was being used against her will or some shit. Or that they were holding a gun to her sick mother's head or some sick shit like that and she had no other choice. That shit isn't just for the movies. There are some seriously fucked up individuals who makes Hollywood look like child's play.

"She's a finance major from Vassar. Coulda fooled me, maybe this is an old picture or some shit. Says here she's been working for the charity for the past year and a half give or take."

"Huh, Dani says she ran into that asshole about a year or so ago. So how did they play it? Did he send Karen in or did he meet her and got the idea. Nah, Crampton said they'd been smuggling for two years. I'm more inclined to believe he sent her in for this purpose. Is there anyway to tell if she's really who she says she is?"

"On it." We had to wait a little longer for his tool to do its thing.
"Nope the real Karen Skeet lives in Greensborough and is married with a young child. The date of birth and credentials are

the same and since this one isn't using her Ivy-league education to steal I'm more inclined to believe that she's the real thing." This Karen was a brunette who looked like a professional as opposed to a recovering alcoholic.

"Let's go I've got the addy." I did a Google earth search and pinpointed the asshole's location. It was a condo so there was more traffic around him than the last one but nothing we couldn't get around. This area was more yuppie central for the younger crowd. There were six condos three and three on a little cul de sac.

The lights were off here as well. Everyone was asleep granted they were even home. There was no real way of telling unless we called and I didn't want to do that. I liked having the element of surprise on my side.

"You guys don't even need to come in with me. In and out in five."
"No way bro you're not killing him."
"Why the fuck not Logan?"

"Use your head Connor. The wrong person go digging and uncover the shit they're up to with your woman's name all over this shit and it leads back to you they'll have your ass pegged in ten seconds flat."

"No problem I already reversed the trail, it leads right back to her." Quinn grinned like the fucking grim reaper. He's another murdering fuck, which is just what I needed on my side right now.

"I don't see why I can't just break both their fucking necks right now and be done with it."
"Because we're not animals. Besides I've got a better idea. When we move the money the men coming in a week will do our dirty work for us. We're here so you can get this shit out of your system but you're not killing them."

Well fuck. We didn't have to neutralize the neighbors on either side. Just cut out the lock on the backdoor to the place and slip inside. We headed up the stairs like smoke and did the same to his door. Inside the others didn't actually hang back but they let me take the lead.

I found them in bed asleep, didn't look like there was any love lost between these two or maybe that's how people usually slept. The fuck I know. I haven't slept without some part of me touching Danielle since I brought her home. Not the time Connor.

I wasn't quiet as I made my way around to his side of the bed. Chump had his woman closest to the door right in the line of fire. I started beating his ass before I'd dragged him completely out of bed. Logan was there to shush her with a hand around her throat when she woke up startled. With the shit these two were into you'd think they'd sleep with one eye open. I guess it's true what they say. Only the guilty can sleep the sleep of the dead after the shit they've done.

"Who are you?" He had got one question in before I threw his ass into the wall.
"Tell me this, did you go after her to fuck her life over huh?" Either he recognized my voice from the one time we'd met or he was one cognizant motherfucker when he woke up because his eyes widened in understanding.

"I didn't. Stop what're you doing?" Is he stupid what the fuck did it look like I was doing?
"I'll tell you what I'm doing. I'm going to beat you to within an inch of your life for fucking with what's mine. Then I'm gonna leave you to your smuggler friends to finish you the fuck off." Yeah maybe Logan had the right idea there after all.

The others were tossing the place while I did my thing. I guess they were looking for any information they could use that we hadn't found at Crampton's. I wasn't too interested in that shit right now. I wanted to obliterate this fucker and his partner in crime. I could hear Logan whispering to her in the background while I plowed my fist into Robert's face. When I was sure he wasn't going to be able to see out of his eyes anytime soon I started on his body.

He'd stopped begging me for his life about five minutes ago when I'd broken his fucking nose. I imagine he was in immense pain from me pulverizing his internal organs. I concentrated mostly on the kidneys. Logan said I couldn't kill him right now he didn't say anything about him dying at some later date from his injuries.

I used all my training to attack only the areas that would do the most damage. It was dispassionate and precise. He was unconscious by the time I realized my hands were tired as fuck. I left him on the floor in a heap and walked over to where Logan still had her. Grabbing her by the throat I pulled her out of his hands.

"What's your real name?" She was shaking like a leaf.

"I already got that info bro let's be out."

"Was she nice to you? I bet she treated you better than anyone ever has in your pathetic life but you were willing to fuck her over. I ought to kill your ass right now." She made a sound of distress as her eyes flew to the bloody mess on the floor and then back to mine. I had to satisfy myself with a hard slap across her face that hopefully loosened a few teeth before Logan was hustling me out of the room.

By the time we got back to the compound my woman was fast asleep so I was able to slip into the shower and wash off most of the evidence. Wasn't shit I could do about my bruised knuckles though so I just doctored them and climbed into bed.

"Connor?" She sighed and turned to me in her sleep. I should probably leave her alone but I needed her. It fucked with my head that while I'd thought I was protecting her something like that was going on behind the scenes. Something that could have potentially taken her away from me. I don't understand that shit as well as Quinn does but from what little I'd seen they'd had her tied up nice and tight with a little bow for anyone who came looking.

I ran my hands over her slowly, softly, gentling her awake with my mouth on hers. She sighed into my mouth and opened up for my tongue. I kissed my way down her middle until I reached her heat. She'd taken a bath after I'd left. Her fresh flowery scent was almost as intoxicating as the scent of her pussy when I'd just fucked her. I preferred her a little dirty though so I got to work making her so.

She moved against my mouth as I tongue fucked her into full wakefulness. Her hands came down to play in my hair as I lifted her to my mouth so I could sink my tongue deeper. When she was swollen and hot around my tongue I eased up her body and pulling her head back so I could see into her eyes I slipped into her. I closed my eyes against the enormity of the feelings that hit me as I started fucking into her body nice and slow.

Folding her close I rocked our bodies in a slow dance of love, whispering words of love and praise in her ears as her body strained up to meet mine. Lifting one of her legs higher on my hip I went in deeper but still kept the slow glide in and out of her until we both came with a groan.

I fitted her body next to mine after pulling out minutes later. "Sleep baby." She was out in seconds.

Epilogue

"What's up brother?" We were all gathered in Logan's kitchen because he'd called and said we needed a sit down. Usually that meant serious business. I was in a hurry to get back to my woman because she'd been acting kind of frisky before the phone rang. And that teasing whisper in my ear just before the phone rang had given me ideas.

I'd almost brushed Logan off but that was something none of us had ever done. Our code was such that when one sent out an S.O.S we all answered no matter what. We'd learned in our time together to put each other first, to always have each other's backs. That's how we'd made it through some of the toughest runs in our careers. That kind of trust was not to be tampered with. I'm pretty sure we'd all be old and grey and still living by that code. But the last time these fuckers called me out of my bed I'd had to lie to my woman about how my knuckles got fucked up.

"I got a call from the C.O." The room fell silent. We were out yes but we all knew because of our team's special skills we would never truly be free. They'd built the team yes, but we'd made it what it was and what it was was an elite force of manpower equaled to none.

"I'm not going. Whatever it is, wherever it is, I'm done." Tyler stormed out of the kitchen as the rest of us looked on. We knew why he felt this way the sentiment I'm sure was shared by most if not all of us; but we also knew no matter what gripes we might have that it wasn't that easy to turn our backs on our calling.

"Go after him Connor." Logan ordered me while the others stayed silent. No one wanted to tangle with Ty when he got like this. He could be a hardheaded fuck when his blood was up about something. "Why do I always get sent to the tiger's lair?" It's true whenever he acts up they all look to me to rein him in, I've got the battle scars to prove it.

I didn't have time to consider the ramifications of what Logan's announcement meant for me. Whatever it is if he hadn't told them to go fuck themselves then it must be bad. "Because you two are more alike in that aspect and you're the only one who can reach him, go get him brother before he hurts something." I left the room and my brothers to go face a man's anger.

He was kicking the wheel of his bike when I came out. "Save it Con I'm not doing it, not this time, fuck them." I let him work off some of the steam he had working there knowing that it was only after he'd gotten most of it out of his system that he'd be able to hear me. It was always this way with Ty. He could get hot at the drop of a hat. I'd once seen him destroy a whole room in less than ten minutes and there'd been no way to stop him. But when the blood was no longer in his eyes and he calmed down a little he was as quiet as a lamb. It was freaky to see. "What's destroying your bike gonna prove brother?" He glared at me before walking off.

"I don't owe those lying fucks anything. I gave them my youth and the best part of me and for what? So some over inflated windbag could sit behind a desk and make money on the backs of our brothers and sisters in arms? And now they want to cut their benefits and shit but they need our help? Fuck that shit, how about I go take their asses out? They're the real enemy the fucks."

What could I say to that? We all agreed, it was fucked what was going on. Most people had no idea how under appreciated the men and women who fought

for their freedoms really were. They didn't
know the sacrifices that were made each and
everyday. But we did it because we believed
in something, because that code of honor ran
deep. Deep enough to overlook the
mishandling of funds and the stench of
corruption, that was even now kept well
hidden from the public. But now wasn't the
time to go there either.

"It's not for them brother, whatever
this is you know it's got to be some fucked
up shit for Logan to even contemplate
dragging us back in. We knew when we left
there was a possibility that it was only a
matter of time before they came looking.
Well it's happening sooner than we thought
but hey."

He kicked at the weeds that had
started growing in Logan's back yard. We're
gonna have to make a run soon with the
lawnmower. "I refuse to put anymore into
this shit. They've taken all they're gonna
get. What's the point of us over there
fighting this shit while they're making
backroom deals with the same fucks we're
trying to eliminate?" Shit this was going to
be harder than I thought. Firstly because I
agreed with him one hundred percent and
secondly I didn't really want to leave my
woman and go anywhere either. This whole

thing was fucked already and we hadn't even left stateside.

"Ty, you know that if this thing wasn't important whatever it is, Logan wouldn't have brought it to the table. You also know that if one goes we all go so there's no point in fighting it. Let's just see what Logan has to say. We all know that the fucks in office are assholes but this is not about them. Chances are this is some shit that can fuck with our citizens and we took the oath brother. God, family, country, hanging up our weapons didn't change that. We are what we are and you can't tell me as mad as you are right now that you're willing to leave our people in a vulnerable position whether from domestic or foreign fuck ups." I knew I was getting through to him when he finally stopped his mad pacing and just stared off into the distance. "Fuck."

I followed him back inside with a slap on the back. The danger wasn't exactly over but at least he was willing to listen to reason. The others were standing around waiting. I know they wouldn't have carried on without us, that is not our way. When you've spent as much time together in the kind of situations we have you get to know each other pretty damn well. I know my brothers and they know me, and that's why I knew that none of them were too happy with this turn of events.

"Before we go any farther, we've got a problem; Connor." I knew what he meant, I was barely holding onto my sanity by a thread. This was the reason we'd all made a pact, the saying goes never leave a man behind. For us that went double, it was fucked to be in the heat of combat with your woman thousands of miles away. It was fucked not knowing every second of everyday if she needed you.

As men we do what we have to, that doesn't make that shit easy. That's why we'd agreed to a man that we wouldn't get hitched before our gig was up. If it had happened, if one of us had fallen in love before now we would've played the hand we were dealt. But luck and prayer was on our side because for the fourteen years that each of us were in, we never felt that pull.

Now though, my ass was in the sling and so was Logan's. How was I going to leave her? I'm honor and duty bound to answer the call there's no two ways about it. Retired or not, my skills were honed in this man's navy, he made me what I am for a reason. I pretty much know they think they own my ass for a lifetime. I'll let them think that until I snap that cord, until then I have to do what I must for my countrymen and women. But how can I leave her?

"Let's hear what they want first then I'll decide if it's worth leaving my woman here unprotected." Zak and Quinn nodded in agreement as we all pulled up a seat. All except Ty who was once again pacing back and forth like a caged beast. As opposed to leaving our women behind as the rest of us were, Ty was the worst. His history made sure of that but that's his story to tell.

"Khalid has surfaced." Everyone in the room tensed. Son of a mother-fucking bitch.

"Where, when?" I was almost at the edge of my seat. This fuck is one of the deadliest assholes to ever walk the earth. The Desert Fox, that's what we'd tagged him. Early on in our career we'd been given Intel but just before we'd been set to smoke him out of his hole in Kabul he'd disappeared.

Since then he'd been attributed the blame for more terrorist acts than any man before him, but always he stayed in the shadows. No one knew where he was or who was hiding him, but it stood to reason that he must have friends in very high places. There was no way for such a well known wanted man to have stayed so well hidden all these years without the help of some very influential and powerful people.

"The Sudan."

Fuck I knew there was no way we were gonna pass this shit up. The chance to bring down the world's leading terrorist. He'd evaded us, and the others who'd come before us for all these years. The only one we'd missed though we were only in on the tail end of that deal.

By the time our team had formed they'd already moved onto the new kid on the block. There had been some assholes on a par with the Fox but none could ever quite take his place. My mind was already on the fact that I had to leave her. Logan had a hard on for Khalid, he hated the fuck with a vengeance. Ever since he'd blown up a school of young girls just before Logan had been able to reach them and lead them out to safety. That was maybe ten years ago but Logan hadn't forgotten. But could he leave Gaby?

"I'm in." Zak threw his hat in the ring first and so it went. Fuck, Danielle. My gut tied itself in knots at the thought of leaving her now when everything was still so new. We'd only just dealt with her ex and his bullshit. She still didn't know anything about that shit. The woman who we'd learned days later was really one Rosalind Haynes from Louisiana had given her some bullshit story about a family emergency back home. True to form my girl had offered her help in anyway necessary but I was there to smooth that shit over.

Haven't seen hide nor hair of Robert in the last few days and it was only a day or so before the ship was due to dock. Now with this shit there was just too much going on at once. My first inclination is to say fuck no. I don't want to leave her here with this shit so up in the air.

"When do we have to give them an answer and how soon will we have to be in the desert?" I broke off when Ty started his shit again.

" We said we'd never do that shit, and this is fucked Logan that you'd even think of dong it. You and Connor have your women now you can't just up and leave them no matter what the fuck. They come first fuck everything else. Fuck these assholes. Fourteen fucking years, I gave them fourteen years of my life and would've given them the whole twenty, and for what? So they can lie to our fucking faces like we're fucking sheep." Tyler bunched his fists as he prowled around the room.

"We're not doing this for them brother, you know this. They're protected, you better believe their asses are covered. We're doing this for each other and for the men and women we pass everyday on the streets. Because we all know they'd sell us out to the highest bidder. As for the girls, you think this is easy for me? I don't even let Danielle drive herself to fucking work and with this smuggling shit and the money moved where they can't find it it's fucked." I had to stop talking because I was only talking myself out of going.

"I'm telling you right now Logan if I find out this is some fucked up bullshit to have us protecting their oil interest or diamond mines or some shit I'm going to put a bullet in some fuck's head."
"I thought you calmed him down Connor?" I shrugged my shoulders at Quinn.
"Hey this is his calm."

"I haven't given them an answer as yet but most likely if we answer the call it will be in a few weeks at the least."

I went home a lot later than expected so I knew she would be asleep by now. I just needed to feel her under my hands. In the next few days I was going to have to get my fill of her, enough to carry me through the weeks ahead.

Fuck, we hadn't had enough time. How could I leave her now when it was all still so new? What kind of warrior will I be? Will I be able to focus or would my mind be back here with her? Will I make unnecessary mistakes? These thoughts and more played through my head as I made my way upstairs to our bedroom.

I stripped as soon as I hit the bedroom door without turning on the light and made my way over to the bed. She'd fallen asleep reading so I removed her reading tablet that was lying on her chest and placed it on the night table before pulling her into my arms. "Connor." Her voice was sleep soft and sexy as she snuggled into m.

"Yeah baby wake up I need you." Her hand made a sleepy foray into my hair as she searched for my mouth with hers. She was naked the way I like her to be when we sleep and I ran my hands over her. Pulling my mouth away I latched onto her nipple and sucked it into my mouth while running my finger down her middle until I reached her pussy. Slipping three fingers inside her I went back to her mouth as she fucked herself on my fingers. "Connor?" her voice sounded unsure as my mouth became ravenous on hers and my fingers plunged deeper and deeper. All I could think about was leaving her, being away from her for all those weeks or months or however the fuck long this cluster fuck takes.

"Get on your knees and whatever I do don't be afraid." I helped her into position and lined up behind her. Her pussy was already wet and swollen from my fingers as I moved my mouth over her. I swiped her with my tongue back and forth while holding her hips in place before sinking my tongue inside. She screamed and grabbed onto the sheets while I ate her, trying to get her taste to stay with me. When I'd made her cum in my mouth I knelt behind her and slipped my cock home. I went in hard and deep on my first thrust. I was pissed the fuck off and fair or not I intended on taking out that frustration on her sweet little pussy tonight. That's why the warning before the fuck. "Hold on."

When she looked over her shoulder in surprise I knew I was doing some shit she'd never experienced at my hands before but still I didn't let up. I couldn't; I was at a place in my head that I'd never been. The thought of having to leave her behind and go into uncertain danger fucked with my head and my heart. If I could take part of her with me I would. For now all I will have are memories.

"I want to look at you baby." I pulled out and helped her onto her back before sliding back into her gently. I looked into her eyes as I loved her. Trying to imprint her beauty on my brain.

"What is it Connor?" Her hand came up to caress my cheek as I shook my head at her. Not yet, let me enjoy this before I shatter us both with the shit I was about to do to her. I'd promised her that I'd never leave her. As much as I was against leaving my woman behind I've come to learn that she's fucking petrified of that shit.

Now I have to break my word. I buried my face in her neck so she wouldn't see the fight going on in my soul. "My Dani. I love you so fucking much. Will you marry me tomorrow if I asked?" She nodded her head yes without question, her eyes worried because she knew something was wrong with her man.

I made slow sweet love to her for the rest of the night, turning to her throughout the night and slipping into her waiting warmth. Each time I turned to her or rolled her beneath me she was there with me. Accepting me into her sweet body without question.

At least I could do that much for her, give her my name so that the child I'm sure I'd planted inside her would have my name.

THE END

Thank you very much for reading

You may reach the author @

Jordansilver.net

amazon.com/author/jordansilver

Jordan Silver is the author of over ninety novels of all genres. Available @Amazon.com and free with Kindle Unlimited

SEAL Team Seven
Logan
By
Jordan Silver

Table Of Contents

Chapter One

LOGAN

"Babe, move that ass faster I'm close, stop fucking around." I had to grit my teeth to keep from shooting too soon. I even smacked her ass to get her going, but she was in one of her moods.

My poor boy was hanging on for dear life, we'd both grown accustomed to her trying to one-up our ass, but I'm all man so she's never gonna win this fight. She's playing dirty this morning though, the little sneak.

She kept teasing me, moving her hips around and around in circles, then lifting up slowly, before dropping down hard on my cock. The sensations were unbelievable as my cock pushed up into her.

Looking up at her as she pulled on her nipples, head thrown back, her flat stomach concaved as she rode me for her own pleasure, I grabbed her hips and tried moving her the way I needed so I could cum.

She's been teasing me for a good half an hour now and I had no doubt it was to get back at me for the torture I put her through when I ate her sweet pussy for an hour. No good deed and all that happy shit.

"Gabriella, fuck, now." She clenched down on my dick so that no matter how much I tried pulling and pushing it made no difference, that's her new trick.

"I've got something for your ass love of mine." I loved being in her like this first thing in the morning. With the birds chirping right outside the window, the sun, trying to make its presence known, and all else was still. It's part of our routine, one I hoped to have for the next sixty years at least.

She rolled over this morning, with a smile on her face, probably remembering the pounding I'd given her the night before. That's all it took for me to pounce. Now I was buried balls-deep as she tickled the head of my cock with her cervix.

On her last downward plunge I slammed into her hard. Her mouth and eyes flew open and already she was bathing my cockhead with her sweet juices. My baby likes her man to do her rough on occasion for all that she's a dainty little thing. I lucked the fuck out there for sure. A fucker like me needs a little raw in the mornings.

Before she could react to my assault on her pussy I switched us over, placing her beneath me with her legs caught in the crook of my arms. She was open to me as I bored into her deeper her sweet cries ringing out in the early morning hours. "Shit Logan wait a minute."

"Uh uh, you had your chance." I showed her no mercy as I fucked into her hard and deep, her pussy wrapped tightly around my cock as it sawed in and out of her.

"You wanna play, huh?" I looked down between us at where my twelve and a half inch rod pinned her to the bed with each thrust. That shit looked massive. I kept my eyes locked there as I started to fuck. In, out in out, side to side, before burying my dick to the hilt in her heated pussy.

She wailed and threw her legs around as her pussy sucked at me, like she was trying to get even my nut sac in there.

"You close babydoll?" Fuck, be close greedy my dick is too happy to keep this shit up much longer.

"Yes almost there." Her voice was breathless as her hips met mine, her ass bouncing off the bed from the hard pounding I was giving her. My kinda sex.

"Fuck I'm there cum with me." I took her nipple between my lips and sucked hard knowing that that was one of her triggers. When I felt the liquid heat of her pussy juices covering me once again, I let go and emptied deep inside her. I felt my balls drain out inside her down to the last drop, as she twitched and sighed beneath me.

I took a moment lying on top of her, pulling her body in close, before dropping to the side and pulling her over on top of me. My girl likes to cuddle after sex so I have to give her what she wants, even though I'm already running late and it's her fault for teasing the shit out of me.

I laid there for a good ten minutes while she ran her hands all over my chest and arms. She was riding the last bit of steel out of my cock like she wasn't quite finished with me yet. Much more of this shit and my rod will be up and ready to go again. She doesn't listen for shit.

"You done?"

"Maybe, why?" She did that cat in heat thing that these southern belle types have down to a fine art.

"Why, because I'm supposed to be somewhere ten minutes ago and if I'm not off this bed in the next five there's a good chance my nosy ass brothers are gonna bust down the door and come looking."

That didn't seem to register too well since she was still doing the bump and grind on my dick. "But I like feeling you inside me." She squeezed around my cock, trying to get a rise out of him.

"Fine, I'm going to do you one last time but then I've gotta go." I pulled out and used my fist to wipe our mixed juices off my rod. "Suck me back to hard and I'll take care of your pussy, but then I've got to go." She was only too happy to get on her knees in the middle of the bed and take my meat into her mouth, totally ignoring my stern look. A little more than a month ago she'd been a virgin; that was a thing of the past. In that time she's tried to get me to teach her everything there is to know about sex. When I wasn't working at the site or running ops with the guys for our upcoming mission, I was riding between her legs.

"You remember what I showed you?" I wrapped her long golden locks around my fist as she moved her head up and down on my meat. "Uh-huh." She opened her mouth wider and prepared to suck me the way I liked.

"Well do it." I hit the back of her throat on my next stroke in and her eyes came up to meet mine. I could see the bulge of my cock in her neck with each fuck I took into her mouth, and her spit and my per-cum was starting to run down her chin.

"Do you want the bed or the floor babydoll?" It took her a minute to ease off my tool so she could answer. "Why, what's the difference?" I played with her chin as she looked up at me with innocent eyes. How could she be such an enigma? "The bed will get you a nice slow fuck, the floor will get you hard and fast, choose one."

She hopped off the bed and landed on the floor next to it on her hands and knees, with her ass in the air, and the pink of her pussy winking at me from between her thighs.

"That's my girl." I led with my dick as I got off and went to stand behind her. I used the thick head of my cock to tease her from clit to slit while she hissed and threw her ass back at me, looking for dick.

I smacked her ass cheek once with the flat of my heavy cock before giving in and sinking into her. She arched her back and hissed when I hit bottom, her legs spreading wider, to take me in deep. "Oh yeah, you're feeling nasty." I planted my feet firmly and bent my knees as I drilled into her pussy, going deep.

"Yes, oh please Logan, do it." I know what she meant, what she craved. If the good people of our little town ever found out that one of their daughters was as wild as this one they'd never believe it.

I pulled her hair back roughly as I surged into her pussy, using her hair like a horse's mane to pull her on and off my rod. As promised it was hard, quick and just a little rough.

It wasn't long before I was emptying my seed in her belly again while she creamed my cock and wailed like I was killing her ass. I kept sliding in and out of her even though we'd both got off, as my dick dripped inside her.

I've been playing it loose and fancy free in her pussy since I took her cherry.

There was no threat of disease and the question of breeding her was of no consequence since she'd practically booked the wedding hall. As far as she was concerned we were already hitched, so who was I to argue? I dripped the last few drops of cum inside her before pulling her head back so we could share one last kiss before we both headed for the shower.

"What's on the agenda for today babydoll?" She gave me a run down of what her day looked like. Now this was not idle chatter bullshit, I seriously paid attention to where she was going and whatnot because of what was going on in the town, things that she knew nothing about.

I didn't want her going into any dangerous situations. I signed off on her plans, which was mostly wedding shit.

I lathered up my hands and washed her body as she stood in front of me. Her body was truly a thing of artistic beauty. High firm tits that were the perfect D cup with the sexiest penny sized nipples, a slender waist that flared off into her hips and a nice fat ass. Her crowning glory is her wild mane of multi colored hair that makes her bottle green eyes just light up.

At twenty-five she's seven years younger than me. Some thought maybe too young and innocent to deal with a man like me, who led the life I did. I really didn't give a fuck what some thought; she was mine.

I'd seen her wanted her and made it happen. The fears of her family were well understood, I am after all an unknown, ex military and I ride a bike to boot with my brothers, which some people automatically perceives as a biker crew, and we all know the reputations bikers have.

As far as they are concerned, the daughter of a prominent businessman had no right being caught up in my world. Their arguments might've worked if she hadn't fallen as hard for me as I had her.

One look and we were both hooked and nothing and no one had been able to stand in our way. Her old man had tried paying me off; he'd almost lost his life for that insult. I still had that shit on video; I'm keeping it for kicks and giggles.

I had of course shown it to her the same day. My little tigress had lit into her dad and moved out of his house an hour later, and straight into my bed. It helped that she was best friends with my new little sister Danielle, my brother Connor's fiancée.

In fact it was because of Dani that we had even met. Like I said, it was lust at first sight, and in spite of my asshole brothers' ribbing, that lust had morphed into something more almost overnight.

With Gabriella it was like being side swiped with a semi truck. There was no real warning, just wham, out of nowhere and I was blindsided. It happened so easily and without much fanfare, that I didn't even know what the fuck had hit me. I think I was thinking the way I always did; I'd hit it and be done in a couple weeks more or less, but one look, one taste and here we are. I knew from fuck one that I was in trouble.

Chapter Two

LOGAN

I hadn't wasted any time getting her into my bed and that's where she's been ever since. The girls keep each other busy when the boys and I are out on patrol, and they both have work during the day. Something I was coming to terms with, since if I had my way, she'd never leave the safety of the compound. Not without me, or one of my brothers riding rough shod anyway.

Her job was pretty much like Dani's something I noticed about this side of the country. People were big on having their kids come work with them or for them or whatever the fuck. Unlike Dani though, this one was the company's buyer or some shit, and this branch dealt in high-end art deals among other things. I can hold a conversation about that shit for about ten minutes before my ears, eyes and every fuck else starts to bleed, so it's good that we have other interest.

So far we'd blended pretty well together, she knew my position on most things, which boiled down to I'm the man, you do what I say and everyone's safe that way. She does have random moments of female crazy when she thinks she can do her own thing and get away with it.

I guess that stems from being raised by parents who thought giving their kid her way in everything was the way to go. With me she's on a tight leash. I think that was one of the things that soured her dad against me in the beginning.

He didn't like that I called the shots. Or more to the point, that his little girl got off on that shit and was only to happy to obey her man.

Men who call the shots have been given a bad reputation in the last few years. That's because some assholes have abused the privilege, but I'm not about to put my woman's life in danger because society was too fuck stupid to know the difference between a man who gave a fuck and an abuser.

I've seen the underbelly of mankind when I was in the trenches. Society can get fucked; I'm tagging her ass from the get. Wherever she goes, I'm gonna know, not because I wanna control her, but because I wanna keep every other motherfucker out there with an agenda away from what's mine, and keep her ass safe at the same time.

Her dad is one of those who don't know the difference, either that or he thinks that's his role and had a hard time relinquishing that shit to someone else, especially someone like yours truly. I'm sure I'm nobody's ideal of their little girl's prince charming; I could give a fuck and told him so in no uncertain terms. If he or anyone else in this town thought I was giving her up because of their fucked up prejudices, they were out their fucking minds.

Things were a little more civil between us these days. I guess a couple of weeks without any contact had been too much for her mother and she had put her foot down. My girl had stood her ground, if her dad didn't apologize to me she would never step foot back in their home again. What she didn't understand was I hadn't punched her father in the face because he'd insulted me, but because of the insult to her.

She was priceless as far as I was concerned and her happiness meant more to me than anything else. If I'd thought for one second that me being in her life wasn't good for her, I loved her enough that I would've walked away, okay that's a fucking lie but whatever. I admit to a shitload of selfishness on my part, Gabriella is the best thing that has ever happened to me, no one or nothing had ever given me that feeling of completeness I get when I am with her, there was no way I was giving that up, not for anything.

I'd given my blood for my country, why the fuck didn't I deserve one of the best it had to offer? Meanwhile I hadn't been looking for her, but that didn't stop me from going all in.

Not even the unmerciful teasing I'd had to endure from my brothers had swayed me; I was locked in there for good. The thought didn't even scare me anymore, not like it did in the beginning when all I could think is 'what the blue fuck?'

The fact that she loved me made life a hell of a lot more bearable than it had been before. I didn't have the best of childhoods, my mother was a truck stop waitress, who got knocked up by a trucker, who used to come through town and sell her dreams. Until the day she told him she was pregnant and she never laid eyes on him again. As a kid, I spent lots of time alone. Being raised in a small- town, people didn't follow the same tenets as big city dwellers.

No one thought too much about a young single mom leaving her five-year old son alone while she went out to make a living during the summer months when school was out. That kid learned a lot about the streets at an early age.

The old guys who hung around at the local bar didn't have any problem teaching him the facts of life. When most kids my age was learning to read and write, I was learning the ins and outs of a hard knock life.

Mom did the best she could I don't hold anything against the old girl. In fact, after I started making real money a few years ago, I'd set her up in a nice little house in the middle of town. It had always been her dream, the white picket fence, and the little flower garden. I made sure she had everything she'd ever wanted, including a cruise every year for her birthday for her and one of her girlfriends. She didn't need to work anymore if she didn't want to, but she liked to always be doing stuff, so she'd taken up sewing, and now had a nice little business.

Some of my old mentors had passed on a lot of knowledge. The less hardcore had taught me that an education was the best escape from Thomasville. The thing is, I never wanted to escape my town, I loved the picturesque small town with the Rockies as a backdrop; no I wanted to escape poverty.

I went into the service where I met my brothers and the commander, which led me here to another small town on the other side of the country, and her, my fucking life.

My brothers and I had our shit together, I made sure of that. And with the inheritance from the commander, we were pretty much set. All that was missing for each of us was a good woman. My brother Connor had found his with my new little sister Danielle and I was pretty sure the others won't be far behind, no matter how much they bitched and moaned.

The only fly in my ointment was the illegal activities that seemed to be plaguing our little slice of heaven. That, and the fact that pretty soon I was gonna have to leave and go take care of something for Uncle Sam, the fuck.

When she was through prattling away at me about everything under the sun, we had a rushed breakfast together. Being in the service had taught me a lot of disciplines and structure and shit, so I was big on doing things a certain way.

Not that I was regimented or anything like that, but I believed having some kind of routine between us would work, so breakfast together in the mornings and dinner at night was a must. We fucked around the clock so I had no fear of shit going dry there. If I hadn't been running late, we would've been at whomever's turn it was to cook this morning, another one of our traditions I aim to keep.

"I want you home before dark and don't let the sunset catch you in the other town you hear me?" I was expecting an argument, she argues me to death about everything, and sometimes I let her, if it's not a big deal, other times, like now, all it takes is a look.

"But Logan we have so much to do. I know to a man it might not seem like much, but planning a wedding is not a nine to five operation." I guess my silence alerted her to the danger she was about to walk her ass right into. I'd told her about that shit, but things were still new and it looked like it was gonna take her some more time yet, to get the hang of this shit.

She looked up from her bowl of fruit and caught the look on my face, nothing sinister, just a raised brow; but that was enough to have her backtracking and acting like she had some damn sense. "Fine, I'll be home before dark."

"The fuck is it that y'all got to do today anyway, build the damn hall?"
"Very funny Logan, I will have you know, we're looking at patterns for the tables and chairs, we still haven't chosen the crystal…"

Her mouth was moving but I wasn't hearing shit. I held my hand up for her to stop. "Sorry I asked." Was Connor really getting involved in this shit? I have got to have a word with my brother; this was some female shit, and no place for warriors.

"I know that look Logan and you promised so don't even."
"The fuck did I promise?" I drank the last of my coffee and rose to leave before she talked me into some shit I was not even interested in, she's good at that shit. Usually she waits 'til I'm inside her to start her shit, but if she's pulling her stunts at the damn breakfast table that means I've been slipping.

"You said we could discuss this stuff and you'd help but so far you always come up with excuses…"

"Uh huh and when did we have this conversation about me having anything to do with this shit, or more to the point, handing over my balls? Just book the church, put on a dress and let's do this shit already." I knew she was gonna have something to say about that, and was in no way surprised by the loud screech. My baby can make some annoying ass noises when she wants to.

I put my shit in the dishwasher and tried to make my escape before she wound down. If that bottom lip of hers starts to tremble she can talk me into pretty much anything, so I needed to be out of dodge in case that shit was next on her agenda. "But Logan…"

"Ehhhh, gotta go to work baby." I kept my eyes forward as I held up my hand for silence and beat feet for the door. Fucking sly ass female, she sped up behind me and I moved faster, it was a bitch move but what the fuck was I supposed to do?

The woman was driving me crazy with this shit. Connor was looking like he was weakening on this front and I'd be fucked if I'm gonna be knee deep in tulle and flowers and whatever the fuck else she's always lecturing me about when it comes to the wedding.

That shit'll just be fodder for Ty and his smartass mouth, and I really didn't want to have to off one of my brothers over this shit. But if he called me bitch made one more time because of this wedding shit, I'm gonna have to cap him.

Chapter Three

LOGAN

"You fucks ready let's roll." They were lined off like sentinels outside in my yard waiting for me. I ignored their disrespectful smirks and grabbed the cup of coffee Connor held out to me. It was his turn for breakfast again I guess, then again since he'd brought Dani home I don't think any of the others had seriously taken up cooking duty again.

It was sexist I know, but I preferred a good home cooked meal prepared by someone who knew what the fuck they were doing, to a half ass job by one of my brothers. The bra burners could go fuck themselves. Gabriella was shy about cooking for them for some reason, but I wasn't about to push her, she'd come around when she was ready or the fucks could eat take out when it was our turn.

"We were waiting for you bro damn, it's getting harder and harder to get a move on these days. Those of us who aren't leg shackled would like to get the day started at a decent hour you know."

Quinn was always the other one starting some shit. It's like he and Tyler took turns being the assholes of the bunch. I took a sip of hickory and headed for my bike. "Fuck you Quinn." The laughter that followed brought a smile to my face. Things had been kind of tense since we'd got the orders that were still up in the air.

We were all just getting into the groove of things here and no one was looking forward to heading back into the deep dark hole that was this war. Especially since we'd already fought this particular fight once before; it smacked of repetition.

Not to mention it was extremely rare to be given a heads-up about an upcoming mission like this one. Usually an order came in and you had to be out in the next five minutes, no questions.

I wasn't too thrilled about that and I'm sure my brothers were probably starting to think along the same lines, but we were all waiting to see which way the wind blows. If anything looks too hinky to me I'd scratch the fuck no questions, I wasn't about to walk my team into some fucked up situation that some asshole in a higher position pulled together out his ass.

It's been known to happen more than the American public may know. That's what happens when assholes start using the armed men and women of the nation as their own personal mercs, evil, twisted fucks.

On top of that we'd made some moves that could set things off here in our own backyard, and we were waiting to see the results from that. After much deliberation we'd gone ahead and moved the laundered money that someone had put in Danielle's name through her family's charity. Robert her ex was still insisting that he didn't know who he was working for and Crampton had given up all he had. Whoever was pulling their strings was still in the shadows, which was a dangerous thing for all involved; it was like chasing smoke.

Our stakeouts down at the pier still hadn't given up anything and the old guys weren't having any luck either. It's as if whoever we were dealing with had eyes and ears all around and knew when to lay low.

I didn't like that theory, it spoke volumes as to what we might be dealing with here and that wasn't good. I guess we could've called in local law enforcement by now, but what were we gonna tell them? And besides, we're not big on trusting that shit. More often than not those fuckers were on the take. How else can you explain an operation that was so well insulated? Nah, I'll hold off on that for now

***

We rode out in formation, some of us on our bikes and some in trucks, according to what role we were gonna play today. Sometimes someone had to make a supply run or some shit, so a bike wasn't gonna cut it. I could see why the people here were still getting used to us we were a militant a little bunch to be sure. Even the way we rode shouted military, do not fuck with us. Add the tats and shit and well you had blueprint for stereotyping.

Quinn and Ty were fucking with Connor in his truck, tailgating him like fucking teenagers as they left through the gate. I waited for the others to pull out ahead of me as I sat my ride. I always ride in the back just in case some shit is about to go down. Cowards hardly ever come at you straight on, so I knew whatever popped off would more than likely come from the rear. I wasn't expecting shit to go there in this little town, but I was trained to prepare for anything, and never let them catch you slipping.

My phone rang just as I turned the key in the ignition. I didn't check the readout because I thought it was my woman. She likes to call and fill my ear with cutesy shit to start my day off, even though I'd just left her body not an hour ago.

"Hey." I was already smiling like a sap.
"Do you know what your commander was up to before he died?"
"Say what?"
"You should really look into that before you go digging into things that don't have anything to do with you. Some of us don't appreciate nosy fuckers messing around in our business." The line went dead. I slammed out of the truck with my hand up in the command position. I was sure they could all see me since we hadn't cleared the fucking property yet.

To a man they all stopped and came towards me, faces already set in stern lines because they knew some shit had gone down. I waited until they were all within spitting distance so my words wouldn't carry.

"Just got a call, don't know who yet, but listen." I'd hit record on my phone as soon as the robotic voice had started talking. The same message replayed and my brothers already had their backs up before it was over.

"That's bullshit."
"Of course it is Connor, we know that. But this hump is obviously up to something. We gotta think, why would they go to all this trouble, for what? Did you hear him say 'nosy fuckers in our business? What have we been sniffing around in lately?"

"Whatever the fuck is going on around here might be more than we first thought. If they're making voice altering phone calls and shit like this is a damn action movie, we must be getting too close. But this crosses the fucking line, what does he mean what the commander was up to?"

Tyler was my wild child. He and the Commander had shared a close relationship, we all did, but Ty is everybody's problem child and we tend to keep them closer than most. If these fucks tried to blemish the Commander's name in anyway I'm pretty sure I'll have a hard as fuck time keeping him from going rogue.

"The money, it's got to be about the money we moved." It was a fuck load of money that we'd found in an account Dani's ex Robert and that Rosalind woman had set up using Dani's name. Quinn was still monitoring that shit to see what popped off, but so far nothing. We all knew that with that kind of money involved it wasn't gonna go down that easy, but it was a risk we'd had to take to smoke the fuckers out. I just thought we had more time, damn. Connor looked back towards his place where Dani was just coming out the door. She looked over and waved with a bright smile, then my door opened and Gaby came prancing out.

"Handle that Con. The rest of you know what to do. Gabriella, come here." She glanced over at me in surprise, probably because of the tone of my voice. The others scattered around the perimeter as she walked towards me. "I need you to stay inside today."

"But..." I just lifted my brow and that shut her up.
"Yes sir." I tapped her ass lightly to let her know I was pleased with her response, before pulling her in to kiss her forehead. "Good girl." We looked over to where I was sure Connor was telling his woman the same thing.

The women headed into Con's place while the brothers met in a huddle in the middle of the compound. "Change of plans, let's make sure this place is secure." I passed my phone off to Quinn. "Check this out, find out how this hump got my number and where that call came from."

Most people don't understand the strength of the technology the armed forces deal with. They see us as civilians without any backing now that we were stateside, but the reality was that my guys and I were always smart.

We brought shit home with us that we knew would come in handy when it came to protecting our asses as well as our families. Some of us had shit in our head that it would take a stick of dynamite to remove.

Each man went about his business making sure our shit was on lock. I called one of the men on the job to let them know we were either going to be late, or not there at all today, and to send someone else out to make the runs. The last job was almost done and we had a few more lined up after this, and were even at the point of turning people away.

All in all things were going fine except for the shit that was going on down by the water. We were accomplishing a lot of what we had set out to do, making strides. I wasn't about to let anything fuck with our program.

My brothers and I had been through the bowels of hell together, they see me as their designated leader and I take that shit seriously. No one was gonna get through me to hurt my family, fuck that.

"Everything looks cool Lo, but I say we take this shit as an eminent threat. Whatever this is I think this was the first volley, which means they're gonna come at us with more unless we back down, and I'm guessing we're not about to that shit right." Zak was usually quiet, but he was always ready for a good tussle. It had been a while since we'd kicked any major ass, except for Con's little skirmish a few weeks ago. Somehow these people had figured out what we were up to, and since the leak hadn't come from any of us, I'm guessing it was the asshole ex, the sidepiece, or Crampton. And since Crampton was bitch made, I'm more inclined to believe it was one of the other two.

"Con we have to go hunting, let's see if your boy was dumb enough to talk. Who do we have in NOLA that can nab the ratchet broad he was messing with?"

There was a lot of throat clearing which told me that I may or may not like what was coming next. The seven of us were a unit, but we dealt with other brothers in arms, sometimes people from other branches. Some of them were more fucked up than others, and we tend to attract the rougher element.

When all eyes turned to Zak I pretty much knew what was coming and so did he, from the reaction we got. "Fuck no, uh-uh anybody else, fuck, I'll go get the skel myself." Damn, I thought he was over this shit.

"Bro, we gotta do what we gotta do, and we don't have time for you to make that run and head back here. Where is she hiding out?" I turned to Quinn because he would be the best one to give me what I needed since he was the one keeping tabs on Rosalind or whatever the fuck she was going by these days.

"French Quarter a little place off Chartres St. The place is old and noisy as fuck and it's right in the middle of the hustle and bustle of the tourist crowd. I guess she learned her lesson last time; but there's one thing she missed, there's a balcony." He grinned at that because Vanessa, the Lieutenant we were planning to send after her, wasn't called Cat-woman for nothing; that chick could climb.

"Tell me you're okay with this brother. We won't do it if you ain't but we need her. Is she stateside Con?" He looked at Zak as he nodded his head and rocked back on his heels with his hands stuffed in his pockets. "Man up bro, stop being afraid of one little woman, what is she four-eleven?" I turned to scowl at everyone's pain in the ass.

"Ty shut the fuck up, who said anything about being afraid?" Zak looked angry enough to chew nails. We all knew the story about Zak and Nessa, well some of it anyway. That was one tale he hadn't shared in its entirety. But we all knew that something had gone down between those two and whatever it was it had ended badly.

The way he was glowering at Ty he wasn't over shit, and knowing Nessa, she wasn't gonna back down either. I need this fuckery on top of everything else. But you gotta do what you gotta do. "Make the call

Con. Zak, I expect you to be on your best behavior." It was short fucking notice but it looked like we were in the middle of some shit, now was not the time for bullshit. Fucking women.

"I'm cool, just keep her little ass in check when she gets here or I'm gonna finish what I started." He walked away after that cryptic note and I was already second-guessing my decision to bring her here.

If I knew more about what had gone down with them I could maybe try to mediate, but I didn't know shit. The only thing I was sure of is that another man wasn't involved, because had it been anything like that, my brother would've been court martialed already, so hopefully whatever it was wasn't too bad.

"Have any of you ever figured out what the fuck went down between those two?" I watched him storm towards the gym we all used. That more than anything told me what kind of mood he was in. Poor sap, she still had him tied up in knots.
"What always goes down between a male and a female Cap? I don't know the particulars but from what I remember about last time, this shit ought to be good. I'ma stock up on beer and popcorn, that shit was

better than the movies, or more like ringside at a Heavyweight bout."

"Ty, anyone ever tell you you're a pain in the ass?"
"Nope, what I ain't is whipped like the rest of you fucks; looks like Zak's gonna be next. Y'all keep that wedding shit away from me ya hear, shit's catching."

Like I said, problem child. He loped of somewhere to give the rest of us peace of mind for a minute. He was joking and acting like everything was cool, but all of us knew to keep an eye on his high-strung ass. He was already wound tight about the Desert Fox business, and this would just be one more thing to bring out that fucker's crazy.

Chapter Four

LOGAN

We sat around in my kitchen all day working out strategy. It might've seemed like a bit much to anyone looking in from the outside, but we knew that every little thing meant something.

You learn that shit fast when you were in the thick of battle, returning enemy fire and your heart went out to the kid you saw trapped in the middle of the crossfires, only to see that same kid detonate when one of your fellow soldiers go to help. A couple episodes of that shit and you learn to be overly cautious about every damn thing.

Outwardly I was cool I had to be. I'd learned a long time ago that the boys followed my lead. It wasn't something that we were conscious of, but it was the truth nonetheless. If I was in a shit mood, they'd pick up on it, and that could sway the day for everybody. So if I let on that I was more upset by the caller's innuendo, then for sure they would be too. So I had to keep that shit close to the vest until I knew what was going on. Then I was gonna fuck somebody's shit up for trying to mar a good man's name.

A man who had done more for his country than most; especially some drug trafficking asshole.

"Okay so this is the first we're hearing about the Commander being involved in anything shady. First things first, we consider the source." I wrote that shit in big block letters on the power point board I had set up.

"Next, we know the Commander, he was basically in charge of whether we lived or died for a huge fucking chunk of our time when we were in, and he never let us down. Aside from that, we knew the man, stand up as they come."

We were all in agreement that whatever this was-was nothing but a smokescreen. I wasn't sure what the locals knew or thought about what we did in the navy. It's a safe bet that the Commander never discussed missions and shit on the outside, but they had to at least know that you had to have nerves of steel to make it through fucking boot camp, farther more stay in for as long as the seven of us had.

"Devon I'm gonna need you to keep your ear to the ground, they seem to trust you around here more than they do the rest of us." That's because he had this deceiving, innocent boy next door look about him. With his nod I carried on.

"Until we know who said what and to whom, we can't really move, but we're not sitting around here on our asses waiting for them to make first strike. Con is right, it has to be about the money. We moved it, they start calling. That was a lot of fucking money; people commit horrendous acts for less so we know what we're up against.

From now on the women are under twenty-four hour guard. There will be no time when they are not under the eyes of one of us. They're always together anyway unless they're going off to work. Con make sure Dani takes a leave of absence or some shit, I'll work on Gaby. They can use the weddings as an excuse."

You'd think in the middle of this fuckery there would be no room for bullshit, but that didn't stop the five of them from making smart ass remarks about marriage.

"Moving right the fuck along, tonight we're gonna start with Robert, aka the douche." I don't know where we got a pic of this guy but we had one up on the board with a death arrow pointed at his head. I didn't have to think too hard to figure out whose handiwork that was. "I'm not sure he has the balls, but we're not taking any chances." They may think this shit was gonna have us running scared, and again, I don't know where they ever got the idea that we were pussies, but that phone call had the opposite affect to what they expected.

We threw around scenario after scenario but the reality was for now, all we could do was batten down the hatches and protect our flanks until we knew who the enemy was.

"You know what I'm thinking, I'm thinking somebody knows about our relationship with the commander. I'm not talking about the town's speculation as to why he left his team his land, but someone knows how any mark against him would affect us not only personally, but because of missions."

"Lo's right; the more I think about that call the more something stinks. We already know that this is no low-end operation they're too good. We can't even get a whiff of who these fucks are, and the people we've spoken to so far don't even seem to know who the fuck they're working for. I'm thinking that phone call was their first mistake, it gave us a little more insight than we had before."

"You're on to something there Con." I looked around at the rest of them, especially Ty who already looked like he was ready for battle, hotheaded little fuck. "Did you make that call?"

I kept my eye on Zak as I asked and almost rolled my eyes at his reaction. He was as prickly as a damn teenage girl on her period over this shit. "Yep, she's on it, said she was getting rusty since her retirement."

"Retirement? I didn't know about this." Vanessa was a little young to retire so that meant something serious had went down. I guess I'll have to wait until she showed up here to get the particulars. Zak seemed as stunned by the news as the rest of us, which meant he hadn't been keeping tabs on her. I wasn't even gonna go there with him right now, because that shit looked like it was gonna take a couple bottles of scotch at the very least.

"You know we never went through the Commander's stuff when we took over. It's still all locked away in the library of his place." Cord reminded me of something I hadn't thought of in a while.

None of us had wanted to go through the old man's personal papers and shit, felt too much like a violation of trust. So we'd locked everything away safely in his old home, which we had pretty much converted into an office with bedrooms and shit.

"What are you saying, that there's something there to verify this shit?" I sighed long and hard at Ty's outburst. This fucker is gonna give me agida. The only time he's actually calm and rational is when we're on a mission, any other time it's like dealing with a psych patient fresh off their meds; ADD fucker. "No Tyler that's not what he's saying. Look, we were all there; we all know the Commander was the salt of the earth. I think what your brother is saying is that maybe we've been coming at this thing all wrong.

None of us stopped to wonder if the old man was privy to any of this, if he suspected something or not. It's worth a look to see what if anything he knew. We just assumed that the old guys came to us first, but what if the Commander, who we know was highly intelligent, and extremely perceptive, was onto whatever this is?"

That seemed to calm his ass down and we were back on track. We decided that there was no point in putting that shit off once the decision had been made, so we sent Candy home early, which translated to her heading to Connor's house, where the women were gathered with their wedding shit.

***

GABRIELLA

"Okay Candy spill." I dragged her through the door after I'd spied her coming. I guess the guys had given her the day off because she was carrying her bag and the whole lot of them had descended on the old plantation house like the feds. "Lordy Gaby let me clear the door at least damn." Like I had time for that.

Dani and I have been on pins and needles ever since we were given our staying orders. It was gonna take me a while to get used to this mess, but with Logan there was no choice. Nothing I tried could sway that man from his path, he's as mule headed as one of my grandpa's old bulls.

I have wedding shit coming out my ears, first he curtailed how many hours I could spend running around, with his be home before dark dictate, and now he'd pretty much put me on house arrest. If I didn't love him like crazy already I'd brain him with something for even thinking he had the right.

"Don't nobody got time for that shit, what's going on over there?" Dani came in the living room with a tray of cookies and tea, like any decent southern belle would at a time like this.

Men are a slower breed, they do not understand the rigors of dealing with wedding plans and making sure that every little detail was just so. Especially when you were planning a double wedding where two of the four participants just grunted and whined when asked for their input.

"Hey Candy, they got you too huh." Dani placed the tray down and sat with her prim and proper self like the lady of the manor. It amazes me that we had grown up together, been taught damn near the same things, and I had broken out of my shell and she hadn't. Don't get me wrong, Dani can get loose with hers if she has to, but she takes a little time to warm up. College had taken care of my good and proper thank you very much.

Being away from momma and daddy for the first time in my life, I'm not ashamed to say that I had gone buck-wild. The only thing I had kept was my virginity, because it had been drilled into me in my mama's milk that that belonged to the man I was gonna marry, everything else was up for dibs.

I drank, smoked, though I didn't like the taste of my first and only cigarette, went joyriding and everything else a delinquent teen with a bank account could get up to. It was some kind of cosmic joke I am sure that I had fallen and fallen hard for a man like my Logan. I couldn't fall for any of the milquetoast mamby-pamby saps in my circle, no I had to go and give my heart to Leonidas.

I had held onto my bad girl persona from my school days unlike Dani who was a born lady down her little pink toes. Logan likes to tease sometimes and ask how comes he'd ended up with the tomboy, but deep down I knew he needed someone like me to put up with his brand of crazy.

"I don't know what all's going on girls, you know these men, they're as tight lipped as they wanna be, but something's lit a fire under their asses. They ain't never had time for going through that place before, never showed much of an interest in it anyway, but now it seems they're hell bent for leather to get to 'em."

"Logan isn't talking and Dani says all Connor told her was not to leave the compound until farther notice. I sure wish I knew what was the big secret. You don't think it has anything to do with one of their missions do you?" I looked at Dani with a little fear in my eyes now. She reached out for my hand and squeezed.

"No, they would've told us if they were going away. I think this is about those night moves." She gave me a look, which I understood very well. Although he men trusted Candy, there were some things that were meant to be kept just between us, if they wanted her to know about their little secret rendezvous they'd let her in on it.

Logan had told me the bare minimum about that as well, and only because I needed to know where the hell he was leaving my bed to go to almost every damn night. It's not like he'd sat me down and talked me through it all nice like either no; if I remember correctly that conversation had gone something like, 'the boys and I have some shit to take care of and might have to leave at night for a while, I won't be gone long, there's nothing for you to worry about.' That was about it.

Candy didn't even ask any questions because she knew better and as much as I was dying to know, the talk soon turned to weddings. But while my two companions were discussing seating arrangements my mind was on what the men were up to. If Logan knew he'd have my ass, but I could never give up a good mystery.

All I needed was to get my girl Dani on my side and between the two of us we might be able to help. How bad can it be? This is Briarwood after all, nothing remotely interesting ever happens here.

Chapter Five

LOGAN

We spent a good part of the day going through the old man's shit and had yet to make a dent in it. Mostly we'd found old letters between him and his childhood sweethearts, and some from colleagues and shit like that, but there was nothing to raise any eyebrows so far. We worked through lunch or tried to, but the women descended upon us and browbeat us into taking a break.

I could tell my nosy ass princess was trying to sniff out what we were doing, but her sneak was as obvious as the nose on her face. Poor baby, it must be hell being surrounded by SEALs when you're accustomed to hoodwinking lesser men with a smile. That shit wasn't about to work, well except maybe with Ty, and since she was still shy about cooking, and the way to his heart was food, we were safe for now.

"Did you get anything done this morning baby?" She was sitting on my lap, swinging her feet as we ate our sandwiches that the girls had whipped up and drank lemonade mixed with iced tea. She looked about twelve with her hair in a ponytail and not a smidge of make-up on. I like seeing her like this, without the damn war paint that got onto everything.

"Nope, nothing at all. How long's this little hitch in my giddy-up supposed to last anyway?" I squeezed her around the middle, because although she said that shit all light, there was a hint of complaint in her voice.

"As long as I say." I waited for it because I know her, she can't leave shit alone for too long, I keep telling her one of these days that shit's gonna land her ass in trouble, but she's still convinced herself that she can get me to see things her way.

The others couldn't hear what we were saying thank fuck, because I would hate to have to deal with their shit if she gave me hell. "Logan we're trying to plan a wedding here. There are things that we need to be on site for, we can't just sit on our asses and expect them to get done. I understand your not wanting to participate, but now you're interfering with what I have to do and that's not fair."

I had to let that shit sink in to make sure she wasn't playing with me, or hadn't lost her damn mind, but she was dead ass serious. A look wasn't gonna cut it this time, but now wasn't the time either.

"We'll talk about this later." I tried to head shit off, the fuck I know about arguing with a female? In my mind, as her man, I lay down the rules, she follows, end of story. "What's there to discuss? I can give up today but…"

What the fuck? "I said later Gabriella." My tone had her deflating which usually would make me try to placate her, but this shit was serious, besides if I start letting her talk me into shit we'd both be in trouble. She wasn't too pleased when they left so we could get back to what we were doing.

"What's the matter Cap, your woman giving you fits?" I threw a piece of bread at Quinn and tried to escape. These fucks like to snick their noses in every damn thing, and the fact that she and I were whispering while the others were carrying on a conversation, would only get their antennas going. "Mind your own damn business you fuck."

"See what I told you, bitch made, both of them." Ty had to duck after making that statement because both Con and I went after his ass. "Say Cap, you do know you're supposed to be the one in the tux right, you too Con." He thought his ass was funny. I cannot wait for him to fall. "As a matter of fact, I do, but I'm thinking of having my attendants, that would be you fucks, wear kilts on account of my Scottish blood."

"The fuck outta here with that shit Cap, I'm not wearing a skirt no matter what the fuck it's called." I knew that would shut him up. I also knew we were all trying to blow off steam before going back in. "Okay guys back to it."

There wasn't any of the usual banter between us; we were all pretty solemn once we passed the door into the private library that we had kept under lock and key since the night we'd buried our old friend.

This is the reason we had been putting this off, it was like saying the final goodbye, something that as tough as we all are, I didn't think we were quite ready to do. For the next few hours there was just more of the same, but then coming on to later in the evening, shit started to take a turn.

"Why the fuck was he writing in code? And check the dates, this was a little before he died, like a few months." Devon passed the ledger type book over to me and the rest gathered around to read over my shoulder.

Something that had been kept between the eight of us was a secret code. We'd all worked on it together and came up with basically our own language. It had been some time since any of us had used it, but it wasn't hard to decipher.

"Shit he suspected something." I ruffled through the pages getting little snippets here and there but I knew we were gonna have to go through it with a fine toothcomb.

"He knew we'd find this eventually, or have reason to come looking, that's why it's in our code. Whoever he suspected is very powerful for him to go to these lengths. Ty make copies for each of us will you?" I passed the book off to him and went back to my digging.

We were all more awake now that we knew we were on the right track. Poor commander, I wonder why he never said anything. We all spoke to him at least once a week when he was alive, even when we were on active we never lost touch, he was our father.

"Did he say anything to any of you about this?" They all shook their heads, which was pretty much what I expected. Our bond was such that there had never been any secrets between the eight of us.

We were each aware of our rank yes, but in the heat of battle, a bullet could give a fuck, so we'd learned to trust in each other beyond the titles. That meant that whatever the old man shared with me stateside, he would've shared with my brothers and vice versa.

＊

We found a few more things that looked like they may be of interest, but then we broke away for dinner because the girls were getting grumpy. They knew some shit was going on but had no idea what.

I, as well as Connor was operating under the fact that they were on a need to know basis when it comes to this shit. They on the other hand like typical fucking females wanted to know everything, so they were playing the role since they didn't get their way. I guess after their little fishing expedition didn't turn up anything at lunch they had decided to change up the act. It was pissing me the fuck off.

I know just how to deal with Gabriella and her bullshit, what Con does with his woman is up to him. She tried coming out of her damn face in front of Quinn and Zak, asking my shit that I had already told her was none of her damn business.

"Are you trying to get fucked up?" She gave me the cold treatment after that. I saw Con whispering to his woman and she was nodding like she had some damn sense. How the fuck did I end up with the hardheaded one?

"Damn, it's like the arctic in this bitch, what did you two do now?" Cord slapped Ty on the back of the head for being stupid and saved me the trouble. The idiot didn't realize yet that when the women get like this it was best to ignore their shit until they came to their damn senses, either on their own, or with a little help. He'll learn, just as soon as he finds one that ties his ass in knots and he learns the difference between a jump off and a wife.

"Taste good ladies, you outdid yourselves." I guess Con decided to play the diplomat, then again that shit might work with Dani, she's easy going and pays heed to her man when he says some shit to her. Gaby on the other hand thinks she can stand toe to toe with me.

Poor thing, I've been letting her get used to me, giving her time to settle in. There was no point in scaring the shit out of her before I even got the damn ring on her finger.

But I was afraid before the night was over she was gonna see another side of me. Especially since she was letting her displeasure show in front of others, that's a big fucking no-no.

By the end of the night when the boys had left and the place was secure, my mind was winding down a bit. And by that it I mean I had more time to think about what the fuck that hump was up to and gave my anger free reign. I sometimes have to hold my shit in check, when you're looked up to as a leader, especially with strong men, you can't always show your hand.

I know in certain situations they feed off of me, and where I'm going in my head, so I have to keep it on the low. But now that they were gone, I didn't have to hold back any longer, I could let my shit out and I knew just how to release the stress.

"You, come 'ere." She didn't know what hit her. She'd been puttering around the kitchen cleaning shit that didn't need cleaning, which told me she had a suspicion that her ass was in trouble.

But whether she knew why she was getting what was coming or not didn't mean fuck all to me. I nabbed her around her neck and pulled her into me for the first mouth fuck. I sent my tongue damn near to the back of her throat before releasing her. "In the bedroom, now." She knew what that shit meant and she wasn't looking too sure of herself as she headed off in that direction.

I started stripping in the hallway and it was safe to say my dick didn't need any direction; he was already on the prowl, sticking out in front of me with a pearl of pre-cum already forming at his tip. She was down to her skimpy panties when I cleared the doorway.

"Leave them." I was in that kind of mood, and I didn't forget that there was supposed to be a lesson in there for her somewhere. Somebody might not get their jollies tonight, I wasn't sure yet. I do know she hates me to leave her high and dry; my baby is a climax freak. If she could cream all over my dick twenty-four seven she would, but a fucker's gotta eat and other shit.

I walked over to her, still holding a little of myself back. I couldn't unleash on her after all, that would be fucked up. But she was gonna get some of it. If she hadn't acted up all damn evening I might've given her a severe dicking, which meant she would've walked twisted for a day at most, but with her bad behavior and my fucked up mood, she was looking at a pussy pounding, and a pussy pounding is nothing to sneeze at.

First things first though! "Kneel." She looked up at me as she got to her knees in front of me. "You know what to do." She knew from my tone that she wasn't allowed to touch me with anything but her mouth. Her hands went behind her back and her head bobbed forward, mouth open wide to take me in. She sucked on my cockhead first, getting her cream, then pulled back and licked from tip to base and back. She nibbled on my dick being careful not to nip me with her teeth too hard before swallowing my shit in one gulp.

My hands went to her hair and fisted and I started face fucking her hard. She made gulping sounds as she tried to keep up as drool and pre-cum leaked all over her face; that was one of my favorite looks.

"Hold it." I was at the entrance to her throat when I stopped her, and then I slowly eased in all the way. There was an art to this shit unless you wanted to hurt your woman; I wasn't into that shit.

A pussy can take more of a beating than a throat I think. What I did do, was flex my cock in her neck until she balked and choked, but with my hands in her head keeping her in place she had no choice but to deal. Lesson one.

I pulled out of her neck and looked down at her sternly as she looked up at me a little more weary now that she sensed my mood. I tapped her cheek with my twelve and a half inch rod and ran the tip over her lips, leaving pre-cum to dry there. "Up on your hands and knees." She climbed onto the bed and looked over her shoulder.

"The fuck you looking for? Eyes front." I knew this way the anticipation would kill her, she didn't know what I was about to do back there.

I eased in behind her and grabbed her ass cheeks and spread. I saw her tense because she knows I said I won't take her there since the one time we tried she was in pain for hours and I had barely got my tip in.

I played with her cheeks long enough to get her worried, and then took my cock in hand and rubbed it up and down her drooling slit. I like the way her hips and thighs jerk a little when I do that, so I did it again. I teased her with my cock tip, using my fingers under her belly to play with her clit while I eased just the tip into her pussy before pulling back.

I kept that shit up for a good five minutes until she started to relax, then I slammed into her forcefully. I had to hold onto her so she didn't slide across to the other side of the mattress from the force of my thrust.

Now she looked back wide eyed like 'what the fuck?' I used the opportunity to wrap her long mane around my fist and pull on her hair hard enough to sting, while going into her belly with the next stroke. Oh she was scared now. "Logan…"

"Shut up." She whimpered and tried spreading her legs wider to ease some of the pressure but a hard slap on her ass soon had her changing her mind. "Stay where the fuck I put you. I want you to think about what the fuck you did wrong while I fuck the shit out of you." The shit probably wasn't gonna work because her pussy was already doing overtime in the leaking department. She was tight as fuck too around my dick, choking me off in her fear.

"Relax your pussy muscles or it's gonna go bad for you." I slapped her ass again when she didn't obey me fast enough.

"I can't, please I'm sorry." I'm sure she was but it was too late for an apology, she shouldn't have started her shit in the first damn place. I used my fingertips on her swollen clit to soften her up a bit.

I nibbled my way around her ear and down her neck, leaving my mark there, all the while plotting to loosen her up so I could put a hurting on her pussy that she won't soon forget.

As soon as I felt the give in her, that slight easing of her flesh, I made my way in there nice and easy; just another one of my tactics to get her to let her guard down.

I turned her head so I could feed her my tongue and slid it past her lips. She sucked as her pussy opened up even more and that's when I struck. I swallowed her screams of disbelief as I let my dick do the talking.

A heavy dick at full hardness can be a serious weapon in times like these, and though she'd gotten her ass in trouble before, it was nothing like this shit.

The secret to this shit wasn't just the pounding either. When your woman was accustomed to being taken care of, was used to loving touches no matter how rough the sex was, you take that shit away she notices. There were no whispered words of praise, no soft smiles, and my touch was as impersonal as it was possible to get. I held even my grunts and moans in check; in short I gave her nothing; just the steel length of my cock butting against her cervix.

When I felt my nuts beginning to draw up, I pulled out of her quickly for my crowning glory. I sprayed the small of her back, tapped the last dregs off on her ass cheek and hopped off the bed headed for the shower.

Her tears started before I left the room. That'll teach her disrespectful ass to show out in front of our family or anyone else for that matter.

Especially since everything I did was to protect and keep her safe. If I gave even an inch with this one I'd spend most of my day getting her out of shit; she's one of those.

She must've hit one of the other bathrooms because when I came back she was in bed, all fresh and sweet smelling. I didn't say shit to her as I got dressed in the dark for what I had to do. I felt her eyes on me but was still too pissed to care. I wasn't only mad at her, but at the situation. This was the very reason why all of us had promised never to settle down while we were in.

I thought we were out of that shit now, but it seemed trouble had followed us here as well.

There was no way for me to get her to understand my side of things, how could she? Most women were accustomed to their man opening up about shit at the dinner table, discussing their day and their business like regular people, we weren't gonna have that, not when it came to shit like this.

I left the room and the house, making sure to secure her inside until I got back. We were moving under cover of dark so no one would know we were off the compound since we were using a secret exit route. I still wasn't too happy about leaving the women here unguarded so we left Cord on night watch. He didn't even grumble about missing the action because he knew how important this was to me and Con.

Robert the fuck had disappeared off the grid for a minute but we found him again. The idiot was so unoriginal that he'd moved to a town over on the other side from the one he'd use to live in before. It was just as easy breaking into his place this time as it had been the last, I guess unlike his partner in crime, he hadn't really learnt that lesson well.

"Hello asshole." Connor waited until he was standing over him in the dark with a penlight pointed at him. He came awake with a start and you could almost smell the fear coming off of him. He sat up like someone had prodded his ass and almost broke the damn headboard. He wasn't looking too good either I noticed, looked like someone had fisted his face. "Who worked you over Robert?" I figured I should try to get at least that much out of him before Con pulverized his ass just for being.

"Not you again, what do you guys want, haven't you caused enough trouble?" "Are you really that fucking stupid? We weren't the ones who got in bed with these assholes that was all you. You're lucky you're still breathing after what you tried to do to my woman, now who the fuck worked you over asshole?"

"I told you before I don't know. You think you're working for one guy, but then he's working for another guy and another and another. I don't know who is who I swear, just please just leave me alone I'm sorry I ever got involved." He wiped his hand under his nose and my stomach turned, what an absolute sap.

"Why did you?"

"Why did I what?" Damn, he's so stupid I almost felt sorry for him. He turned his frightened eyes my way, I guess he figured anything was better than Con. "Why did you get involved?" We hadn't really got much out of him the last time, but then we hadn't yet realized how big this thing really was. Back then we were more focused on the money laundering thing and why Dani's name was being used.

"It was fast money."

"How did they approach you?" I kept my voice civil unlike some people who were looking at him like he was a specimen they'd like to extinguish. "I told you already the last time."

"Tell me again." I got closer to the bed so he could see what there was of me to see. We were all painted up pretty good and covered in black from head to toe. I guess it was our approach that had given us away.

"Someone contacted me, I guess they knew about me and Dani…"

"Don't say her fucking name."

"Con…" I gave him a look, which I'm sure he missed in the dark, but he got the message, stand the fuck down. I expected him to pound this douche into dust any second but I was hoping to get more out of him first.

"Uh…" he looked at Con like he was a two headed monster and moved closer to my side. "Okay um, they knew about the charity and that I might have a way in.

They said she wouldn't get hurt I swear." Again he looked at his own personal monster before carrying on with the story. "We were only supposed to move some numbers around, no one would've ever known if you guys hadn't gone snooping. That last time wasn't the first time we'd done it, we'd made a few dry runs before to see how things would pan out."

"Get to what we wanna know before this one takes your head off." Con was looking like he was ready to go all Samurai on his ass, and I wasn't sure I wouldn't let him. This guy was a real piece a work. "Like I said, someone contacted me."

"How, by mail, email, over the phone how?"

"Oh, they called the first time."

"And why did you take the offer?" He got the beady eye syndrome then. You know, when the eyes get smaller and start flitting around like prey looking for a predator.

"I was in a tight spot okay, I needed the money."

"Who knew you needed money?"

"My bookie I guess, why? You can't be thinking it's Clancy, that fool wouldn't know how to run a set up like this, I'm telling you, these guys are professionals."

I was inclined to believe the idiot and the more we pushed him the more convinced I was that he was telling the truth. He was just another hump who'd fallen in with the wrong crowd. For me, I'd just leave his dumb ass alone and be done with it, but Con had an axe to grind. "Let's go sailor." He gave the douche one last glower before following me out the room.

"Why won't you let me end him?"

"Because it's not right?"

"The fuck you care?" I tried not to laugh because I knew what his problem was, it was eating him up that Dani had once been with this guy, but I can't have my men going around killing off exes, how many virgins were they expecting in this bitch anyway? That brought my mind back to my own pain in the ass.

"Women are a pain in the fucking ass." I signaled to the others to fall in from their positions in the dark outside the townhouse as I made my way to the truck. "Okay I'll bite why do you say that? Gaby giving you fits?" I could hear the laughter in his voice, disrespectful fuck. "When isn't she giving me fits? What the hell is wrong with them, well not yours, Dani's a saint, I ended up with the menace." He stopped short and looked at me with his mouth open before breaking out in laughter.

"What the hell's so funny? She is." The others wanted to know what the joke was so I filled them in while Con tried to compose himself. Of course I had to listen to all of Gabriella's virtues and how a beast like me should be glad she'd even spit in my direction.

"Fuck you Ty, you're just hanging on for those cheese biscuit things Dani says she makes." Which I have yet to taste myself, because she's got problems, fucking nut.

"And, your point? All I'm saying is that both little sisters could've done a lot better." Con and I had to listen all the way home in the truck with the rest of those idiots to how lacking we were, and how much better off our women would've been if they'd chosen one of them. The mood was so light it didn't even matter than we hadn't learned anything more than we'd already known. Well except that we were right in our thinking that this wasn't a small operation.

That led me to thinking about what else they could be in to. If we followed the waterway to the neighboring towns will we find more of the same? How did they come to choose this place anyway? Was it a local? That possibility was looking more and more real.

"We're idiots; of course it's someone local, or at least one of them is. How else would they have known about Dani's charity and now the call about the Commander? Not to mention Robert the douche said they knew about his little gambling problem."

That changed the subject again and we put our heads together trying to figure out who had that kind of pull in the small town. Both Con and I were dating the daughters of two of the town's leading families, but I didn't see them for this, and

Con had already vetted his in-laws when that whole thing had gone down.

We were looking for someone else and I was pretty sure it wasn't Gaby's dad, but I was still gonna look to be absolutely certain.

We hadn't gone that deep into the ledger we'd found or the other papers as yet. So far all we had was that the old man had suspected something was going on down by the water. There were a lot of dates and numbers that we were gonna have to figure out at some point, but no smoking gun pointing to any one person in particular.

The commander also wasn't a foolish man, so if he was onto something he might've left us the ledger with our secret code, but there's a good possibility there were other writings somewhere else, more well hidden. The fucking place was huge I wouldn't even know where to start, but maybe there was something in the book.

"I think we have to get to the bottom of that ledger and soon. The sooner we translate that shit, the closer we will be to the truth. If the old man suspected something then this thing might've been going on for a while. We need to find out what he saw, what made him suspicious, because we all know he wouldn't let something like this rest."

"I'm with you there Lo, looks like we got two breaks in one day, first the phone call, tipping us off to the fact that we're getting too close and now the ledger." Connor sped through the night headed for home and our women and who knows what the fuck else. I was getting really tired of the bullshit. In the service you pinpoint the enemy and take that fucker out. I didn't have time for this bullshit.

Chapter Six

LOGAN

It was full dark when we pulled in. Cord said all had been quiet and there was nothing to report. We made one last round around the perimeter before calling it a night. I slipped into the house quietly so as not to awaken her, and got undressed in the dark. Out of habit, I made the rounds around my place as well before heading for m woman and bed.

I got in on my side and since I was still a little pissed at her, didn't pull her into my arms the way I usually do. I guess I wasn't quiet enough because she stirred behind me. "Logan?" She snuck up to my back and did her kitten shit where she's all cute and cuddly. Sneaky ass.

"What is it?" my voice was stern and uninviting because if she made the wrong move, or the right one depending on how you look at it, I'd be putty in her damn hands and tonight's little lesson would be in vain.

"I'm sorry I was bad I won't do it again."

"Yes the fuck you will. Go to sleep." I'll forgive her in the morning. Right now I had a misbehaving woman to train.

***

I rolled over early the next day before the sun rose. She was still sound asleep with tear tracks on her face. Poor baby, she must think I'm really mad at her. I don't remember ever not holding her all night since we started sharing a bed. She was so beautiful in the early morning light that filtered through the windows, and so fucking young. She certainly didn't look like she was able to take on a man like me, but she did it very well. My badass baby.

I made my way under the sheet that she had around her hips. Damn she has the prettiest skin, soft and supple with a hint of honey from the summer sun. I kissed her hip once before easing her onto her back. She sighed and settled as I held my breath.

Don't wake up, not yet. I checked to make sure she was still asleep. I wanted to take my time and enjoy this, but if her greedy ass were awake she'd rush me to get to the dick.

"Damn baby what the fuck?" Her pussy was a red puffy mess. It looked like I'd literally pounded her with my shit. I studied her for a minute to make sure she wasn't torn or some shit, and tested her skin with the tip of my finger for heat. I'm gonna have to make this shit up to her. That's what happens when I turn off in the middle of a punishment, I can go too far. Damn Logan you fuck. The one person you're supposed to have control with you lose it.

I ran my nose along her flesh and inhaled her scent. My morning wood got even harder at the sight and smell of her. I opened her with my fingers and inspected the damage. I must've been really ice last night because I didn't realize I was hitting it that hard.

I looked down at my cock trying to do a Jedi mind trick on his ass to see if he would behave, but that shit wasn't even close to working. He'd already smelt his girl and there was no putting him back in the gate. I'm gonna have to give her the softest fuck in creation, or she'd walk bow legged for a week.

I licked her folds before opening her slit and letting my tongue go inside. I was careful not to be too rough as I let the flat of my tongue taste her morning dew. She made waking noises when I took her ass in my hands and lifted her to my mouth. By the time she came fully awake I had my tongue buried to the hilt and my fingers digging into her ass.

I took care of her the best I could, tonguing her pussy's soreness away as I pressed my cock into the mattress for some relief. She wasn't fully awake yet, but there was a smile on her face. She knew if her man was giving her an early morning tongue bath that he couldn't be that mad any more. I'm such a damn sap.

She moved against my tongue, slowly at first, and then the pleasure hit her and she went wild. I like the wanton moves she makes when she can't control herself. The way she spreads her legs wider without having to be told, the way her nails dig into my scalp as she tries to keep me just where she needs me. I especially like the way she moves, like she's fucking herself on my tongue.

I pressed my cock into the bed because she wasn't ready to take me yet, not by a long shot. So I tried to keep my dog on its leash while I pleasured her with my tongue until I had taken some of the sting from the night before out of her abused pink pussy; well it was more like red now but...

"Can you take me now?" My mouth and jaw was tired as fuck and I know her greedy ass would keep me down there with my face buried in her snatch all day, it wouldn't be the first time, but I had shit to do. Her answer was to tug on my shoulders to pull me up her body. One last check showed that she wasn't as beaten up looking as she was when I started, but she was still a little swollen

I eased my cockhead in slowly, sort of testing the waters so to speak. She was a tight fucking fit, tighter than usual. "Baby, if this hurts you gotta tell me and I'll stop."

Her lying ass nodded but I knew she was full of shit. I measured her pain and discomfort by watching her eyes myself. That's how I knew to stop when there was only about six inches, half my dick, inside her; anything more and she started flinching.

"Wait a minute love." I pulled out and reached for the side drawer. I rummaged around until I found the cock ring I was searching for and slipped it on to the desired length. I eased back inside her with more confidence, this way I was sure not to hurt her.

Sometimes I get carried away when the pussy's good, and the pussy's always good. I didn't want to forget and slam my whole length into her and hurt her unnecessarily, this way the ring would block me from going too far.

Unlike last night, this was a slow sweet ride. I held her close with her face in my neck with one hand on her ass keeping her close, and the other around her shoulders. You couldn't get a thin blade of grass between us that's how close we were.

"I missed you baby." I'm not a complete ass I know how to make my woman feel her worth. "I missed you too." She squeezed me a little tighter as I cautioned myself not to get too rough.

When I came, I brought her over the edge with me. We stayed locked together like that for a long time until the birds started chirping and I started moving inside her again. "You too sore for this?" She shook her head no and pushed her pussy harder onto my cock. "Quit it before your hurt yourself." I tried slowing her ass down. "I want all of you, please Logan, I can take it I promise." I studied her eyes and tested her with a harder stroke before pulling out and removing the ring.

I was still a gentleman when I dipped my dick back into her though, but she had other ideas. Her nails bit into my ass, she planted her feet in the mattress and her pussy took over. "Gabriella, fuck."

For five minutes she fucked herself on my dick, I didn't move, didn't do a damn thing but hung over her as she got what she needed out of me. She laughed like a loon when she came. I like when she does that shit. "You done?" I slammed into her, cutting her off mid laugh. "Oh shit." Yeah!

I pulled her nails out my ass and held her hands down on the bed over her head. "Wrap your legs around my back." She hurried to obey and as soon as she did I started fucking. I was riding high in her pussy, hitting the back of it with each stroke, making her cream the way she does. She begged me to fuck her harder, but I kept it to a decent pace so as not to hurt her again. "Shh baby it's okay." She was reaching for her climax and close to tears because I wasn't going faster to help her out.

She growled some shit at me that got her a slap on the ass before I flipped us over.

"Go ahead greedy, take what you need." Her eyes lit up and she bit into that bottom lip of hers which meant I was in for it now.

That's her 'I'm about to be a bad girl' look. She started out slow, lifting herself on and off my pole, then rocking herself back and forth, looking for her sweet spot with my dick. When she found it, it was off to the races. Still I held her hips to control her wild movements, but I didn't try to stop her.

"Uhhh, harder Logan, faster." Her head went back on her neck, her tits pushed forward, and beads of sweat were starting to form on her skin. I wasn't thinking when I sat up suddenly to reach her tits with my mouth, but that seemed to be the right move.

It sent my dick deeper into her, hitting her spot even as I sucked her nipple into my mouth hard. She gushed all over my dick, riding hell bent for leather. "Oh it's so good, feels so good." She did her babbling shit while I fucked up into her, chasing my own cum.

I felt it rise up in me, hot and sweet and blasted her insides. It was like a tidal wave this morning, a never ending fountain of jizz spewed up inside her while I pulled her down hard onto my rod until my nuts were empty. She kept moving to get the most out of my still hard cock until she damn near exhausted herself. "Hop off." I tapped her ass to get her moving. "You need a shave let's go."

She lifted off my dick and plopped down on her back beside me. "I'll just lie here, you do it." I kissed her forehead before rolling out of bed and heading bare-assed for the bathroom.

"Two minutes, be in here." She mumbled something and rolled over onto my pillow, burying her face in my scent. I watched her for a hot minute, enjoying the feeling in my heart. Never in a million years, not even after seeing Connor get taken down, did I ever think this shit was in the works for me. Now I can't imagine life without her in it.

Isn't it strange how that shit works? How you can go from accepting and believing one thing about yourself to knowing something else entirely? When she wasn't tying me in knots, she was making me crazy. It seemed like twenty of the twenty-four hours I was given in a day were now consumed with thoughts of her. Everything was about her, what she needed, how to keep her safe, and a whole host of other shit that I never thought to be dealing with ever in this lifetime.

I'd seriously thought that my brothers and I would settle down peacefully in this little slice of heaven and live out our days away from the chaos and mayhem we'd endured while in the service. I don't think any of us ever expected to settle down and have families though we talked about it back in the day.

We had too much shit going on, had seen too much of the worse of what mankind had to offer. Now I'm looking forward to planting my kid inside her. The shit doesn't even break me out in a cold sweat anymore.

She pranced into the bathroom with my seed drying on her inner thigh, and her hair flowing wildly around her shoulders. "Let me clean you up first." Who would've thought that one of the highlights of my day would be washing her body? For some reason I get a huge thrill out of grooming her. She stood still while I washed between her legs getting her nice and clean for her shave.

Of course as soon as she was clean and sweet smelling, I knelt at her feet and with the water running down on my head and back, lifted her leg over my shoulder and tongue fucked her again. I'd only planned to get her off one last time before we started our day, she didn't need to be riding my dick anymore for the day, but she started making those fuck me noises and tugging at me to come get some.

I stood and slid in in one smooth motion. Pinning her against the cool wall, I kept one of her legs over the crook of my arm and left the other on the floor, while I fucked her with my whole dick and sucked hard on her nipple. "Oh fuck oh fuck oh fuck." Have you ever seen a good girl gone bad? That shit is a big fucking turn on, turning little Ms. Priss into my own little cum addict.

With her tit in my mouth and my dick buried to the hilt in her pussy it didn't take her long to cum. As soon as she came down I released her tit and whispered in her ear. "I want to cum in your mouth." I pulled out and she dropped to her knees just in time to catch my first load on her tongue.

Then my little debutante covered just the head of my cock with her lips, held them closed tight and sucked, as I offloaded in her mouth. "Show me." She held her head back and opened her mouth before swallowing while holding my eyes with hers. "Naughty girl." I pulled her up finished cleaning her up and tried my best to stay the fuck away for her pussy. I had shit to do.

After I was through with her I took care of myself before stepping out and getting the supplies ready for her shave. Fuck, I'm gonna be late again. I looked down at my boy and he was remembering that swallow and looking for seconds, greedy fuck. Between my dick and her greedy ass pussy I'm headed for an early grave.

Chapter Seven

LOGAN

"Devon and Cord, you two have first watch, we can't let the job go too many days without us being there, and we're not leaving the women here alone." Of course they nodded their agreement and the rest of us headed out. I missed her ass already and we hadn't even cleared the gate.

This was more about leaving her alone while all this shit was going on than anything else. We were gonna look through the ledger this evening after dinner, but we couldn't leave the job alone too many days in a row since it was coming on to the end and we make it a point not to do shoddy work. The only way to make sure of that shit was to handle things yourself.

Business wise we couldn't complain, things had taken off in ways that none of us had expected, not in the middle of a recession anyway, but so far so good.

We did good work and that spoke for itself, not to mention our reputation seemed to be spreading in the right circles and that shit goes a long way. My phone rang as we were on the road and I thought, 'not a fucking again.' But I recognized the number.

"Hey Lo, I just heard from Nessa. She's moving in tonight, should be here tomorrow, next day the latest." I whistled over the phone, I'd expected at least a couple days wait, but I should've known better.

One thing about Vanessa, she gets the job done. "Sounds good, how's our boy?" it's not like I expected Zak to do anything foolish, but when it came to men and women, I was beginning to see that that shit didn't follow any guidelines I'd ever encountered. Pretty much everything else on earth had a playbook except that.

"He seems cool, I didn't tell him yet though, I'll get on it as soon as we get to the site." We hung up and I paid attention to where we were going. We weren't expecting to be ambushed or anything like that, but we weren't taking any chances either. The hump hadn't called back and nothing else seems to have been done, but if they were on to us, we had to be on the alert.

At the site we looked over what had been done in our absence the day before and I was glad to see that the men and women we had working with us hadn't slacked while we weren't here. That was always a good look and meant we could promote men and women as needed.

Each man went to his own thing to get the job done. Nothing like hard, back breaking work, I'd take this shit over the jungles of the world any day, and I never thought I'd be saying that shit. In fact until a few weeks ago, before we got the call about the Desert Fox, I was kinda getting itchy about being out of the loop. Now that I had Gaby, I was looking at that shit different.

As I pounded nails my mind wandered between the shit that was going on and Gabriella. She was all focused on this wedding shit and I knew before it was all said and down, she was gonna have me like a little bitch, then Ty won't ever shut the fuck up about bitch made and all the other bullshit anecdotes he came up with.

I wanted to give her the wedding of her dreams, but when the fuck did that involve me getting all the way involved in that shit? I thought all I had to do was give her cash, show up on the day and say 'I do' and be out. Connor that fuck had been with me on this when the girls first talked about doubling up, now it looks like Dani had worked on his ass and if he fell then my woman was gonna get her tits in a twist if I didn't. I'd have to hear all about how I don't love her as much as Con love Dani and all that other female shit they use to make us stupid. Fucking female.

"Whose go is it?" it was lunchtime and I had pissed myself the fuck off with my own thoughts. I threw my gloves to the side and emptied a bottle of water with one swallow. "It's hot as a bitch in this fuck. The fuck are you fools looking at?"

"What's up with you Cap, somebody piss in your Wheaties or some shit?" Zak and his tongue twisting ass, when he does talk he gives my ass a headache. "The fuck are you talking about?"
"Your face bro, you mad about something?"
"No, it's Dani and this wedding bullshit."
Why the fuck that should make them laugh was beyond my ass, I think the sun was too hot or some shit.

"What does she want you to do? You not talking about that kilt fuckery again are you?" I gave Ty the stink eye for being an asshole. "No she wants me to help pick out flowers. Somebody agreed with me that we weren't getting involved in this shit, but now it looks like they're all in.' Connor the fuck didn't even have the decency to look ashamed.

"Told you about those bitch made fuckers you can't trust them."
"Can somebody please keep his ass off the TV, he never learns anything good from that shit." I'd like to meet the fucker that taught Ty that bitch made shit so I could bitch slap their ass into next week.

"Look Lo, the way I see it, this wedding shit is only for one day. I say give the girls what they want this one time and get on with our lives."
"See, bitch made."
"Whatever asshole, all I'm saying is that when your woman looks at you all gooey eyed and say 'but baby why don't you care about our wedding?' You show her that you fucking care."

"You've lost your fucking mind, we do this shit they'll have us doing some pussy whipped shit next. Don't you get it? with you it's the eyes with me it's the fucking lip, just don't look in her eyes unless you wanna get trapped into doing some shit you don't want, that's how I deal with that one and her shit."

"I don't know Lo, it doesn't seem like such a big deal to me." I caught the look on his face just in time.

"Fucker are you setting me up?" I looked at the rest of them as they started exchanging fist pounds. "I told them you'd never go for it. Fuck you I'm picking out flowers, Dani knows better than that shit the fuck."

Woo, thank fuck I was beginning to wonder about my brother. "So whose turn is it to get lunch, and we never discuss this wedding shit again."

"Con's."

"The fuck is it always my go, Ty you're up."

"Uh-uh brother, I had Monday, later for that shit." He was a little more annoyed than the situation warranted, which caused some raised brows.

"What's with you bro, you on the rag?" I have to keep an eye on this one for more reasons than one. Lately he's been getting agitated more easily. I thought it was because of the mission that's been hanging over our heads, but this didn't feel like it had anything to do with that.

Quinn's stupid ass grin told me I was missing something. "What?"

"He's afraid of the little hottie that works at the diner." I rolled my eyes when the fuckery started. It never ceased to amaze me how grown men who'd served together in some of the most dangerous situations known to man could degenerate into high school pedantic assholes when it came to females.

"Fuck you I'm not afraid of anyone." "Are you blushing Ty, what the fuck?" "Give me the damn list Lo; asshole." That last was thrown at Quinn along with a left hook, which he ducked. "Never a dull fucking moment, and on that note." I turned to Zak who looked like he was deep in thought about something. "Zak, Vanessa will be here sometime tomorrow or the day after, we cool?"

He didn't look too sure there for a second and I wondered again just what the fuck had gone down between those two. From what I could remember, the two of them had been hot and heavy there for a while, which had been surprising considering the deal we'd made with each other as a team. I guess it had been acceptable because Vanessa was one of us, maybe not the same branch, but we were fighting for the same cause.

Unlike a civilian female she would understand the rigors and the ins and outs of the life.

Then one day it was like world war fucking four and the only reason things hadn't escalated was because the shit went down while we were on a mission and both of them had to be mindful of their rank and where the fuck they were. After that, nothing! I don't think he even mentioned her name after that last day. As mush as I like Vanessa, if there were any other way to do this, I would've gone with it.

"I'm cool Lo don't start worrying about me I'm a big boy. Just let's get to the bottom of this shit once and for all. I feel like there's too much bullshit going on around us just lately, and we came here hoping to get away from that shit."

He composed himself very well but he wasn't fooling me. Hopefully whatever was going on between those two could be resolved this time. For now, I tabled it and focused on the issue at hand.

"I'm with you brother. The rest of you keep your eyes and ears open. Shit, I shoulda sent someone else with Ty." I wasn't thinking, didn't think that anyone would go after one of us, especially not in broad daylight, but still. "From now on we do everything in twos until we've resolved this shit."

Our talk with Robert last night only made me more uneasy. When there was that much secrecy involved and for so long, that left some serious implications. The only ones I know that could keep an operation like this under the radar for so long were governments and big time corporations.

Dealing with either is always a pain in the ass, and sometimes the only way to dismantle the shit was to cut off the snake's head, literally.

"You think the commander found anything? If he was on the case you know he'd never give up." We all had an opinion on that, and were pretty much in agreement.

The old man would never have left any stone unturned if he thought there was something illegal going on, especially in his little town. "He got sick though remember, so that could've brought his little PI game to an end. Whatever he found though it's a safe bet that we're gonna find it in the ledger or somewhere else in the house. I think it's time we went through the place, maybe give Candy a few days off with pay. Dev can handle the books for that long at least, can't you Dev?"

"Of course Cap, I say we table everything else and get to the bottom of this shit. The job here's almost done, not much more to it but the superficial stuff anyway and we have the right people for that." The guys all nodded their agreement and I guess that was that.

Ty came back with the grub and he didn't look any worse for wear so I guess the hot little number that's been giving him fits for a while hadn't done him any harm.

For someone with so much damn lip, that boy sure had a yellow streak a mile wide when it came to that one little girl. Now wasn't the time to rib him about it though, we had a lot to deal with. Of course the talk turned to our little night missions and the fact that we were still no closer to finding out what all was going on there, and none of us were going to rest easy until we did.

It was a pain in the ass to go around in circles when you were accustomed to taking care of shit in and orderly and timely fashion. "My only problem with the whole thing is not knowing shit. How can we let the women walk around freely when we don't know who the fuck is who? It could be someone they know and trust. If that is true, and we know these people are onto us, then their asses are in danger."

"Well we know it wasn't Robert the ass that snitched so I guess it was the woman. But with both of them claiming not to know who's pulling their strings where do we start to look?" I looked to Quinn after Ty's little speech since he was the one in charge of tracing the call. "So far that shit's bouncing off of a million different places. Whoever these people are they're good, we're not gonna get them that easily that's for sure. I can get to the source, but it's gonna take time. They have a shitload of interfaces blocking shit."

"So we're dealing with hi-tech shit is what you're saying, almost as good as ours." "Basically, yeah." Shit, just what I was afraid of.
"Damn, that confirms my theory. This isn't a mom and pop operation, not some low-end dealer running shit.

Not that we thought it was, but it would've been nice if we caught a break. If the shit had been going on for as long as we believe, not to mention the way they set up Dani's family charity, that shit takes brains and skills.

Someone very powerful has a hand in this shit, and I'm afraid their next move is gonna be to use the Commander and his memory in some way not to our liking before all is said and done. If that should happen, I want everyone to keep their head. Ty, I'm gonna need you to go to your happy place." I got the finger for that one but I still gave his brothers the look over his head and received their nods of understanding.

Everyone knew to keep an eye on him, it was one thing to let him hotdog it in the hills of Kabul but the streets of Georgia were a whole other story. "We know the man, so nothing they say is gonna matter.

We know how this shit works we've done it ourselves more than once. It's all blowing smoke, a way to keep us focused on their bullshit while they do whatever the fuck it is they're trying to do here."

"Agreed, no one goes off base here. We all keep our heads and stay focused. No one does anything without all of us knowing about it; no one goes off on their own anywhere. For the next little while we're on lock. They might not be expecting us to take it that far, but that's what the fuck we're gonna do, we're gonna treat this like any other Op."

Connor had gone into command mode. I guess he'd given this shit a lot of thought. It was different for both of us; we had women to protect now. This shit was fucked

None of us were too much into the job after that and it was no surprise when we knocked off right on time. I wanted to get back to my woman and eyeball her to make sure she was okay. I'd put an icepack between her thighs before leaving the house this morning and ordering her to keep her shit iced until it didn't look like she'd been in a knock out bout with the champ. I'm thinking a good tongue fucking when I got through the door might be just the right medicine. Speaking of which, I pulled my phone. She answered on the first ring. "Hey babe, you got any of that cream on your pussy, you know the ointment shit?"

"A little why, you told me to remember?"
"Yeah I know but I'm on my way home and I'm feeling like dessert before dinner, so why don't you go get yourself ready for me huh?" I could see her fucking blush through the phone. How anyone that liked to ride my dick the way she does could still have a shy bone left in her body was beyond me.

"Okay." Damn she sounded like I was fucking her already. I couldn't wait to get my mouth on her shaved smooth pussy. Damn, my dick was leaking already before I even got the key in the ignition. I ended up speeding and hoping no one pulled me over because there was a sure bet I wasn't gonna stop. You'd think it had been days instead of hours since I'd had her, but suddenly I missed her like crazy.

Chapter Eight

LOGAN

Since bringing her home my routine has changed up a lot, women will do that to ya. I left the boys as soon as we cleared the gate and headed for home. It had only been about ten minutes since I gave the heads-up, but damn. "Imagine what you could've done with a whole hour." I kicked off my shit kickers and pulled my sweaty shirt off over my head before tackling my jeans.

She was spread out on the bed, naked, pussy glistening because she had started on herself with her fingers; she wasn't allowed to stick anything else in there but me. "Open." My eyes were already glued between her thighs on her hotspot. She opened her legs wider and bent her legs slightly so I could get a better shot of her fingers as they glided into her already slippery pussy. I loved that sound; that wet sound. My mouth watered.

She drew her fingers out and my eyes flew to hers as she pushed them past her lips and sucked. Damn, I almost whimpered at that shit. I took my cock in hand and stroked, getting some pre-cum in my palm for lube. She diddled her clit and her breath hitched as her eyes followed my hand.

I knelt on the bed between her thighs as we watched each other. "Feed me." She fed me her sticky fingers and I reached down for one of her tits with my free hand.

Leaning over, I sucked her tongue into my mouth before moving down to her nipple. Her hand came down and joined mine, stroking my meat to fullness. She was soon pushing my hand away and scooting down on the bed so she could take my cock in her mouth. I loved fucking her face like this with her in submission under me while I kneel over her.

I love to watch her force most of my length into her mouth and try to deep throat my shit. She used one hand to feed my cock into her mouth while fucking herself with the other. I pushed her fingers away and replaced them with mine. She was tight and hot as I added first two then three fingers into her.

My cock twitched but I didn't want in her mouth this time, when I cum I want to be buried balls deep inside her, I was in the mood to breed her, and I knew just how I wanted to do it, the old fashioned way.

"I want you on your knees." She was only too happy to oblige. I helped her get into just the position I wanted, her ass high and chest low. Opening her up I was happy to see she looked much better than this morning, instead of the angry purplish red she was a nice blend of reddish pink. I inhaled the sweet honeysuckle scent of her pussy before letting my tongue come out for a dip.

Her pussy was already talking to me. You know that in and out thing pussies do when they're hungry for cock, like a breathing organism. I thumbed her pussy deep with both thumbs before pulling them out and going back in with my tongue.

I pulled her ass back hard so that it was spread around my face as I buried my tongue in her pussy, sucking up all her juices. I love eating her pussy from behind; her reaction gets me every time.

I hope to fuck no one was walking around out there because she was already starting her shit and I hadn't even given her the tip of my dick yet. When she started riding my face and tearing at the sheets I decided to fuck with her. I used one of my thumbs, still wet from digging inside her hole, to tease her ass.

I used the fingers of the other hand to play with her clit as I tongue fucked her to orgasm with my thumb in her ass. She went off like a shot, filling my mouth with her juices. I didn't wait for her to come down, just reared up behind her, adjusted her ass for deeper pussy penetration, and slid the dick home.

I hit bottom and started to fuck. Her pussy was like an oven, hotter than usual, shit felt fuck awesome as I tried to get my dick past the lining of her stomach.

I don't know what it is about her, but whenever I'm inside her I want to get deeper than I've ever been in anyone else before. It's like I was trying to find a way to meld us together forever or some sappy shit. Reaching around I took both her tits in my hands and squeezed gently, her pussy flexed and juiced. "Ride my cock; like that." She pushed back against my rod, nice and slow at first before speeding up. By the third slide she was slamming herself back on my cock hard enough to shake the bed.

"Baby…"
"Don't stop Lo, it doesn't hurt I promise." Her voice was breathy and sexy as fuck. I'd stopped moving, letting her get her pleasure, but I had to join in the fun. "I'll try not to

hurt you." Her harsh movements back and my strong strokes forward soon had us in a nice rhythm. Her poor pussy was going to be sore again. I held onto her tits trying hard to be careful as I fucked into her like a battering ram while she pushed back and wailed.

I imagined my whole length going into her belly over and over and wondered how the fuck she was taking me with her tiny little ass. She on the other hand was acting like she hadn't had dick in a week and rode my shit raw. I felt her body tighten and her head snapped back just before the warmest pussy juice gushed all over my cock. "That's it, cum on my cock like a good girl." I growled in her ear before taking a nip out of it, and that set her off again.

I went in search of that place deep inside her, that rubbery surface with the tight ring that makes my dick hurt so good, her cervix. When I found it I forced my way in, making her screech bloody murder. "I'm going to breed you tonight."

My eyes closed and I fucking roared as I flooded her pussy walls with my seed. "Fuck yeah, ride it out baby." My little naughty debutant was trying to get the last of my jizz inside her by sliding on and off my still stiff pole.

Her body was overly sensitive to my touch, which meant she was in that multi orgasmic phase she gets into sometimes. I kept my dick inside her and let her do her thing until she could stand for me to touch her again.

"You still hungry baby?" She whimpered; that was answer enough. Poor baby she was in heat. I pulled out and turned her over before climbing back between her thighs and guiding my dick back into her with my hand.

Her eyes were glazed over and her mouth hung open as she fought for breath. I stole what little she had left by covering her mouth with mine and feeding her my tongue as I started a nice slow ride in her pussy.

"I love the smell of your sweat Logan.' She sniffed me as I fucked her, that shit was hot and only made my dick twitch inside her. She licked the salty sweat from my skin as she wrapped her legs higher around my waist and tilted her pussy for a harder fuck. "You want more? You want me to do you harder?" She nodded and bit into her lip.

I lifted up so I could see down to where my dick had her pinned to the bed. My long angry pole looked obscene as it sliced into her soft pink flesh. Her bare pussy was plump and sweet the way it wrapped around me, sucking at my meat greedily for my cream. "I'm gonna cum so hard in your pussy babe."

Her body did that shaking shit it does when she's about to have a massive orgasm. That shit only goes to my head and makes me shoot hard as fuck, which I did ten seconds after her pussy went into overdrive.

I nutted so hard I almost put my damn back out. That's that young pussy, young tight and fresh. "I think I'll fuck you for dinner too, I'm in the mood." She squealed and giggled when I went after her neck. It felt so good inside her sperm soaked pussy I figured I'd stay there until my boy felt like playing again.

"You missed me?" I played with the hair around her face. At times like this, when the need had been fed and I could think clearly again, the love I had for her would rise up inside me and choke the shit outta me. "I always miss you Logan."

And then she says something like that, or something equally sweet and I want to give her the fucking world. I hate getting sappy and shit but it makes her eyes light up when I make an ass of myself, and after last night I figure now was as good a time as any to act like a damn sap.

"I love you Gabriella." See, her eyes lit up like the fourth of July and her arms came up and around my shoulders, pulling me in for a kiss. "I love you too." This time was slower than the last. We kept our mouths sealed together as we both moved to our own rhythm. Her soft skin glided across the smooth Egyptian cotton of the sheets as I fucked into her with long deep strokes. Her nails dug into my back as I held her ass in both hands, lifting her onto my cock for each stroke.

"I love the feel of your pussy like this, when my cum is already inside you doing its thing. Tonight I'm gonna fill you to overflowing."

See, fucking sap; her too good pussy is gonna make me stupid yet. We whispered to each other and shared soft touches in between long meaningful kisses. What the fuck? if she wasn't enjoying herself on my dick so much I would've upped the pace, try to get my damn manhood back.

When I came this time, I held her
head in my hand as I sucked on her tongue.
Her pussy quivered around my cockmeat
just as I was emptying my balls inside her
again. "I'm not done with you yet. I'ma hit
that pussy all night." She howled with
laughter the way I knew she would, she
loves that kinda talk, the shit tickles her ass.

We spent the whole night in bed until
it was time to make the rounds with my
brothers. "Sorry you missed dinner baby."
I'd just given her the last of my strength
with a quick hard fuck against the shower
wall. "It was well worth it."

She wrapped her arms around me, as I
was about to put my shirt on. Her towel
almost slipped and I was contemplating
bending her over the bureau for one last shot
before my doorbell rang. "Cock blocking
fucks." She thought that shit was funny.

"You stay in this house while I'm
gone if you wanna talk to Dani call her on
the phone." She looked at me like she had
something to say but was afraid of my
reaction. I'm not too fond of that look.
"Speak." I ran my hand over her hair before
kissing her forehead.

"Nothing, it's just, Dani's right across
the way, why can't I go see her?"

"Because when I leave I'm putting this place on lockdown and I'm sure Connor's doing the same. I don't know what the fuck is gonna go down tonight, but I know when I get back I want you in my bed waiting. Now kiss your man so he can go do what he gotta do."

She didn't argue with me this time, and she had a point. It made sense to leave the two women together, but you never give your enemy a sitting target. If anyone came here, not that there was a chance in hell they'd get past our security measures, but just in case, they won't know where to hit and that might buy us time.

Chapter Nine

LOGAN

Tonight was the night the ship was supposedly coming in and we'd done all we could to secure the area, but we'll see what we see. I wasn't sure that they would show with everything else that was going on. There was way too much going on at once if you ask me though, and it was never too good to have too many irons in too many fires at once.

"I have the sneaky suspicion after that call that these fucks are gonna be even more careful than before. They know we're onto them now, I'm not feeling too hopeful about tonight." I made the announcement when I stepped out the door to my waiting entourage of pains in the ass.

When we'd conversed with Robert and the other misfits last time this was the date they'd given us for the pick up. Now with the money gone, and them knowing who knows what, since we had to wait for Vanessa to bring Rosalind in to tell us what she'd told them, we were just going just in case.

They'd be dumb fucks if they showed up tonight and we'd already decided they weren't that. We know they hadn't made the move already because we'd been keeping an eye out.

"Damn Lo, give it a rest already, you're getting as bad as Connor, damn." They were all trying hard not to grin behind their hands. "What the fuck are you talking about Ty?" Like I didn't know, even when we were in the trenches these fucks were always talking shit, nosy fucks.

"Took a long nap did you brother?" Quinn can be part ass too when he wants to be, but I chose to ignore them all as we moved towards our bikes. "I don't know what you're talking about." I hopped on my ride and waited for the rest of the gossip committee to do the same. "You never turned the lights on buddy, it doesn't take a rocket scientist to figure out since no SEAL worth his salt would take a fucking nap in the evening."

"Fuck you, fuck all of you, except maybe you Con." That was only because he got as much shit as I did.

"He's the one who started it." I gave Con the stink eye after Zak's announcement, but he held up his hand like he was innocent, somehow I didn't believe him, could be the smirk he was trying hard but failing to hide. I guess it's true what they say, misery loves company and his ass was tired of being the only one.

We did our thing, easing down to the street before the boardwalk, lights out. We left our rides in one of their hiding places, we never leave them in the same place all the time, too easy. There was no one around, the town was literally asleep and had been for a while now. There were distant lights farther away, probably porch lights and shit, but closer to the water there was nothing but dark.

"Feel how peaceful that is." It's one of those nights where the sky is a blanket of dark blue velvet, barely a star to be seen, no other brightness, but the light of the moon reflecting off the water. I could sit here with my girl and enjoy the cool breeze on a warm summer night, if some fuck wasn't using my spot to run his illegal shit.

The shots came from above and went wide. My men were in motion already, as we hit the ground. "Are you fucking kidding me?" I didn't have to speak, just with hand motions I sent Zak and Tyler around and behind where the shots had came from. The rest of us crawled on our bellies towards the boardwalk, staying in the bushes, guns drawn.

The shooter was on a side angle to the water, which means we were heading to cover but would still be in a position to take the fucker out if the others didn't get them. "Alive." I uttered the word into the watch I had on my wrist that doubled as a communication device.

There was another spate of gunfire, which seemed not to be aimed anywhere in particular, unless you were laying down fire to subdue. I looked at the others like 'what the fuck!'

"Who the fuck do they have out there, Barney Fife?" There came the sound of running feet and tussling, followed by an expletive and a few thumps. Zak came striding back with a gift, which he thoughtfully dropped at my feet. What the fuck is this?" It was a damn kid.

"Who the fuck? What are you doing out here kid?" The boy couldn't be more than seventeen, shaking like a leaf with terror in his eyes. I would feel sorry for his little ass if he hadn't just taken shots at me.

"Were you the one shooting?" he nodded and looked around like he was about to shit himself. "Why?" I cold practically hear the kid's bones rattling together.

"They told me to."

"They, who's they?" I knew what he was gonna say even before he formed the words in his damn mouth. I'm tired of chasing fucking ghosts. I'm especially tired of coming up against this shit over and over with no results. "I don't know sir, they didn't say." My men were keeping their eyes peeled to the surrounding area while we had our little chat, but it was like I said, they weren't dumb enough to show up here tonight.

"You don't know them but yet you came out here in the middle of the night to take shots at me and my men because they asked you to." He started shaking harder and looking for an escape route of which there was none. Ty was looking at him like he wanted to put one in him and the others were in position to block all routes of escape.

"They said they would hurt us if I didn't, I swear sir I didn't know what else to do, that's why I shot wide, I didn't really want to hurt anyone. They tried telling me that it was part of some night raid game, but I knew better, I've seen stuff on TV ya know." Now he was babbling.

"Kid what the fuck are you talking about?" he opened his mouth to speak but I held my hand up for silence. "Start at the beginning." He wiped under his nose and tried to compose himself. I saw myself at his age and my heart gave a little. That shit was dangerous as fuck, you never identify with the enemy, no matter where or who, but there was something about the kid.

"Okay, my friends and I were messing around down here a few months ago. We weren't supposed to be, but we thought it was fun to hide out here and steal a few smokes. These guys came, they didn't know we were here at first and we didn't even hear what they were talking about at first I swear. But when they noticed us they went ape shit. It was really scary when they put on the things on their faces and came after us."

"What things on their faces?" Was this kid reciting a movie to me or some shit? He looked from me to the others and down at the sand and brush. "Those military mask things they wear in the movies." I looked at my brothers over his head as he carried on with his story. "They were scary enough to begin with, but when they put those on it was like one of those horror movies you know. Then they roughed us up a little, not much, they just wanted to know what we heard. Then they asked our names and I was so stupid I gave them the right information, my friends didn't though; they were smart." He wiped his nose again.

"Have you ever seen these guys before?" He squinted in thought and shrugged his shoulders before looking out at the water.

"Maybe, that night I thought one of them looked familiar but it wasn't his face, it was the way he moved ya know, I don't know how to explain it. There aren't that many bodybuilder types around here ya know, so he kinda stuck out. I know they're not from around here though and when I asked the Commander if his friends were doing some kind of training here in town he seemed surprised." Well fuck that changes things now didn't it?

"You knew the commander?" Everyone was paying attention now, as the kid seemed to relax a little, sensing that just maybe his stupid ass might make it out of this alive.

"Yeah, Don, he was a cool old guy, but when I asked him I could tell he didn't know what I was talking about and then he asked me all these questions, kinda like what you're doing now. Then he got real quiet like and I don't think he was too happy." He did that sniffling shit again, reminding me of his youth. "Go on, what else did the commander do?"

"He played it down ya know, the way adults do when they wanna keep something from us kids, but I knew it was something big because he seemed deep in thought when he told me to head on home and stay away from the boardwalk for a little while at night, but he sure did ask a lotta questions, like a lot. I wish I'd got a better look at the guys' faces but I didn't, I couldn't even describe the tattoos because it was dark and they were partly hidden under their sleeves, but I think they might've been the same."

"And you say this happened a year or so ago?" He got sad and picked at the grass before nodding his head and looking at me for the first time. "Yeah, just a few months before Don died.' I didn't like how the way he said that shit made me feel, and from the restless movement around me no one else did either.

The commander had supposedly suffered a heart attack out on his boat; fuck me no. I looked at my brothers and barely contained the rage that was just beneath the surface. The same question was reflected in their eyes and the winds had just shifted.

I questioned the kid some more until he gave up all he had. "How did they talk you into this, how did they find you?" "They knew my name, just looked my family up in the phonebook I guess. They told me it was a game and that the bullets weren't real, they were these new type of bullets that the army was trying out or something like that, but I knew it was a lie, because when I practiced the cat died."

Fucking kid started crying, what the fuck was this shit? I let him get it out of his system before going on to tell me how he was contacted by phone, how the package was left for him a few days ago and how they convinced his dumb ass to do it. Apparently he wasn't as dumb as he looked because he'd shot wide and long.

"Why you, why did they choose you for their little experiment?" "Because I'm the best marksman on my reserves team I guess, and because they knew that if I didn't do it they'd tell my mom what I'd been up to down here a year ago and she'd skin me." Something was off as fuck, why would obvious professionals send a kid to take shots at us?

"Fuck let's move." I grabbed the kid and we high tailed it out of there just before the place went to shit. The explosion was loud and lit up the night sky like fireworks, hopefully most of the town's folks would think that that's what it was.

The whole fucking boardwalk and a good chunk of the beach was gone. "Fuckers used C4. Ty clean him up." The kid puked himself and I didn't even wanna know what that smell was that was coming from him. "Fuck outta here, little shit took shots at us let him wallow in his shit." I gave him a glare which he ignored as we watched the night sky light up. "Fine, he's on the back of your ride, let's get the fuck outta here before the brigade shows up." He grumbled some shit before collaring the kid and heading for the water.

I wasn't surprised when I heard the splash and the loud complaint from the kid. They met us back at the bikes and Ty was contemplating tying the kid behind his bike and dragging him back, fucking nut job.

We headed back keeping to the side streets with our lights out. This shit had just taken a turn. All the implications the kid made had my radar on high fucking alert.

Military, it sounded like military, but which branch, who and why?

It was definitely no newbies running this shit; it was too organized, too secretive. And the way they went after us tonight, took someone with a head on his shoulder and balls. One thing I wasn't dwelling on too hard, not yet anyway, not until I've had a chance to talk it over with my brothers. The commander had suspected something, and then the commander had died. I'm gonna have a fuck storm on my hands of my suspicions turned out to be true, we're gonna have to do some serious digging in the next few days.

The kid was scared when we clanged the big ass gates shut behind us, locking him in. I could kinda see why the town folk were so interested in what was going on behind these walls.

First, the shits were higher than regulation, but we pulled a few strings and got shit taken care of. The gates were special made titanium, wasn't shit getting through there for all that we'd had them designed to look normal and not like the military grade shit they really were. There was no way too see in from the outside, and the houses were situated in such a way that no one knew exactly where each structure was. Add the fact that the walls were reinforced with a material that prohibited any kind of radar and we were sitting in fucking Knox. This is the reason for leaving the girls home and not letting them go to work or anywhere else. They were safer here than anywhere else.

Chapter Ten

LOGAN

Back at the compound we all headed for the commander's place without question. It was the first time since the night we'd buried him that we were going in like this. Even when our homes were being built we preferred to sleep outside in tents than to invade his territory, but somehow this felt right.

I knew from their somber moods that we were all on the same wavelength. I just needed the kid to tell me what he knew and what if anything he could remember from back then.

I didn't lift the shields on my house yet and neither did Con, until we were in there with eyes on their asses I don't think either of us were gonna feel comfortable doing that. It wasn't a small thing that we were shot at tonight, I knew our blood was still up, which meant Gaby's pussy was in for a workout again, damn. I'm gonna owe her and she's probably gonna try to hit me up with this wedding shit again, fuck.

We headed for the study and Con went right for the liquor, which was right where the old man had left it on the sidebar. Each man nodded yes to his silent offer and he poured seven snifters of cognac. "Sit." I pointed at the kid who was looking around at us in awe.

"He told me about you guys." His eyes went around the room and I'm sure the granite looks in my brothers' faces was probably making him shit in his drawers. "The commander talked to you about us?" My voice was more frightening than disbelieving I think, as he swallowed and his eyes snapped back to me.

"Some, no top secret stuff or anything, he just always told me that you were stand up guys and if I was ever in trouble…that's kinda why I couldn't shoot you you know, because I know he liked you guys and he was a good guy, so you must be good guys too right."

He fidgeted in his chair when there was nothing forthcoming, but all our minds were working. The commander would never discuss our missions, but he wasn't big about talking about us period except to a select few.

There was another shared look before I answered the kid again. "Why didn't you come to us then?" He looked back over his shoulder again before scooting forward in his chair with a whisper.

"I think they're watching me, my house I mean, and my phone sounds funny. I would've come I promise, but I didn't want to risk it. I don't even know what I'm supposed to do now that I've botched it." He looked miserable the little fuck and I as reminded that he'd puked and shit himself not long ago. "Get the kid some clothes." I directed it to Cord who was the one most likely to adhere seeing as how the kid had shot at us and the rest of them were an unforgiving bunch. He didn't look too pleased by my request either though. "He looks fine to me the little fuck."

"Cord!" Sometimes my brothers make me tired, all of them. I threw back my cognac and rested my head against the chair back. "Fine, but he gets any of his shit on my clothes I'll skin his ass."

He marched out of the room his massive shoulders straight, feet stomping. The kid must be scared shitless surrounded by all this testosterone. But instead he seemed amazed, just what the fuck had the commander told him anyway? "There's a little bathroom down the hall go clean up."

"I know where it is." That got a few raised eyebrows. The commander never let anyone in his place as far as we knew, but it seemed he and this kid were close. "I wonder why the old guy never told us about this kid?"

"Probably never had time. Remember we were supposed to come out and then we got called away?" Devon was pacing back and forth, I wasn't worried about him though, I kept my eye on Ty and gave Con the look that had him moving closer to our problem child.

"Yeah, and he'd said it was urgent, we just put it down to his health after he passed but what if it was about all this?"

When the glass hit the unlit fireplace mantle I wasn't surprised. I knew it wouldn't take long for everyone to start putting the pieces together and coming up with stink. "Con."
"Got him." He moved to crows Tyler against the wall while the others moved into position just in case shit went south. I heard Cord returning and called out to him. "Keep the kid out Cord we're dealing with Ty." His

'fuck' told me he got it; I didn't have to explain.

"Murder, they fucking killed him the spineless fucks. I'm gonna cut off their heads and piss down their motherfucking throats before this is done." There was wet in his eyes which I knew with Ty was as dangerous as it gets. Next he'll go cold, just flat cold and heaven help us if he reaches that stage because there isn't fuck any of us can do if he does. "Ty, we don't know that…"

"Fuck that Cap. Military mask, the kid tells the commander, the old man starts digging the old man dies. Didn't we all question his death in the beginning? Didn't we all comment on how strange it was that he'd died from a heart attack when he'd been healthy as an ox the last time we saw him? And we let him down.

They fucking killed him and we built fucking houses and went on like nothing happened." I saw the change come into him then, his whole body locked down and his fucking eyes went dead. Con stepped away because he knew the signs. Our boy was here but gone.

"And there he goes, fucking ice." Con looked over his shoulder at my words with that look of resignation he gets whenever his dog pops his leash. "Don't worry Con we'll all keep an eye on him." Fuck me I need this shit.

***

We couldn't let the kid go home yet so after we'd questioned him some more and were all coming down from our adrenaline high, we headed for our respective homes. Cord surprisingly enough, volunteered to put the kid up for the night.

Ty hadn't said fuck one after his outburst, which meant I had a powder keg on my hands, and the only thing keeping the general population safe thus far was the fact that we didn't know who the fuck.

"Logan." Her soft whisper smoothed out some of the rough edges as I kicked off my shoes and shed my clothes. I climbed into bed and pulled her into my arms.

"I need you baby." There were no words exchanged between us, I went straight for the pussy. I pushed the sheets away from her sleep warm body and dove right in with my tongue. She wasn't allowed to wear anything in my bed except one of my old tshirts, but definitely no panties, I liked knowing my fingers and anything else was just a slip away from her entrance, no barriers.

I lifted her onto my tongue and growled into her pussy as her taste flooded my senses. She was already moving like a wanton, her nails digging into my scalp. "Ohhh Logan, please."

Damn, greedy bitch never lets me get my fill of pussy juice before she starts her shit. A nice hard slap on her ass was no help; that shit only made her wilder. "Yes, spank my ass." This little girl is an enigma she can go from zero to fifty in the blink of an eye.

I pulled my tongue out her snatch before she scalped my ass and flipped her over none too gently. She was ready for me, canting her ass just at the right angle for the dick to go in. I hit her spot with the first stroke and she sprung a leak.

"Oh fuck yeah, tight hot pussy." We were both gone, I was working off whatever the fuck was going on in my head and I'm guessing she'd been having sweet dreams or some shit because her pussy was hungry as fuck. She was taking me in deeper than usual at this angle and my dick was a happy camper, I hit the rubbery surface of her cervix and that's where the fun begun.

Her scream was more like a growl and her body shook uncontrollably as she spasm all over my cock. I wasn't even close to finished, so I let her ride her shit out before fucking into her hard again, over and over.

"I'm going to fuck your pussy raw, then I'm gonna eat you 'til you cum again and again." That set her off again and she squeezed my cock. I pulled out and latched my mouth onto her pussy so I could drink from her.

She rode my face as I ate her out from behind, before kneeling behind her and slamming home. "Ugh, Logan, so deep." She arched her back and pushed he ass back, spreading her legs wider to take more of me. I like this shit. The sheets were literally torn off the bed as we fucked each other and I still hadn't cum.

It was going to take me a while; it usually does when I get like this. When she wound down from her third or fourth orgasm I pulled out and put her on her back with her legs over my shoulders and her pussy tilted up for the dick.

My dick was extra hard as pre-cum dripped down onto her pussy lips. I opened her cunt with my thick cockhead and slid in nice and slow, feeding her half my dick while she whimpered and moaned. "I'm going into your belly." I warned her one-second before fucking the rest of my dick into her. She was bent double with her arms pinned above her head, total submission. I attacked her tits with my teeth next, leaving my mark behind as I suckled her hard, going from one plump nipple to the next.

My dick bored into her like a battering ram as I fucked out my frustration and anger in her. She stayed with me every step of the way letting me know she wanted to be fucked hard.

She did some kind of gymnastics with her pussy and put a crimp in my shit. "Fuck!" I came like a fountain in her pussy and damn near killed her as I pounded out my lust on her poor little body.

I let her legs drop, but I didn't pull out, just laid on top of her with our lips locked together and my dick dripping the last of his offerings inside her deep wet cavern. I didn't want to leave her and she wouldn't let me go, so we stayed like that until we started fucking again, into the early morning light.

Chapter Eleven

CONNOR

I woke to a strange sound and hit the floor running when I realized what it was. My heart was in my lungs and I was already breaking out in a cold sweat.

"Danielle, baby, what the fuck?" I barely got the words past the fear lump in my chest. I moved towards her slowly, not sure what the fuck I was supposed to do. I'd never seen her SICK. I knelt on the cold hard marble of the bathroom floor where she was already sitting leaned over the toilet.

"Did I hurt you last night?" I tried to replay everything I'd done in my head, I hadn't been any rougher than in times past. Yes I was a little fucked up because of what we were beginning to suspect about the commander's death, but I wouldn't have hurt her.

She was shaking her head and holding her tummy, looking green as fuck. She used the last of her strength it looked like, to flush the toilet, before I picked her up. I helped her get cleaned up and she just folded into me with her head on my chest.

I held her there with a hand behind her head while I tried to understand what was going on. I hurt because she hurt, but in a few seconds I was gonna switch to pissed if I didn't get some answers. Not pissed at her of course, but pissed at some fuck. I take good care of her so she doesn't get sick. I load her up on natural vitamin C and shit.

"Baby talk to me please; what's going on?" I felt her head and neck but she wasn't hot. She fucking groaned like I'd twat punched her and sent my ass into panic. "Connor, don't move so much." What the fuck, I wasn't moving. I shushed her the best I could and lifted her in my arms.
"I'm taking you to the doctor." I laid her on the bed and had to count to ten before I could get myself under control. She looked pitiful. Her skin was clammy to the touch and she grabbed her tummy and did that groaning shit again.

"No Connor please, I don't need the doctor. Just let me lay here for a little bit and I'll be fine I promise." Her voice didn't sound like she was going to be fine and I wanted to yell and scream like a little bitch.

When she started crying I was done. I climbed onto the bed as easily as I could and tried taking her in my arms but she balked. "What the fuck." I pulled my phone and sent out an S.O.S to my brothers, this was some team shit. I remembered to cover her up in time as I heard their feet running from all directions outside. They came through the door like they were expecting an invasion.

"What is it, what's wrong?" Of course Logan led the charge. Cord had the kid there with him and at my raised brow he sent him out of the room.

"Go wait out there kid." He pointed to the general area of the living room. "You leave this house the lion Connor keeps in the backyard will eat your scrawny ass." The kid bleated like he really believed that shit.

"I don't know what's wrong she's sick." I think I was about to fucking cry. Last night when I came in she'd been asleep. I'd been out of my head a little I admit, what with Tyler going off the rails before I could reel him in, and thinking that these humps had ended the old man. It was a lot to take in all at once.

So when I came to bed and pulled her under me, I may have been a little more than she's used to. I replayed the first, second and third time I fucked her and couldn't see where I'd fucked up. Could it have been when I had her on her hands and knees? That was the last time and I was the roughest then I think, but only because her pussy fucking owns me when we're in that position and all I can think about is getting deeper inside her.

But she was right there with me, egging me on, begging me to do her harder, faster. Now my brothers were standing in my fucking bedroom looking at my dying woman because I was such a fucking pig. I wanted to tear the hair from my head, but I couldn't move because it seemed any kind of movement hurt her.

Gaby came rushing into the room with her hair still wet and her shirt buttoned all wrong and shit. Lo tried to snag her but she evaded his ass and headed for the bed. Dani picked up her head and looked at her and the two women shared some kind of look that us men didn't know what the fuck.

They reached out to each other and Gaby climbed on the bed on the other side of her and took her hand. "Careful, don't shake the bed." I didn't even look at Lo to see what the fuck was going on with him. Brother or not, I'm pretty sure he wasn't too pleased to see his woman on a bed with another dude no matter what the circumstances. "Okay everybody out, you too Connor" I gave Logan a look after his woman had lost her damn mind.

"Bro, handle your shit." I love Gabriella and all but she's fucked if she thinks I'm leaving my woman like this. He started calling her over. "Babe come on, get outta there." She just looked at all of them lined off in my bedroom as if ready for battle. Ty was looking pissed as fuck like he just needed an excuse, any excuse to start blasting some shit. Dani started that groaning shit and then the two of them started whispering to each other. "Gabriella swear to fuck, if you know what's wrong with her you better tell me."
"Con."
"Fuck that Lo, if she knows..." Gaby leaned over and whispered in my ear. I didn't mean to jump off the bed.

I pointed my finger at Dani who was looking close to tears. "You're with child? You're going to be uncles." I was in a state of shock when I turned to my brothers with the news. It took their thick asses a minute to get it before the backslapping and congratulations kicked in. I turned back to her and knelt next to the bed this time.

I'd heard stories about morning sickness; apparently this shit was vicious. "I'm sorry Connor." She was a mess.

"What, why?" I was a little slow it seemed because I had no idea what she was talking about, why would she be sorry? If she…no asshole don't go there. "Because you weren't ready I thought…"

"Shh, shh, of course I'm ready, I told you so didn't I?" Gaby climbed off the bed and headed for the door, but I wasn't paying her or the others any mind. "Come on boys let's go find something to eat." They all left the room, but Ty was soon back with a Ginger ale. "Gaby said this should work for now." He was whispering like we were in church.

I was still kneeling at the side of the bed with her hand in mine, not sure what to do next. I wanted to be inside her again, that's what I wanted, I don't know why the urge, the need was so strong. I helped her sit up to sip her drink, and miraculously she seemed to transform after a few sips of the shit. "You okay now? I'm gonna have to have a talk with my son about this making his mama sick business." I smiled to try to ease the tension in my chest before placing the almost empty can down on the nightstand.

We sat like that for a while whispering to each other as the news sunk in that I was going to be a father. "Is this real baby, you're sure?" She nodded her reassurance against my chest that was already swelling with pride.

I told her about all the things I was going to do with my son. All the things his uncles and I were gonna teach him. She was looking and sounding better already, and my dick was on the hunt. Looked like she had the same idea too.

"Do you think you can do me real soft so the others won't hear?" She nibbled my fucking ear. What the fuck was she carrying in there, Damien? She was like a whole new person. I looked from her to the door and back before going over to close and lock it.

She pulled her nightgown, my t-shirt, off over her head and laid back with her legs spread. I didn't know what the fuck, but I was going with it. "No don't Connor, just come inside me, I need you inside me." She wouldn't let me warm her up. "Fine." I wasn't sure about this shit but I went with it because that seemed like the thing to do in this situation.

I just simply pushed my boxers down and released my cock to slip inside her. She was warm and wet but I didn't have time to think about how the fuck she got that way because her pussy grabbed me and sucked me in. I couldn't pound fuck her the way I wanted to because of my son, and because of the six nosy fucks inside my kitchen.

"Fuck baby, your pussy's hot." Damn I never felt anything that good in my life, hot, wet pussy. I stroked into her nice and soft as she dug her nails into my ass. We had to keep our voices low and so I buried my face in her neck, closer to her ear. "Does that feel good lil mama?" She pushed her pussy harder onto my dick and moaned into my neck.

"Yeah clench that pussy for me. I want to feel you cum on my dick." Her body grew hot and her pussy gushed. "I'm gonna fuck you all day, they're gonna need a crowbar to get me out this pussy." I was on some sort of high I realized. I was going to be a dad, me and Dani had made a baby. Fuck, just the thought had my sap rising. I ground into her harder, lifting her leg around my hip to open her up more for my long dick. She was taking me like a champ this morning, her pussy nice and pliable.

"Fuck I'm cumming already, cum with me." I made sure she did by placing my hand between us and circling her clit with my thumb. I had to catch her scream in my mouth when she went off and bathed my cock again. My eyes crossed and my back locked up as I emptied what felt like a gallon of my seed inside her. "Yes Connor, fuck me." Oh shit.

Chapter Twelve

LOGAN

I stood off to the side and watched her with my arms folded as she puttered around Connor and Dani's kitchen. I gave each one of the ungrateful fucks sitting at the table the death glare to let them know there will be consequences if they made her feel bad about her cooking. I wasn't sure what she could do in the kitchen since she'd been playing it shy up until now, but whichever way it went these fucks had better not hurt her feelings or I'll shoot their asses.

"Ty you fuck sit down." He was hovering like a starving orphan. At least he wasn't looking like murder central any longer, shoulda known his greedy ass would be like this. He just grinned at me like a simpleton but I wasn't sure I trusted that shit either. The kid was acting like he was stuck to Cord's side and my brother for once wasn't trying to get away, weird. He caught me looking and shrugged. "Kid's got brains, you should see what he can do with a piece." I just lifted my brow at him but he interpreted that shit easily enough.

"I wasn't worried about him trying anything, I could snap his neck without blinking." The kid swallowed hard and I realized I didn't even know his name.

"Did you get a name at least while you two were bonding?" what the fuck was going on around here anyway? "Davey. His family lives in that little pink and blue house on the edge of town."

We'd all seen the place, who could miss it? There was a garden out front that looked as big as the place itself, and though the place was sagging a bit, the general upkeep was good. It was the unusual color in the middle of all the other brick houses that made it stand out though, and gave the impression that some very unique people lived there.

"Your parents gonna come looking for you?"
"Ma'll be at work, she leaves early so she probably doesn't know I never made it home, but sis might." That seemed to scare him a little. "Afraid of your sister are you?" He nodded as his eyes went towards the platter of pancakes my woman was bringing to the table.

"Fuck that smells good." I forgot all about the kid and his fear of his sister as I watched the others fall on the cakes like hungry wolves.

"Oh fuck, you've been holding out." Tyler gave me the stink eye as Zak reached for a couple to plop on his own plate. "I bet Lo the fuck knew she could do this." He closed his eyes and sighed as he chewed on the buttermilk pecan pancake. I was smiling like a proud papa at her and she beamed from ear to ear. She didn't need words to tell her how they felt about her cooking, the grunts and groans not to mention Devon stabbing Quinn in the hand with his fork when he reached for the last one on the plate was enough.

"Here you go Davey, I was wondering what you were doing here. Susie knows where you are?" she sat the kid and gave him his own plate. "What the fuck, where's mine?"

She patted my cheek like an imbecile and grinned, she was full of herself because the boys liked her shit. "I saved the best for last." I stood at the stove while she poured more batter onto the griddle and then pulled a shitload of bacon out of the broiler. "Ty sit the fuck down." Geez this fucker and food!

Con and Dani soon joined us and she wasn't looking so green anymore, in fact she had a nice glow about her and Con was looking like king of the walk. Fucking douche interrupted my morning session but it looked like he'd not missed out. Fuck there's going to be a baby. I walked over to my brother and hugged him.

"Congratulations bro this shit is amazing." The others soon joined in and the talk turned to babies and all the shit they were gonna need, and my eyes went to my woman as I imagined her round with my child. My dick sprung up and leaked. I was tempted to drag her outta there but shit turned into a mini celebration.

Con held Dani on his lap like he was afraid to let her go and Ty and Zak teased her about blowing up like a whale soon. Even the kid was grinning and smiling like he was part of the crew and for a little while there, we weren't thinking about the shit storm that was about to unfold.

I let them enjoy the last bit of happiness before we had to get back to the trenches. The kid was another extra worry, now that he'd done his part, I didn't know what the fucks had planned for him, so I couldn't just cut him loose. I would've left him with the girls, but with Dani pregnant that was a fucking no-no. If the kid even sneezed wrong Con would cap his ass.

In the end we headed back to the commander's place and had the kid call his sister and give her some story about leaving early. With that squared away we got down to business trying to piece shit together.

We hadn't heard any sirens until long after we'd come back last night, so chances are no one had seen us leaving the area in such a hurry. I was half expecting a phone call any second, unless they thought we were brainless assholes who had fallen for their trick.

"I think last night was more of a warning than anything else. They couldn't have believed that we'd be that fucking stupid." We had the kid in front of the TV with headphones on so he couldn't hear what we were discussing. Although it seems he was tight the with old man, he was still an unknown and there was no way I was gonna trust him with shit. As long as he was here there were going to be eyes and ears on him at all times.

"Maybe, but we can't sit around and wait for them to try again. From everything the kid said we know the commander was onto something." Con was going through the ledger again interpreting what was written there and breaking down the code.

So far we knew that the kid had brought the situation to the commander and he in turn had picked up the scent. There was definitely a military presence involved, but so far all the old man had written about was speculation. But he was convinced that someone very high up was involved.

"It looks like he was digging for a while guys, and knowing him, he would've been asking questions. He would've been smart about it, but if that got back to the wrong ears it could be why they killed him, if they killed him."

Connor looked at Ty who was already getting restless again. "We're gonna take this shit one thing at a time. First we have to decide what to do with this kid, he can't stay here indefinitely and we can't just cut him loose."

"His parents won't mind if he stays here with us, we'll just come up with a story, tell them we're taking him under our wing." I gave Cord my 'what the fuck' look because he was acting like one of the pod people. "Come again, since when do you wanna babysit?" Every mission we ever had that involved getting some diplomat's brat out of shit, he was the first to grouch about babysitting. Now he's acting like it's the most natural thing in the world to take on this kid.

"Look, all I'm saying is that from listening to him last night, we can work it. It's not that they don't care, but they need a break, that sister of his sounds like a real handful, maybe we'll be helping them out.

Besides, they know he was cool with the commander and he says he spent a lot of time here before the old man died, so it's worth a try." Huh, I'm not sure what the fuck but whatever. I shrugged my answer and went back to looking through the old man's belongings for anything else that might help us.

The women were at my house today and the place was on lock. We'd given the workers the day off; they can have a long weekend. Thank fuck the job was all but done and only needed the cosmetic finishes before we handed it over. One less thing to worry about.

Just as I expected, the phone rang with the same unknown bullshit as before. "Yeah." I motioned to the others and the place went quiet except for the squeaking of

the chair the kid was swiveling around on as
he watched cartoons.

"Sorry we missed you last night, until
next time. You can consider that a pre-
warning, next time we won't be so
generous."
"Is that what that was, you army boys have a
lot to learn. There were holes so wide in
your little scheme my brothers and I walked
right through them. It wasn't even as good
as a made for TV movie plot. And who uses
kids to do their dirty work, what are you a
bitch?" Come on asshole lose some of that
control.

"Listen you seadog, that will be the
day when one of you could get one over on
us. You think you can outsmart me, better
men than you have tried. Stay out of our
business or next time one of your women
will get it, or are they trained as well?" His
laughter rang out as he hung up. I took the
phone away and hit replay again. "Did that
fuck just threaten my pregnant woman?" Ah
shit, fucking tunnel vision.

"Con keep it together, the girls are
safe as long as they stay inside you know
that. We have to figure out what the fuck
we're dealing with and do it fast though

because they're not gonna wanna stay cooped up for long."

I know Gabriella and her wedding shit is gonna be a problem, but I couldn't worry about that now. "He's army, no marine would refer to anyone as a seadog and the air force is full of elitist dicks who wouldn't know what to do with this shit. If they were navy the commander would've sniffed it out, so I'm going with army."

"Fine but that still doesn't tell us who what or why?" Ty got up from his chair to pace as the others all looked to me for answers. "That's where the power of deduction comes into play. We need to find out what base is near here, who's running it and get the dynamics of the place, the ins and outs so to speak. It would be perfect if we could get someone on the inside that don't have a clue what the fuck we're up to, so we could have eyes inside."

"We could offer some sap a weekend job or some shit, maybe a reserve, then work on him. Nah, that'll take time." Ty was thinking on his feet as were the rest of us, but we all knew it wasn't going to be that easy.

"Vanessa is supposed to be here with the Rosalind woman tonight, let's see what we can get out of her. In the meantime let's get to work." Before we could get started on anything the buzzer for the main gate went off. Everyone turned to look at everyone else. "Who's expecting a delivery?" Everyone shook their heads including me. "Who the fuck?" Quinn pulled it up on the computer and panned the area.

"Shit, that's my sister, that's Susie." This kid was really afraid of his sister. I couldn't see why, she looked like about a hundred pounds and she was about a good two inches shorter than her brother, who looked like he was about to shit himself. "I'll get her."

Cord was out of his seat and headed for the door. What the fuck were we supposed to do with all these unknowns running around? The rest of us headed out at a slower pace with the kid bringing up the rear. If he was gonna hang around someone was gonna have to help him find a pair.

"Listen asshole I want to see my brother, until I see for myself that he's okay I'm not moving. Now get the hell out my way before I call the cops." Cord was standing arms crossed, legs braced in front of the pint size pixie with the behemoth attitude. "I said move dickhead." His eyes went wide when she poked him in the chest. The rest of us just stood back and watched while her brother groaned.

"I'm okay Susie, I'm right here." He moved out from behind us so she could see him, and see that we hadn't mauled him or whatever the fuck it is that she'd expected.

The girls heard the commotion and peeped out the window but knew better than to step foot outside without getting the all clear. Cord's gruff voice brought me back to the situation that was going on around me.

"And I said you're not getting by until I search you, now turn your little ass around and head out, you've annoyed me." I'm pretty sure everyone else had the same dumbfounded look on their face that I did. I've never heard Cord be anything but courteous to a female before, usually he's their biggest champion. The kid started to move forward but Quinn pulled him back. "Stay out of it."

The two in front of us squared off like two warheads, she was breathing fire and he looked like…what the fuck? I had to change tactics and take her in again. Okay, she was about five one five two tops, wild chestnut colored curls that seemed to go in every direction, and cat green eyes.

Her skin was that porcelain shit that people write about and if her little nose turned up any higher it'll touch her brow. "Are you seeing what I'm seeing?" I asked Connor out the side of my mouth so the kid didn't hear me, and especially to keep it away from Ty. I might be wrong, but I was pretty sure I wasn't.

"Yep, if Ty catches on there's gonna be hell to pay. Then again it might distract him from plotting mayhem." That's a thought. Now I know all my men, down to their little peccadillos and if I were not mistaken I would swear my brother was fighting a serious case of lust. It was the way he was holding his body, the way he was scolding her yet protecting her from the rest of us.

That's Cord's thing when it comes to a woman he's topping. I've never seen it look this intense before though, and never with someone he hadn't already taken to his bed.

"Try it shit for brains and I will kick you in your nuts so hard you'd have 'em for breakfast."
"Geez Susie would you quit it? You see I'm fine, now go on home and I'll be there later." She withered him with a look but it

seemed all her venom was reserved for
Cord. Ty the nosy fuck came to stand beside
me and from the way he was squinting I
knew he was onto something. "Well fuck
Cap, is it the water? What the fuck?" He
hightailed it back to his place, the jackass,
while I got the others back on track.

"Alright the rest of you, break it up,
we've got shit to do."
"Is that what I think it is?" Quinn pointed
his chin at Cord and the female who were
now in each other's face."
"Looks like."
"Fuck, Ty's right, I maybe should look into
getting some sort of repellant. How long did
it take this one?" Devon started backing
away like he thought the shit was catching.

"Far as I can tell this is the first time
they've met."
"Well shit." that was Zak's pithy parting
shot and I didn't even want any part of his
fuckery.

"Come on kid, looks like you're with
me for the duration." I looked back at the
two of them and felt almost sorry for the
female. If Cord had he scent she was in for
it, that brother is a controlling fuck if I ever
met one. "How old is your sister again?"

"Twenty-one why?" he looked back at them but I put my hand on his shoulder and dragged him off to my house.

At least she was legal because chances are from what I'd just seen out there, it wasn't going to be long before she was topped. Damn, maybe Ty the fuck was onto something, maybe there was something in the water.

Chapter Thirteen

LOGAN

The day had been long and the night promised to be longer. Cord was the main attraction, he and the female that was caught between shooting daggers at him with her eyes, and mooning over him, that shit was making my teeth hurt.

The kid had proven himself to be more of a bottomless pit than Ty, by eating me out of house and home all afternoon, while the women fawned all over him like he was three. Connor was understandably preoccupied with his woman and their unborn child, and we'd already had a meeting, all of us, about the need to protect them at all cost.

Security was beefed up and Connor was working on getting her to stay home until we got shit squared away. I knew Gabriella was gonna give me shit, but I was gonna insist she stay her little ass put too. We were taking a break and every man was off doing his own thing.

Cord had taken his new shadows with him and I was alone with my woman. Things were gonna be a little hectic around here for the next few days, and I needed her cooperation.

"Babe I'm sorry, but you're gonna either have to put your wedding shit on hold, or do that shit online."

I guess she took offense to me calling it 'her wedding shit', if the way she posed up like a bantam rooster was any indication. "If you don't want to go through with the wedding all you have to do is say so. I can just pack my stuff up and leave. You obviously got what you wanted and now why buy the cow when you can get the milk for free right? Jus so you know, there are more than a few men waiting to take your place." She threw the pen down on the coffee table and folded her arms like she was fucking grown. I waited until she felt the frost from my glare and looked at me.

"You on the fucking rag?" she gave me a look that I did not easily recognize, one that I did not like one fucking bit though. "Come 'ere." I grabbed her neck and turned her over the arm of the couch. "Logan quit it."

"Shut the fuck up." Just that easily she'd pissed me the fuck off. Like I didn't have enough shit to deal with she's gotta get lippy. I pulled her little flirty skirt up around her waist and tore the thong off her ass. It was no trouble getting my dick out by just pushing my jeans down around my hips.

I wasn't even gonna take the shits all the way off. That nice slow loving I'd been planning to give her for lunch was a thing of the past. I swiped my fingers through her dry pussy a couple times until she moistened up. Not her usual leaky faucet, but enough for me to get my meat in without hurting her too much.

It was a tight fucking fit and her hiss when I eased in to the hilt told me all I needed to know. "How many times I gotta tell you about your fucking mouth huh?" The 'huh' came right before a slam that sent my dick right into her deep end. I eased back and fucked into her hard over and over again, until she was babbling out an apology.

"I told you to shut the fuck up. I don't wanna hear shit." I took my dick on an adventure in her pussy, hitting places I don't think I'd ever touched before. I was aware that she was crying and telling me how sorry she was, but that shit didn't mean fuck. Her hardheaded ass needed to be taught a fucking lesson. I kept one hand in her hair and the other on her hip guiding her on and off my dick, and made each stroke count.

She tried pulling off my dick, but my hand in her hair held her in place. "The fuck you going?" I slammed into her over and over again before reaching around and teasing her clit. Just as her body started to wind up I removed my fingers from her clit, pulled out of her pussy and came in her back.

"Think about what the fuck you just said to me, and next time you won't get off so fucking easy." I left her ass crying on the couch with her skirt up around her waist and my seed running down her back. The fuck outta here! "Don't even think about leaving this fucking house." I slammed out the door done. Who the fuck was she talking to anyway?

***

I was too pissed to think straight and the others seemed to notice that when we reconvened. No one said anything to me about it until a good hour later when I'd cooled down a little. She'd tried calling me in that hour and my phone had dinged with a few texts in that time that I was sure were from her, but I ignored them. I'd had time to think while I was pissed, but not about my woman and her fucking PMS melt down.

No my mind had gone over all the things that had been going down here lately, and some things just weren't adding up. I stepped away from everything in my head for a hot minute. Things were changing for us, most of them good, some were a little fucked, but nothing we couldn't handle. I was going to be an uncle soon, that was a giant step in the right fucking direction if you ask me, and before anything else was done around here, as the designated head of our little family, I'm gonna see to it that our boy came into a peaceful world.

It didn't matter what was going on around us, we were never gonna lose sight of the greater purpose of us being here. We'd earned this little piece of heaven, and I aimed to see we got it.

"I'll be right back guys." I knew they thought I was headed back to my house to fix whatever the fuck had gone wrong between the last time they'd seen me and now, but my mind wasn't even on that shit.

Instead I called one of my contacts to see about the mission that was hanging over our heads. I needed to get that shit squared first and foremost, and was more than a little surprised by what I learned. He couldn't tell me much about something he knew nothing about, so it was a short fucking conversation. I'm not in the habit of keeping shit from my men so we had a little huddle and I conveyed what I'd learned.

"What the fuck, that doesn't make any sense. He of all people should know something about the mission." There was a heated debate about the implications of this, but the boys and I decided to shelf it for now, since there was really nothing else we could do. But it was passing strange that someone as high up in authority as he was, had no idea what I was talking about.

More alarming was the amount of time between the call-up and actual deployment; that shit's just not done. My guy on the inside didn't sound too pleased by the shit either, or the fact that he knew nothing and was only now hearing about it from me. Something was way the fuck off.

Granted it hadn't been his division that had contacted us, and sometimes these things were kept close to the vest, it was still weird that he hadn't heard a whiff of what was going on. Either the shit was more volatile than we'd first thought, or someone had got their wires crossed somewhere.

Either way it looked like we had bought some time, which with the news of Con's impending fatherhood, was most welcome. Chances are we'd end up scrapping the mission because of this turn of events. It was a hard call to make, but we worked together or not at all, and I wasn't about to take my brother into combat under these circumstances.

We'd done our bid ten times over and were free and clear. It would've been a favor in the old man's memory, but getting to the bottom of this shit now took precedence as far as I was concerned. It was more important to me to make sure our own backyard was safe than some hellhole in some remote part of the world that would just go back to the same old same old ten minutes after we cleared out.

While I'd been taking care of that, each of the men were taking care of other things, gathering more information. We now knew that the closest base was ten and a half miles away, which wasn't far at all, and that the man in charge was well known and respected.

He ran a tight ship and was known as a hard ass stickler for the rules type. If this was coming out of his house he didn't know about it, and that was a little hard to swallow with a reputation like his, you can't have it both ways. But neither was I ready to start pointing fingers at anyone.

The day dragged the fuck on since we had nothing else to do but wait. Vanessa was bringing in the woman and we were all chomping at the bit to see what if anything she could tell us. "You need to go talk to your girl bro, she looks miserable as fuck." "I don't have time for this shit now Connor, I've got more important things on my mind."
"Yeah, more important than her? Look, I know they can be a trial, and heaven knows Dani knows every fucking last one of my buttons to push, but they're ours bro.

They're the best fucking things to ever happen to us in this fucked up life." Happy motherfucker, soup to nuts he'd be trying to wring Dani's neck in a day or two when she starts giving him fits again. "Ty is right, you're pussy whipped." I smirked as I walked away. Maybe he had a point.

***

I read her million and one texts on the way to the house, each of them a different variation on I'm sorry. Fucking female will drive me to drink. She was in the house curled up on the church wrapped up in a blanket like a mummy.

I wonder how Con knew she looked miserable, which she did. She probably called him over to set him on my ass which was a neat little trick she and Dani had; play monkey in the middle. I didn't say anything just stood over her until she looked up at me with red eyes, and a blotchy nose. My perfect baby, fuck.

I picked her up and sat her on my lap and not once did I complain about how fucking hot it was outside while she was wrapped up like we were in a Deepfreeze or some shit. Maybe her pussy hurt, serve her mean ass right. "Do you understand why I got so mad at you?" she nodded her head against my chest and sniffled. "You can't tell a man like me that there are other men lined up waiting for you. First thing I'll do is go find every last one of those motherfuckers and de-ball them. Then I'd skin your little ass and tie you to my bed for all time so no one else could ever get at you."

"It's not true Logan, I was just hurt because you seem to always want to put off the wedding." I held her closer because I understood how she could misinterpret shit.

I haven't been exactly forthcoming in the last few days because I don't want her stressing about this shit, but I didn't know her mind was gonna go off the fucking rails.

"Babe I'm not trying to put off the wedding, there's some things going on that me and the guys need to take care of before we can relax again. I don't want you involved so I'm not gonna tell you any more than that, just stop with the crazy okay. I want to marry you, more than anything in this world I wanna marry you, come 'ere." I could hear Ty in my mind calling me bitch made but I didn't give a fuck.

I turned her around on my lap and fought with the blanket to get to her skin. When I had all her pertinent parts free, I fingered her pussy until she was sighing into my neck, then lifted her enough to seat her on my cock.

"I need your tit in my mouth, now." Now it was her turn to fight with her clothes to get me what I wanted. "Feed it to me." She held her tit up to my mouth as she rode my cock with my hands on her ass.

" I love the way you ride my cock, like you're enjoying the fuck out of it." And she did, all those horse-riding lessons came in handy when she got on my dick, she had great muscle control.

Her tits seemed a little fuller in my mouth; she was probably close to her period, that'll explain her attitude I guess. "Are you tender?" I hefted her tits in my hands as I pushed up into her. "Not really a little tingly but nothing bad."

I went back to mauling her flesh as she dripped all over my dick. There were no rushed movements, just a nice slow up and down, in and out that made us both happy. "I love you baby."

Her pussy tightened around me and she wept in my neck. "I love you too." I rolled my eyes where she couldn't see. Just why the fuck was she crying, who knows? I held her a little bit closer and let her tit for her lips, and when she started a nice slow cum, I bit into her neck to mark her, let her know she was mine all the way.

We ended up fucking one more time on the couch, this time I had her on her back as I drilled into her and whispered words of love and encouragement to her. I don't know why the fuck I bother going upside her damn head when she acts up, because I end up putting in more time making up for that shit in the long run; high maintenance pain in the ass.

"We straight?" I flicked off the water and stepped out of the shower where she'd just sucked the last of my energy out through my dick. She sure knew how to make it up to her man.

The sun was gonna be going down soon and then the real fun would start, our visitor was gonna be here a few hours after that. "Oh shoot, I gotta start dinner."

She slapped on her lotion and whatever the fuck else she used to make her smell fuckable before rushing out of the room. "What's the rush?" Granted after that five star breakfast I couldn't wait to see what she could do with dinner, but she was acting like there was a fire. "I wanna cook for the guys tonight. Breakfast was such a big hit I don't feel any of my old fears anymore." Poor baby, she looked so excited I didn't have the heart to tell her that if you feed wild animals they always come begging for more. I'll just have to knock some heads together and make sure they know not to fuck with me on this shit.

She threw on jeans and a white button down top, just some shit she pulled out of the walk-in closet, but made her look like she were getting ready for a magazine shoot.

"Flawless." I like the way her eyes went all dreamy when I cupped her nape to hold her in place for a deep long kiss. "Don't overdo it okay baby, just throw some scraps on a plate, they'll appreciate it." She gave me the bitch brow and jetted. Fine, I tried. I left the house in search of the hoard of wild beast that would be descending on my home in about two hours or so. The fucking kids were still here, but there was nothing to be done about that now, at least Davey had to be here for his own protection, the sister, well, that was another story.

We ended up meeting up in the yard. No one wanted to go to the old man's place because we had all unofficially decided tot take a break since there was nothing else to be done for now.

Connor was the last to join us, I'm guessing in the next few months it's going to be like that. The decision not to go anywhere was getting easier and easier. "Listen up, Gabriella's in there making some kinda spread." The pigs started rubbing their bellies and grunting already.

That would be Ty the ringleader, Devon and Quinn. Zak just smiled and Cord was looking over at where the two kids were setting up to play ball. When is the last time any of us had used the court? It had been a while.

"I don't want you freaks overworking her with this shit, or this would be the first and the last time." Connor had had to have this same discussion weeks ago, for all the good it did him, I figured I could at least try.

"What's she making Cap?" how the fuck should I know? "Tyler, come back here you greedy fuck. How's Dani doing bro, we need to do something special for her soon, a baby is a big fucking deal."

"Yeah it's called a shower and the women usually take care of it, bitch made." Ty shook his head while the others laughed at his antics. "Fine, but in the meantime we need to have a celebration, just a nice night out somewhere. Even though the mother to be can't drink we can still go out somewhere to celebrate the fact that we're gonna be uncles and Con's gonna be a dad. We're not gonna hide out in here from these fucks forever. We need to figure out what to do with the kid, the asshole didn't mention him when he called, let's hope he just thinks the kid missed or we got the drop on him." I looked around at each of them and everyone seemed to be in agreement.

The more I thought about it, the more it seemed the kid was just collateral damage, not really a threat. If they suspected him of talking to the commander, they had to know by now that he didn't know shit, but I didn't think so.

From what the boy had described, it seems like the old man had been very crafty in their dealings, only meeting at certain times of the day, and never being seen talking together in public.

"I say we work on getting the kids home tonight, tomorrow the latest, we've got enough to worry about without the added stress." Cord shifted from one leg to the next and I waited, but he didn't say a thing. Talk soon turned to the situation with the Desert Fox and when we all put our heads together, it really didn't make sense.

The thing about dealing with the military, unless you were the headman in charge, nothing had to make sense, you just followed orders. Our only saving grace is that we were out, and had been doing it as a favor. But there was nothing that said I had to take my men into a fucked up situation if

I didn't want to. They may try to shame us, but that shit never works. We had too much to live for these days.

Chapter Fourteen

GABRIELLA

"I'm telling you, there's something major going on, and I think it has something to do with that explosion we heard down by the water the other night." I was putting the last stir on my whipped potatoes; with one last taste on the tip of my finger it was ready.

Dani was sitting on one of the kitchen stools at the island sipping on a ginger ale; it seems her morning sickness had got its times mixed up. "Did Connor say anything to you?"

"Nope, and I would stay out of it if I were you. These guys aren't like what we're used to Gaby, Logan will go upside your damn head if you go meddling in this stuff, trust me, I know. I can't even ask Connor about what they're doing without getting a lecture and a warning. If I were you I'd forget all about it they know what they're doing." I checked on my NY strip to make sure they weren't overcooked and turned off the heat under the cast iron skillet I'd brought from home.

It was my nana's and had been in my family for generations. My Bourbon pepper cream sauce for the meat was next, the beans had already been blanched. I started to get a little nervous. "Maybe this wasn't such a good idea, maybe I should've waited." I went into panic mode I've been doing that a lot lately.

"Shush Gaby, we both know you can cook your ass off, stop worrying, did you see them at breakfast?" she rolled her eyes at me, and lifted her can to her lips. I looked down at the row of steaks on the platter that I'd covered with foil to keep the heat in and my chest got tight. This was my new family, what if they hated it, I was actually close to tears. "Dani." She must've heard the panic in my voice because she left her perch and came over to hug me. "This isn't about dinner is it hon?" I could only shake my head against her shoulder.

"It's the wedding, and everything that's going wrong, and Logan keeps getting mad at me because I can't keep my big mouth shut, and our beautiful wedding is going to be destroyed.' I said all that in one sentence and felt a little relieved to get it off my chest.

"That's it, I know what I have to do."

"Uh-oh, I know that look, that is the look that got me grounded more than once in this lifetime girlfriend, oh no." She's such a worrywart. "No-no-no, this is gonna be good I promise. Don't you want to have the wedding you've always dreamed of? And how amazingly cool is it that we've found brothers to marry and that we can have a double huh? But there's one fly in our ointment, whatever is going on down at the boardwalk. Now if only we can take care of whatever it is."

"Gaby, if the guys can't do it what makes you think we can?"
"Because the boys don't know our little town like we do, it's probably just some kids messing around.

Remember what we used to do down there when we were teens? It's the same thing; it's just that kids today are more advanced than we were. We had bonfires and firecrackers, these little delinquents probably have homemade bombs, I mean look who they've nabbed already, Davey. We both know what he and his cohorts get up to."

"I don't know, Connor seems to think there's more going on." She bit her lip but I could see her weakening, just a little more and I'd reel her in. "Yes but like I said, that's only because they don't know this town like we do. Our boys are SEALs babe, they're trained to see danger in everything, shoot Logan would childproof the house for me if he thought he could get away with it. Sometimes at night he takes me through all these scenarios of what-ifs. I now know the theory of how to get out of every sticky situation known to man.

But am I ever really gonna need them here in Briarwood? Come on. Look. It's our job to show these guys that they can take off the riot gear, that we're perfectly safe. Unless you wanna be under house arrest every time something goes wrong in a fifty mile radius."

"Fine, but we're being careful." She put her hand on her tummy and I had my first doubts. Nah, it was nothing I was sure, just Logan being overprotective as usual. If I wanted that wedding that I've had mapped out in my scrapbook since I was ten, I'm gonna have to do this. With my mind made up I went back to my sauce feeling ten pounds lighter.

**

LOGAN

"For the love of fuck, Ty chew." It was no question that dinner was huge hit, she'd really outdone herself. There wasn't an unloosened tab in the place. She had the biggest fucking smile on her face and that's all I cared about, though I could wish the wildebeest at my table had some damn manners.

"What's for dessert?" I closed my eyes and counted to ten, there's no point in trying to control his greed. She got up from the table and headed for the kitchen and I got up to go help her. "Cap sit your ass down, no hokey pokey while I'm waiting for dessert. If you're anything like Connor we'd end up waiting half an hour while you do who knows what in there, and some things just don't taste the same cold."

"Ty, learn to cook or better yet find a woman who can, that way you don't have to worry about what goes on in my kitchen." "Ooh nasty, I'm just saying."

He wasn't fazed by my tone, not even a little bit. I ignored his dumb ass and went in search of her to help. She was bending over taking something out of the oven and I eased up behind her and rubbed my dick into her ass. "Logan you'll make me drop the cobbler."

She placed the pan on the rack and turned into my arms. "They liked it Logan, they liked my food." I didn't have it in me to tell her that that bunch would eat fried sawdust, but it was good that she could actually cook or they'll talk about her, my brothers have no fucking etiquette whatsoever. "Yes baby I know."

Before she could open her mouth to prate away at me I swallowed her tongue while pressing my cock into the junction of her thighs. "Let's feed them real quick and get rid of them so I can have my dessert."

I nibbled my way to her ear and bit down gently before going back to her lips. "Logan we just did it like a few hours ago." That didn't stop her for reaching for my mouth or grinding her pussy onto my cock. "Your point?" Ty started pounding his hand on the table in the next room and started up a chant for dessert. I heard the kid start to laugh before he joined in. "I'm gonna skin him."

I helped her take the little mini crocks of the bubbly peach concoction out to the table after she'd spooned mounds of homemade whipped cream on top. My baby's a fucking gourmet, which means that while Dani's dealing with her pregnancy, my kitchen's gonna be like the fucking mess deck. By the time I got rid of them it was already getting late. I wasn't sure what the night would hold, but I knew I didn't want to face it without her sweet taste on my tongue, or the memory of her pussy wrapped around my cock.

That's how we ended up in bed with my dick in her mouth and her clit on my tongue. I had her on top of me in the sixty-nine and she was going to town on my dick. If I didn't know better id swear she wanted something from me.

I licked her clit until it was nice and plump in my mouth, then tongue fucked her until she squealed and creamed all over my face. I blew air into her pussy before opening her up with my fingers and going back in with my tongue.

When she was nice and sopping wet, I eased her head away from my dick, which made her grumble until I held her head down on the mattress while searching out her hole with my cock. "Right there." I sighed as I eased into her pussy.

It doesn't matter how many times I've had her, it's always exciting and new, that first feel of her. I gave her a variation of nice and slow and hard and rough. Each time she'd get used to one I'd switch up on her until she was screaming and tearing at the sheets.

"I wanna see you when I cum." I pulled out and flipped her onto her back, driving my dick back into her before she could even miss me.

I like this position. In this position I could take her breast in my mouth, kiss her lips and dig as deep into her pussy as I wanted, all of which I did now.

The orgasm hit me out of nowhere, an emotional cum. It was just having her under me, knowing what she meant, all of that combined to give me the sweetest cum of all. She felt my seed burst into her and that set her off so that she clenched and released around me as I emptied my nuts into her belly.

I had visions of a little me running around as I rested my still hard cock inside her walls. We'll talk about that shit later.

***

"I'm hoping she can shed some light on this shit, cause so far we're catching at our tail." Word had come in that Vanessa was on her way with the sub. The kid and his sister were still here, I knew why he was here, but there was no real reason for her to stay after she'd ascertained that her little brother was perfectly safe. I did gather though in the time that she's been here, that she is one over protective sister, who seems more like a mother to the boy than a sibling. If we weren't in the middle of this bullshit, watching her and Cord dance would've been funny as hell too. He was looking at her almost as much as she was eyeing him, but neither of them was about to let the other catch them at it.

"They're here Cap." Ty was on lookout, which means he was monitoring the street around our place. We had it under surveillance for at least a hundred feet or more in some places, which meant no one was getting close without us knowing it. I walked over to the laptop he was monitoring and looked over his shoulder as we all sat around in the commander's place, which had suddenly become headquarters.

"Is she coming in hot?"
"Nope but I only see one body in the vehicle, no wait." Another little red dot

showed up on the screen and all I could do was shake my head. "Let's head out, you two stay here and don't touch anything. The place is wired so we'll know if you even move out of this room." We started to head out but Cord stopped to have a word with the fire-breathing dragon.

I would love to have heard what he was saying that had her going hot and cold in one second flat. When she swung at him and he caught her arm and laughed I knew he was a goner.
"What the fuck Cap?" he scowled as he almost walked into me, since I'd been standing behind him watching the byplay.

"She's not your usual type bro."
"I don't know what you're talking about."
Yeah that's why red was creeping up your damn neck, lying ass.
"Sure you don't, just watch yourself, that one looks like she'd kill you in your sleep."
"I'm not afraid of one little girl, she's more talk than anything else." I'm not ready for this shit; he was totally fucking gone.
"She's tiny though Cord, damn." Not that my woman was any bigger, it's just that Gabriella and Dani for that matter, may not be tall, but somehow their personalities made them seem more mature, more able to handle men like us.

This one seemed to be all ballast.
"And so fucking young."
"Are you trying to talk me out of something
brother?" he stopped walking as the others
went ahead.

"Never bro, not if she's what you
want. I'm just saying that you're part ox,
part elephant, and she looks like a high wind
would blow her away." I had to rein it back
in because if he wanted her I wasn't about to
put a damper on it. It's just that I am over
protective myself, and she did seem rather
young for all her bravado earlier. I just don't
want to see any of them hurt. I want each of
us to find what I'd found with Gaby and
Con had with Dani. And who knows, maybe
I was making more of this than there really
was, but then again I don't think so. I could
almost feel that shit in the air.

Vanessa gave the signal for us to open
the gate and we all stood around as it slid
back to give her entrance. She stopped in the
middle of us and hopped down with a big
grin. It had been some time since we'd seen
her, almost a year I think, if not more.
However long it was, it was way too long,
she was good people.

"Lieutenant." I walked over for a hug
and at the last second hoped like fuck that
Gaby wasn't spying on me from somewhere

in the house. If there's one defect in my baby, it's her wide jealousy streak. She doesn't give a fuck who it is, and no amount of explanations work when she gets that shit in her head. "Captain, it's good to see you." I patted her back and released her before my Tasmanian devil came running to put her down. I hadn't told her too much about what was going down, just that we were expecting a visitor and I expected her to show her all the hospitality due a guest.

Gaby like I said gets her hackles up when there's a female involved, and she doesn't trust shit. I can't say as I blame her because I'm the same way with her. I trust my brothers with my life, and still if I felt one of them was getting too close to her, as innocent as it may be, I'd go for his fucking throat.

She walked around the back of the van, hitting the sides as she went. We walked around with her and stood behind her as she pulled open the double doors. All that could be seen were the two eyes opened wide in fear. Vanessa hopped up into the van and pulled Rosalind up by one of the ropes she had wrapped around her body. "Damn Lieu, what the fuck?" Ty the jackass was already sipping on a beer like he was really waiting for action.

I'd sent Zak on a chumped up mission slash errand because he was still acting like a bear with his paw caught. I don't know what it is about women that makes otherwise smart men fuck dumb. As soon as the time for her arrival drew near he started getting twitchy.

"The sub was getting on my damn nerves so I decided back here was best. I assume you wanted her here in one piece?" That's why we like Vanessa, even though she was a marine.

She'd worked with us on an Op in Kabul, that's where we'd all met. We'd seen her mettle then when she'd put her life on the line for another SEAL. That situation had worked out but it could've easily gone the other way. That was all that was needed to bond her as friend for life though, until some fuck went wrong between her and Zak.

She dropped the woman on the ground and was about to say something else when she stopped. If I hadn't been looking at her I would've missed it, damn. I literally saw the moment she sensed him.

Her whole body went loose and then tensed in a split second, she looked like a cartoon character the way she'd just shutdown in the middle of what she'd been doing. I did notice though that she didn't turn to look at him, but she knew exactly where he was.

Damn, this is going to be some shit. I hope I didn't open a can of stink because what just went through her was real fucking real. I'm gonna have to have a serious talk with my brother. I don't think he had any idea what that woman had in her for him, he couldn't have let her walk if he had. Whatever had gone down, I'm thinking she wasn't the one to call it quits. I'm gonna have to deal with his ass in the next few days while she was here, but fuck he can be a hardheaded ass, this was not going to be a walk in the park.

Looking around I realized that the others had noticed it too, and no one was making any wise cracks, in fact no one was saying anything. The only sound that could be heard was the moaning, or complaining that was coming from behind the gag that the prisoner was wearing.

I waited to see who was gonna break first, but he didn't say anything and neither did she. Now I remember why they had such a tumultuous relationship in the first place; they were both thick as fuck. I rolled my eyes and picked the woman up by her bound hands before removing her gag. She looked around in fear, because although she might not have seen us that night, she had to know that this was more of the same. Connor the fuck wanted to work her over because of what she'd tried to do to Dani, he didn't care that she wasn't sporting a dick; he just wanted answers.

Ty would slit her throat if he thought she knew who was behind it and was refusing to talk, and I'm not too sure about the others. "She's not staying in the commander's house. Tie her ass up in the yard somewhere." Damn, I hadn't even asked the question.

"Now Ty, we need to treat our guest with a little more decorum than that, this is the south after all." I didn't know where the fuck to take her but he was right, she wasn't stepping foot in the old man's place, it would be an insult. "Well she can't stay with me and I'm not sure I trust any of you with her overnight, so what do you suggest? Other than tying her up outside like a canine."

"Let's just question her first, the question of where she stays might not matter, not if we end up slitting her throat for being stupid." Fucking Connor, bastard can hold a grudge like nobody's business.

Of course she opened her mouth to scream and before I could stop her Vanessa very obligingly throat punched her. "She does that a lot." She brushed off her hand while the woman gagged. I'm surrounded by fucking animals!

***

In the end we went with the old guest cottage behind the old man's place and chose Devon as night watch since he was the only one not bitching about something, though that didn't mean he was any more trustworthy. This woman's life was in danger no doubt about it. "Cord take your charges back to my place." They'd been so quiet this whole time I'd almost forgotten they were there, but I didn't need anyone in our business. They'd both been frisked and were both clean and besides, they knew the girls so there was no worry that they might try something.

Still, I called my woman with orders. "Those two kids are coming back to the house, either of them try anything aim to kill, remember to protect Dani and the baby."

"Who is she?" Dammit, I need this shit. Why would a woman who looked like Gaby, and who knew that she had her man tied all the way the fuck up in knots suffer that jealousy shit?

"Fuck babe not now, she's Zak's." Her harrumph told me she didn't give a fuck what I said and I was gonna have to deal with her shit later. She hung up on me, but at least she was in a fucked up mood, anyone tried anything she'd take 'em out. My sigh was long suffering because I truly was about at the end of my rope. Not with Gaby and her shit, but with all the up in the air bullshit that had been going on lately. "Let's get this over with."

I led the way to the cottage that hadn't been used in over a year and had that smell of disuse about it. There were sheets over everything once we turned on the lights. "Okay, we didn't have much time last time, but we need some answers and you're gonna give them to us."

She opened her mouth to speak from her place on the dusty floor in the middle of us, but I held my hand up. "Before you open your mouth to lie I think you should know that we know a lot more than we did last time and if you bullshit me, I will let one of these fucks slit your throat since we know these guys killed our commander."

Her eyes gave her away before she opened her mouth again. "I had nothing to do with that, I was just the scapegoat for the money thing." Her eyes were even more afraid than before and I felt the shift in the room. It was one thing to suspect and quite another to have verification.

Con moved to stand next to Tyler but I wasn't sure he was the only danger. She might not have offed the old man herself, but she was in bed with the fucks who did it. "Tell me everything you know, from the moment they contacted you, to now." She swallowed hard and looked around for an ally, there was none to be had. Right now I might be the only thing keeping her alive.

"What guarantee do I have if I talk? These people are vicious, if they even know that I'm here they'll kill me." I didn't stop Ty when he moved towards her. "What guarantee do you have that I won't cut your lying tongue from your head right fucking now?" he brandished his knife and she tried to escape through the floorboards. "Now talk bitch and make it good, I'm not like my brothers here, you're a waste of space that I won't mind offing and dumping somewhere,

I give a shit that you're a chick." I gave her time to compose herself and get used to the fact that her life depended on what the fuck she said in the next five minutes.

"Okay, okay. Robert approached me, we knew each other from gambler's anonymous or one of those deadbeat things, I was so high at the time I don't remember which. I don't know, I guess in an off moment I'd actually told the truth about myself, how I had lost everything because I'd embezzled funds and the only reason I hadn't done a longer stretch is because I'd been so good at it that the feds had recruited me for a job.

But my life went into a downward spiral after that and I started using and drinking and everything in between. I don't know how Robert got in bed with those guys, he never said and we never really got into it. I just knew that they needed money moved and he knew I was good at hiding large sums of money under the radar.

Her came up with the idea of using the charity, and I kinda got the impression that everything was local, though no one ever said, just from some overheard conversations everyone seemed to know everyone. I wasn't part of the whole smuggling thing, anything I know about that is just hear say."

She looked like she was really afraid that we were gonna ask her to testify or some shit. "We're not asking you to stand up in a court of law and point fingers at anyone, just tell us what you know." No because these fucks were never gonna see the inside of a courthouse, not if I had anything to say about it.

"Yeah, okay, like I said, Robert brought me in to work the money angle, he set up the meet with his ex." Her eyes went to Connor and she lost a little color, and with good reason. "When you refer to her in the future you will use her name, it's Danielle, the woman you had no problem setting up for a fall is Danielle and she isn't his ex anything."

Oh yeah, she'll be lucky if she makes it out of here alive. "Sorry, okay Danielle, he set it up with Danielle so that I could get the job. I swear I wanted to change my mind after I met her, but you don't know these guys, they don't care about anything or anyone."

"Tell me about these guys." I moved in closer, now we were getting somewhere.

"I don't really know that much the one time
I saw one of them by mistake they almost
killed me. Robert had let it slip that they
were having some kind of meet, not him,
just the guy that's in charge and one of the
go-betweens I guess. I got nosy, I wanted to
know who we were dealing with because
that was a lot of money and I wanted some
insurance just in case things went south.

I was even playing around with the
idea of going to the feds." Lying ass, the
feds never entered your mind. Even now the
signs of a true junkie were riding her hard.
She was sweating from more than fear, her
eyes were blood shot and her skin had that
clammy unhealthy look an addict gets over
time.

"This guy you saw, tell me about
him."
"Uh, stocky, with a low haircut, military I
think, not very tall five-nine I'd say. It was
the way he walked though that stood out,
and the tattoo high up on his arm." I looked
at the others, sounded like the same asshole
Davey had seen down by the pier.
"Go on." you could hear a pin drop in the
room, no one so much as twitched as we
listened to her recitation of what she had
seen that night. "I remember his voice, it
didn't really go with this body type, kinda

girlish like but there was nothing girlish about the way he went after me.

It was only the other guy who stopped him from snapping my neck I'm convinced, and only because he said it would be too messy."

"This other guy what did he look like?"
"That's the funny thing, I never saw him, he stayed in the shadows, but I remember the smell of his cigar it had a sweetish smell to it; and his voice, very authoritative."

She didn't remember much more after that and believed me we grilled her, if she'd had anything more we would've gotten it out of her. "Can I go now?" She looked at Vanessa who looked like she'd like nothing better than to scalp her ass. "No, you're staying here for at least tonight, we'll decide what to do with you in the morning."

"But I've told you everything I know, why do I have to stay here?"
"Because you're a lying bitch who'd sell her own mother for a dollar and we don't trust your ass." I think it's safe to say Connor did not like this woman.

"I need a drink. You, stay here, I think you should know your friends are watching this place so if you try to leave they'll most likely take you out. That's if you get past our security, which I guarantee you you won't. Put her out."

She held up her hands when Devon moved towards her with the needle. That ought to knock her out for the next eight hours or so. I ended up having to drag her to the couch myself since no one else was willing to, before we headed out the door.

"Let's get the women and go have some fun, I need it after this shit, and we're supposed to be celebrating, fuck this." I checked my watch, it was getting late but the little spot we'd found in the next town over didn't close until about three or four so we were good, unless the girls were tired.

"Cord you cool with us dropping the kids off?" he had to think about it which told me more than words where we were at. "They're safe enough, I didn't pick up anything when I did a run through, but I think we should keep an eye out for the next few days just in case."
"Fair enough."

Chapter Fifteen

LOGAN

For some fucked up reason the kids didn't wanna leave, the female especially seemed the most reluctant though she tried to play it off. I noticed she was no longer breathing fire, she seemed calm as fuck compared to when she first arrived and I wondered what the fuck Cord had said or done to her in the past few hours to tame that beast.

I introduced Gabriella to Vanessa, which helped to calm her ass down a little, but she still clung to my arm like she was marking her territory. Even though we'd checked and double- checked the area, we were still careful as we headed out of town. We rode in three vans funnily enough with three couples in one and then two and two in front and behind for security. Zak and Vanessa still hadn't said fuck all to each other but I noticed that he'd been quick to jump in the truck with her when she followed the girls.

The night was the usual balmy clear skies with a nice breeze and the women were acting more excited than the rest of us, like we'd held them prisoner for a month instead of a couple of days.

Vanessa was involved in the conversation like the three of them had known each other since birth, especially when it came to talk of the baby. I watched Zak in the rearview and that fucker was hanging onto every word.

"Hey Lieu if I didn't know better I'd think you've done this before." She stopped in the middle of her sentence and looked around like Bambi caught in the headlights. What the fuck was that about?

"No captain, just my experience from being around my sisters and cousins with their pregnancies." Zak looked at her like he wanted to fall on her in the back of my damn truck but I didn't say a word, whatever he had brewing I was pretty sure it wouldn't be long before it came bubbling to the top.

We reached the bar and it looked like the place was still hopping, the weekend was just getting started so that could be the reason for the overflowing parking lot.

We hadn't been here since the night I'd snagged Gabriella in fact it was the first time we'd really been anywhere in quite a while. "Okay crew, you know the deal, have fun and we'll pick shit up tomorrow." The ten of us headed in the doors and straight for the tables in the corner. Con and I pushed a couple together with our backs to the wall and a clear view of the door, which is our usual. The bartender hailed us and without being told started lining off our drinks of choice.

Ty stayed at the bar for now and I let him because I knew he was working through some shit, so I took off my captain's cap and put on the fiancé cape.

Con and Dani were already off in a corner smooching and pretending to dance and Gabriella was smiling, that's all the fuck I cared about. I saw the little one that was on Ty's dick walk in not long after and looked at my sneak.

"What did you do?" She gave me the 'who me' innocent bullshit look but I wasn't buying it, especially when she raised her hand and beckoned her over. Dammit, why are these women always playing an angle, and when the fuck did she have time to call her between the time I'd told her to get dressed and the time we left the house? Fucking women.

I looked over at Ty and wondered if I'd had the same reaction to Gabriella, as he and Vanessa seemed to have to their mate. I was pretty sure he knew the second she walked in. Some strange shit has been going on since we came to this town. If I didn't know better I'd swear the old man was up there playing matchmaker or some shit.

***

TYLER

I don't know why she does it to me but she does. If I see her hear her or smell her, I'm transported to another place, another time and I'm not myself. It's almost as if she's haunting me with her very existence and I can't shake it off. Sitting at the bar with a couple of my brothers throwing back a few, trying to unwind from the fucked up day we'd had she walks right in.

I didn't have to turn around to know that it was her, every hair on my body stood on end and my cock started throbbing, that was always the way, even if I didn't see her, just from my body's reaction alone I always knew. My own personal alarm!

Her voice reached my ears as she greeted one of her friends, I knew how this was going to play out, she'll pretend that I wasn't here she'll say hello to my brothers and sisters and pointedly ignore me. Maybe I should've taken her up on her unspoken offer a few weeks ago, but I wasn't ready for her kind of fun. She's the marrying kind and I'm just not ready to slip on the noose. And at the rate these fuckers were dropping, I knew if I even entertained the thought I'd be a goner. I wasn't blind. I'd seen the way Cord reacted to that Susie girl who if you asked me was a candidate for a lobotomy.

Yes Vitoria Lynn was hot, she was sweet as fuck too from what I'd seen, but she wasn't for me, too fucking innocent. Besides she was a tiny little thing, which seems to be the only thing this town produces. Then again Nessa wasn't from here and she wasn't that much taller than the others come to think of it. Maybe that's just the type of woman we attract; the dainty kind that looked like a hard fuck would break them in half.

I watched her out of the corner of my eye as she flirted her way across the room. Every guy had his eye on her whether he was alone or with someone, she just had that kind of effect on the male of the species. That was another reason for me to steer clear. I'm a hotheaded bastard, I know that better than anyone else and if she ever fucked around and flirted with some other man I might snap and do her harm, so it was best for all concerned if I just stayed the fuck away from one Victoria Lynn Delaney.

I could see my brothers watching me covertly but when you've spent the last ten years or so in very close proximity to men in tight quarters you get to know them so they weren't fooling me one bit. Logan left where he was with his nosy ass and made his way over to the bar where Devon and Quinn had been keeping me company.

"Kill it boys."
"What Tyler?"
Logan was always the ringleader always the one pushing.
"I'm not going there okay so kill it."
My brother Connor and his woman were in the corner smooching as usual so I had two less nosy fuckers to contend with. My new little sister Danielle is relentless, she couldn't understand why I wouldn't give her

friend a chance. She believed that since she had my brother wrapped around her finger that it was only a matter of time before the rest of us fell. Now there was Gabriella and she was giving me looks, fucking set me up.

I was listening to them but my attention was completely on her as she made her way to the table where Gaby and Nessa were sitting talking. Zak was on the wall not too far away pretending not to be watching Nessa and I felt the noose tightening around my neck.

"Just what the fuck is it about this town?" I didn't have to expound, they knew exactly what I was talking about.
"I don't know brother, but I can tell you, it doesn't pay to fight it, just go with the flow, it's a lot easier. Logan the pussy whipped was full of advice but I seem to remember a time when he was singing a different tune.

LOGAN

The night wasn't turning out to be half bad. Everyone seemed to be having a good time except Ty who seemed to be grumbling in his beer. He had his eye on Vicky the whole time even though he was slick about it, and thank fuck she had ignored my little upstart's suggestion that she dance with the next man who asked her to. I wasn't trying to get kicked out of the only decent watering hole in a ten-mile radius.

So it didn't look like Ty was gonna fold tonight but there was still a lot of fodder for my shits and giggles. Like Dani trying to convince Con that it was oaky for her to have a half a glass of wine, and him having a conniption, funny shit. Or the way Cord was mooning into his mug, like he'd lost his best friend, good times.

"It's already late." What the fuck? Vanessa's raised voice came out of left field. "I said you're not going and that's final." "Who made you the boss of me Zachary? I can go where I want when I want and with whom I want." "Try that shit and it'll end bad for you swear to fuck."

"Alright you two break it up." Fuck Ty was right, it was like watching the Tyson Holyfield bout all over again in techni-fucking-color. "What seems to be the problem?"

"She thinks she's heading into the next town over to find a place to stay, and this asshole's been sniffing around her all fucking night." He glowered at some poor smuck across the room who probably had no idea that his life span was now being counted in minutes. I need this shit.
"I am going to find a place to stay and you can't stop me." Well now, she wasn't backing down and I know for a fact that he won't so we're in a pickle. Just once I could wish for a female who wasn't so damn fearless and ballsy, it's like our size didn't matter, they all still think they can take us on.

"Uh Vanessa he has a point. We have more than enough room at the compound. You can stay with Gaby and me or Con and Dani or…"
"She's fucking staying with me." Okay cowboy who's arguing? Damn.
"I am not." When he stepped into her like he was giving serious thought to popping her one I figured I'd better intervene.

"Okay, listen, we can't do this here first of all, and second, Nessa, none of us are gonna let you go off on your own. Let's get back to the compound and the question of where you spend the night can be solved there."

She didn't agree with it I could tell, but she caved because I'm pretty sure she knew Zak didn't have any give in him worth a damn.

We headed back to the compound feeling a lot lighter than when we left and I just wanted my bed. Tomorrow promised to be another trying day because we still weren't any closer to figuring this shit out and I couldn't shake the feeling that we were racing against the clock.

We ended up having to drop Ty's future whatever home because she'd taken a cab there at my woman's suggestion, sneaky fuck. I wasn't really worried about where Vanessa slept as long as it was within these gates, so as soon as we were all safe inside I left the rest of them to their shit.

Ty was still griping about being cornered, but I knew what his problem was. Somebody had given his little filly pointers and she wasn't putting up with his shit. The two of them had played the ignore game all night until it was time to leave, and the way she spoke to him there at the end, permafrost.

I dragged my pain in the ass off to bed and left the rest of them to their own recognizance, tomorrow was soon enough to deal with their brand of fuckery.

Vanessa cussed out Zak at the top of her lungs as he dragged her ass off to his lair, to the entertainment of Ty who was over his snit it seemed. I heard one last complaint for the night, this time from Devon who was supposed to be watching over our guest for the night.

"Babe, what the fuck have you been telling that girl?"
"What girl?" She wanted to play dumb.
"You wanna play dumb fine, but when she pushes Ty too far I hope you're willing to bear the consequences." That seemed to put a little hitch in her giddy-up. "What do you mean, he wouldn't really hurt her would he?" it would serve her right if I left her with that impression in mind, but I couldn't do that to my brother.

"No, but if you push him into a corner you might not like the results. And for fuck sake don't tell her about flirting with other guys, you trying to get her ass killed?" now she was back to worrying, good, maybe now she'd stay her nosy ass out of other people's shit.

"I don't see what's the big deal. You gave me a hard time now look at you." She got jokes. I got sidetracked when she pulled her jeans down and off. "What's that you got there?" she had some kind of gem hanging from her clit.
"Oh Dani and I were bored waiting around so we pierced each other's clits."
"You did what?"
"It's a joke, it's just a clip on." I grinned because I could already imagine the fun we were gonna have with that.

"Leave it on." we both rushed onto the bed and I rummaged around in the nightstand for some goodies. I got out the ben-wa balls and some lube.

"Open." She spread her legs for my mouth and I climbed in between them to warm her up. I used my tongue to get her off and just as she was cresting, I slipped the balls inside her, using my finger to push them as far up in her as they would go.

Next I teased the little diamond in her clit with my tongue while shoving my thumb in her ass. She was in heaven. She started fucking my face even before I got started on her pussy.

I went in search of the beads with my tongue but they were too far, so I satisfied myself with eating her out until she came in my mouth. I nibbled her flesh as she wound down, leaving my mark on her thigh her hips and her tummy, making my way up to her tits. I slipped my cock into her as I took her nipple into my mouth, and felt the balls rolling around in there at the tip of my cockhead.

"Oh Logan that feels so nice." I went deep on each stroke, knocking the balls together inside her. She was juicing all over my dick and tearing the skin from my back in her lust craze.

I wasn't even doing her hard, I didn't need to, the added sensation of the beads and the ring in her clit had her continuously cumming on my dick, who was as happy as he'd ever been.

"Raise your legs up here." She wasn't paying me any mind so I lifted her legs myself and held them open and high at an angle so I could fuck into her however I wanted. Her eyes rolled back in her head when one of my strokes went too deep and her body started to convulse. "Oh shit, oh fuck." I tried to pull out but her body went into some sort of lockdown and trapped my dick inside. Her pussy quivered as she jerked and the movement had me spewing a jet stream of cum inside her that seemed like it would never end.

"Baby, talk to me, come on." She was out of it and I still had to wait for her body to relax to pull out. I ran into the bathroom for a wet cloth and tried to bring her back that way. Her breathing was normal and her pulse wasn't accelerated, and it took me a minute to figure out that she'd fainted. I didn't know what the fuck to do, should I touch her, try to wake her what?

She came to five minutes later, the longest fucking five minutes of my life. I started to pull the beads out and her body did that shit again and scared the fuck outta me. She stayed awake this time thank fuck but I'm thinking that's it for the beads.

"What the fuck happened? my heart was in my lungs and this one was grinning like a Cheshire cat. "Oh Logan it was amazing, we have so got to that again." Not in this fucking lifetime.

She stretched and reached out for me, which meant her pussy was still hungry. My boy had gone into hiding because he thought he was in trouble. "Since you scared the fuck out of him, you get him back up." She rolled into me with a nasty smile on her face; fuck I forgot her and alcohol, oh well.

"No problem honey bear." I just rolled my eyes at her drunk ass and let her do her thing. When she licked my dick down to the nuts with her juices and mine still on it, I knew what kinda mood she was in.

She likes when I kneel over her with my dick in her face while she reclines against the pillows. I fed her my cock little by little until she had a mouthful, then I fucked into her throat slowly. I held her head in my hands and throat fucked her until she gagged with pre-cum running down her chin. I wasn't going anywhere near her pussy again with my dick, so I used my fingers to get her off while she sucked the skin of my dick.

When my dick started to jump on her tongue and her pussy tightened around my fingers I pulled out of her throat and sprayed all over her tits. All in all it was a good night.

Chapter Sixteen

GABRIELLA

"So here's the deal, we have got to find out what's going on down by the water. So far we know squat and this affects our lives as well." Dani and I and our new friend Vanessa were sitting around drinking coffee while the men folk were out and about doing who knows what.

"I don't think that's such a good idea, and whatever you're gonna do I can't know about it because I ought to know better." "Oh come on Vanessa, you're like one of them if you go with, you can be our protection. Besides, we're not doing anything, just going to see what they missed."

Dani wasn't looking too sure either but I knew how to bring her around. I had to work on this Vanessa person because Logan had left her here with us, knowing him she was supposed to be more watchman than pal, but later for that. I have a wedding coming up in a few short months and all this cops and robbers mess was interfering with my program. "They don't even have to know we went anywhere.

They left on an errand didn't they? It's just a quick trip to the pier and back." I'd dragged as much information out of Davey yesterday that I could and knew that something had gone down but he wasn't saying what.

I did garner that the guys had been down there looking for something, I just don't know what, and now they had that awful woman that used to work for Dani locked away in the cottage. Since no one was talking I figured it was up to us women to figure out just what in the Sam hill was going on; and with Vanessa being G.I Jane and all, why not?"

"Gaby I'm with Vanessa, we don't know what all is going on down there, I think we should leave well enough alone." she's just afraid of Connor, but who wouldn't be? I wasn't even gonna think about Logan's reaction if he found out about my little side trip, but he wasn't gonna find out because we were gonna be gone and back before he came home.

"Fine, if you two won't go with me I'll do it by myself, but I bet you there's nothing going on down there but a bunch of kids acting the fool." I just wanted to go and catch them in the act so that we could put this whole mess behind us and move on.

I'm sure if I had the proof that there was nothing really going on that Logan would settle down and help me plan the wedding.

I got up from my chair and headed for the closet to get my shoes. The sun had been down for a few hours and it was almost full dark. Logan and the guys had gone somewhere to check out something and he said they wouldn't be back for a couple hours at least.

The woman was under lock and key and no one said anything about us having to watch her. I figured if I made the move to go, that these two would follow. "Let it be noted that I'm doing this under duress."

"Yeah, I knew I was gonna like you Vanessa." Dani was still looking doubtful but I knew she wasn't gonna want to be left out, and I was right. "Your ass is still getting me into trouble, I'm telling you, these men have radar. They're gonna know the second we leave the compound."

"You need to stop watching Sci-Fi, now come along." I took her hand and pulled her along before she chickened out. I had a moment's pause when I remembered the baby, but soon squashed it. I'm sure I was right, there was nothing to worry about.

***

LOGAN

"What the fuck?"
"What is it?" Connor reacted to the tone of my voice, and the others raised their heads from their positions in the brush, surrounding the place we were told we might be able to find the man that fit the description we'd received from both Rosalind and Davey.

"Check your watch Con." I didn't even need to explain as he looked at his and had the same reaction, before we were both heading for our rides. My mind went into combat mode as the others fell in behind us.

"What's going on?" Ty was the first to catch up with us.
"The girls are on the move." That sent everyone scrambling for their bikes as a thousand scenarios went through my head.

It wasn't a breech because each of us had a special alarm on our phones that would've gone off if someone had got past the perimeter, so where the fuck were they going? Had someone tricked them into leaving? It's the only thing I could figure since I'd told Gabriella not to leave the house.

I couldn't afford to let anger, or fear, rule me now, not until I had eyes on her and knew that she was safe. After that, she'd better have a good fucking excuse for what she was doing away from where the fuck I'd left her.

"They're heading for the water." Yeah, like my shit wasn't already twisted enough, Quinn's words had me fighting to rein it in. We weren't too far out, maybe a half an hour, but every second felt like torture.

Quinn and Dev were keeping us up to date from the van as they followed behind. "Shit Lo we've got to move, they're on the run." Quinn's voice in my ear was like a dagger to the heart and we were still ten minutes away.

"Is Vanessa with them?" That was Zak, I knew he knew we had no way of knowing since we hadn't tagged her, but chances are she was, since we'd left the three of them together. I started praying as we sped through the night. No one said anything as we waited for updates from the van.

We came in sight of the pier or what was left of it just as a scream rang out and carried on the wind. Two figures were running on the beach in the dark, two men were after them, and two other figures seemed to be locked in combat. I jumped off my bike while it was still in motion and ran towards the two in front, while Zak headed for Vanessa who we rightly assumed was the one doing the fighting. Connor bypassed both of us and was on one of the assholes while the other grabbed Gabriella and put a gun to her fucking head.

I stopped short with my hands raised as chaos ensued. The others came up behind us. "Everybody stay where you are." He was desperate and a desperate man is a dangerous fucker.

His eyes were going all over the place like a cornered rat. I'd seen that look a time or two. Usually before some asshole did something stupid that got him dead. I wasn't too fond of the idea of Gaby seeing me in

action, women tend to get squeamish about
that shit.

"Okay, no one's gonna do anything. I
won't ask you to let her go because she's
your only bargaining chip, but I will ask you
to think. There's only one way you're gonna
survive this." I didn't look at her, couldn't.
Con had the other asshole subdued and had
passed Dani off to the others, while Zak had
taken over kicking ass from Vanessa.

"As I was saying." I brought my
attention back to him. "You kill her, I break
your fucking neck, you die. You let her go I
give you my word I'll let you live, after we
have a little discussion about you putting a
gun to my fucking woman's head. Before
you give me your answer, I suggest you do a
head count. Right now one of my brothers
has a scope centered on your forehead." He
looked around in a panic.

"Shh shh, don't do that, he might get
twitchy fingers and shoot, and I really don't
want your brain and shit all over my woman,
so let's keep a cool head here." By then Con
and Zak were bringing their guys into the
circle.

A quick glance showed me that none
of them were the one we were looking for,
but they were definitely military, the hair,

the build, the carriage; all dead giveaways. I looked back at my quarry who was sweating profusely and not looking too sure of himself. She was crying and shaking but I couldn't take that shit in right now, I had to save her life so I could wring her fucking neck for being stupid.

"Give me my woman." He looked around at all of us, and his two mates who were beat to fuck.
"No, everybody back off." He started backing up in a panic.
"Don't do tha...well fuck." She screamed loud and hard when the blood sprayed all over her face.

Cord had gone for the hand with the gun instead of the head, which was just as well because I wasn't sure how we would've explained that fuckery. I didn't go near her right away because now that the adrenaline was kicking I was beyond pissed.

The asshole was writhing on the ground holding his wrist but I left him to the others. Connor was consoling Dani and Zak was reading Vanessa the riot act. I moved towards her, not sure what I was gonna do, I couldn't even see through the haze that was over my eyes.

"Logan." She called out to me with a fearful voice but I wasn't hearing shit. I was about to tear her little ass up for putting herself in danger. I made some kind of move towards her but a fucking tank got in my way. Connor, fucker knocked me on my ass.

"Stay down Cap, you've gone FUBAR." He stood over me looking down as the others came to join him. "Yeah Cap, you stay your ass where you are."

Ty was looking down at me with a look of worry on his face. I'd only seen my brothers react this way once, when I'd lost someone on the battlefield and had lost my shit. What the fuck happened? It was as if my mind had taken flight or some shit. I looked around me not sure of what the fuck and it all came back. I had been about to strangle Gabriella's little ass.

I took a deep breath and closed my eyes, willing my heart to come back into my chest.
"Ty get your damn foot off my chest you ass." The danger had past. She was still in trouble but not as bad. Zak was shooting daggers at Vanessa with his eyes and I wasn't sure she wasn't in danger too.

"Come on let me up, I'm not gonna hurt her." I could hear her crying and it tore at my heart but I wasn't about to fall for that shit. Fucking infuriating female.

"You sure you cool?" I just nodded my head as they stepped back. I must've really been out of my shit because I don't even remember anything before feeling Con take me down.

"Con how's Dani, the baby?" I stood to my feet and dust the sand off me. "They're fine, she just has a stitch in her side. I'm gonna run her into the emergency room as soon as I'm sure you're not gonna do anything stupid."

"I'm cool brother let's get your girl looked at. We'll keep these three on ice." Devon and Quinn had already taken them to the van and Cord had come down from his hiding place. I realized I hadn't even needed to tell my team where to go or what to do, we'd all just fallen back in the way we do.

Half of us followed Con and his woman to the hospital while the others went to stash our prisoners, who were in deep shit because they were about to miss curfew. Too bad for their asses, right now they had bigger worries.

***

Dani got the all clear and I commended Connor for his restraint. I could see he wanted to tear into her, but she'd had enough of a scare for one night so he was taking it easy. My pain in the ass however was not about to get off so easy.

I had already dragged the story out of Vanessa who had come to the hospital, and since she was feeling guilty, she shared it all. I should've known mine was the ringleader, that she was the one who'd talked the other two into this fuckery.

She was way too quiet and that could be because I was ignoring her. I'd put her in the van instead of on the back of my bike and I knew that had to sting, but I was too pissed. She tried approaching me at the hospital but I ignored her ass. The second time she got too close I leaned over and whispered in her ear.

"Stay the fuck away from me, I'll deal with you later." That really threw her ass in a tizzy. She could've been killed could've gotten others killed, like what the fuck.

We left the hospital and headed for home. I don't know what the fuck was going on, but Zak dragged Vanessa's ass off as soon as we got back to the compound. I didn't even try to intervene and neither did any of the others.

We were all just happy that they were okay. I stood around long enough to be sure Zak wasn't gonna lose control, because when that fucker goes quiet, it usually means trouble. It took me a while to figure out he was fucking her and not killing her five seconds after the door closed behind them. "Alright come on you pervs break it up." The others were just hanging around in the yard listening to shit like they were at the movies. I shook my head as I walked away.

"You know, the rest of us didn't sign on for Family Ties, this was supposed to be a bachelor compound. In less than a year you three weak fucks have gone AWOL for pussy and fucked everyone else's shit up."

Ty was in bitch mode again. He sounded grumpy and it wasn't hard to figure out what his problem was; fucker was running scared from the little beauty down at the diner.

I could tell him there was no sense in running. There was some shit in the water here in Briarwood that was designed just for us, or so it seemed. There was no other explanation for it. Sometimes I think the commander knew what he was up to when he left his boys this place. The way we were pairing off one after the other with our soul mates was something beyond. Still, can't have the boy raining on our parade.

"Ty go get your ass laid and stop being a pest." I went in search of my own woman; it was time to work off some of this anger between her thighs. Her pussy stayed on the injured list these days. Her hardheaded ass didn't seem in any hurry to learn any lesson I sought to teach her.

Now she'd fucked up but good. After tonight, she'll learn not to disobey me again. I still had to go deal with the three assholes on ice, but first things first. "Don't hide little girl get your ass out here." I knew her game as soon as I got through the door.

The lights were off and the place was still, too fucking quiet, like there wasn't another breathing soul here. That's some shit she used to do as a kid to hide from her folks when she was in trouble. Maybe if they'd spanked her ass instead of fucking timeouts I wouldn't have to deal with her shit on a bi-daily basis. I had less stressful days in the Navy for fuck sake.

I got my belt and went in search of her ass when she didn't show. I wasn't quiet when I opened the million and one doors in the place, or when I walked through the closets. I must've known I was gonna end up with a princess, because what the fuck did I need with walk-in closets as big as the damn bedrooms? "Gabriella, front and center, now." Not even a peep. It took me damn near ten minutes to find her.

Her ass was in a cubicle in my closet. "Get outta there." I snapped the belt that I had folded in half. Her eyes were glued to the leather and she wasn't looking like she was about to climb outta there anytime soon.

"Did you hear me?" she opened her mouth about to scream. "You do that shit it'll only go worse for you, now get your bad ass out here and take your licks. You wanna do the crime, do the fucking time. How many times must I tell you? If you're not willing to bear the consequences, don't do the shit that's gonna get your ass beat."

"But we were only trying to help." "Yeah, and whose idea was that?" Her guilty look as she crawled out of the space was answer enough. "Uh-huh, you just cost your friend an ass whipping cause I'm sure as shit Connor's just as pissed off as I am. Do you know why I tell you not to do the things I tell you not to?" I pulled her along behind me to the bed.

She was already sniffling but her ass didn't get anything to sniff about yet. I sat down and pulled her down across my lap hard. "I asked you a damn question answer me." She tried picking her head up but I pushed it back down before stripping her jeans halfway down her thighs. "For my own good, to protect me." Now she wants to sulk.

"So what the fuck were you doing down there?" I brought the belt down across her ass before she could answer me. "No Logan, no." I wailed her little ass until it went red. "Move your damn hand."

All the fear came rushing back, seeing them down there unprotected, knowing we were dealing with something very sinister but still having no clue as to what the fuck. How could she do this shit to me? If I live to be a hundred I'll never be as scared as I was tonight. Seeing that fucker with a gun to her head will haunt me for many nights to come.

"If you ever do anything like this again I won't only beat your ass I'll take you back to your father's house." I didn't realize

I was this fucking pissed until I got my hands on her. I'd stopped spanking her ass long enough to talk so that she might hear me this time. "I can't have that shit in my life. My life is about order, structure. There's shit in the world that my woman have no right being a part of, if I tell your ass to stay out of something you stay the fuck out." I sat her up on her sore ass and left the room.

"Logan." She beat tracks running after me until she caught up with me at the door. Her face was a mix of terror and despair and tugged at my heartstrings.

I felt like a fucking ogre and she's the one who fucked up. Looking down at her, one thought ran through my mind. "We're not having any fucking daughters." That brought her up short. "What?" Like I'm telling her shit. That look had just shown me what a little girl made from her and me would do to me, fuck no.

She rubbed at her ass and pouted, how the fuck was she supposed to learn shit if I kept melting like putty in her hands? "I'm pissed at you, don't give me that look." She snuggled into me with her sneaky ass and all I could do was sigh and wrap my arms around her.

"You have to listen baby, there's no negotiating that shit, you fuck up again like this we're done." Yeah right you fucking sap, you wouldn't make it one day without her under your ass. But she didn't need to know that shit.

She seemed to believe me because she held on tighter and soaked my damn Henley with her shit. I held her while she cried and blubbered an apology into my chest. "But Logan it's not fair, you get to put yourself in danger but you won't let me help you." I rolled my eyes before pushing her away so that I could look down at her.

"Were you born with a dick?" She shook her head no. "Thank fuck or I'd have to kill your ass and bury you out back. Listen up, you're a girl, you're my girl, you don't protect me from shit, I protect you. Your mom rules your dad like a fucking third world dictator, that shit's not gonna happen here, ever.

I make the rules, I do the protecting and all the other shit my nuts have ordained to be my job as a man. Now stop the bullshit and just do what the fuck I say from now on, and don't forget, no fucking female offspring."

"I'm pretty sure that's on you." I looked down at my dick, which was now pressing against my fly. "You hear that buddy? It's up to us, no girls." She cleared her throat and gave me a look that I did not trust. "What?" She hugged me tighter and shook her head. "I can't tell you yet, I'm not sure yet." I'm fucked if I understand any of that shit.

"What are you not telling me?" I held her face up by her chin so I could read her eyes. She wasn't sad I could tell that much, but there was something going on there. "I'm pregnant." What the fuck? I think things went dark for a minute or two before life came back into focus.

"You…you're pregnant, and you went running around down there tonight?" She wasn't expecting that shit. I think I was just trying to buy time, to process the shit she'd just told me.

I didn't know what to do next. I wanted to call the boys together to tell them about my son, I wanted to take her back in the room and fuck her or maybe not fuck but make love to her. I didn't know I was going to be this happy at hearing those words. Never knew there was more joy to be had other than winning her for myself.

Dropping to my knees I laid my palm over her flat tummy. "Shit baby, he's in there?" Fuck had I hurt him when I spanked her ass? "We have to go to the doctor." I started dragging her towards the door. It didn't register that it was late at night and the doc's office was closed. We could always go back to the emergency room. "What why? I have an appointment next week."

"What if I hurt him just now?" She smiled and caressed my cheek like I was the village idiot. "You didn't, I kept him protected the whole time I was over your lap." She's doing a lot of fucking protecting around here lately.

Logan Epilogue

LOGAN

"Unghh." I love the way she grunts when I pound her. She gripped the sheets so hard I thought they'd rip, but I didn't stop battering her pussy with my steel hard cock. Her legs shook and almost gave out on her when I changed up and went in on an angle.

"Mine…mine…mine." Oh yeah, it was one of those moments. That shit came out of nowhere and hit me like a freight train. Next thing I knew I was biting into her neck like a wolf with his mate, marking her on the outside as I scalded her pussy inside with hot jizz.

Ever since she'd told me about the baby I've been hard. Each time I think I'm done with her, my dick stands up and I have to fuck her again, it's some kind of phenomenon. I dropped down on the bed beside her, puffing like a steam engine coming into the station.

"Your pussy is gonna be the death of me." She crawled onto my chest and I held her close and kissed her hair.

"You still mad?"

"Yes." She didn't say anything for a long time. "I'm sorry Logan I won't ever be that stupid again I promise, I learned my lesson."

She's so full of shit. I've come to accept that Gabriella is always gonna be in shit, she's a magnet and that's all there is to it. I'm just gonna have to keep my eye on her for the next seventy years or so, and heaven help me, any kids we share. I placed my hand over her flat stomach and some of my anger and fear drifted away. A baby, fuck me, there really is something in the water.

"I gotta go tell the guys." I jumped off the bed and grabbed my phone while she lounged back on the bed. I took enough time to grab a quick shower before heading out after calling them for a meet. We still had to deal with the assholes before the night was done, and I had a feeling that shit had just heated up.

"What's the big emergency Cap? Some of us need to unwind after the shit your woman put us through." Ty was gnawing on some type of meat bone as we waited for the others to join us. Con came next and we watched him say bye to Dani in the doorway before coming over.

At least she didn't look any worse for wear and I could only surmise that he was taking it easy because of his son.

The others soon came, all except Zak who was probably still in his woman. "Gaby's pregnant." I didn't bother leading up to the shit, why bother? It took a minute for it to sink in but when it did, the air shifted around us. Everyone was excited and the news went a long way to alleviating the stress of what we'd dealt with in the last few hours.

Ty of course had to make his feelings known. "It's got to be the fucking water, either that or the shit's catching." The idiot started backing away like we had the plague.

I smirked at him because from what I saw last night his time was just about up. I watched him the whole night as he pretended not to be watching Vicky, but I wasn't about to say anything because knowing his hardheaded ass, he'd deny her just for that shit.

Zak finally came waltzing out his door, but for a man who'd been busy, doing what he'd been doing, he sure didn't look rested. "What the fuck is wrong with females?" Uh-oh. He didn't even stop to find out what was going on, but kept going towards the cottage where we'd stashed the three idiots in a separate room away from the woman.

"Damn another bitch made fucker."

"Tyler would you shut the fuck up?"

THE END

SEAL Team Seven
Zak
By
Jordan Silver

Table of Contents

Chapter i

ZAK

This damn female is gonna make me crazy, but then again what's new there? She's the only one of her kind to have ever gotten under my skin, and shit didn't look like it had changed much in the two years or so since I'd last seen her. I slammed out of the house and left before she made me lose my fucking mind again. She'd only been here a short while and already she had me ready to turn her over my damn knee.

Now wasn't a good time either, since my brothers and I were dealing with some bullshit in the small town that we now called home. Shit had just taken a more serious turn, and we needed all our concentration on that. Not on annoying ass females who didn't know to quit while they were ahead. I was so pissed at her, I forgot all about my brother Logan's call. The fact that the others were standing around out there meant it was something big too.

Oh well, too late, I was already half way to the cottage where the three assholes we'd caught earlier were awaiting judgment. The little scuffle I'd had down by the water had barely whetted my appetite; I needed to knock some heads together.

Part of me knew I was running from what had just happened in my bed, and part of me still had some shit to work off. It's been a while since I'd been that fucking scared and last time had been because of her too. She was my weak spot no doubt about it, and it didn't seem to matter that we'd been apart for so long, seeing her again had brought it all back.

All those old feelings that I swore to myself over and over again were gone. I knew as soon as I saw her again that I was full of shit, that I'd just been fooling myself. I'd buried my head in the sand so to speak, kept moving one day at a time, putting one foot in front of the other, but I see now I was really just going through the motions.

In life there was one man made for one woman and vice versa. The first time I met her I believed that wholeheartedly, and even after our separation, I still believed that shit.

There was no getting away from it, she was mine and I was hers no two ways about it. It was as if the past two years had not happened, all the bad feelings in between had disappeared between her thighs. We had awakened something long dead in my bed just now. Something that I had thought long buried.

The memory of what we'd just shared, her over me, with her long beautiful mane trailing over my chest, as she took my cock, was imprinted on my brain, erasing the last memory I had, of her walking away. That shit still cut deep whenever I allowed myself to think of it, but for whatever reason she was back in my sights again and I wasn't about to let that scene play out again. I assured myself of that fact for the one-hundredth time.

There was no force on earth that could take her away from me again. The last time had almost finished me off. I'd let her go for her own good, because if she'd stayed with things the way they were, I would've ended up destroying her or myself. At least that's one of the things I've told myself over time, but there was a whole lot of other shit involved in that mess that wasn't that easy to explain.

I'd run the gamut of emotions where Red was concerned over the years. From wanting to go find her and drag her back by her hair, to never wanting to lay eyes on her again. I'm not the kind of man you can say certain things to and she'd crossed the fucking line back then. It's a given that things had gone down the way they had because we were in the thick of battle when she started her shit, and my hands were tied. Now she was on my turf.

She's a brave fucking soul though I'll give her that. Funny thing is, I'd talked myself out of going after her for the last time not too long ago. Something I never shared with my brothers, since I never discussed her, never mentioned her name after the day we split.

In a million years I never expected to be inside her again. When we'd parted on such volatile terms last time, I thought for sure that was it. I'm not big on second chances, I'm a hard fuck, but I've had to be. I've seen too much, been through too much to play certain games. It was the hardest thing I'd ever done in my life, letting her go. But at the time I was too fucking pissed to think about the consequences. I'd let my anger get the best of me and said some fucked up things that I couldn't take back after she'd come at me with her bullshit.

My life is about discipline and order. One of the first disciplines I'd learned was to let my word be my bond. Vanessa is the only person to ever fuck with that in more ways than one. The only person to ever make me want to go back on what I'd said. I guess love would do that to you, make you fuck stupid. And what we'd had back then was the real deal.

Too bad no one ever told me that that shit could make you strong as an ox one minute, and weak as fuck the next. I wasn't too big on love and its rollercoaster bullshit, but it didn't seem like I had much choice in the matter, until she left and damn near turned my shit upside down. It was only after she'd left that I'd realized what it was the I held in my hands.

That my pride didn't matter when held up to the love I felt for her. But by then it had been too late. Now she's back and I have a feeling deep down in my gut that this time she's not getting away.

I'd warned her once, but I guess she lost sight of that shit when my brothers sent out the call. Too fucking bad for her. I'd given her-her freedom once, no fucking way I was doing that dumb shit again. That shit had almost destroyed me. I'd gone into a downward spiral that had taken all my brothers' strength combined to bring me back from the brink.

It had taken some time before I realized that I was on a suicide mission, taking unnecessary risks. It was only because those risks could've hurt my brothers as well that I had harnessed myself.

It was hard as fuck living without her. After only having her for a short time it felt like I was missing the best part of me. I faced death everyday, but nothing hurt as much as the loss of her. I was on the brink of madness more than once, questioned my sanity and my reason for living like never before. All the shit I'd thought was soft in others, I found myself falling into; and then out of that confusion bred hate. I waffled back and forth between hating her and loving her so much it fucking gutted me.

Back then I had promised myself never again, I'd never give a woman that kind of power over me again, and here I am, not even twenty-four hours since she walked back into my life, with her pussy juice drying on my nuts. It felt good as fuck though I can't lie.

The feel of her was just as I remembered: that soft flesh wrapped around me the same way it always did, and drew me in. And it didn't take much to have all the old feelings come rushing back. Feelings I'd thought long buried and forgotten were once again at the forefront of my mind.

***

Like the first time I'd ever laid eyes on her. It was the wolf whistle from some other fucker on the base, in the middle of the desert, that had drawn my attention. I remember the hot sun beating down on us as we were winding down from a drill in a bitch of a heat wave.

I'd turned to see what all the fuss was about when the murmurs started after the whistle. Fighting men are part dog, part hyena, they'd howl at a fucking snake if it looked good enough. Especially when you've been in the middle of bum fuck nowhere for weeks, waiting for the action to kick off. I've seen less disciplined men pine away for the taste or feel of pussy. Me not so much.

It was her hair that caught me first. Either she'd grown too hot sitting in the transport that had brought her and the rest of her team in, or she was just happy to reach her destination in one piece, but she had taken off her head gear and loosened her braid.

All I saw was a rainfall of red trailing down to the top of her ass, and oh what an ass it was, fuck me. Then she turned and looked right at me and poleaxed my ass. No joke, I think my world stopped for a second or two. Quinn likes to say he saw the second the lightning bolt struck. He said there was nothing in me for five seconds at least, like I'd gone away somewhere, before coming back to myself.

He could be right, because I remember shaking my head as if to clear it, but not being able to take my eyes off her. Everything else went still; even the din of the men's voices had ceased to penetrate. I even forgot I was in the middle of a war. All that was there was her. I was intrigued and pissed the fuck off at the same time. My brothers and I had a deal, no serious relationships while we were still in. We all took those things seriously, whatever we'd promised each other as men. But looking at her, I felt the threat. No other woman in all the years since we'd made that pact had come close to making me want. And I knew as sure as the sun was shining, that I was about to break that promise.

She didn't only make me want after one look, she made me crave. I was already formulating the upcoming arguments in my head of what I was going to tell the others so I could have her, and I didn't even know her name, knew nothing about her. None of that mattered though; all I knew in those first few moments was need.

It didn't escape my notice that she too seemed have been stopped in her tracks, to be hit by the same phenomena that had struck me where I stood, as she stared back at me. It was only the intrusion of the noise around me that had snapped me out of it, and when I moved she started to blink again like she was coming out of a stupor.

I honed in on her like a wild beast on his mate's scent, locked her in and caged her off from the other males that were there, with just a look. My body reacted strongly to her scent the closer I got to her, like I knew her somehow, but that couldn't be, I would've remembered her.

I didn't say anything to her for the longest while, just stood there gazing down at her, not giving a fuck what the others in the camp must be thinking; all I saw, all that mattered was her. I felt a sense of calm come over me, followed by the need to mate.

I remember feeling almost desperate to get her alone, to get her away from all of those male bodies. Men who had been comrades a short ten minutes ago were suddenly a threat. I became aware of others vying for her attention and almost committed murder.

I wanted to take my piece and shoot the fucks for even trying, but common sense prevailed. I think they got the message to back the fuck off when I bared my teeth at them though, and they all fell back.

My brothers like to remind me of that shit too on occasion, well they hadn't in a while, not since we'd called it quits. Back then I'd wanted the day to come to an end so that I could learn everything about her; and then I got pissed the fuck off that she was there, which made no sense.

I hated the fact that this woman who had made me feel, was here in the middle of this hell. What her being there meant suddenly registered and I wanted to grab her up and get her the fuck out of there and back to the mainland. Back to safety until u could come get her when my tour was over. But I knew that shit wasn't about to happen.

I'd heard the stories of the hot shot marine they were bringing in, hadn't paid too much attention though, because what the fuck did I care? But everything I'd heard came rushing back and I hated all of it. I hated that she was good at what she did, so good that they were bringing her in to send her on special ops with us.

I hated that she was a beautiful woman in the middle of all these men when everything in me told me she was mine. I especially hated that her CO had a reputation for fucking his female subordinates, and rumor had it that it didn't matter if they were willing or not. The very thought of it made me contemplate murder.

It was amazing looking back, how quickly everything had changed. In literally the blink of an eye I saw my life change, saw everything I wanted, with her in the center of it, and I didn't even know her name. "Red."

I reached out and touched her because I couldn't help myself and the next words I said to her pretty much sealed our fate. "No one will ever have you again but me." I never dreamed that she might me innocent, but I knew for damn sure somebody would die if anyone else ever came near her again.

She was the first woman I'd nicknamed in my life and the only one to have tied my guts in knots. I fell fast and fell hard that day. And in the weeks that followed, after I'd taken her cherry three days after we met, we'd been inseparable. Well as much as that was possible while on an Op.

I spent my days watching her back more than my own, with a ball of worry in the pit of my gut. And at night I spent what hours we had left 'til morning light buried inside her. Trying to exorcise the worry and fear I had for her between her thighs.

I'd been like a dog in heat back then, we both were. And though I tried to shield her from the lascivious jests of the other men, it was no secret what we were doing, it was written all over our faces. Whenever we could find a dry place to fuck I would take her down. I don't know if it was being the thick of it or what, I just knew that where before I'd been more than happy to go without, now I found myself wanting her every free second and sometimes not so free ones.

My brothers had covered my ass plenty back then, and it helped that we were on a mission where there was a lot of waiting involved. So while we waited, I spent as much time as I could buried inside her.

Back then it didn't matter how many times I came inside her, I wanted more, always more. She was like my own personal elixir, a tonic that I needed at least three, four times a day.

Every free moment we had I was inside her, and she let me, never turning me away. When she bled and was in pain and I couldn't have her, I laid beside her and held her close with my hand pressed against her tummy, willing the pain away. Three days later I was pulling her under me again, by then I had been ready to fuck the wind.

I'd taken the rubber off that first time after I'd felt her barrier on the tip of my cock. I'd never put one on since, and she'd never asked me to. Then again by the time I nibbled on her neck and got my fingers

between her pussy lips she was too far gone
to care.

It's what I remembered most about
our time together, the feel of her bare skin
against mine, that and the way my heart
always seemed out of sync whenever she
was around.

She'd been my first and only virgin.
And the only woman I'd ever taken
bareback. She was also the first woman any
of us had messed with that the others
seemed to automatically know was off limits
for the usual jokes.

No one even questioned the
seriousness of the relationship, and after I
explained it to my brothers they were very
accepting of it. Maybe because she wasn't
the average woman that I would have to
leave stateside, who knew nothing about
military life, or maybe because they sensed
that I would die without her, who knows. All
I know is that from the first, I never wanted
her out of my sight.

We'd been on one furlough together.
I'd dragged her off with my brothers and I to
a beach in Riad, away from the battle and
the death and destruction. We'd spent the
whole weekend in bed together until she was
sore. Even then I'd licked her pussy until

she wasn't hurting anymore, just so I could fuck her again. Only stopping when she cried from the pain.

Once we'd tried playing tourist, but we'd lasted all of fifteen minutes before I was hustling her back to the hotel. I've never fucked anyone as much as I fucked her that weekend, not before and definitely not since. It was the only time we'd had together like that, before things had fallen apart not long after.

Because I couldn't get over my fear of her getting hurt, not to mention wanting her away from this asshole that couldn't keep his eyes off her ass and had almost caught my bullet. If it hadn't been for Lo and Con I would've probably ended up in a military prison for the rest of my life because of that fuck. In the end I'd settled for kicking his ass once we were all back on domestic soil. I have Ty to thank for that, but that's another story.

We'd argued and both of us had been out of line, and just like that, we had unraveled. The shit had happened so fast and been so unexpected I don't think I'd believed it was real until the pain set in. I'd missed her so fucking much in those first few days after she'd shipped out, that I thought I wasn't gonna make it.

If I were a drinking man I would've found my way to the bottom of a bottle. But because I wasn't that weak, not to mention the six men I called my brothers were like fucking sentinels watching over me, I made it through.

I had to come to terms with a lot of shit quick if I wanted to survive. I was still in love with her yes, didn't think that shit would ever change, but I'd made up my mind to live without her, even if it meant spending the rest of my life alone. That shit had been easier said than done though. There were plenty of nights when I'd plotted her abduction and all the other ways I was gonna get her back. Then my stubbornness would kick in and I'd say fuck it.

Now she's back and I feel whole again. If that fuck Tyler ever got a gander at what was going on in my head in the last few days he'd be on my ass with his bullshit for sure. I find myself caught between smiling like an ass at absolutely nothing, and scowling into the wind. All with a fucking hard on that wouldn't quit. Just having her near these last few days have been like a reawakening or some shit.

Chapter ii

ZAK

When Lo had said the women were on the run, and I knew that she was with them, all the old fears came flooding back. Then seeing her in hand to hand with that asshole I'd wanted to tear him from limb to limb after I got her out of there. By the time we got to the hospital I was coming down from the rush, but there was something brewing in me.

She'd slept in the other room the night before, but when I dragged her off when we got back to the compound I knew that was dead. I'd lit into her as soon as the door was closed, and she'd fought back. Big mistake.

She'll never understand my need to protect. In her mind she was a soldier, a fighter, to me she was my woman, soft, gentle, to be cherished. It was the same old argument.

This time, I cut that shit short. I pushed her back against the door and just tore her pants off before fighting with my own. I didn't even take the time to prepare her; it had been too long. Just one swipe of my finger between her folds, my teeth in my favorite place in her neck, and I slid in. I had to take a second to appreciate being home again. And then the fucking started.

I hadn't given any thought to whether or not we could be heard, and when her tightness wrapped around me I didn't really care. "So fucking good. I missed this, missed you; never again." I was rambling but I didn't care.

How could I have forgotten how amazing she felt on my cock? Her nails dug into my scalp as I battered her sweet pussy up against the door. I bit and sucked my way down to her tits, which seemed much fuller than I remembered, but I didn't have time to dwell on that shit.

I was starved for the taste of her on my tongue. I wanted to do everything at once, that's how I ended up pulling out of her and getting to my knees in front of her, pulling her onto my tongue so I could tongue fuck her to orgasm in my mouth.

"Zak, please, oh damn." Her body trembled from the force of her lust as she tried to pull me back up her body. I wasn't ready. I opened her up with the tip of my tongue, and sucked her clit into my mouth while bringing my fingers into play. I slipped three of them deep into her while licking on her love button. Only when her juices burst forth on my tongue did I stop feasting on her flesh.

I pulled her down to the floor right there and mounted her from behind. With one hard thrust I went as deep in her pussy as I'd ever been, making her cry out as she creamed all over my cock.

This used to be our favorite position, me mounting her like a wild beast, taking her down, overpowering her, breaking her to my will. I fucked into her like a madman, trying to bond our flesh together.

My teeth found its place in the flesh of her neck as she fucked back on my cock, her sweet pussy sucking me in deep. "Can you feel me, I'm in your belly? Tell me you want me there."
"Yes Zak you know I do." I loved that hitch in her voice that told me she was gone.

My hands ran over the smooth flesh of her back and around to her tits. "Brace." She remembered. Her knees went a little wider, back arched, and hands planted firmly, with her ass tilted in the air. With her hips held tight in my hands I went wild. I had two years of buildup to work off and my dick knew he was in his happy place again. There was no real finesse to my strokes, but it was just like being back in the saddle again. Her body felt softer somehow, more pliant. I don't remember being able to get this deep inside her without causing her pain, but now she was taking me in with maybe just a slight discomfort, but no danger.

"Oh yes please don't stop." Her pussy trembled around my cock as she came again but I was just beginning. "I want to taste you again." I pulled out without warning and clamped my mouth over her leaking pussy, sucking all that nectar into my lungs. I pushed my thumb into her ass the way I thought her to like and she rode my face until she was flowing into my mouth.

When she came down again I rose up behind her and ran my dick up and down her slit to her asshole, dipping just the fat head of my cock into her ass and giving her a few teasing strokes. "Later, I'll take you there later, right now I want in your pussy again." I slammed back into her and her screech was music to my ears. I smacked her ass none too gently as I rode her pussy making sure to feed her all of my dick with each stroke. "Fuck me Zak please fuck me."

It was all I needed to let go, where before I had to be careful not to hurt her, I now slammed my whole length home in her belly. I had to grab hold of her hair to keep her planted on my cock, when her knees started to give out.

So with one arm wrapped around her holding her tit, and the other fisted in her hair, I rode her pussy like a rodeo king as she bucked and moaned under me. When I came, I thought that shit would never stop. It was the way her pussy squeezed and released around me, the way her ass shook with her climax, it was everything about her that sent me to a place I'd never been before, not even the last time.

I came twice in one go, something I'd heard of but never experienced. I leaned over her back in amazement as I tried to catch my breath and take in the wonder of it all at the same time. After we both calmed down a little, I picked her up and took her into the bedroom, where I'd started on her all over again. In between fucking her twice more, we'd talked and she'd just started to piss me the fuck off when Logan's call came through. "Stay here." I wanted to find her in my bed when I came back, something I was looking forward to doing for a long, long time. With one last kiss and a heart that was finally beating right again I left the bed.

"Where are you going?" I looked over at her as I pulled my shirt on over my head. She looked like fuckable sin and all I wanted to do was climb back inside her and stay until the dawn.

"Logan, we have to deal with this latest problem. I hope you know that that was your one and only fuck up. I don't want you running around getting into shit, and I especially don't want you getting those two involved in shit that could get them killed." Where was the anger coming from? I knew on some level that it wasn't just about this, that there was a whole lot more beating beneath the surface.

"How is this my fault?" She stormed off the bed naked and looked around for her clothes that were still on the floor in front of the door. "First of all, I can take care of myself, and second, I told you it wasn't my idea. I knew this was a mistake, why did I think this time would be any different?" I didn't like where this conversation was going, I wasn't interested in hearing how difficult I was to get along with or how over the top my ideas of the man woman dynamics were. I'd heard it all before in fucking Kabul.

"You're about to tread on very thing fucking ice, we're not in the desert surrounded by a platoon young lady, watch yourself." She got so turned around apparently, that she went back to the bed when she couldn't find her clothes.

"It doesn't matter anyway because I need to be getting back soon." Is she fucking kidding me? I just glared at her until she started to fidget. "

What the fuck are you talking about, you're not going anywhere." She knelt in the middle of the bed with the sheet pulled up to her chin, her hair wild around her shoulders, her eyes shooting fire. "I can't stay here Zachary and you can't make me."

"What's in New Orleans?" She got real quiet and my gut twisted, I'll fucking kill her. "I asked you a fucking question, who the fuck do you have to get back to?" I advanced on her and her eyes went wide. Oh yeah, this wasn't the SEAL and the Marine now, this was a man and a woman, and she knew better than to try pitting her strength against mine. "No one, it's not what you think." Confusing ass female, at least I got what I wanted.

"Hold that thought, we'll discuss this when I get back. There's no way off the compound so don't even try, and if you should so happen to find a way, I will find you, do not fuck with me on this Vanessa." She had a few choice things to say, but I tuned her out since I needed to go see what the hell was up.

I thought we were leaving those three to stew in their own fear until much later, but it looked like there was a change of plans. I hated that torn feeling, being pulled in two directions at once, but she wasn't going anywhere, and the sooner I dealt with this fuckery the sooner I can concentrate all my efforts on marking her for good.

Once I do that, there's no way she'll ever get away again. It felt good as fuck having her again, and I aimed to keep it that way.

***

But now I was back to being pissed because of her damn mouth. How could I have forgotten her penchant for getting under my skin with her hardheaded ass? She never fucking stops and almost two years apart hadn't changed shit.

I heard the others coming up behind me just as I hit the door. I was in the right kind of mood to deal with this shit though, and so I kept going. It had been quite some time since I had my foot in someone's ass, and with all the shit that was going on lately, I knew it was only a matter of time before I blow. Better they get it than her.

That pent up anger I had against her and the way things had ended between us only needed an excuse, a reason, to run free. If that day ever comes it's going to be a dark fucking time I know it.

So I have to be careful here for the next little while and channel my anger and energies in a different direction. I wasn't about to give her a reason to want to leave, because even if I had to chain her to my bed she was staying. I wasn't about to lose her a second time, fuck that.

I put that shit behind me and headed for the room where we'd stashed the prisoners. They were chained to the wall thanks to Dev and Quinn's handy work. The woman could still be heard griping about her conditions a few doors down. How the fuck did she expect to be treated after the shit she'd done?

I knew none of my brothers were dwelling too hard on the fact that we now suspected these fucks or whoever they worked for of killing the commander. We like to deal in facts so the sooner we can square that away, the better. It was looking more and more like we might be on the right track there though, which was in no way good for these three.

We'd been on the lookout for the asshole who seemed to be in charge, at least on this end. From the meet the Rosalind woman had described it seems like the really big fish might be an out-of-towner or some shit; we were still working on the logistics.

Lo had come up with a plan and the rest of us had agreed, it seemed sound. He'd contacted someone we knew we could trust, whose reach stretched across all arms of the country's military. With him on our side we'd have more legroom, and one hell of an ally.

The plan had been set and we were on our way to weed out these fucks from their little hidey-holes. Of course we had to scratch that mission because the fucking females had decided to play Colombo or some shit.

After I'd fucked Vanessa to within an inch of her life the second time in my bed, she'd told me their hair brained idea and how it was they came to be down there in the first place. I only had enough time for one hard smack to her ass before Lo had called, but that was enough to let her know what she had coming.

It didn't matter that it hadn't been her idea, she should've known better. Now she was giving me shit about having to get back to NOLA and acting all secretive about why.

When I was buried to the hilt inside her with my hand wrapped around her throat she swore to me she hadn't been with another man, so I knew that wasn't the reason for her wanting to go. The reality is, had it been, I wouldn't have cared. She'd been mine for a long time, and it took seeing her again to realize that she'd always been mine, even when she wasn't with me. The shit that had gone down between us had more to do with my needing to protect her as her man, and look out for her, than anything else.

She had these ideas about the roles we were supposed to play, that hugely differed from mine, and we'd had a heated difference of opinion on our last mission. That shit had involved another dick, but I see now that it had been unreasonable of me to want her to transfer from her unit because her CO had the fucking wandering eye and it was wandering more often than not in her direction.

She was a marine, she had no real control over where she went and shit like that, and the bastard hadn't actually done anything yet. But all I saw was that another man was after what's mine and I reacted like I typically do.

Once she reassured me that she wasn't in an all fired hurry to get back home because of a man, I decided to let her live. Fuck I just came in her, more than once. That shit stopped me in my tracks. Not that I thought she had any diseases or any shit like that, I knew she wasn't promiscuous, I'd been the first man to have her. I wouldn't even let my mind go to the time we'd been apart, I have to trust that she was telling me the truth. I can't deal with that shit, not now anyway. Dammit, she better not had let another motherfucker put hands on her. I was tempted to go back and confront her again, but the six men at my back reminded me that we had business to take care of. I looked over the men for my prey.

"Hey you, asshole, you look like you're in charge." I pulled the idiot I'd already beaten to a pulp up from the floor. His eyes were already swollen shut and his lip split. If he lived, he was gonna have a hard time explaining those bruises, granted his CO wasn't the one in charge of this whole operation.

"You wanna tell me what the fuck you were doing chasing our women?" The others closed the door and stood back, this was my show.

Chapter iii

ZAK

They were tougher to crack than we expected, and had an overblown sense of themselves, but we got what we wanted. We hadn't expected them to fold too easily. Whoever was in charge would've chosen the best for the job.

He had to in order to keep it running this smoothly for this long without any fallout. I worked them over in both body and mind until I had them just where I wanted them, and we knew which of them could be easily separated from the herd. Now all I had to do was some homework on our boy, and put the screws to him later.

They were feeling pretty good about the fact that they hadn't named any names, but they'd given us plenty without even realizing it. All in a day's work! I left the rest of them to clean up that shit and headed back to the house where I'd told her not to leave.

I'm gonna have to tag her soon, because I did not want to come back one day and find her ass gone. Her stint in the marines was up. I hadn't had a chance yet to find out what that was about.

All I cared about was the fact that there was nothing she had to do stateside that she couldn't do from here as far as I could see, and this time I wasn't taking no for an answer.

Like I'd told her, she couldn't get off the compound without me knowing, unless one of my brothers betrayed me, and I knew there was not even a remote possibility of that shit happening.

I quickened my pace the closer I got to the house, suddenly ravenous for her again. My dick perked the fuck up at the thoughts in my head, of what I was gonna do to her. I heard the water running in the shower when I hit the door and smiled.

A shower sounded real fucking good right about now. I stripped on my way to the master suite and left my clothes where they fell as I made my way to her. I took a hot second to enjoy the view of her in my shower. I let the sweet feeling rush through me, before pulling the door open and stepping inside behind her. My arms went automatically around her waist and pulled her back into my already hardening cock. She stiffened up a little before relaxing under my hands.

"Umm, my soap smells good on you." I buried my face in her neck and sucked as I rubbed my already leaking cock into her ass. I let my hand drift down her middle to between her thighs and sunk three fingers inside her pussy.

"You were almost virgin tight when I fucked you earlier, you said you're not rushing back to a man, but I've gotta ask. Who did you fuck when you were gone?" My other hand came up and around her throat without any conscious thought on my part. When she didn't answer a red haze started to form and my fingers tightened. "Red..."

"No one, I swear, no one...you?" I felt her body tense as if expecting a blow. That's one thing about her; she can never hide from me, her body gives her away every time. She might put up a good front, pretend she doesn't care, but I know better. "No, no one." Her body relaxed again and I hid my smile in her hair before going after her neck with my teeth again. I don't know what it is, but I've always got a kick out of marking her while I fucked her. I loved knowing that other men could see my stamp on her; it was like tagging her pussy for the world to see. The world or any other dick that thought he stood a chance.

There were no words needed when I bent her over, put her hands flat against the marble walls of the shower, and surged into her from behind. All without releasing the hold I had on her neck with my teeth. She went up on her toes and spread a little, not much, just enough to make it easy for her to take the pressure.

She moaned and shook on my cock and I hadn't even started yet. Her pussy, that glorious pink meat between her thighs gripped me like it knew me, like it was waiting for its owner to come claim it again. "You ever let another man inside you I'll kill you." She came on my cock and flung her head back on my shoulder, her mouth turned up for my kiss. That's what I like, when she gets loose and freaky, I can do anything I want with her when she gets like this.

I fed her my tongue and gave her a little time to play before taking it back and sucking hers into my mouth. She fucked herself on my cock hard as I concentrated on teasing her clit with my fingertips, while playing in her mouth. "I wanna fuck you everywhere, it's been too fucking long." I pushed her forward so that her arms were braced against the wall and her ass was pushed back against me. I held her hips in my hands as I started to fuck.

"Twelve inches for one little girl." It never ceased to amaze me how she was able to take all that dick in her tiny pussy. Vanessa has a big personality, but she's a very tiny person. She tops off at five one, red on blue, and skin so milky white I used to worry about her burning to a crisp in the desert.

Now I fucked into her nice and slow from behind as that ass that had attracted me like Pavlov's dog from the get, pushed back into my belly. My hand fisted in her hair as I pounded into her sweet cunt hard and deep. I had to wrap my other hand around her middle to hold her up when her orgasm ripped through her. "That's it, show me how much you want this, cum on my dick."

"Zak, Zak…"
"Right here baby right here, let it go." She was close to tears as her body went into free fall. I felt her insides quiver and her limbs begin to shake. "No one else, ever." I

couldn't bear the thought of anyone else having this with her.

How the fuck had I convinced myself that I could spend the rest of my life without her, without this? The thoughts in my head went straight to my dick and instead of easing off so she could enjoy her orgasm, I sped shit up and fucked her through it.

She was really up on those toes now and all that could be heard beneath the sound of water hitting the walls was the slap-slap of our hips as I piston in and out of her.

I was riding high in her pussy, hitting her spot and beyond with each stroke until she started doing that whimpering shit I remember. It's a cross between fuck me harder, and please take it easy on my poor pussy.

I'm one of those sick fucks who like a little pain with his pleasure, and once I found out she liked that shit too, it was a match made in heaven. At this angle I was going into her belly, she used to say I was pressing on her ovaries. I listened for the little pussy hurt sounds she makes because that usually lets me know when I'd gone far enough.

"You've got a lot to make up for so don't even think about telling me to stop, two fucking years." What is it about this woman that can flip me on a dime? One minute I'm lost in the pussy and the next I'm pissed the fuck off because she'd destroyed us. I doubt she knew just what the fuck she was getting herself into when she decided to come here.

Or did she expect this? Maybe I was looking at this thing the wrong way, only time will tell. I finally heard that whimper in her voice that told me it was time to pull back.

When it came I held still to let her get used to my length and weight inside her, before starting to move again. She hissed but her pussy was flowing and her ass was moving back and forth pulling her on and off my dick.

I looked down between us at the length of my cock as it disappeared into her, her juices and mine coating my meat as it slid easily back and forth, pulling her pink pussy lips out with each outward stroke only to have them disappear again when I went back in.

"Does it still hurt?" I was looking for blood on my cock, it wouldn't be the first time, but I didn't like that shit even though she said it was natural for someone my size, I wasn't sure about that shit. She shook her head no, her voice trapped in her lungs from the pleasure.

"Why did you let me cum inside you?" I wasn't sure if she was on the pill this time, she hadn't been the last time, but that was another story. We were a million miles away from home and everyday could've been our last, people tend to think different in those kinds of situations. But this was different.

There was no excuse; we were both a little older and a lot wiser. "I like to feel you." Her innocent answer given so softly was almost more than I could take. I hadn't expected her to be that honest about it, thought for sure she would try to hide from me.

I slipped out of her and turned her around in my arms so that I could see her. With our eyes locked together, I picked her up and wrapped her legs around me before reaching down beneath her ass to put my dick back in her. "Ride my cock." She did her best in this position to take as much of me inside her to play with as she could, teasing the first few inches of my dick with her silk walls, but I was soon ready to fuck her into the marble floor. "Quit fucking around baby."

That's when her playful side came out. I'd forgotten how she likes to tease the shit outta me when she gets into a certain mood, hadn't been expecting that to show up anytime soon either. Her head went back on her shoulders as she tightened her arms around my neck and moved her pussy on and off my cock.

I lowered my head and took one of her nipples into my mouth, her nipples were always sensitive to my touch and I felt the answering pull in her pussy. She came on a long sigh, but that wasn't enough, I wanted more, I wanted her screaming. The way she used to when we were stationed in the desert and I had to cover her mouth with my hand or make her suck on my tongue so that no one could hear her wild moans while we fucked.

Here there was no need for that, so I went to work on that shit. I leaned her back against the wall as the all but forgotten water washed down over us, and fucked her like I meant it. Her eyes went wide when my cock went in full tilt on one stroke. She wasn't laughing anymore, now her bottom lip was caught in her teeth as she accepted my cock that looked like it was splitting her in half. I planted my feet, grabbed her slender hips, and fucked.

Chapter iv

VANESSA

This is dangerous, I know it is, know I'm headed for a serious collision course with disaster, but I can't seem to stop myself. Just twenty-four hours here and already I'm under his spell.

I knew there was a chance this would happen, and I wonder now if I hadn't secretly wished for it. I knew as soon as I heard his brother's voice that the road led here and still I came. This was only going to complicate things.

If they hadn't called, I don't know if I would've ever gotten in touch with Zak again. I missed him every day that we were apart, but we were both so full of stubborn pride, that neither one of us wanted to give in.

I think now that we were both dumb, but hindsight and all that. And there was more, so much more. I felt that hitch in my chest again. The one I've been getting ever since I set out to come here.

As I lay here under him, sore, tired, excited, and waiting for that moment he turns to me again, and he will; I let my mind drift, but not too far. Why shouldn't I take this time for myself?

Why shouldn't I enjoy this thing that I had thought never to feel ever again? When he'd asked me earlier about other men I wanted to laugh. How could he not know? Just the thought of anyone else getting that close to me was repulsive.

I'd given it some thought, boy have I, but in the end I could never go through with it. It was as if he were always there, or the specter of him, shadowing me. There were nights when the loneliness was so hard to bear that all I wanted to do was disappear.

The worse was when I imagined him with someone else, some other woman enjoying what we had. That would usually tear my heart out and send me into a downward spiral that would last for days. In those first few months after I'd walked away because he'd forced me to with his hardheadedness, I thought I would curl into a tight ball and die. I never knew loneliness could feel like that. Not even when I was in some of the world's most dangerous locations, did I feel the despair I did then. "What're you thinking so hard about?"

I turned my head, which was about all I could move since he had me pinned, to look at him. That's one of the things I like most about Zak, the way he uses his strength to protect me even in the safety of our bed.

I don't think he ever realized, ever knew what it meant to me back in those hot, sweaty tents, when he'd finish making love to me at night, and instead of rolling over and going to sleep like I'd heard of more times than I could count, he'd literally cover my body with his, but always being careful not to crush me. "Nothing."

He quirked his brow which meant he didn't believe me, but thank heaven he left it alone. I closed my eyes but that was no help, he always did see more than anyone else. Now that the heart pounding, heat intensifying, sexual marathon was at a lull, all the old worries were coming back. We were both out of the service now, and that had been the biggest issue we had back then, that and his insane jealousy. Zak is one of those men that believed his woman was his and his only and dared anyone else to even look. It got so he didn't even want anyone else within a mile of me, or one man in particular. Turns out he was right about him, maybe it was just his natural instinct that had shown him something that I couldn't see. But at the time all I saw was his need to control me and everything else around him.

Now I get it, then I didn't. Men like Zak and his brothers, because of the things they see, the horrors they've had to deal with, it makes them see life different to the rest of us. Even me who'd seen combat, had never experienced the same mind altering hell that they've been through. I could appreciate that now, but two years ago I couldn't.

Back then I thought if I was woman enough to join up, then there was nothing I couldn't do. And when he tried reining me in, I'd broken the tethers so to speak and never looked back, well not physically anyway. Emotionally I'd left everything that I was back in that desert with him.

I knew the only reason I'd been able to escape him so easily was because we'd both been called up at the time, and there was nothing he could do. But I had no doubt had we been stateside he would've fought me tooth and nail, and I would've given in. There were many days and nights in between then and now that I wish I had. When his hand started moving on my body again it was the easiest thing in the world to just turn into him and let him take me. The soreness between my thighs was forgotten along with everything else, I'll think about it tomorrow.

"Put me inside of you." I pulled his body over mine and spread my legs to receive him. At his command I reached down between us and felt his heated length against my palm, stroking it a few times before leading the leaking head to my opening. I was wet and ready for him, like always.

I didn't think of the risk as I felt his fat cockhead split the lips of my sex, didn't think about anything else but him as he pushed all the way in, stopping halfway to let me get used to him. It was always like that, he always had to be careful not to go too deep too fast, though now it seemed I was able to take his whole length easier than I could two years ago.

I started moving with his first stroke, lifting my body up to meet his as he started off nice and slow. It would be so easy to think that the fire had burned down to a cinder, but I knew better. It didn't matter how many times he had me, we were always hot for each other, whether it was the first round or the last.

"Your pussy feels so fucking good baby." I reveled in hearing things like that.

Liked knowing that he found such pleasure in being inside me. I added a little twist, tightening my walls around him the way I knew would drive him crazy.

His growl set me off, and then his teeth biting into the same spot as before took me over the edge. He held still while I rode the crest and I knew what was coming next.

As soon as my breathing calmed a little he pulled out and flipped me over onto my stomach, keeping me pressed into the bed with a hand in the small of my back as he surged back into me.

"Oooh." He always went too deep in this position, but I liked the little bite of pain it caused. I felt every ridge of his cock as he fed it to me while straddling my ass. I wanted to get up on my knees to ease the pressure on my organs. "Stay, I want you right there; you hurt?" I nodded my head because I couldn't speak.

"Take it." I didn't have a choice, and didn't need one after the third stroke. "Um, that's it, take my cock like a big girl." Why does his words make me so hot? When he's in me like this I love his caveman, take charge ways.

It's only when the clothes went back on and real life intruded that I had a problem with his way of treating me like the little woman. Now I was enjoying the hell of the way he took me over and fucked me like a man possessed.

By the time he came in me my limbs were all but ready to give out. That's why he had to pick me up from the bed and take me into the shower, where he held me close as the water ran down on our overheated bodies.

***

ZAK

I woke with a start until I felt her body next to mine, and the night came rushing back. I didn't have time to be lying around in bed. We were supposed to be letting the men go today.

We couldn't keep them here indefinitely because the army would come looking for the fucks, and since we'd ascertained that they were just patsies, there was really no need to hold them.

How they explained their bruises to their superiors was their problem, and we were hoping that that might lead to something; maybe someone would start talking. Plus we had found a way to make this work for us.

She was still asleep and no wonder. We'd fallen off about three hours ago after an intense night of lovemaking, and she was out cold. I on the other hand was feeling more energetic than I had in quite some time. Even with all the shit that was going on, having her here, made life seem worthwhile again. The only other thing I was really interested in now, was finding out what, if any part these three played in the death of the only man I'd ever really looked up to as a father figure. I knew that shit, when it was discovered, was going to cause all hell to break loose, because none of us were gonna let that shit go.

But for now I was more than happy to find comfort in her body. It had been a while since I'd had that.

I took a quick shower and got dressed, wondering if I should let her sleep in or wake her up. I'd already disabled her van and had put a tag on her while we were fucking, so she wasn't going anywhere, but would she even try?

I knew she was gonna have to go get her stuff at some point, women hated leaving shit behind for some fucked up reason, but that could wait. I planned on asking the girls to take her shopping for some shit later, to tide her over until. But first we had to make sure it was safe.

I left her and headed for Logan's place since Gaby was making breakfast today. I hope these women never catches on to the fact that we'd basically divvied up kitchen duty between them since they'd got engaged. If I had to go back to eating the swill my brothers concocted I'd lose my fucking mind. In the last couple of months we've been eating like kings, but now with Dani's morning sickness, which according to Con came at all kind of hours, she wasn't too good around the scent of food, so Gaby had taken up the mantle.

I didn't even know if mine could throw down in the kitchen, we hadn't ever discussed it. Thinking of her staying here, being a part of all this, made my heart do strange things in my chest. It strengthened my resolve not to let her go.

"Hey AWOL, what's got you frowning?" Ty met me halfway from his place to Logan's. I ignored his bullshit, that's one of his many insults, that Connor, Lo and I went AWOL for pussy, I can't wait for his turn to come.

It looked like everyone was getting a late start today because Logan and Gaby both looked like they were fighting to get into their clothes when we walked in.

She had a pretty blush on her cheek so there was no second guessing what the hell had been going on before we showed up, and he was still trying to get his hand on her ass.

"Lo, cut the shit, your time is over buddy, it's eating time now, what's on the menu?" Swear to fuck Ty has problems. He all but shoved me out of the way to get to the table. The others came straggling in with Con holding Dani like she was an invalid.

"Damn sis you look green." I pulled out a chair for her and looked at Con who looked like he was ready to kill someone over this shit.

"I have to run her into the doctor's this morning, I'm not putting up with this shit no matter how normal she says it is." The two of them started bickering, which was funny as hell, because Con wasn't listening to a word she said.

"Hey, Bullwinkle, it's natural for a woman's body to do that while she's with young. Don't embarrass us, what're you gonna do, run to the doctor every time she pukes?"

Ty the expert put his two cents in. I'm pretty sure if he doesn't stop his shit either Con or Lo is gonna put his lights out. The only reason none of us had taken his ass out as yet was because we knew this was his way of not dealing with what we suspected had happened to the commander. A pain in the ass Ty was better than crazy Ty any day.

The talk was light as we sat around drinking cups of coffee while we waited for whatever Gaby was gonna dish up this morning.

One thing about these Southern Belles, they knew how to put a meal together. It was almost surreal sitting here like this, shooting the breeze, talking bullshit, like Ty teasing Cord about moping because the little firecracker wasn't here, when all the while there was a shit storm brewing.

Of course we didn't discuss shit in front of the women, they didn't need to know and after last night I'm pretty sure they'll keep their asses home. I knew I didn't have to tell my brothers not to share any of this with my woman, she was out of the marines and she damn sure wasn't putting herself in the middle of this shit, not while I'm around.

I was pleasantly surprised when the door opened five minutes later and she walked in looking all nervous and shit. But when our eyes met she gave me that shy smile that I remembered so well and came over to sit on my lap.

That I did not expect and I had to kick Ty the nosy fuck under the table to get him to keep his trap shut. The idiot started humming the wedding march and rolling his eyes around in his head. "I have to leave today." She said it low enough so that no one else heard.

"No." I shut the fuck down and concentrated really hard on not getting up and destroying my brother's kitchen. She wasn't doing this shit to me again; fuck that.

"We'll talk later, but you're not going anywhere."

She looked scared, uncertain and I didn't know what that was about, but one thing I did know, no matter what, she wasn't leaving me. Lo seemed to sense that something was up and asked me in that silent way of his. I just shook my head slightly at him, but I knew there was no putting him off.

We'd all grown accustomed to sharing everything with each other over the years; it was just natural for all of us to be in each other's business like that. I guess once you'd faced life or death with someone you tend to see the small shit as nothing.

"Excuse us." I'd lost my damn appetite. No one said anything as I stood from the table and pulled her along to the door with me, but I could feel their stares and knew they were gauging the situation for danger.

I wasn't feeling homicidal yet so they relaxed and went back to what they were doing. That was the one drawback to being so close to people that knew you so well. My brothers would stand in the way if they thought I was a danger to her, and that shit could get ugly.

I didn't stop walking until we were back at the house. As soon as we were safely behind doors I turned to her, caging her in with both arms on the wall beside her head.

"I want you to listen to me, don't say anything just listen. Did I or did I not tell you that if our paths ever crossed again in this life or the next I was keeping you, and your worries and fears be damned? Answer me." Fuck Zak you just told her not to speak.

"Just move your head yes or no." She nodded her head looking miserable. "I asked you if you had a man waiting for you back home, you said no. Not that I would've given a flying fuck, other than to beat the living shit out of you for cheating on me…" She opened her mouth but I cut her off. "I know what you're gonna say but I don't give a fuck.

I haven't been able to even look at another pussy, much less fuck anyone else in the time we've been apart, because what we had was real. If you told me it was that easy for you to let some other dick top you, I would've strangled your ass no joke."

"Now back to this bull-fuckery, I don't know how much you know about shit like this, but it is in poor form to spend the night with my dick inside you and then get up the next day with 'I'm leaving'. If I did some shit like that to you, you and the rest of the bra burning fucks would be up in arms, not gonna happen.

At some point after things have cooled down around here, I will take you to get your shit, until then you stay put. If you have a job to get back to I suggest you call whoever the fuck is in charge and hand in your resignation, you can fax that shit in duplicate. Call your landlord, work shit out until we get there, we'll pay the rent for a couple months until I can get there. I can't get there now because you see what the fuck is going on, work with me here, what the fuck?"

She held her hand up like she was in class or some fuck, and asking the teacher for permission to speak, cute.

"Talk." I know she was dying to roll her eyes at my high handedness, but she had the good sense to restrain herself, which was a good thing because I wasn't in the mood.

"You do realize I have a life right, and that I can't just pick up and move here just because you say so." I just looked down at her as she stood in front of me with her adorable self. I see she had forgotten who the fuck she was talking to. That shit might've worked once because my hands were tied, but not this going down. She was mine; all the way mine.

No one else had ever had her but me, that meant something in this fucked up world we lived in, it meant something to me. How can I get her to see that she had nothing to fear because of my over possessiveness? She should know that when it came to me, she was the safest person on the earth, but I wasn't about to give in, not even a little bit. There was only one way for us to work, and the sooner she got that through her thick fucking skull the better.

"This isn't a fucking democracy Red, you had your shot I let you walk, now you're here, end of story. Let's eat." I pulled her along behind me because as far as I was concerned the conversation was dead. "Zak wait, there's something…" I stopped and looked back at her.

"What is it?" What the fuck, she looked scared as fuck, and that in turn made my heart almost stop. I softened immediately and took her little face in my hands. "What is it baby are you sick?" Please don't let it be that, anything but that, fuck. I started to pull her into my chest to offer comfort.

"No I'm not sick, it's nothing like that." She stopped and bit into her lip, looking worried as fuck. Whatever it was it was weighing on her heavy. "Tell me what's bothering you and I'll make it stop." I didn't even have to think twice about making that offer, there was nothing I wouldn't do for her, nothing. She shook her head and took my hand in hers. "It's nothing, I'll call mom later and have her take care of it for me." I wasn't sure if I could trust that smile on her face, but I let her drag me along behind her.

Chapter v

ZAK

The others were already acting like the pigs they were when we returned, but thankfully Gaby had save us some. "You two okay?" Logan gave me the big brother's watching look and I just nodded my head and sat my woman next to me after kicking Ty off his chair.

"The fuck?" he didn't let go of the bacon strip he was inhaling; greedy fuck. I made her a plate before getting my own and dug in. The others started asking her shit about what she was doing back in NOLA and shit about why she'd timed out so soon from the service.

Some of her answers were sketchy at best, but no one pressed her, it was just like old times. Except there was no mortar in the background and no impending danger.

Gaby and Dani who was looking like part of the living again, were asking her questions about her time in the service and some of the hairier escapades she'd been a part of. The conversation was making my gut burn but I kept my lips sealed. I didn't want to start world war fucking four by airing my true thoughts and having to battle the fucking suffragettes. These fucking Southern blossoms can be vicious with their tongues.

I just listened and glared at my idiot brothers whenever they encouraged her when she told one of her tales. We all knew she was badass, that she was a demolition expert among other things.

"Well those days are behind you now; thank fuck." What, I couldn't hold it in any longer. She just did her eye roll bullshit, like I gave a fuck.

After breakfast we left the women at Lo's place and headed back to the cottage after I gave her ass a stern warning. I wasn't too sure that Gaby wouldn't talk the other two into some shit.

She seemed to have wedding fever and not even Lo's threats seemed to be working. He did whisper some shit in her ear that made her pout right before we headed out, so maybe we'd have some peace today for fuck sake. "So brother, you and Nessa?" I knew what he was asking as the others slowed down to hear my answer. "If I have anything to say about it, yeah." They each offered their congratulations in some way or the other, and Ty of course started his bullshit.

"Who the fuck is that now?" Someone was at the gate? Quinn checked his watch and looked at Cord. "You expecting company?" Cord looked fifty shades of confused as he shook his head no.

"It's your girl and her brother." He didn't even wait for the rest of us to react, just started walking towards the gate to let them in. "Hold it." That was Logan for you, he didn't give a fuck kids or not, he wasn't trusting shit.

"Zak, check the perimeter." That was easy, all I had to do was pull that shit up on my phone, it was like Google earth but with a twist. "We're clear, it's just the boy and the girl."

Cord went ahead as the gates slid open. We were already standing in formation just in case, but the gates closed again behind them without incident. Davey came towards us while his sister stood in front of Cord. What a pair, it was like watching a cartoon or some shit. He towered over her by a mile, but it wasn't just his stature, it was knowing what kind of man my brother was, and seeing him with someone so tiny.

I hope he knows what the fuck he's doing. Plus the fact that she has a mouth on her, somebody better keep an eye on that shit.

"What's up kid?" he looked to where his sister was still talking to Cord before turning back to Lo. He looked worried as fuck too. "There were soldiers in town earlier, I think somebody's missing or something."

No wonder the kid looked like he was ready to shit in his drawers. Cord came over to us with Susie in tow. "Con, Lo, Zak, I'm leaving her with the girls, these two are scared."

"I'm not…" she puffed up and started to get huffy.
"Quiet." She piped down. Damn, how come I can't tell Red that shit and have her stand the fuck down without giving me headaches?
"What about the boy?" Lo asked as Con and I nodded our agreement. If Cord trusted her around our women, then there was no question, plus I'm pretty sure Vanessa could take her if she had to.

"He's in this, no use keeping him out." He had a point. The kid had shared some shit with us about the commander's last days that we hadn't known about, and wouldn't have without him. "Fair enough."

Lo gave his consent as I called Red to give her the heads up that the girl was coming. Then the rest of us stood back and listened as Cord lectured her on how to behave while she was out of his sight. "You have got to be shitting me. I'll meet the rest of you pussy whipped honchos in the cottage."

Ty walked off shaking his head. I'll deal with him later; right now it was more fun watching the drama unfold.

"What do you think I am two? Look, my brother and I may not come from money and we may not be as lofty as you and your friends, but we do know how to act. We know how to eat with utensils too, and look…" she opened her mouth and showed him her teeth, "We have all our teeth and we're hard workers." Oh shit.

"Brothers and sisters." That's all he said and confused the hell out of her. I for one was wondering where the fuck all this calm was coming from. Cord isn't exactly Mr. Cordial for all that he's the quietest one of the bunch. "What, what are you mumbling about now?" She looked at him like he was crazy.

"They're my family not my friends, and no one ever said you weren't good enough, now be my good girl and come along." She folded her arms and looked ready for battle.

He picked her up and threw her over his shoulder. What the fuck? I just looked at the others and followed after Ty. "Lo, Con, you two are the leaders of this outfit, I'm hoping you're keeping your eyes on that shit, because that right there, is a domestic situation waiting to happen." I thought I had problems.

***

We had already decided on which of the three to turn. It was easy enough, you find the weakest link and you turn the screws. But we had to use common sense, we couldn't let the other two know what we were up to, so we separated them. He was hungry, hurting and scared. "So, Adrian, let's talk about your future."

I pulled up the file we had on him on my tablet. "Is this your family? Cute wife, you wanna live to see her again I suggest you not fuck with me on this." He started sweating and I hadn't even begun.

"You say you don't know who's calling the shots and we believe you, for now, but we're gonna need you to do something for us. We need a man inside." He opened his mouth but I held up my hand.

"Hear me out, there's no negotiating, you either agree or you don't leave here alive. And in case you're thinking of reneging once you leave here, know that we have someone already in place to watch you. I'm guessing right about now you're trying to figure out how the fuck you got yourself in this fix? This is what happens when you go south. As far as I'm concerned you're a piece a shit who doesn't deserve to live, but we might be able to use you, you try to fuck us on this and we'll bury you. You won't see us coming, but you'll feel the impact two seconds before you're dead."

"It doesn't matter anyway, they probably already think we went AWOL." He really is a nervous fucker, and a liar too. That could get his ass shot before he even left the room.

"No they don't you're on leave for the weekend all three of you, and that's your only freebie, lie to me again and I'll slice your nuts off. You'll live, but that pretty little filly won't have any uses for you." He got the picture.

"What do you want me to do?" Lo came off the wall and stood over him making him shake even more in his boots. "It's simple, you're gonna get word to us when there's something going down. You're gonna keep your ears and eyes open and keep us informed.

Any more surprises and you're gonna be the one to get it, from downwind." He knew what that shit meant and one of his buddies had already seen what Cord could do with a gun from a distance.

It had taken damn near the whole night but Lo had been able to set something up with one of the old man's oldest and dearest, who wasn't too pleased when we told him of our suspicions.

Because this man straddled the great divide between all factions of the armed forces, and was one of the only human beings who did, he was like our very own secret weapon.

We'd found his name in the codes and the commander had basically told us where to go if something happened to him, like a fucking blue print. It's like he knew he was getting in way over his head coming on to the end, and that said a lot, because the commander was a smart fuck.

When we laid everything out for the chief, he'd acted as though he knew a lot more about us than we'd expected. The funny thing was, he knew about the kid as well. Well enough to ask about him.

We made shit look good by working over the other two as well, just to avoid any suspicion on their part, but we didn't offer them the same deal. Their backgrounds had shown that these two were criminals in the making before they joined up, men like that were in it for self and was damn near impossible to turn. We blindfolded them and took them out through the secret door in the back wall.

Dev and Ty took them back to the beach where we'd found them and just left them there. Whatever they did from there was up to them. We went back to the ledger and digging through the old man's papers and shit to see what else we could find that might be of help.

We knew that he suspected drug trafficking, but he'd seemed to think there might be something a lot more sinister going on as well. Some of his notes didn't seem to make sense; they referred back to the Vietnam War and the heroin trade that came out of that.

"Whew." I held up the paper I was poring over. Each of us had grabbed a bunch to go through to make shit go faster. "What you got brother?" Lo and the others turned in their chairs to look at me.

We'd given the kid grunt work to keep him occupied but he too looked up. I studied him for a second but then decided what the fuck. He wouldn't be here if we didn't trust him, and since the old man had trusted him, that was enough for us.

I waved the sheaf of papers in the air. "There are some big names on this shit. If I'm reading this right, then this shit goes way back and there are some heavy hitters involved." They all left their seats and came to look over my shoulder where I'd been decoding my part.

I knew what their reactions were going to be before they started reading. "Fuck me this is bad. Total lockdown right fucking now." Every man headed out to his post leaving the kid scrambling behind us. "What is it, what's going on?"

"Shit I forgot about him and the girl..." Lo was about to tell us what to do there but Cord butted in before he could get the words out.

"They're staying in, we'll think of something to say to the mother, but she's not going beyond these walls until this shit is squared."

Okey dokey then, I guess that answers that. Con was riding herd on Ty but for once he didn't seem to be on the verge of mayhem. Instead he was deep in thought, which under the wrong circumstances could be worst. "I never liked that family, a bigger bunch of fucktards I have yet to see." At least he was speaking intelligibly.

"Ty you cool?" I needed to make sure he was okay before I headed off to do what the fuck I had to do. Con and Lo's women lived here. Cord had already laid down the law where his apparent woman was concerned.

I had to go secure mine and make sure that she knew there was no way for her to leave now, not only because I didn't want it, but because it wasn't safe. I went and took care of my part of security, which was making sure that all the cameras we had linked up were in fine working order, and that all the communicating devices were up to code. Then I went to find her.

I found her in the living room with the other three and I don't know what the topic of conversation had been before I came in, but they looked guilty as all hell. I just quirked my brow at them and called her over with the crook of a finger. The others broke into laughter making me eye the cups in front of them, but I knew Dani wouldn't be dumb enough to drink while carrying Con's kid or he'd wring her neck, so it couldn't be that.

"She'll be right back." I walked her out of the house and headed to ours. Ours, I like the sound of that. I sat her down at the island in the kitchen while I grabbed a drink. One thing about the south, it can get very hot, very early in the day. "Something came up while we were going through the old man's papers.

Something that makes us believe that anyone who's been involved in this thing in anyway may be in danger. You can't leave. Not that I was gonna let you, but now it's official, no one leaves for the next few days at least." She got that fucking panicked look on her face again.

"Those guys, they saw my face, would they go after my family?" I had to think on my feet, something else I'd been taught over the years.

"I doubt it, too messy and they seem to like things contained, plus I doubt they were paying that close attention."
"But they killed the commander, that's what you think isn't it?" She was up from her seat in a panic and freaking me the hell out.
"Yes but that's because he was getting too close. What is it, what's wrong?" She moved past me on her way to the bedroom.

"And you're sure it's safe here?" What the fuck was going on with her? "Yes I'm sure." I followed her with my mind full of questions.

"I have to do something." She got her phone and sent off a text. It took everything in me not to snatch the shit and see who she'd contacted. I was gonna have to work on my trust issues. I'm pretty sure she wouldn't have texted some other man in front of me though so my rabid meter was on low.

"Something you wanna tell me Red?" I hate secrets, secrets get people dead in fucked up ways. She bit her lip and looked everywhere but at me. "Not now, later." She got up on her toes and kissed me. Uh-huh, fuck is she up to?

I held her hips in my hands and tried not to glare her into a heart attack. "Is this something you're gonna tell me later gonna piss me off?" she patted my damn chest like I was ninety. "Maybe, but it's a good something I promise." She tried moving away again but my dick was on the rise. He'd got a whiff of her and for him that meant pussy was on the menu. Besides, it had been at least four hours since I'd been inside her.

I walked her backwards towards the bed and took her down with my mouth on hers. There was a lot of fumbling around going on as we tried to get each other naked without releasing our mouths.

She seemed almost desperate, like if she didn't get me inside her soon she was gonna die or some shit, so I helped her out, well almost. First I needed my favorite snack, so I lifted her to my mouth and dove in tongue first.

I growled in her pussy and made my tongue dance until her juices flowed. That shit was coming faster than I could swallow, and pretty soon I had a mouthful of pussy juice and an iron hard cock in my hand.

She was moving wildly beneath my tongue fuck, so I gave my boy a few strokes with my hand to keep him happy, while I let her ride out her pleasure. When her legs stopped shaking like she'd been shocked, I climbed up between them, lifted them high and wide, and fucked into her with all twelve inches. Her back arched off the bed and her mouth fell open in a silent plea. I eased back out of her womb and teased the entrance to her cervix with my cockhead. She tried covering her pussy with her hand. Too late, he was already in there. "Zak you beast, shit-shit-shit." Her mouth was complaining, but her ass was already moving.

I bent her double so I could nibble on her tits as I slid in and out of her pussy with deep long strokes. She juiced all over my cockmeat as she took me all in, her pussy packed tight with cock. Her fingers played with my scalp as she held me in place against her breast.

We rolled around on the bed until she ended up on top so she could ride. This wasn't the easiest position for her, even though she was the one in charge, too much dick for one little girl. But as usual she did her best, taking as much of me as she could until I took over and used her hips to pull her down fully on my engorged cock.

Her ass picked up speed when I pressed down on her clit with one thumb while teasing her ass with the fingers of the other hand, and then it was off to the races. That's the thing with my girl, once she gets going, I better try to keep up, she can handle her shit. I watched her little body as it shook and swayed over me, a fine sheen of sweat forming on her chest as she fucked herself on my cock until the cum boiled in my balls and shot out and into her without warning. "Fuck-fuck-fuck." I slammed up into her as I pulled her hips down hard, shoving my whole length home as she cried out and squeezed around me.

I sat up and wrapped my arms around her, drawing her in close so I could soothe her. Sometimes like now, her emotions get too high, and she cries. I held her, twisting and turning so that we laid on our sides still connected. I didn't move my dick inside her, just held her and murmured to her soothingly until she quieted again. "You okay?"

Her answer was a nod against my chest. I kissed her forehead, gave her one last squeeze, and slipped my semi hard dick out of her. "Damn your pussy's red." I kissed and licked her hot pussy before rolling out of bed and heading for the shower. I wasn't giving her one because I liked the idea of my scent on her for the rest of the day, but I did get a wet cloth to hold between her thighs to relieve the sting after I was done.

"I gotta get back baby, just mind what I told you okay and keep your head down." I left her and headed back outside. My mind had already switched gears and moved on to the next issue. Dev, Quinn, Ty and Davey were the only ones in the mansion when I got there.

"Where's everyone?" I went back to what I was doing before Lo called a halt. There was a deeper sense of urgency now. I knew we were playing it cool, but beneath the surface we all knew that we were sitting on a powder keg. The names on that list were no small time drug dealers. If they were involved in whatever this is, then we were in the middle of some serious shit.

Now I was convinced more than ever that they had done the commander. If word of this shit ever got out, it could overturn a lot of apple carts, and men like these would do anything not to let that happen.

"The other bitch-made douchebags are sniffing around their women most likely." Ty looked at the kid. "Hey kid, scram." Davey looked at Dev and I before leaving the room for the kitchen. Since we'd been spending so much time there lately the sisters had stocked up and the kid did eat a lot. "What's with you, why'd you nix the kid?" Quinn scowled at Ty.

He looked over his shoulder to make sure the coast was clear. "What the fuck are we gonna do about Cord and the sister?" "What do you mean, what the fuck do you wanna do?" He threw a few peanuts in his maw and rocked back in his chair.

I kinda knew what he was getting at, I'd had the same thoughts myself after all, but there really wasn't a damn thing to be done. "She can't handle him, those two are like oil and water.

We all know how Cord gets with a female; he's nuttier than squirrel shit. And the way he looks at this one, she's not like the others. Still, I wanna go on record as saying this shit will not go down well."

"We don't know that." Dev, who come to think of it seemed to be the only one other than Quinn who didn't have a woman on his scent was still pretty laid back. "Brother are you serious, have you seen the way she tries to talk back to him? We all know where that shit's headed. Somebody better check his fucking house for a playroom or dungeon or whatever the fuck. All I know is that little girl is in some serious shit." I'm not sure what the fuck he expected any of us to do. I guess because he was running scared from his own little filly he thought the rest of us should too.

"They'll be fine, can we get back to work now, seeing as how I'm the only one not with a female on my dick at the moment?" Quinn grouched as he turned back to his computer screen.

"You and me both brother."
"Yeah you keep telling yourself that Tyler, but as much shit as you talk, your ship is already sunk." I hid my grin as the two of them went back and forth with that shit. By the time Lo and the others showed up we were back to work trying to piece shit together.

Chapter vi

LOGAN

Things are heating up in more ways than one. I'd had to move fast after finding the commander's instructions in the codes, but we were finally getting somewhere. So far we hadn't found what it was that he had uncovered if anything, but we knew he had been on the right track.

Zak's findings today had changed things up a lot, put a whole new spin on things. If what the old man had suspected is true, then we were dealing with some dangerous fucking individuals. The men themselves may not be much; I could take those fuckers with my bare hands in my sleep.

But that's usually the way with these types. No, their strength came in the form of the power they wielded.

They had money and standing not only here, but internationally as well. It had long been rumored that these fucks were in bed with the devil, as far back as the first world war. If you ask me, if you wanted to trace the axis of evil, all you need do is study all who gained from that shit. After I'd sent my brothers off to secure our home I went in search of my woman. I needed to look at her and reassure myself that she was okay.

I knew there was no way anyone was getting in here to harm her or any of my family, we'd seen to that shit when we built the place, but still. These players were nothing to sniff at, they had access to everything the army did and wasn't shy about using it on their own. We should know, we'd seen some questionable shit when we were on the job.

One thing we'd learned as a unit was how to survive. When we'd been building this little haven we'd put a lot of security measures in place.

One, because Ty was convinced that one day the threat would come from our own, and two, we didn't trust one fuck. I guess Zak and Con had the same idea as I because I saw them both leading their women off to their homes. Cord came up beside me and I braced myself. It's always the quiet fuckers you have to watch out for. "Something on your mind brother?"

"I'm keeping her." He kept walking ahead towards my place and I closed my eyes for a second for some damn peace. I need this shit. Ty the ass is gonna start his fuckery any minute now, as soon as he catches wind of this turn of events, and that girl is a menace.

She's cute, no doubt about it, but she's got a mouth on her, and knowing Cord and his…fuck I'm not going there. I guess Zak was right, I'd have to keep an eye on that shit. Poor girl, I almost felt sorry for her.

At least Gaby stood a chance with me, I had some give. That fucker didn't have any, and I imagine that if she was the one he'd chosen, her life had just been derailed. Maybe I can have Gaby have a talk with her about how to mind her man. What the fuck am I thinking? She needs help in that department herself.

Fuck it; I just have to resign myself to the fact that the peace and quiet we'd all been in search of when we came here was a thing of the past; fucking women. I took enough time to lecture her about staying inside and most importantly not giving me any shit about having to stay inside for the next little while. Of course she gave me shit and asked me a million and one questions, but when there were no answers forthcoming she calmed down. Not that I trusted that shit, but with the clock running, I didn't have time to sit on her ass. So with one last warning I left her to head back to the others.

***

ZAK

"So, now we know one of the players involved, how do we figure out the rest, and are we still trusting the chief?" When dealing with shit like this, with these kinds of players, it was always best to keep shit close to the vest. I trusted the men in this room with my life, but I wasn't about to trust anyone else. So far the commander seemed to have trusted the chief, but that was then and those two had a different kind of relationship. The chief certainly didn't have any allegiance to us, and was only doing us a favor because of his ties to the old man. But if that particular family was involved, then there was no guarantee that we could trust anyone in government, which meant we were close to being fucked.

"We'll keep digging. As it stands we have no reason not to trust him, and we don't have any reason to, other than the old man's word.

We'll play it by ear and see what we see, but we need him for this, we just have to play it smart. I want everything we have on these fucks, the world knows the eldest son is part asshole, part fuck up, but what else do we know?

Who's next in line to inherit? That's what we have to find out. All their business dealings, even the ones that are listed under dummy corporations, we need ASAP. Zak, Quinn, I'm gonna need you to go deep on this one, do a thorough search, don't leave any stone unturned. Davey you're here because the old man liked you, you fuck with us on this we'll bury you."

The kid looked at Cord and swallowed deep before turning back to the task Lo had given him of running a search on off shoots of the family's holdings. We all got back to work on our individual piece of the puzzle. With security boosted, it meant the women didn't have any privacy, so whichever house they were in, whatever room, was running on a loop in the background.

We left the sound off to give them at least that much, but they were gonna be under a microscope until we got to the bottom of this shit.

I hit on something not even an hour later, but it wasn't what I'd been looking for. I sent an alert to all of them except Davey with the warning not to react for the kid to see, and then I shut down what I'd been working on.

Lo and Con turned to look at me with their brows raised and I walked over to the printer to grab the paper I'd printed out. "We'll be right back kid." He barely picked his head up and went back to what he was doing, just happy that he was involved.

"What is it, what did you find?" Ty with his impatient ass hounded me as soon as we cleared the door. I just passed the paper off to Lo and the others waited for him to read it before passing it around. "Oh shit." Cord had the strongest reaction. "Both of them? No wonder the kid's so fucking good with a gun, it's in his blood." Cord looked a little green around the gills when reality kicked in. He walked away and bent at the knees.

"How sure are we about this?"
Connor passed the paper back to me.
"The old man seemed pretty sure, but I don't think he got as far as the DNA test, as you can see he was setting it up right before he died. I'll keep digging but I don't think he ever did anything, otherwise those two would've said something."

"I wonder why he never said anything about this to any of us."
"According to this he didn't have a chance to."

I'd stumbled across a notation in one of the old man's files about this suspicions that he was the father of not only Susie, but also her little brother Davey, who was three years younger. I had no idea about their family dynamic other than there was always talk of a mother and no father, but I couldn't imagine the man I knew letting his kids go without his name. He'd taken each of us under his wing and been more of a father to us than the men who'd seeded our mothers, so it was hard to reconcile him with this new development.

"Shit, we need to find out one way or the other, that would make them our responsibility. Cord how're you doing buddy?" He looked determined as fuck and I could only imagine that he was trying to come to terms with the fact that the woman he was planning to take to his bed might be the daughter of the man he'd looked up to as a father. That might put a different face on things, knowing his proclivities…

"This doesn't change anything, she's still mine."
"Alrighty then, at least if this is true we no longer have to worry about you killing her by accident." Ty can be such a shit.
"Okay, how the fuck are we gonna do this?" I wanted to keep shit moving.

"Easy, we get some hair and have a lab run the tests on both of them, then we talk to the mother and find out what the fuck was going on. I'm guessing no one in the town knows about this because those two don't have a clue. I can see where she gets her guts from though. Cord you have my blessing." Lo clapped him on the back and the big lug actually blushed.

"Damn the pussy whipped, bitch made list is getting longer by the day. Who's left now, just Dev, Quinn and me? You fuckers are sad, look at you. I'm buying bottled water from outta state."

We all just looked at him because he was so fucking delusional.

"You know what they say about the one who barks the loudest."

"Fuck you Con, that's never gonna be me. I'm footloose and fancy free, ain't no pussy gonna tie me down. And after seeing the way you four fucks have been led around by the nose here lately, no dice."

"Who's being led around by the nose asshole?"

"Con are you serious, you walk around behind Dani like a dog in heat, and Lo, Gaby has your nuts in her purse somewhere. Zak's always been part ass when it comes to Nessa, and don't get me started on this fucker here. He hasn't been able to tell his head from his ass in three days." He pointed at Cord, who looked like he was two steps away from ripping his head off. "Whipped, all a you." He walked away after sneering at us.

"Okay, I've had enough of his shit, I know we're on lockdown but is there anyway to get Victoria Lynn here?" It was time we brought that boy down a peg or two. "I like the way you think brother." Logan clapped me on the shoulder as we followed the pain in the ass back inside. At least his little diatribe had lightened the mood.

We were all looking at Davey a little different when we walked back in. If I know my brothers, we were all thinking the same thing. If they were the commander's he and his sister, they were ours now.

***

VANESSA

I have to talk to someone but who? I don't know the girls that well for all that we've been thrown together, and I wasn't sure I could trust any of the guys not to spill the beans before the time was right. I hadn't planned for this contingency, even when I was coming here it never entered my mind that it would come to this. That was stupid of me I now admit, but the call had come out of nowhere and it had never occurred to me to turn them down. No matter what had happened between Zak and I, the guys had always been kind to me, and if they needed a solid there was no reason not to.

Now I find myself in the worse possible situation ever, because not only was I stuck here now; but I wanted to be. Zak was always going to be Zak; I knew that now. I had a better understanding of why he was the way he was, because now I had that same over protective streak running through me.

When I think of all the time we'd lost because we'd both been too stubborn to listen I could cry. And now I stand to lose everything again. In a few hours I will know for sure one way or another. I could only hope that things turn out better than I expect, but I wasn't holding out much hope. Zak wasn't exactly the most forgiving type, and there was no guessing which way he'd go with this.

"Hey you okay?" Dani came and sat next to me in the window seat of Logan's home, where I was sitting gazing off at nothing. The guys had laid down the law so to speak, so we were pretty much under house arrest. "Yeah, just working out some things in my head." I had pretty much made up my mind that I wasn't going to tell anyone anything about my little problem. I'd just wait and see.

"How are you feeling?" I benched my own issues and turned to the other woman who was trying to hide the fact that she was scared about everything that was going on and not doing a very good job of it. No wonder Connor watched over her like a bear with a cub, it was cute to see, and gave me a little bit of hope for my own situation.

"I don't know. I'm excited and scared and happy all at once. I'm pregnant and unmarried and I can't leave my house because a bunch of crazy people, are out to get us apparently. Not to mention the fact that Connor has lost his mind and has a list a mile long of my dos and don'ts, mostly don'ts.

Other than that I'm peachy, but we were talking about you. Are you planning on sticking around?" I was wondering how long it was going to take before someone came right out and asked me that. Zak didn't count, besides he never asked, more like ordered.

"I don't know, I want to but…" I cut myself off before I said too much. It was only fair that Zak should be the first one to know, but boy was I dreading what was coming. With Zak things could go either way, he could be very understanding, or he could go off the rails completely. It was too late to turn back now though, I'd already set the ball in motion and in a few short hours my life was going to be changed forever. Hopefully it would be for the good.

I was almost tempted to call my mom and tell her not to come, but in the end I buckled down and let it be. Please just let it be okay.

***

DANI

"I think something's wrong with Vanessa." I'd left her in the window seat and headed back to the living room with the others. "What do you mean, is she sick?" Gaby stopped halfway to her seat. We were just sitting around cooling our heals since the men had pretty much forbidden us to do anything more than sit and look at the four walls. Connor was being even more of a tyrant than usual and I despaired of having a moment's peace for the next few months until the baby came. I've never seen such a strong man lose it over a pregnancy before in my life.

It's like we were transported back to the seventeenth century when conditions were tentative at best and the birth rate was a lot sketchier. As much as I tried convincing him that everything would work out fine, he wasn't having it. And now with this new development things were going to be a lot worst.

Now we were cooped up in the house under strict orders to stay put, with two relative strangers. I liked Vanessa, she seemed cool and she tried to protect Gaby and I from those goons the day before, which more than upped her in my estimation, but she seemed troubled somehow.

"No not sick, but there's definitely something." I took the cup of tea Gaby passed me and waited until she was seated. Susie as usual was just taking it all in. We knew her and her family from the town of course, but we'd never had occasion to hang out together, so we didn't really know that much about her. She seemed okay, even though I got the sense she thought Gaby and I were idiots for letting the men boss us around.

From what little Connor had let slip, if she was sniffing around Cord she was in for a rude awakening though, because apparently, he was worse than Connor or Logan, if you can imagine that one.

"I think she and Zak used to be an item once before and something went wrong, and now they've been thrown together again." Gaby folded her legs beneath her and took a sip of her tea after imparting that little tidbit. I could see where that might not be the easiest thing, especially since these men didn't seem to have much give in them.

"The two of them seemed to be getting along fine at breakfast; no there's something else going on." Whatever it was we weren't gonna figure it out by guessing so we moved on to talk of the wedding.

"I know one thing, Logan had better figure out how we're gonna get to the dress shop for our appointments in a couple days or there's gonna be hell to pay."
"Oh hush Gaby, you know darn well that you're not gonna step foot off this property if he says no; besides, we're in enough trouble as it is so don't you go getting any ideas."

"Shows how much you know. These men are crazy about babies haven't you noticed? Lo will let me get away with anything because I'm carrying his son. You should see him, totally gone."

Vanessa came back into the room just then and I wish I understood the look on her face. I'd noticed it when we were on the way to the hospital talking about babies; there was definitely something there. But as soon as it appeared, it went away.

"Yeah I know, Con's the same way, but that don't mean he won't go upside my head if I try a stunt like that again. So no more of your brilliant ideas."
"Really, I'm surprised at you two, letting these men run roughshod over you; and you call yourself southern belles." Gaby and I both looked at little Susie and burst out laughing.

"Girl we've seen you making eyes at Cord, if you think our guys are bad, from what I hear he's worse." She turned red as a cherry and didn't say anything more, which only made us laugh harder. The talk soon turned to the guys and who was the worse of the bunch when it came to being dictatorial.

Gaby, Vanessa and I were each convinced our guys were the worse, Susie, after she overcame her shyness, swore that her Cord as she puts it was a saint, an angel among men. Poor thing, bless her heart, she'd learn.

"Quinn." Vanessa said it out of the blue.

"What, no way." She just nodded her head as she sipped on her own cup of tea.

"Yep, I'm telling you. I've been around these guys in the heat of battle. Now don't get me wrong, they all have their shit that would make you wanna throat punch them every other second, but that one, he's got an extra something going on just beneath the good boy next door surface. And you know what they say; it's always the quiet ones. Now Cord, he's another breed of animal, I'm sorry Susie but you're gonna have your hands full there."

After that we pretty much degenerated into a free for all and I soon forgot all about Vanessa and her issues and even the fact that we were being held prisoner in our own homes.

At the end of the day I don't think any of us would have it any other way. I know I wouldn't change my position for anything in the world, not if it meant not having my Connor. It was strange that only a few short months ago I was the only female in this sea of testosterone and now I had three new sisters to help me deal.

I was actually pretty excited for all of us, even with the danger that played on the outskirts of our lives. Because I knew, that if these women found with the others what I had with Connor, what we were building here was going to be spectacular.

Chapter vii

ZAK

It felt like she'd been hiding from me all day. Every time I came within breathing distance she found somewhere else to be. I was getting pretty fucking tired of that shit and was looking for her to set her ass straight when I came up on her and Logan in some sort of secret meet, they were standing way too fucking close.

I stopped short and took it in, willing myself not to go off kilter, which is usually my first response. There was a strange vehicle parked just inside the gate, which I totally ignored because the scene looked all fucking wrong to me. Cool it Zak; fuck that.

"What the fuck are you doing?" I started moving again with purpose. Now rationally, I knew there was nothing going on. I knew that Lo would never poach on my shit, and since she didn't have a death wish she wouldn't play me false. But irrationally, I didn't like anyone that fucking close to her and they all knew it. So far everyone had respected my boundaries, but with the way she'd been acting and now this, it was a bit much.

They both turned and looked at me and I knew something was wrong. Lo started to walk towards me with a look on his face, and then he sent out the call for the others. It was this special whistle we all used when one of us needed the whole team on some shit. It was rare as fuck to hear it here though.

"What the fuck Lo, what's going on?" I looked at her, at the fear on her face and nothing was computing. I started to go to her but he got in my way and shit started going haywire in my chest. From their body language I knew some fuck was wrong, but I had no idea what. She wasn't bleeding, didn't look hurt, she didn't look anything but fuck scared.

Then I saw movement, like something was on her chest or some shit. What did she have there a pet? Swear to fuck I thought she had a pet monkey clinging to her. I started to turn back to Lo to ask him what the fuck, but she turned completely around to face me. It was a baby. She had a baby? I felt something inside me twist painfully and a roaring started in my head. She had a fucking kid with someone else? My life dimmed in and out and I went hot and cold before nausea set in. I could hear Lo speaking but couldn't make out the words. She fucking lied to me; that's the only thought I could hold onto at the moment.

When I could feel again, I moved towards her, to do what I don't know; all I knew was the rage the beat in my chest. I'd never laid hands on a woman before in my life, but in that moment I knew I could kill her.

There was blood in my eyes as I went for her, but then the kid picked its head up and looked dead at me. It was like getting hit in the chest with a brick. My world did a three sixty and my knees almost went out from under me. I looked from her and back at the kid who was staring at me, and back again.

"Who the fuck is that?" I pointed my finger at her accusingly. I knew who it was with just one look, but I couldn't quite bring myself to accept. I was looking into a replica of my face; only this one was attached to a mini female. I looked back at Vanessa in shock and disbelief. "You unconscionable bitch." Now I know I was gonna fucking kill her.

"Zak no." I heard Devon scream my name, heard running feet, but I didn't hear much else until hands were pulling at me. I struggled against them as they all rushed me. My world was all confusion in that moment. I couldn't see, hear, nor think.

My heart rate exceeded the norm and I went into shutdown. Total fucking combat mode. I was in enemy territory again at least that's where I went in my head. I think I had to, to protect my mind from utter darkness. "It's okay brother we've got you, stay down." I heard Lo's voice in my ear, close, too close.

"Look at me Zak, I said look at me." I looked at Lo and the others who looked worried as fuck. What was going on? I was fighting hard to hold onto reality. "That little girl is seeing you for the first time, who knows when she grows up what the fuck she will remember. Let her first memory of you be a good one brother, you owe her that." Little girl, I had a little girl. It all came rushing back.
"She's mine?" I knew the answer already, but I needed someone else to say it out loud so I'd know I wasn't losing my fucking mind.

"Yeah she's yours." I studied his face to make sure, Lo wouldn't lie to me, and the others were already nodding their heads too.

A million things went through me in that moment. Isn't it funny how your life can change so drastically from one minute to the next? My whole life I'd been taught to think on my feet, this was no different. I was already moving things around in my head, already making a place for my kid.

I heard the women come outside and go to Vanessa after Con made a phone call, but she no longer existed for me. I'ma strangle that bitch first chance I get. Yeah, that sounds about right; but first things first.

"You can let me go now, I'm not gonna do anything." He studied me for a good minute before nodding and standing back. I got up and dusted myself off and accepted the claps on the back from my brothers as I made my way towards them. The women were all standing together in a huddle, protecting mother and child. Vanessa looked scared as shit, as she should be. I wanted to wrap my hand around her neck and squeeze, but I showed none of what I was feeling outwardly. The others might catch on eventually, but for now I used all my training to keep my face blank and my body loose. I stopped in front of her but I didn't even see her, my eyes were for the pintsized version of me.

I reached out and took her, but Vanessa tried to stop me by hanging on tighter. "Let go Vanessa." It's all I said to her but it was my use of her name that had her letting go of our daughter in surprise. She knew I had to be pissed, I never called her by name otherwise, it was always Red, or Nessa. I took my baby girl and walked away with her calling my name and my brothers cautioning her to give me space. When I was a few feet away I stopped and without turning to look at her, asked her the only thing I wanted to know from her. "What's her name?"
"Zakira."

I buried my face in my daughter's hair as I walked on. She had my hair when it wasn't shaved down to the scalp. The same wild curls that went every which way, and my eyes, fuck she was all me. She looked up at me so trustingly with her wet eyes and my heart flew out of my chest and into the little hand she had curled against me. I picked up that hand and kissed it. "I love you Zakira."
I went into my house and locked the door.

Chapter viii

VANESSA

"You fucked up royally, I don't even know what to say to you and she isn't mine. You shoulda known he was gonna go ape shit." I was sitting in Logan and Gaby's kitchen trying to come to terms with the scene that had just unfolded outside.

Yes I had expected Zak to be pissed, but I hadn't expected the look of unbridled hatred in his eyes. I wasn't sure I would ever overcome that, and now he had my daughter, and had locked himself away in his house. I felt the disappointment from the men around me, even as Gaby, Dani and even little Susie hung close and tried to offer me comfort.

"I know you're all mad at me, but try to understand, I didn't do this to hurt him…" "This is a conversation you're gonna have to have with him. We're not gonna go against him on this and you know that. I don't know your reasons for doing what you did, but I do know my brother, and right now, you're fucked." My body jerked at his words. "Hey, there's no point in me sugar coating that shit. Just take a deep breath, accept that you were wrong, and know that he's not gonna be satisfied until he gets his pound of flesh."

"But that's not fair..."
"Nessa, you had his fucking kid and didn't tell him, do you not know who the fuck you're dealing with here?" Well when he put it like that, yeah, but still. I wasn't the one passing out ultimatums two years ago. I wasn't the one who was too pigheaded to give even an inch. I refused to cry in front of these men, men that I had served with, and gained their respect. "If he isn't back with her in one hour I'm going over there."

"Uh, I'm thinking that's a big fucking no-no." Tyler dropped down in the seat next to mine. "Listen, Lo gave you the harsh truth, now I'm gonna give you a little hope. The only way for you to get through this, is to keep your head down, do not give him any shit on this or he will eat you alive.

And I'm sorry to tell you, but you won't only be fighting him, that's just the way it is. It might not seem like it now, but you're one of us, you gave us our first niece and that means something, so we're gonna go to bat for you. Just don't do anything that would make it seem like you're going against him, or this bunch will be on your ass like a condor on carrion, the women included."

"Ty, you're not helping."
"I'm just trying to be honest Con, what the fuck?" My head was starting to hurt worse. How had I handled things so poorly? I had thought for sure that after the last few days and nights, after we'd reconnected, that he would've handled this better, I guess I was wrong. I kept seeing that look on his face, replaying the moment it took all six of his brothers to take him down, and now my little girl was with him. Not that I thought he would harm her, but he was so angry.

"This isn't right, whatever she did, that's her baby." Gaby wrapped her arm around one shoulder and Dani the next as they turned to look at their men. Both Logan and Connor sighed and rubbed their foreheads.

I wonder if any of them realized that over the years they'd picked up each other's mannerisms, or that they finished each other's thoughts. I could do with some of that camaraderie myself, but Ty was right, this bunch will stick together. And even though the girls were trying to be supportive of me right now, when it was all said and done they'd side with their men.

"There's no point in all of you getting your panties in a twist, because at the end of the day, Zak's the only one you have to watch out for, and in case you've all been under a rock for the last little while, that fucker's not the sanest motherfucker in the pack."

"Ty for fuck sake would you stop? We're trying to diffuse the situation not make it worse." Logan tried to cut him off but we all knew he was telling the truth. "Yeah, good luck with that. Nessa, if I were you, I'd let this shit play itself out, nothing you think will work is gonna. You're not dealing with the average Joe here and you know it. What you did is fucked no two ways about it, and trying to pretend any different isn't gonna help." He glared around the room at the others. I guess I didn't have to ask how he felt about the situation; I can only imagine that Zak felt ten times stronger about it.

I sat there with a hole in my heart and a weight in my gut as everyone threw around ideas of the best way to handle the situation. "I'm sorry I brought this here with all that's going on." Shit, I had all but forgotten that they were dealing with something here. "Are you kidding me, you were right to bring her here." Connor knelt next to my chair and patted my knee. "Look, shit's all over the place right now, you feel cornered and scared, that's understandable. But no one in this room wants to see anything happen but what's best for you and our niece. Just do like Lo and the jackass said, keep your head down, don't give him a reason, please don't give him a reason."

They all had their own little piece of advice, but I couldn't really take anything in. Two years ago Zak had given me an ultimatum that just wasn't doable for me at the time. He wanted me to opt out of signing up again, which I couldn't do. I had a plan you see, had it all mapped out, and wasn't about to change it because I'd fallen in love.

Maybe if he hadn't been so forceful about it. Back then I resented the way he thought he only had to say something to make it so. I wanted his respect as a marine, wanted him to see me as something more than a bedmate, which I knew now wasn't fair, he'd never treated me as anything less than his.

In the end I'd had to do what he'd wanted me too anyway, only it was for different reasons, and it was too late for us. Now my mind was full of what-ifs and all the ways I could've handled the situation. Only now when it was too late did it make sense to do things different, at the time it had seemed like I was making the right choice. Isn't it funny that now in the face of things it seems like the worse choice I could've made? I hate hindsight.

I bit my tongue to hold back the begging and the pleading. They were right, I needed to give him time, just not too much; my heart can't take it. I'd lost him once, and it looked like I might lose him again, but I couldn't bear to be separated from my baby, and I know Zak, if he gets mad enough, he'd go that route, and he had the connections and the resources to do it.

"Please don't let him take her away from me." The wall of silence was answer enough. If it came down to it, they were on his side. I closed my eyes and begged for strength as silent tears ran down my face.

The thing about it was, there was so much more. I could tell him the whole truth, but wouldn't that destroy him? I know him this he might get over, but there were some things a man like Zak could never live with. And if I tell him the truth about why I never got in touch with him back then, he'd lose it for sure. No better not ever let that secret out...

***

CORD

"You've got to do something." I knew she was going to follow me outside; that's why I did it. I was proud of her for holding her tongue in front of the others, not showing her displeasure or her fear, but I wanted her to come to me always. "This is not for you little Susie. There are things going on here that you know nothing about." I stayed away from her, okay like a few feet. But that was a lot considering I wanted to reach out and take her in my arms and...no Cord not yet, remember who you're dealing with.

Even before the suspicion that she might be the old man's daughter, I knew I had to take it slow. She was like a dainty little bird, one wrong move and I'd bruise her wing; I could never have that. "It doesn't matter, that's her baby, it's not right." She's so fucking young, and even with all that mouth of hers, so naïve in some ways. I'd seen the fear in her back there when my brothers were telling Vanessa how things really were.

For someone who wasn't accustomed to men like us, it could be a bit daunting. But I never wanted her to be afraid of me. "There is more than right and wrong in some situations baby, leave it alone, everything will be fine I promise."

She looked like she wanted to argue; in fact I was mildly surprised that she wasn't railing away at me in her usual way. Maybe she was catching on to the fact that when she did that, she was only putting herself in danger, that I was fighting everything in me not to take her too soon.

"This hurts you, I'm sorry." I didn't look at her, had been cautioning myself not to for the past few hours. I'd already started conditioning her to me, not sure if she knew it or not, then again how could she? I'm sure she was innocent of such things. The thought that she might not be had me reining it in. There was a way to tell these things without asking, and by my powers of deduction the feisty little nymph was as innocent as a newborn lamb. My cock started to thump the way it had been since the first day we met. I knew it wouldn't be long now before I had her under me, before I tamed her to my will.

I reached out for her arm and pulled her around in front of me. I felt her pulse race under my fingers. "There's only one thing you need to be thinking about now. In a few days I'm going to claim you. I'm going to take you to my bed and fuck you until I leave my scent in you. And this, all this, will be a distant memory."

She looked a little shell-shocked but I was sure I could knock that out no problem. "I've been dying to do this." I took her beautifully amazing face in my hands and lifted her mouth to mine for the barest of touches. I

t started out that way. I was just going to taste her because the wait was killing me. But the feel of her lips under mine was like a shock to the system.

"Fuck me you're sweet." I ran my tongue over her lips and she opened up like a baby bird to take my tip inside. I felt my body straining to hold back, not to go too fast too soon. "You make me tremble, no one else has ever made me feel this much this fast." I held her in place with a hand around her neck.

Not too hard, but not too light either. I was testing the waters to see how well she could handle what was to come soon. She relaxed under my touch and looked up at me in the moonlight.

"Give me your mouth again." She
didn't hesitate, just got up on her toes and
swept her lips over mine until I took over. I
let her feel the length and hardness of my
cock through her clothes, rubbing myself
against her over and over until I felt the give
in her.

"Go on back inside now before I take
you before it's time." She wasn't too steady
on her feet when she lifted her arms from
around my neck and stared up at me. "Go."
She turned and walked away and I bent at
the knees. "Fuck; please let me go easy."

***

CONNOR

I could feel the heat waves coming off
Dani and her new posse, but I was sure she
knew better by now than to come at me. I
was pissed as fuck and trying my best to
hold it in. Fuck yeah I agreed with my
brother. I'm the first to tell them when
they're wrong, but this shit is fucked up.

If Dani had done some shit like this to me, her ass would be on fire. I don't care what happened, and I'm a hundred percent sure it wasn't as bad as all that, because he's my brother and I just know, nothing justifies keeping his kid from him all this time.

She couldn't pick up the phone during the pregnancy, after the birth, who was there when my niece was born? She had a fuck load of time to come to her senses and I'm sure it was probably tearing Zak up right now thinking about all that.

Gaby had said her piece and Susie had just come back from following Cord outside no doubt giving him her thoughts on the subject, but if Dani opened her damn mouth about this shit I'll blast her. She must've seen the look on my face because she calmed the fuck down. I beckoned her over to me and when she reached me I pulled her in and with one hand on my child that was even now asleep in her womb, whispered in her ear.

"I don't want you getting upset, you get upset I'm gonna get pissed and that's gonna be it for you and your new playmates. We'll deal with Zak and work this shit out, you do not let your sisters talk you into shit."

I felt it was better safe than sorry when dealing with this bunch. Fucking Gaby was already looking like she was loaded for bear and I wasn't in the mood for anymore bullshit.

"Are we clear here?" She nodded her head and I looked down at her to be sure we were on the same page. I know my girl, she takes on other people's shit and though I didn't want Vanessa to feel out numbered I didn't want her thinking that what the fuck she had done was acceptable either. These women were a fucking handful as it is they didn't need to be getting any more ideas about how to fuck with our heads. Better they learn now the consequences of fucking with a man and his kids.

My mind switched to my brother and the shit he must be dealing with right now. We all knew what family and kids meant to each of us, what being there meant to us. Right now I'm pretty sure he was hurting and beating himself up for something that I was pretty sure wasn't his doing. I wasn't about to let that shit go on for too long, fuck that.

"Alright you lot let's go beard the lion in his den." I waited until Cord came back in from outside, doing who knows what the fuck, since he looked like he'd just gone a round or two. I didn't even wanna think about that fuckery.

Ty bypassed the rest of us out the door, muttering something about babies and some fuck else. I gave Dani one last look of warning over my shoulder before following the men into the night. When it's not one thing with these fuckers it's another I've known more peace in fucking Baghdad.

Chapter ix

ZAK

We sat watching each other for a good five minutes. She was studying me, and I was studying her, and wondering what the fuck? She couldn't talk yet but the baby sounds she made as she pointed at my face or patted my cheek were music to my ears. I'd already checked her over to make sure she was okay, that she had all her fingers and toes, and I wasn't sure what the fuck she was looking for, but she was looking me over pretty hard herself, and babbling away.

"I'm your daddy." Those words sounded foreign and I had to clear my throat after saying them. She patted my cheek and grinned with about six teeth showing. How the fuck do babies do that shit? I didn't even know her, but already she was everything. Just like her fuck of a mother; I'm not thinking about that female, not now, I just wanted to concentrate on my daughter. Shit, I needed shit, didn't babies need food and shit, and clothes she needed clothes.

I picked up the phone in a near panic just as there was a knock at the door. I approached it cautiously just as I heard the phone ringing outside. Cool, I'd been calling Quinn. I opened the door to find all six of them out there. They didn't even wait for an invite just all filed past me. "Hey don't hog the kid bro." Ty reached for the baby and I found that I didn't want to let her go. "Selfish fuck hand her over." He held her like a sack of potatoes and I snatched her back.

"That's not the way you hold a kid, and watch your damn mouth around her." Shit, how was I gonna pull this shit off? I didn't want my little girl growing up cussing up a storm, but being raised around this bunch, and I'd be fucked if she was gonna be raised anywhere else, there was a good chance she was gonna have a potty mouth.

"This is how you do it." I showed them how to hold her as they all stood around looking at me like I'd suddenly grown an extra head or some fuck.

"Okay Mr. Expert, hand her over." I let him take her but kept an eagle eye on his ass. No one was saying anything so I had a pretty good idea what was on their minds. I folded my arms and leaned back against the counter. "If you're here to plead her case you can all get the fuck out." I glared first at Logan and then Connor.

"Oh yeah that's gonna work. What say you calm the fuck down and we come at this shit like men? First off, only you and Vanessa know what went down between you two, and knowing you-you didn't make shit easy on her back then. Whatever happened, and whoever did shit to whom, the reality is there's a baby involved.

You two obviously still have feelings for each other since and pardon the intrusion, she's been in your bed since she got here." Logan as usual took point, but he wasn't telling me shit I didn't already know.

"We're here to make sure you're thinking of this thing rationally, and that you're not gonna make any hasty decisions. Whatever her reasoning, you need to at least hear her out, that's all we're asking." I waited to see if he or any of the others had anything else to say but got distracted by Ty for a hot minute; the fuck was he doing? I shook my head and ignored him as I turned back to Logan and the others.

" I hear everything you're saying but I don't give two fucks what happens to her, now if that's all the door's that way. Ty bring my fucking daughter back here." The idiot was heading out the door with my Zakira. Lo sighed long and hard but I was sure he knew it wasn't gonna be that easy. They changed tact and concentrated on the baby. Six grown men making faces and talking like idiots just to get a smile out of their niece.

They passed her around, each of them holding her like a bomb that was about to detonate. Quinn came over to me, "you were calling me before what's up?"
"I need to make a run, she needs stuff, like clothes and food and shit. I can't leave her here because I don't trust her fucking bitch of a mother…"

"Bro, watch what you say, don't let your anger make you say or do something that you'll regret later. She gave you a kid, whatever else happened or will happen; remember that. She could've thrown your kid away and you would've never known."
"I'd fucking strangle her with my bare hands." He had a point, but I wasn't in the mood to hear shit.

"Congratulations by the way, she's a beauty, my first niece. You beat Lo and Con in the baby pool."
"Shit I did, didn't I? Isn't she perfect? Look at how good she's being with her uncles." I

felt proud as fuck at the fact that my kid wasn't a screamer, that she was studying them as much as they were studying her, that's my kid. "Okay it's my turn again." Ty wrestled her away from Dev and the two of them grinned at each other. Just my luck my kid would choose him, after me of course.

"Damn bro we are so fucked, a girl? What am I supposed to do with a niece?" He looked at me the way we usually did him when he burped at Dani's dinner table, then he turned to Logan and Con.

"You two fucks better have boys, there ain't enough bullets in the county to deal with this shit." He went back to cooing at the baby who was about the only one who found his ass funny, if the way she was beaming at him was any indication. I'm pretty sure he got caught in one too many mortar attacks, or some fuck from his childhood totally warped him.

"So, what's the plan?" Logan watched me like a hawk. That fucker sees too much so I had to play it cool. The plan was to murder her bitch of a lying ass mother and bury her ass in the sand. Barring that I didn't know what the fuck, I hadn't thought that far ahead.

"The plan is I'm keeping my kid no matter what. Other than that I don't know and I don't care." At least that much was true, and even though they may not agree with the way I did things, I knew my brothers were behind me one hundred percent. That didn't mean they wouldn't try to talk me out of shit, but they would back my play when the time came.

"Okay, things are changing up around here at the speed of light. We have a young girl and boy to take care of, two pregnant women, and now a baby. This, my brothers, is the hardest fucking mission we've ever been on. We don't half step where security is concerned. We still have the whole weekend ahead of us so let's get ahead of the game. Zak we need you on this so you're gonna have to come to grips real soon brother, you can't lug the baby around with you."
"You wanna bet? She stays with me."

I knew we weren't planning on going out this weekend, that most of what we were doing was on the comps and going through the old man's files so she could stay with me. "I could work from here if needs be but she will not be out of my sight at any point from here on out until she's about twenty-fucking-five years old."

Right now it might be hard to tell whom she belonged to since Ty and Dev were busy fighting over her, but I was all clear in my head. As of a little more than an hour ago my mission in life changed. My only fucking purpose now was to secure and protect that little girl. Fuck everything else, especially the mission that was looming in the background with the desert Fox; fuck.

My kid started to fret so I took her from Dev, who had been in the middle of cooing at her. She stuffed her hand in her mouth and looked at her daddy all miserable and shit and I forgot everything else.

"What's wrong with her?" I looked at the others who were all stumped. I was tempted to call one of the females but I didn't trust their asses right now. "I think that means she needs changing." Quinn tried sniffing her. "Get the fuck away from her." I moved her out of the way. "Fuck is wrong with you?"

"Language." Lo studied her like he knew what the fuck he was talking about. When she started eating my shirt I think we all knew what was going on. "She's hungry, what the fuck am I supposed to feed her? I don't have anything in the house." I was about to go into total panic as my brothers threw around ideas.

"How about asking her mother?" I gave Con the death glare and headed for the fridge. I showed her an apple but she just kicked her legs and fussed even harder. Everything I showed her she turned away from until I was ready to pull my hair out at the roots.

"Hey, she came with a bag." Ty pulled his phone and made a call, and from his end I knew he was talking to the deceitful bitch who'd had my kid for over a year and didn't tell me. "Bad news bro, she's still on the tit. Only mother's milk. Apparently she eats that soft shit, but around this time it's you know…" He circled his chest with his face going red. Fuck this. They were all watching me like 'what the fuck are you gonna do now asshole?' "Everybody out." They looked at me like 'what the fuck' but I wasn't in the mood to trust anyone right now. I knew Lo and Con might be on my side, but their women could talk their asses into anything.

"What do you plan to do? You can't just let her cry herself out from hunger, and you don't have a tit full of milk." I glared at Lo because he thought his shit was funny. "Very funny, I'll take care of her thanks, now run along."

Ty stopped short like he wanted to argue but I pushed his ass out the door with the rest of them. What the fuck was I gonna do? I hadn't figured in this factor. I walked up and down with her thinking, until her screams grew louder.

"Okay baby, daddy will take care of it." I found a way to secure her while I ran next door. "I'll be back in two minutes I promise." Merciful fuck who could stand to see a kid cry? Her eyes were large pools of water that tugged at my heartstrings and broke my fucking heart in two.

My face and everything else changed as soon as I cleared the door and headed out into the night. The yard was already clear but knowing my family, they were already congregated together somewhere trying to decide my life for me. No one was getting any sleep tonight I was sure. I heard the din of voices coming from Lo's place and figured that's where she was. I opened the door and all eyes turned to me.

"You, come 'ere." I didn't wait for her answer, just turned and left the way I came. No one said anything but I knew they were all thinking plenty, nosy fucks. She followed behind me without uttering a sound, which was just as well because if she said the wrong thing right now with the mood I'm in I might snap.

I held the door open for her when we reached my place where I had sat my daughter on the floor surrounded by cushions until I got back. "Feed her and then get the fuck out." I didn't even look at her when I walked over to the baby and picked her up from the floor.

Her poor little face looked pitiful with tears and I promised myself that my kid was not gonna have too many reasons to cry in the future.

This one looked like she wanted to argue but one good glare soon had her getting her act together. She took the baby out of my arms and the only reason I let her was because I couldn't feed her my damn self. My plan was to keep her as far away from my kid as possible, just like she'd done to me. "Where the fuck are you going?" I'm trying not to curse in front of my little princess but these fuckers around here aren't making that shit easy. "I'm taking her into the bedroom to feed her."

"No, you can do it right here where I can see you. Like I'd trust your ass out of my sight with my kid." She got huffy and headed for the couch but who gave a fuck? I stood over her while she took her breast out and the baby latched on like she'd been starved.

My body reacted and pissed me the fuck off, which only made me want to be more of a dick to her. "How long before she doesn't need you for that anymore? Isn't she too old for that?" I did the math and my kid had to be fifteen months old give or take. "What was she eating when you were gone?"

"I expressed milk for her, that's why I kept telling you I had to leave, and no she's not too old. Mama breast fed me until I was two so I planned to do the same." Another nine months think again. Nine months, my mind went off the rails for a hot minute before I reined it back in.
"What do you mean, what's that express shit, is that good for her?" I didn't know shit about babies. She went on to explain about breast pumps and temperatures and my eye started to twitch so I held up my hand for quiet while my baby girl made gurgling

sounds like she'd been on a ten mile run and was finally getting some fluids. "Fine." She looked dejected and I knew she had a shitload on her mind that she wanted to say to me, but I was seriously contemplating knocking her head off her shoulders no joke.

Zakira wound down and the nipple popped out of her mouth and right into my view, making my dick do the one eyed salute. Fuck him; I'd rub one out before I go near her ass again.

"You can leave now." There was no intonation in my voice; the shit was dead, just like my feelings for her.
"I can't, what if she gets hungry again later? She usually has one more feeding in the middle of the night." She looked almost hopeful, like she thought shit was gonna be that easy.
"Do that express shit you mentioned earlier."
"I don't have the stuff." Uh-huh.

"Write a list." Everything she came at me with I had an answer for. I wasn't sure how I was supposed to go to the twenty-four hour Wal-Mart and take care of my kid at the same time, but I'll figure it out. I should send her ass, but I couldn't see sending my kid's mother out in danger, no matter how pissed she'd made me.

We didn't know if we were being watched or not, and I was sure the secret passage was still good since we'd blindfolded the assholes when we released them earlier so I'd use that. The only problem was what to do with little Zak until I got back because I sure as fuck wasn't gonna risk taking her out there.

I took her out of the incubator's hand and did that burping shit I'd seen people do after feeding a baby. "You can't keep me away from my daughter Zak, we've been apart for too long already, she needs…" "Are you fucking kidding me? You're gonna tell me what my kid needs when you kept her away from me all this time?

You had my kid out in the fucking world and I didn't even know she existed. I move across the globe, putting my life in danger to make the world a better place for other people's kids, and never knew that I had one of my own to safeguard, to protect. You can get the fuck outta my face now before this shit gets ugly." I didn't care about her slumped shoulders or the tears that were gathering in her eyes. She fucking gutted me. Only someone who had no fucking regard for me could've done something like this to me; fuck her.

How was it possible to hate and want someone at the same time? This whole thing was so confusing. I hadn't really had time to take it all in yet, to put things in their right perspective. All I knew right now is that I was a dad. I had a little life that was a part of me to take care of for the rest of my life.

That was going to be my main focus from here on out and everything and everyone else will just have to take a backseat. What the fuck I was gonna do with these feelings was another issue altogether. They'd only just been reawakened. I'd opened myself up to this shit, forgetting that she'd fucked with my insides once before, fucking female.

I inhaled my baby's innocent scent from her hair and felt some of my anger melt away. I'd forgotten to get the list from her incubator but that was okay, that's why we had the Internet. I held baby Zak on my lap while I booted up and surfed the web looking for what I needed to take care of her. I did some searches on single dads of newborns and toddlers and shit just to get some pointers and didn't feel too bad by the end of it.

There was a lot of shit that needed doing, but I didn't let the enormity of the situation get to me, I'm a SEAL for fuck sake, I can do this. I'll just pretend her mother no longer existed, tell myself I had to do it all myself, and go from there.

The baby babbled away at me and tried getting into shit on my desk. I sat in wonder, as she climbed all over me. I'd made her; she was mine. How fucking cool was that?

Even more than the anger I felt towards her mother, the love I felt for this little being was overwhelming. It didn't even matter that I'd only just met her for the first time a few short hours ago, the love was instantaneous and real. Life had a whole new meaning. Now it was more important than ever that we take care of whatever was going on in our backyard. My kid as well as the others that were on the way weren't gonna grow up in anything but peaceful surroundings. I'd fought for that shit for strangers; I could do no less for my own.

***

I thought long and hard about how to get the shit I needed and was hit by inspiration. Serve his ass right, kill two birds with one stone. It took some doing because I didn't want anyone else knowing what I was up to, but I got what I needed. She didn't even ask any questions, just said okay and see you in a few.

"See, daddy took care of everything." She was drooping and I found that I didn't want her to go to sleep just yet, I wanted her to stay up and grin at her old man and babble away some more.

I sat on the couch with the weight of her on my chest and fell more deeply in love. In less than a day she'd turned my whole world upside down and moved everything else out of the way. The road ahead might not be easy, but with the books I'd ordered and my brothers there to pitch in, I had no doubt I'd get it. All I had to do was survive the teen years and it was a go. Shit, that was a long fucking time away. What was life going to be like in the intervening years? Would I fuck up and turn her into a heartless bitch like her mother? Damn Zak, you're gonna have to get ahold of this anger.

She reacted to my mood and fussed a little, until I soothed her with a hand rubbing up and down her back as I hummed to her. I let my thoughts go and just enjoyed the feel of her and the newness of fatherhood. I dozed off myself and came awake with a start when I heard the others heading back. The fuck did they want now?

Chapter x

ZAK

She was out cold poor little mite, and
I put her on a comforter on the floor and
surrounded her with cushions and shit the
way I'd seen on the net. For the first time
since I first held her I breathed a little easy.
She was so tiny and helpless and so fucking
perfect. I rubbed my heart where a pain had
started. Please don't let me fuck this up. I
said the quick silent prayer before heading
to the kitchen where the others were filing
through the door. "Shh, keep it down, baby
Zak's asleep."

"You're not planning on calling her
that are you?" Cord shook his head as he
headed to the fridge for beer. Ty went into
the other room to look in on her like he
didn't trust me to know what I was doing.
"She can't sleep there, I think her mom has
stuff for her that her grandma brought
earlier."
"I don't want any of that shit in my house." I
could tell by all the eye rolling and
muttering going around that they didn't
agree with me but whatever. If it were any

one of them, Vanessa's lying ass would already be buried out back somewhere and we'd be coming up with a cover story.

Cord passed around the beers and I weighed the odds against how long she might stay down and how much one beer might impair me. When I caught them looking at me like they knew exactly what I was doing and found the shit funny, I gave them all the finger and took a sip.

"What do you fucks want now?" It didn't escape my notice that they were standing in formation like they were expecting some shit to jump off. "If you'll remember, you kicked us out when we were in the middle of a discussion." Lo quirked his brow at me.

I knew it was burning his ass that I'd done that, we weren't in the habit of dealing with each other like that, but shit was different this time. My little girl was involved and no one was taking her from me.

"There's really nothing to discuss and each of you know it, every last one of you would do the same. Lo, Con, you're about to become dads, tell me you would do this shit different." They relaxed a little, but there was still an underlying tension. Ty was rolling his eyes like he was being put upon. "The fuck's wrong with you now?" He looked at his watch, back into the room where the baby was sleeping peacefully and then back at me. "Nothing, when's she getting up? I got something to show her."

This… "Ty she's not on the clock, she's a baby you ass. Kids wake up when they're good and ready; and you're not waking her up."

Fucker was hopping from foot to foot like he was antsy about some shit. I turned back to the others. "Look I appreciate that this is a fucked up situation all around, but it wasn't my doing. Nothing I said to her back then could make her believe that this shit was okay, this was her fucking way of getting back at me."

Did she really hate me this fucking much? The fuck I care. Oh you care. Shut…the fuck…up.

"Is it, are you sure about that brother? Do you remember where we were two days after you two split? We went off the grid for four and a half months." Logan had a point but still, there were a million ways she could've got word to me, especially afterwards when we'd been back on domestic soil.

"I don't buy that shit, she had ample time, two fucking years and she doesn't say a word. That's part of me in there, the best fucking part and I wouldn't have known about her if you hadn't called that..."

"Hey!" They all got in my damn face. "Fine, had you not needed that she devil's help I wouldn't know I have a daughter. I don't care what any of you say, she was fucking wrong and I never did anything to her to deserve this shit. My fucking kid spent a whole fucking year on this earth without me there to look out for her." Each time I thought of it I wanted to wring her fucking neck 'til it popped the fuck off. So much could've happened to my little Zakira. The thought left me cold.

"Zak we agree, and we've told her so, but the fact remains we can't leave this shit like this indefinitely. We're dealing with who knows the fuck what from the outside. We can't have dissension among each other in here. Nessa can be a big help to us on this..." I'd like to punt her ass over the wall for being fuck stupid.
"She can do whatever the fuck she wants, just make sure she stays out of my sight and far the fuck away from me." I didn't let his long drawn out sigh or the shaking head

deter me. I'd fight every last one of these fuckers if it came to that.

"She's her mother Zak, you know how women are about these things. The situation is already strained as it is, I'm just saying that you need to keep a cool head and be rational."

"She's a mother, I'm a father; her rights do not outweigh mine I don't give a fuck what the world says. She had a year or more with her all to herself, let her deal with this shit now." We all heard the buzzer go off and switched gears. "Who the fuck?" Logan checked the monitor on his watch.

Someone was at the gate and from Lo's reaction when he checked I had a pretty good idea who it was. I'd all but forgotten the little surprise I'd organized for Ty, and though I wasn't in the mood for a good laugh at his expense any longer, I wouldn't mind a little light entertainment. Or something to take the focus off my ass for ten minutes. I checked on my baby and then followed the rest of them outside. Victoria Lynn pulled in and hopped down from the truck that was a mile too wide for her. She must've been a sight, sitting behind the wheel of that tank. She started offloading

baby stuff as Cord and Dev who were
closest moved forward to help.

"The fuck…what did you do bro?"
fucker was already sweating.
"Nothing, I needed baby clothes, you told
me to get baby clothes." No he didn't but he
was so twisted he won't remember who did
what. She made a point not to look at him or
acknowledge him in anyway, and just to
fuck with him I picked her up in a bear hug.
I looked at him over her head and he looked
like he was gonna take me out barehanded.
If I were three I would've poked my tongue
out at him.

I put her down again and it was very
telling the way she looked at him as she
fixed her clothes before moving away from
me. I hid my grin behind my hand and
pretended not to notice shit just like
everyone else was.
"Hi guys so we have a baby on board huh,
where is she?" She lugged bags into the
house while the rest of us followed with the
heavy stuff. "What do I owe you Vicki
Lynn?" She passed me the receipt and I
fished out my wallet and counted off some
bills to cover everything plus a little extra
for her time. "Oh no Zak that's too much."
She tried giving it back to me but I wouldn't
take it. When she tried to force it into my

hand Ty almost lost his shit. "He said he didn't want it." His eyes were glued to the spot where her hand touched mine. She sniffed at him and turned away.

At this point everyone had seemingly forgotten all about my drama for the moment and was totally focused on these two. She looked in on the baby and cooed and this ass got a pained look on his face. He could talk all the shit he wanted to, his eyes never left her. I walked over next to him and nudged him. "What're you waiting for brother?" I pointed my chin at her as she bustled around looking into the bags she'd just brought.

"Fuck bro I…" He broke off whatever it was he was going to say, and I felt almost bad for setting him up when he closed his eyes as if in pain. It's funny, but as pissed as I was at Vanessa, I wish to fuck that my brother, that all my brothers could feel at least once, that deep abiding love I'd once had for her. Then again if it was all gonna turn out like this maybe they were better off. He pulled himself together and just shook his head and took a swig of his now warm beer.

I heard the women coming and moved in front of the door. Gaby, Dani and even

Susie looked like they wanted to kick my ass. "What do you lot want?" My brothers might try to kick my ass for being less than polite to their women, but I wasn't in the mood to deal with their brand of fuckery.

"We're here to see the baby, in case you've forgotten, we never did get a chance to say hello." Gaby seems to be the designated mouthpiece. Good luck with that. "She's asleep, come back tomorrow and leave that one somewhere." I pointed at Vanessa before slamming the door in their faces. I don't give a fuck; let their men deal with their meddling asses.

"Fuck bro, you do not want to start a war with these women are you fuck stupid?" Lo looked like somebody had gut punched his ass. I'm beginning to think Ty was right about him and Con; they were almost unrecognizable.
"Damn, the pussy whipped battalion is at it again. I got your back Zak; don't listen to them. These women need to learn their place."
"Oh do tell Mr. Hotshot, and just where is that?" If this fucker runs from her I'll never let him live it down, and that looked like just what he was about to do.

Instead of tucking tail and hightailing it out of there though, he gave her a look that said plenty. There was enough heat behind that shit to roast a whole cornfield. I felt almost like a voyeur witnessing the shit. "Damn bro tone that shit down, there're other people here."

I looked at the others to see if they'd seen it as well and they had. Poor Vicki Lynn was trying to figure out what the fuck had hit her, but she regrouped fast enough.

"He is so gone." I whispered that shit to Quinn out the side of my mouth. "Didn't really believe it until just now. You think he knows?" why the fuck were we whispering?
"Yeah, but that fucker's gonna fight it tooth and nail." There was a lot of throat clearing after that and I was hoping the rest of them would get the hell out and go deal with their women, but no such luck, they wanted to talk. Vicki Lynn made a joke that she should spend the night so she could look after Zakira and I thought Ty would have a conniption.

"That's okay Vicki Lynn, I think you should stay with Dani and I for tonight." Everyone looked at Ty to see if that was acceptable and his shoulders relaxed a little even though he looked like he was chewing on nails.

She soon left thank fuck before he became postal, and they started their shit with me again. Thank fuck the baby woke up again and they got distracted. "I know we have to deal with shit, but I'd like to take some time to get to know my daughter. I'll do my part around here of course, that goes without saying, but what say we table any heavy conversations about me and the…me and her mother for another time."

"Hardheaded fuck." Lo pushed up from his chair.
"Or we could do it now and I could tell you to get her out of here before I snap and break her fucking neck, choose your pick." I went after my kid and left them to see themselves out. I was over the shit already. It had only been a few short hours, though it felt like a whole lifetime had passed, but it wasn't enough time for people to be hounding me like I had shit all worked out already.

"It's okay little darling, daddy's here." She was muddy so I set up the laptop near her new changing table, and went to YouTube. I followed the instructions to a T and pretty soon my baby girl was freshly powdered and smelling like a baby again.

Now all I had to do was figure out how to feed her and we were in business. I loved the weight of her on my arm, loved the way she already clung to her daddy like she needed me.

We stayed up and talked. Well I talked mostly she just babbled and nodded her head like she knew what the fuck I was saying, in between trying to eat her feet. "Daddy's gonna teach you how to shoot but we gotta wait until you're about six or so.

That way anybody fu…ahem, anybody messes with you and I'm not there, you can handle shit yourself." That sounded about right to me, and I'm sure the others would help me show her all the ways to protect herself. My chest burned with the thought of all the years that were to come and just what the hell we were gonna face.

As the hours wound down and I figured it was coming on time for bed, she wasn't looking like she was going anywhere anytime soon.

She kept worst fucking hours than a night watchman, what the fuck? It's not like she had a job to go to or some shit, but she had no regard for my feelings as she stayed up all night either cooing or fussing.

Around bum fuck o'clock she let up a howl that had me scrambling, this only after she'd dozed off for what seemed like two seconds. When nothing worked to get her to sleep I went knocking on Logan's door. The incubator was there waiting like she knew I was gonna come knocking. "She's hungry."

We went through the same routine as before, only this time I paid attention to more than her tit and my hard dick. Like the way she held the baby all loving like, or the way she smelled her hair. I especially noticed the way Zakira clung to her; the bond was hard to miss. Good, I hope her guts hurt tonight when I kick her ass out and she has to be without our daughter. Let her wonder how long I was gonna keep them apart, just like she'd done me.

I let her stay until the baby was asleep; I'm not stupid. Then I had her express milk with the new pump I'd had Vicki Lynn pick up. I didn't stay around for that shit; I gave her space.

But as soon as she was done and I had a few bottles lined up, I showed her to the door. I didn't give her a chance to say whatever the fuck she was opening her mouth to say to me, just held my hand up and closed the door.

No I didn't feel one ounce of remorse, there was no room for that shit next to my anger. I missed the fuck outta her when I crawled into my lonely king sized bed not long after though.

Instead of thinking back and trying to make sense out of why she'd done the things she had, I read through the books on babies. People had some fucked up ideas if you ask me, but hey, I'm no expert. I stayed up long after she'd finally gone down for good, worrying about how the fuck I was gonna make her world perfect. I knew one thing for sure, my kid was not gonna be raised by anyone else but me, and anyone who thought different were out of their fucking minds.

***

Shit, it felt like I'd just dropped off when I heard movement coming from her side of the room. I wasn't comfortable having her away from me, so I'd set her crib up in the corner of my room. "Ty what the fuck are you doing in my house so early, wait how did you get in here, did you break in?"

I had everything on lock so her damn mother couldn't get in. I didn't forget that she was a Marine and all the shit they'd taught her with their sneaky asses. I rubbed the sleep from my eyes as he lifted the baby from her new crib. "Did you wake her?"

"Uh-uh she was up." He was already going in for a smell of her hair.
"Lying ass she was up all night, I know she's tired and the book says if you interrupt their sleep it makes them cross."
"What book, she came with a manual?" he looked like he actually believed that shit. I just shook my head and left the bed.

The book I'd stayed up all night reading said she might be hungry and wet or dirty first thing so I needed to take care of that. She wasn't crying yet and Ty was telling her some shit about how to sight her gun, swear to fuck. She just cooed and laughed and gabbed away at him while he taught her to say his name.

I washed up real quick in the bathroom sink and went back in the room where he was telling my kid tall tales about shit he'd supposedly done. "Give her here, I have to change her diaper." He watched every move I made and questioned me up one side and down the next. "How'd you learn how to do that? Shit looks confusing."

"Seriously? You can build a bomb but you can't figure out how to put a kid's nappy on?" he just shrugged and took her away from me after I kissed her little head. I went and got the formula I'd bought and a bottle of her mother's milk just in case. As soon as the coast was clear I was kicking her lying ass out, so it was best I start weaning baby Zak off the tit now.

I would ask one of my sisters how to do it, but they weren't too happy with me so I was for self. There was a knock at the door before Lo pulled it open and stormed in, followed by Con, just as I was reading the instructions on the can of formula.

"What do you two want?" Ty scowled at them like he fucking lived here and pulled the baby closer to his chest as he came into the kitchen. They both ignored him and looked at me instead. "Bro, you've got to come to terms with this shit and fast." They made a beeline for their niece and started making kissing noises. Babies, like women, turn men into idiots. If I had my camera I'd YouTube this shit. I finally caught on to what he'd said since it felt like my body was moving but my mind was still playing catch up.

"Why what's wrong with you two?" Like I didn't know.

"Our women kept us up half the night complaining about your shit. Now I'm all for you standing up and all that, but not when it interferes with my shit if you know what I mean." Lo looked like he'd slept rough.

"What he means is that when a man grows accustomed to a certain reception from his woman, he doesn't like being thwarted by a fucking nonexistent headache on account of his brother is being an unreasonable asshole." Con covered the baby's ears as she nibbled on Ty while her formula was being heated.

"Damn bitch made one and two, it was only one night, grow a pair." Ty held Zakira protectively like he expected them to snatch her and give her back. At least I knew I had an ally.

"You stay out of it, you didn't have much to say last night when your little filly had you in her sights. You might not be pussy whipped...yet, but you're something. I think I see a yellow streak under his Collar Lo what you think?"

"You're lucky I got my niece in my arms or I'd kick your ass." I rolled my eyes at the three of them and got the bottle. "Give her here." I wonder what the fuck was wrong with Tyler; he was acting like he didn't want to give up the kid, domesticated fuck.

I sat and held her the way the book had said to. I stayed up all night reading that shit which was fine, since my baby girl fussed half the night. I think she might be teething, I'm not sure; I have to read some more. I refuse to believe that it's because she missed her mother. She has me now; she doesn't need anyone else. She wasn't too happy with the formula, she only drank a couple ounces, so I got her mother's milk under duress. I wasn't sure how she could tell the difference, but when she leaned back against me and played with her toes while sucking it down like a wino at a bar, I figured it was going to be a while before I could talk her outta this stuff.

Thank fuck Con and Lo switched gears and concentrated on the baby instead of trying to make my ass crazy. "Did you get her that food in a bottle stuff? I think her mom has some." I gave Con the death glare and he piped the fuck down. I'd already told them that I wanted nothing from the she wolf but they were still trying. "I had Vicki Lynn pick some up, but as soon as I can make a run I'll get the shit and make it myself. The book says fresh is best."

"What book, why do you keep saying that? I thought babies were like...you know, play it by ear, trial and error, that kinda thing."
"Ty what the fuck, were you raised by wolves?"
"Close enough."
I moved my kid closer to me and out of his way, because no joke, he had a serious attachment to her already. I could just see him teaching her all his bad habits, and next thing you know, no one would want to be around my kid either on account of she'd have his damn mouth. I think I might be too late though, because he started making faces and she grinned around her bottle and waved her limbs in the air.

The others came straggling in one by one and I got the distinct feeling from all the sighs of relief that they didn't trust me to make it through the night with my little girl. Disrespectful fucks. It wasn't long before my kitchen was full, and everybody seemed to have a damn attitude. Ty, the baby thief was waiting for her to suck the last dreg through the nipple before he was ready to take her from me.

"She needs a bath, it's going to be hot today. The book says a bath and powder." He just nodded and headed for my room and her stuff. "Who's cooking?" Dev pulled up a chair while I passed the baby to Lo so that I could go fill the tub with water. "What do you mean, isn't Gaby cooking?"

"Didn't you two tell him?" "Tell me what?" I came back out and left the water running after Quinn's statement. "The women are on strike, they're not doing shit until you talk to Vanessa and straighten this shit out." I need this shit first thing in the morning.

"What the fuck, can't you two control your women?" I shoulda known some shit like this was gonna go down. I took my daughter from Logan just in case he got any ideas and headed for the bathroom, with Ty hot on my heels, with what looked like a couple hundred different bottles of shit and rubber toys. He hovered like an old woman while I got her undressed. "I don't think you're supposed to do it like that."

"Do what like what Tyler? Look, how many kids do you have?"
"None asshole." He was huffy.
"Exactly, I have one, and this is how you're supposed to do it."
"You don't know shit bro. How is she supposed to sit in that big tub? She'll drown. Aren't you supposed to get her one of those plastic tub things that fit in the sink?"
"No you ass she's too big for that." He grumbled some shit under his breath that I was sure wasn't very flattering but I ignored his dumb ass.

He wanted to climb in with her but couldn't figure out how to do it without getting his clothes wet, and I'm pretty sure he knew I'd skin his ass if he dropped down to his skivvies in front of my little girl. In the end we both settled for kneeling next to the tub and keeping an eagle eye on her as she splashed away with her toys.

"Aren't you gonna tell me to make peace so you can have decent food again?" He gave it some thought, and for the first time since the baby came, he grew dead serious.

"No." That was all he said, but I could tell that he had more on his mind. "If it was me, I would react the same way, maybe worst. It doesn't matter what went down, as long as you weren't an abusive asshole, she had no right to keep your seed from you. I don't think you should shut her out forever, because that's just fucked, but I understand your need for some distance now. Just do me one favor, whatever decision you make, please put baby Zak first."

"Is that what you're doing brother?" "Yeah." He can be such a pain in the ass sometimes that it was hard to remember his beginnings and how hard they had been. I clapped him on his shoulder as he picked up the little pink washcloth to bathe my daughter. The moment was over almost as soon as it begun because he started his shit again.

"Dude, what the fuck kinda frou-frou shit is this?" He looked at the Disney character washcloth in distaste. "What? It's for girls." "She's a SEAL bro, get camouflage or some shit next time." This fucker is certifiable. "I better go through the clothes you bought, I bet it's more of this pansy ass shit." "What the fuck did you want me to buy, fatigues?"

He fought me to death about every
damn thing until I wanted to drown him in
the one foot of water in the tub. For
someone who had spent exactly four hours
in the presence of a baby, he sure was an
expert. "Ty, it says no tears, it's not gonna
hurt her." The ass actually tried to put some
of the shampoo in his eyes to check. "Give
me that jackass." I snatched the bottle from
him and lathered up her hair while he
grumped.

"You know those people lie just to
sell shit, fine if it hurts her though, we'll
sue." I wasn't even paying him any mind
because he'd obviously lost his. When her
bath was over he rifled through the bag of
stuff that I'd ordered on line and had Vicki
Lynn pick up. "See, I knew it, nothing but
girly shit." He settled on a pink and brown
set and fought me to dress her. I wasn't sure
what the fuck was up with him, but I was
gonna start taping this shit. When we'd
deemed her decent enough, and my poor kid
was looking like what the fuck daddy, we
headed back out to the kitchen where the
others for some reason were still gathered.
Davey had joined the crew and was already
munching away on an apple.

"What, they kicked you out too?"

"Nah, I left when they started the man bashing thing, I didn't think that was right." "Man bashing, who's man bashing?" He turned to look at Ty whose face was starting to look like a thundercloud.

"All of them, those women are mean. It's like they forgot I was in the room even, or they don't see me as a man." Poor kid, he looked hurt. "Don't sweat it kid, that bunch is part of the neutering party, they've already de-balled these fucks." Con smacked the shit out of Ty for that one, but the rest of us unattached men found that shit hilarious.

For some reason my place had become command central so with my kid strapped to my chest in her new sling, I sat around the kitchen table and got a rundown. Life hadn't stopped because mine had been derailed and shit still needed to be dealt with. We sent Davey on a trumped up errand that was sure to take thirty minutes or so, in order to discuss some things the he didn't need to know about. Hopefully the women would take it easy on him, unless they'd gone full rabid. Fucking females. "Wait did anyone remember to feed that chick in the cottage? It was my turn last night and I got distracted." Not that I was too busted up about it, but still.

"We let her go early this morning, this shit is bigger than her, or this town come to think of it. If they know we had her and they go after her, that's the price she pays for getting in bed with them in the first place. Cord where are we with the hair samples for the kids?"

Lo was at the stove trying to whip up something. I felt bad that it was because of me that we were back to gruel and grub, especially since we weren't sure if it was safe to go into town for a bite, but a man's gotta stick to his guns.

Cord passed him two separate envelopes. "I took that from them while they were asleep." Inside were two locks of hair. "Cool, now all we have to do is set something up so we know if we can trust the chief or not. My gut says yes and I always follow my gut, but we've got too much at stake now to take chances." He looked at little Zakira who was taking it all in from her place on my chest.

She seemed to have some weird fascination with her toes. I'm gonna have to read up on that shit because she kept pulling off her socks to get at them and stick them in her mouth.

"How do you plan on doing that?"

"Not sure yet, but we'll think of something. I'm hoping to find something in the commander's files that we can use, something that maybe only those two would know about."

This shit was getting more and more complicated. If I thought that it would be better for my daughter to be somewhere else, if I was sure I could send her somewhere safe, I would do it in a heartbeat, even if it meant giving her back to her mother. But with so many different variables at play, there was no way I was gonna make that move. I wouldn't even send Vanessa out there and I hated her guts.

"I got another call from the asshole last night, and no we still haven't been able to triangulate the calls."
"What, why didn't you tell me?"
"Because brother, it was your first night with your baby girl and there was nothing you could do. I'm telling you now." He put his phone on the table and pressed replay so that the tinny robotic voice came through for all to hear.

"Hello my friend, I see you've been busy. Too bad the little pigeons you netted weren't of any use to you, better luck next time. Oh by the way since you have decided not to adhere to our warning to stay out of our business, we have decided it's only fair to go ahead and expose your old commander for what he really was, and by so doing, discredit your whole team. All that hard work for nothing." There was a very sinister laugh at the end of it before the line went dead.

"Hold it, that 'hello my friend' where the fuck have we heard that before? That's not American speak."
"You're right, see, one more clue to add to the puzzle."
"Yeah but how much time do we have to put this puzzle together? I say we go back to the beginning and put everything together from scratch starting with when the men first came to us. Then we add in what we've found so far from the commander, factor in what Davey knows and see what we've got because so far, we ain't got shit."

Chapter xi

ZAK

The brainstorming begun, and we all threw around ideas. There was no immediate worry because we all recognized the call for what it was, a fishing expedition. On calls like that you listen out more for what's not being said than to what is. So far we knew that the men we'd released hadn't told them anything useful, more to the point, the one we were trying to turn hadn't spilled his guts.

That could mean also that the chief was on the up and up since he was our man inside and knew what we were up to, but Lo was right, with what was at stake we needed more than that.

"That phrase, 'my friend' that's middle eastern, most of them say it like that so that's no help, but who do we know or have had run-ins with in the past that would feel comfortable enough to call us like that? And that knows about our relationship with the commander?" My mind was still working thank fuck, I was afraid that I wouldn't be able to switch gears as easily as I used to, but that hadn't changed. I just had to compartmentalize shit in my head. I kissed my baby's hair because she was being so good and not complaining. Then again that could be because every so often one of her uncles would stop to tickle her or make faces at her.

Lo's oatmeal was sitting like a lump of cement in my gut so I knew it was only a matter of time before this bunch mutinied and turned on my ass. And the closer it got to lunchtime I was waiting for one of the greedy fucks to break.

Davey was back and adding his two cents along with the rest of us, and it was amazing how easily the kid held his own. It wouldn't surprise me at all if it turns out that he really is the commander's, but I guess we'll know one way or another in a couple of weeks at least.

We hadn't seen hide nor hair of the females but when the baby started rooting around on my chest I knew that shit was about to change. She'd made it pretty clear as shit that she did not care for the formula, but maybe I could sidetrack her with some strained peas, or one of the other equally repulsive fuckery they had for her to eat.

"Here Ty hold her." He was only too happy to snag her as I went to get her food.

Feeding time became a whole production with everyone pitching in with their ideas after I strapped her into her high chair. I blocked them all out and concentrated on my girl who seemed happy enough with her lunch thank fuck, and the storm that I had sensed brewing was delayed.

I was sure that I was gonna have to see her mother at some point though, before the day was over, if I wanted to keep my little girl happy. The price you pay to be a good dad.

When they started giving each other looks and then eyeing me down while Ty was playing airplane with her spoon, I knew what was coming. We'd pretty much came up with a plan of action and were now playing the waiting game, so it was back to Zak's intervention.

I waited to see which tact they were gonna take before losing my cool, because I was over the shit already. It had been less than twenty-four hours and already everyone was acting like I should have all the answers. I had a few but I was pretty sure

that none of those were the ones they
wanted.

"So, back to more immediate matters,
what have you decided to do about your
situation?" Lo sat forward in his seat with
his hands clasped between his knees. That's
his 'I'm a reasonable fucker until you fuck
with me' pose.

"I thought we had decided to give me
some time." I kept my tone even so that my
little girl didn't react. I'd noticed that
already her eyes flew to me when she heard
my voice, and according to my tone she'd
either smile or look a little bit unhappy.

"Yeah, but that was before the women
got involved. Now it's a fact that I don't
mind dressing Gabriella down when it's
warranted and you best believe that I will
nip this shit in the bud if it goes on for too
long, but you've got to understand. We've
put them under house arrest, put a crimp in
their wedding plans, which apparently is all
that's needed to turn the female of the
species into rabid dogs. On top of that shit,
we've got one of the nation's leading
families on the hook for some nefarious
dealings in our backyard, now is not the
time for you to go bat shit. Do you follow
me?"

"I don't see how any of this shit has anything to do with me and my kid. We're safe in here, we saw to that when we were building the place. We've dealt with more formidable opponents in the past and always came out on top.

The women need to learn that not everything is about them, and that sometimes one of their ilk is fucking wrong and I personally will not bow to their bullshit so I can eat a fucking home cooked meal. So if you're asking me to give in and forgive before I'm ready, the answer is no." My voice was still calm, and my girl was enjoying her game with her uncle Ty.

"Will you at least talk to her? Dani says you made her feel like a...what did she call it? Oh yeah, a nursing maid or handmaiden or some such shit. Said you had her feed the baby and then kicked her out. Don't forget two of your sisters are pregnant and their hormones are out of whack. Every little thing sets them off, and I guess seeing one of their own treated like that has flipped their switch or some shit." The fucker was reaching.

"You really want me to deal with her now? Fine, I'll deal with her, go get 'er." Dev's 'oh shit' wasn't soft enough, I still heard that shit. Lo wasn't looking too sure anymore, but since everyone wanted to back me into a corner, I'll show them how that shit feels.

I wasn't worried about the women and their shit, I knew they'd come around eventually, but Vanessa needed to learn a lesson. What she did was fucking wrong, not to mention irresponsible. She was a marine, she'd seen some of the same shit I had. On top of that she knows what kind of man I am; how could she claim she loved me and not know? So she had to know that keeping my kid from me was the wrong fucking move to make.

"Do you promise not to do anything stupid if I bring her here?"
"I promise not to kill her if that's what you're asking, but whatever I choose to do you lot will stay out of it. This is between me, and her."
"I don't know Zak you can be so fucking hard."
"That's the deal, take it or leave it. I'm not the one forcing the issue remember?"
"I trust him Lo let's go, he's not gonna break the code no matter how pissed he is right Zak." I just smirked at Con as they headed for the door. If only he knew. I'm a diabolical fucker when it comes to her; she

knows it even if they don't. We'll see how much she wants her daughter, we'll just see.

***

     I gave strict instructions that no one was to come anywhere near my home while this conversation was going on. They wanted to hang around but it was my way or no way at all. Ty, who seemed to be going through some sort of life change, was the last to leave.

     "If you two are going to be getting all loud and angry maybe I should take baby Zak." It was like the invasion of the pod people or some fuck. "Ty, get a grip what's with you bro, she's mine, she stays with me. We'll see you later I promise."

     "Fine, but if things get out of control call me and I'll come get her."
"Why don't you go spend some time with Vicki Lynn?" I knew that shit would light a fire under his ass and get him the hell out of my house. I'm gonna have to remember to take this shit out at a later date and have a good laugh over it. I'm not sure what the equivalent to baby whipped was, but

whatever it was he had it. She had him wrapped around her little finger already, which meant I was never gonna get rid of him.

I hate like fuck that they were forcing my hand so soon. If it were up to me, I'd make her ass sweat for at least a month. In fact, if we weren't dealing with the shit we were, I would've taken my kid off somewhere just the two of us already. I was trying to come to terms with my anger, to put the shit in perspective, but it wasn't gelling for me.

I couldn't wrap my mind around the way things had gone down. The one thing that I kept coming back to was why. Was it because she hated me that much, was she really the afraid of me, what?

Nothing in our past gave me any answers and I was left with a gut full of confusion, and more questions than answers. Only Vanessa knows why she'd done this shit and I wasn't sure if I was ready to believe her or listen to her reasons. I held the baby closer to my chest and rubbed my chin across her soft curls. One thing was for certain, no matter, what, she stays with me.

***

VANESSA

When Logan came back and told me that Zak was ready to talk, I wasn't sure if to be relieved or more worried. I was suddenly more afraid than I had been and nervous as hell. My whole life was about to be decided in the next few minutes and I slowed my pace as I made my way across the yard from Logan's place.

The girls had tried to build up my confidence, but I could tell that even they weren't too sure of the outcome. I couldn't read the men's faces since they were so hard to read, so there was no point in trying.

I tried to work out a strategy in the short time it took me to get from one place to the next but it was no use, my mind couldn't hold a thought. I tried to imagine a life without my daughter, or worst yet, a long drawn out court battle between her father and I with her in the middle.

The problem with that is that I kinda blamed myself for this. They were right, I'd had more than enough opportunities to tell him about the baby, so why hadn't I? That was the million dollar question, and the thing that Zak was gonna hang me with.

It wasn't fair though that I should lose them both again. I'd long conditioned myself to life without Zak, but at least I had Zakira to fill the void. Now if he had his way I wouldn't even have that. I know Zak I know how hard he can be when he wants to be. My heart felt sick and my pulse raced in fear the closer I got to his place. I knew one thing I wasn't giving up without a fight. And if it were at all possible, I would fight to keep them both.

*** *** ***

ZAK

I'd had a lot of time to think last night while I was reading and surfing the web for information. One of the things I kept going back to for some strange reason was the whole pregnancy thing. I watched other men loving on their wife's or significant other's rounded belly, and the envy welled up inside me.

Now I never gave much thought to such things before, shit never crossed my mind. But seeing it played out in front of me, I wanted it. It made no sense whatsoever since twenty-four hours ago it wouldn't have been on the top of my to-do list. But since I was already a father, one who had missed the whole deal, I felt cheated. That was just one more thing for me to lay at her feet.

Lo and Con were gonna get to enjoy their kids from beginning to end. Already I was privy to the secret looks and touches they shared with their women. I saw the way Dani and Gaby glowed whenever my brothers touched their tummies. No doubt it was all-good for the women, but I knew my brothers enjoyed that shit too. I had missed out on that. I held the baby closer as my heart broke a little at all that I had missed. I know some people might say that it didn't matter, that she wouldn't remember. But I'd seen those men speaking to their women's tummies and the book said the baby could actually hear in there. Mine should've been the first voice she heard. "I'm so sorry baby, sorry daddy wasn't there from the beginning. I promise I won't ever miss any more of your life."

I had to face some hard truths. One, did I want to deny my child her mother? The answer was no. I knew my anger is what was holding me back from even considering giving her a chance, my anger and my deep sense of betrayal.

She'd lain in my bed, let me cum inside her again, and never once let on that she'd had my child. Who does that? I knew it wasn't because of our past that she'd done this. So what I'd been possessive and over protective, it wasn't in an abusive stalkerish kind of way. I'd never given her reason to believe that she'd ever be anything but loved by me. Our only problem was her unwillingness to leave the service. I was terrified of something happening to her, and I'd been afraid from some of the stories I'd heard about her CO, that she might end up a statistic. There was more than one rumor going around about his way with his female subordinates, and I wasn't about to let that shit happen to her.

When I'd threatened to talk to him, she'd had a fit. Told me she could handle herself. That's when I'd given her that stupid ultimatum. I was pissed and frustrated because my hands were tied.

The navy doesn't look too kindly on it's men going after other officers whether they're from another faction or not, and especially not in the middle of battle. In the end we were two hotheaded people who didn't have any give in them. Had we been stateside I'm pretty sure I would've brought her little ass to heel, but that's not how that hand played out.

We'd parted on those terms but it had always been my intention to go get her when we came back. Then things had gone to shit. We'd been sent into the desert under deep cover for four and a half months, no way to contact anyone on the outside. Then not long after we came back to the mainland the commander had died, and things had been topsy-turvy again. In between building the compound we'd been sent out on mission after mission and by the time we came back here for good, we were barely settled before the shit down by the water took our focus.

I hadn't known what was going on in her life, hadn't even known she'd retired, but always in the back of my mind was the thought that one day I would go after her. It never once entered my mind that she might be with someone else. What we had had been so strong, that I just knew deep down inside, that just as there was no one else for me, there could never be anyone else for her. I never expected in a million years though, that she would've borne my child without telling me.

"Hey baby girl how you doing?" She grabbed my face and babbled away at me all the while stealing a little more of my heart. I watched through the living room window as her mother left Logan's place. I didn't want her seeing her and kicking up a fuss, so I had to move quickly. I was already working shit out in my head as I went. I was going to treat her like just another hostile I had to take down. She had me the man once; she fucked that up, now she could deal with Zak the SEAL.

The first thing I did was lock the door so she had to knock. She wasn't gonna just walk in like she was welcome or some shit. Next I got every toy that I'd bought the baby and put her in her crib with them before taking the monitor out to the living room with me. It was almost naptime anyway, so she should be fine. I was setting the scene, letting her know her place in our home, our being mine, and Zakira's. Mostly I just wanted her to see how it felt to be left out in the cold.

When the knock came I took my time getting to the door. I opened it up and stepped back without a word. She looked nervous as hell as she looked around for the baby. "Thanks for agreeing to see me Zak I…" I held up my hand before she could go any farther. One part of me wanted to hear her out, and another didn't give a fuck about what she had to say. "I didn't agree to see you to listen to your bullshit so save it. The only reason you're here is because you owe me and I intend to collect."

"Owe you, owe you how?"
"You might wanna tone down that fucking attitude or you can turn around and leave the way you came." I turned and headed for the living room leaving her to follow or leave, her choice. "Fine, I'm listening." Why is it that when it comes to kids women always think they have the only say? Is that what the fuck the world is like? A man's seed doesn't count for anything? I'd like to see any fuck grow without the seed, fuck that.

"You wanna know what you owe me, you owe me a fucking kid, a pregnancy, the whole fucking deal. That little girl in there was made from love. Whatever else followed I never touched you with anything less than that. Because of you I'll never trust another female again as long as I live, so that means if I want a son, he comes from you, the same place his sister came from. After that you can get the fuck away from me and my kids." Yeah, that shit sounded fucked up when I said it out loud, but she'd taken me there.

"Why would I agree to that, that's insane do you even hear yourself?" I guess her girls had filled her head with bullshit; she wasn't expecting me to be this hard. They probably thought if they put the screws to their men their men would in turn burn my ass. They had no idea what the fuck they were dealing with here, and apparently neither did she.

"You want to have anything to do with our daughter that's the way it's going to be. You robbed me of the whole experience, now we'll play do overs, that's the offer and the only one you're gonna get."

Her sadness almost made me fold, but I buckled down on that shit. Maybe if she'd told me when she first got here, like that first night when she slept under my roof, I would've heard her out. But she didn't, instead she laughed with me, fucked me, and kept her damn mouth shut. And I'd cum inside her more than once. What if I'd bred her again? I didn't like the way my body reacted to that thought. It didn't seem to care that she was a lying thieving bitch. Fucking traitor.

"Who was with you?" I didn't think I'd remember the questions since they'd all left my head with the anger, but they all came flooding back. "I'm sorry?"

"During your pregnancy, who was there to support you?"

"My mom mostly, some of my friends."

"How was it?"

"I don't understand." The book had talked about all the different stages and how different women dealt with different issues. "Were you sick a lot? Was she a healthy baby, what?"

I listened as she told me about battling morning sickness and being afraid of the delivery and all the other shit that women apparently went through. I kept my expression blank so that she had no idea that with each word she was digging her grave deeper. I should've been there.

And when she told me about some fellow marine doing the Lamaze classes with her and being there in the delivery room when my fucking kid was born I almost killed her right then and there. If I'd been contemplating taking it easy on her ass that shit sealed her fate.

The baby seemed to sense her and started fussing in the other room. She made a move to go towards her and I stopped her. "You wait here." I went into the room and got her, taking my time changing her diaper while she fussed and looked at me accusingly. Fucking females, they learn that shit from young.

"Don't give me that look you, I'm doing this for you." She gave me a look that swear to fuck looked like 'yeah right daddy' before putting her fist in her mouth and butting her head against my chest. Damn I love her so much already it's scary. So you can imagine how much her mother loves her. Fuck you and her damn mother.

I walked back into the living room where she was already preparing herself to feed Zakira. It was like I wasn't even there as she reached out for her. The two of them reached for each other and the baby latched onto her tit like it was her lifeline. I realized I was jealous as fuck.

This was something I couldn't give my kid, something that she seemed to desperately need. It pissed me the fuck off and I had to stifle my anger, even as I was drawn to the sight before me. I didn't look away this time, just stood there watching, taking it all in.

It was easily one of the most beautiful things I'd ever seen, but it only made me wonder what else I'd missed. I watched as she switched Zakira from one nipple to the next, and my mouth watered at the little bead of breast milk that was left behind. My dick, which had no sense whatsoever was already sniffing around for a hole to fill, he didn't give a fuck about me, or my hang-ups. I was so overtaken with what she was doing that I didn't stop her when she went to take the baby into the bedroom. I followed behind her like a lovesick puppy or some fuck, my anger fighting against my lust, and lust was kicking the fuck outta anger.

"I need your answer now." I wasn't gonna give her time to run back to her girls and let them fill her head with shit. This was between her and I plain and simple. She closed her eyes and I almost caved, almost, but not quite, at the defeated look on her face. I couldn't forget what she'd done, wouldn't let it go.

Her answer was a simple nod of her head and a blush. Thank fuck, I let out the breath I wasn't aware I'd been holding. "Don't ever do that breast feeding thing in front of anyone else, especially not another man." She looked a little taken aback but I wasn't about to give her any explanations. It was bad enough that I still cared, but the thought of any other man witnessing what I'd just seen was enough to cause me to commit murder.

Since my dick was already hard from watching her feed the baby and it felt like years instead of days since I'd had her, I was more than ready to get started. I made sure Zakira was really asleep in her crib, before taking her hand and leading her to my bed. She followed a bit tentatively at first but then I felt her relax. "One more question." This shit had been plaguing me since I'd first seen her feed the baby. "I sucked on your tits a couple days ago and I didn't taste anything, how are you feeding her?" just mentioning that shit made my dick ache. Fucking sap, I was still hot for her snatch even though I knew she was a conniving bitch.

"I dry up for a few days if I don't feed her for a while, but it comes back in if I go back to feeding her." I didn't understand any of that, but I left it alone. "So if I take you in my mouth right now there'll be milk?"

My hands were busy while I was talking, and my dick grew hard as a pike at the thought of getting my mouth on her. I tore her top off and she jerked in surprise. "You won't be needing this." If she only knew what I had planned for her she'd run screaming, but I wasn't planning on giving her the chance.

Her breasts held new meaning, now I knew why they seemed fuller. They were there for more than my pleasure. I played with her, teasing her tits but going nowhere hear her nipples. I wanted to bring her to fever pitch, wanted to make her crave me, the way I'd once craved her and had stupidly started to again.

I was no longer sure what I was madder at, the fact that she'd had Zakira without me, or that she'd been here for days and not said one fuck to me about being a father. It didn't matter right now though, she'd agreed to my terms and I was going to hold her to it.

"Touch me." Her hand came up and touched the fly of my jeans, tentatively at first until she grew brave. I slid the bra strap down her arm and bent my head to suck on her nipple. The rush of milk burst on my tongue and I almost pulled away in surprise.

The taste was surprisingly sweet, no wonder my little piglet liked it so much, I wouldn't want the can shit either if I were her. I sucked on her tit softly at first and then did what I'd seen Zakira do and went to town. I was afraid of hurting her, but my fingers playing through her pussy folds came away wet.

I got my cock out and into her hand. She didn't need any instructions as she fondled my balls with one hand while stroking my cock with the other just the way I liked, as I sucked the milk from her tits steadily, working back and forth from one to the other. She spread the pre-cum from my cockhead over the slit and down until her hand was moving smoothly up and down. I fingered her pussy with three big fingers stuffed deep inside until her pussy juice pooled in my hand.

I pulled my fingers out and fed them to her. "Suck." She almost inhaled my fingers as she jerked my cock even faster.

I laid her out on the bed, marveling that I could be so calm, so gentle, when there was a barely contained rage beating away inside me. I was torn between wanting to put my head between her thighs and feasting, or wetting my dick. My dick won that round. I eased her thighs open more and slid between them with my rod in hand. I let the head go on the hunt and he sniffed the pussy out on the first try.

I teased her by rubbing my pre-cum filled cockhead against her wet slit before lodging just the crown inside. "Beg." "What?" She was already fiending for my cock, her body moving on its own accord trying to suck me in. I held myself back until she gave me what I wanted, but she was hanging tough.

"I said beg." I sucked on her nipple and pressed down on her clit and that was all it took. "Please Zak, please." I wasn't sure if she was begging to be fucked or begging me not to make her beg, I didn't care. As soon as the words crossed her lips I fucked into her. Fucking ambrosia.

I had to grit my teeth to hold in the growl of pleasure. It didn't seem to matter that I was pissed at her, my body wanted her, but I wasn't happy about it. I didn't want to give her anything more of myself, but I was fucked if she was gonna keep herself back from me. I nibbled my way to her ear as I stroked into her nice and slow.

Her tits were leaking milk onto my chest, and I reminded myself to clean her up before we were done, but first. "I'm going to stay in your pussy all weekend. Thanks to your girls acting up, I've convinced the guys to give me the whole weekend to work our shit out. Only there's nothing to work out is there? You're gonna give me a son." I fucked into her hard and pulled milk from her tit onto my tongue before lifting my head to look down at her. "I'm going to fuck

one into you before the weekend's over."
She cried out and came on my cock. "Oh
yeah, you like that don't you, like the idea of
me breeding you, again.

I tried to detach myself, to not feel the
pull of her pussy, or the way my heart beat
rapidly at being this close to her again. I
refused to kiss her even though I knew how
much she likes that. Instead I licked the spilt
milk from her chest and sucked her tits until
I'd had my fill while her pussy tried to pull
the cum from my balls as she came a fuck
load on my cock. I could get used to the
taste of her, better leave some for my
daughter though.

Just for spite, I stopped moving and
glared down at her when her pussy stopped
quivering around my dick. "That was a
freebie, you don't need to enjoy this to give
me a kid." Her eyes opened wide and she
tried turning her face away. "Oh no you
don't, look at me." I waited until her eyes
were on mine and fucked my way to an
orgasm, making sure not to hit her spot or go
anywhere near her clit. I dripped every last
drop inside her before pulling out. "Don't
move." I found a sheet and tore it in strips.
When she saw me coming she tried rolling
off the bed. I grabbed her and pulled her

back, straddling her with my thighs, and holding her hands pinned to the bed.

"If you fight me, the deal's off. I will find a way to get you out of here safely and that would be the end of it." She held still but the look she gave me told me all I needed to know. "You mad? You can lay here and think about what the fuck you did." I tied her down and got off the bed, suddenly disgusted with the whole fucking situation.

"You can't leave me here tied to your bed Zachary."
"Until your ass is bred, that's exactly where the fuck you'll stay." So what I'd lost my fucking mind, people ought not to fuck with a SEAL, we've got ways and means. "And just in case you're thinking one of the others will come to your rescue, think again." I was planning on keeping everyone away from here for the weekend at least, after that we'd see.

She started to argue so I walked back over to the bed and stood over her. "Keep your voice down, I don't want my kid knowing about any of this shit." Her eyes were spitting fire but she had the good sense to keep her mouth shit. I didn't like the fact that seeing her tied up and spread out for my pleasure made my dick weep. I wanted this shit to be about planting my son in her and nothing more. I'm pretty sure Zakira had been made in love, and look where that shit got me, apparently it didn't matter.

"You look tired why don't you take a nap." I moved away again but she seemed like she was in the mood to argue. She really didn't get it. "You know you can't get away with this Zak, what do you hope to achieve? You can't keep me here forever." That's what she thinks.

"If you open your mouth to me again, I'll shove my dick in it, I don't wanna hear shit you have to say." I pulled the sheet up over her nakedness so my daughter won't see it if she woke up, and headed out of the room.

***

I went about my day same as usual with one ear pricked for my daughter's cries when she woke up. I'd bought one of those high-powered monitors that allowed me to leave the house and still hear her. I knew today we were gonna go through the last of the old man's papers and finish deciphering the code in the ledger. We still had a business to run and had no intentions on hiding out from these assholes. We just needed to make sure that the place was secure enough for the women and now my daughter.

Everything seemed to be coming at us all at once, and for men who were accustomed to getting answers, it was a pain in the ass to be playing the waiting game. We still didn't know who had told these guys that we were onto them, or that we had been the ones to move the money.

The Rosalind woman as well as Robert swore that they weren't the ones who'd talked, so that still left a dangling string. Try as we might we hadn't been able to come up with an answer to that question, short of the place being bugged which we knew wasn't possible.

Shit was taking long because we had to piece everything together. So far the best leads we had was whatever the commander had left for us, but that wasn't enough. We could go after the family there were ways to that, but with what? All we had were speculations, no real hard evidence. And as much as we were all convinced of their guilt, that wasn't enough to even get an arrest. For me, with my kid now caught in the middle, it was simple. Find out what they knew and whose strings they were pulling, and take the fuckers out.

"Where's Nessa?" Quinn met me halfway across the yard.
"She's taking a nap." I was going to be fielding that question a lot in the next few days. He gave me a disbelieving look but didn't take it any farther. "Where are the others?" I didn't see the guys, usually on a Saturday we'd be puttering around doing lazy day shit, but since this shit had started we hadn't had too many of those.

"We were waiting for you, we're running a drill just to be on the safe side. Con and Lo are trying to figure out how safe it is to let the girls go to work next week, they're gonna be running drills any minute. Cord and I are gonna do a scouting run to see if we're under some sort of surveillance and Ty and Dev are gonna go into town and see if anyone's talking. Apart from that our main concern is the baby and making sure she's safe here."

"What the fuck does that mean? She's not going anywhere." We'd reached the commander's place by then where the others were congregated. Lo looked up at my outburst.

"No one said she was hothead, we were just throwing around ideas, we have to make sure the women and the baby are safe here. We still don't know how these humps got onto us, and at this point it doesn't matter how, the fact is that they are. We're gonna do a run on Candy, she's the only one coming in from the outside, the only unknown except the kids and the humps were onto us before they came into the picture."

"I don't know Lo, I don't see Candy for this."
"Neither do the rest of us, but the fact remains, she's the only constant from the outside, and we all know there're ways of getting to someone without them knowing it. Someone could've slipped something in her bag, under her skin; there are any number of ways for someone to tag her without her knowing it. We've done it enough to know how it's done."

Shit, I hadn't thought of that, hadn't let myself think about the fact that we could be dealing with someone as high-tech as that. "We're not dealing with small time drug runs here are we brother?" He shook his head no as the others got restless. Just what the fuck was my kid caught in the middle of? "Okay what's the plan?"

"We're going over this whole place from top to bottom with a fine tooth comb. They have some way of knowing that we were making runs down by the water. We went over that place before we put our own eyes down there and there was nothing. Now they knew the commander was onto them, there's no reason to believe they knew the old man was gonna leave the place to us, but now we're here. Say they figure the old man had been keeping some kind of records or something, now here we are. They'll know that we'll find it eventually. I'm just guessing here, but we've got to start somewhere, I'm tired of these humps having the upper hand."

Chapter xii

ZAK

"I have some thoughts on that. I say we sweep the place yes, but so far we've been playing defense, what say we start playing offense for a change? None of us want to play hostage to these fucks, so far it seems like they've been calling the shots, but what have we really got to lose here? Let's secure the place, make sure there's no way for these fucks to breech and go full tilt after their asses. Because I don't know about the rest of you, but I'm not about to be playing hide and seek with these fucks. I'm not too thrilled about my kid being caught in the middle of this shit, not to mention the girls."

"You've got a point Zak and my mind was running that way, that's what we were discussing before you got here, but we're gonna need you one hundred percent on this brother, no distractions." I knew that shit was coming, and I understood his reasons for saying it. "I'm cool, the sooner we deal with this shit the better." I didn't let my mind go to the woman I had tied to my bed, or the fact that my shit was just beginning. "Glad to hear it. We heard back from the chief, he passed the test."

"Thank fuck, Cord told me what everyone was going to be doing what's my gig?" As if I didn't know.
"Follow the money. The account we pulled it from has a million layers but it's one of our only leads. See what else they had going on there if anything." My brothers got up to each go about his business and I felt a little better that everyone wasn't so focused on me anymore.

I checked the monitor to make sure the baby was still asleep. I'd remembered to turn it off while we were having our little talk, but now I had an idea. I booted up the secured computer and put in the numbers from the offshore account and started running a search with variations. "Can you hear me?"

I was pretty sure she could, but wasn't expecting her to answer. "I know you can. Are you thinking about what you did, how you robbed me of my seed? Are you worried about what I have in store for you? You should be."

I've been thinking, always thinking, and I knew it was going to be quite some time before I got over this mad. Maybe at some point in the future I'd move on and the sting wouldn't be so bad, but as of right now, that shit was all consuming. "I've decided that I like having you tied to my bed for my pleasure. I especially like the fact that I can do anything to you. I can exact my vengeance on you at my leisure. I've been thinking, why stop at one son, why not two?" I had to cut that shit out and get back to work when my own thoughts were starting to fuck with me.

I wasn't about to become a slave to her pussy, that's not what this was about. By the time I was through I was gonna make her crave me. My plan is to enslave her, mind, body and soul. I left the computer running and headed out when I heard my daughter starting to fuss over the monitor. Back in my bedroom I barely spared a glance for the naked woman in my bed as I changed Zakira's diaper. I knew she was gonna want to nurse soon, so I got her set up in her highchair first to feed her before she started fussing.

I had a bit of a dilemma on my hands now too. My dick was hard as fuck from just the thought of Vanessa's naked ass tied to my bed, but I wasn't about to fuck her with my kid in the room. I draw the line at that depraved shit. There was only one thing to do, I was gonna have to move the crib into the room next to mine. Since her mother was the only one I had been worried about breaking in and taking her it was safe. I cleaned her up and put one of her toys on the tray hoping it would keep her occupied while I moved her stuff.

With that shit out of the way I took the baby into the bedroom where I had her mother tied to the bed and put her on the tit after she started to fuss. Vanessa was looking at me the way we're taught to look at our captors in war. "That shit's not gonna work on me, I already know you remember, you're the woman who stole my fucking seed." I said the words soft so that the baby wouldn't hear. "Talk to our daughter so she knows you're okay." I wasn't sure if the baby would notice the difference, but I wasn't taking any chances. Then again my little piglet didn't seem interested in anything else but her milk.

Without thinking, my hand came up and started to knead the other tit. I was fascinated despite myself. I watched my little girl suckle until she fell asleep, and without giving it any thought, my head lowered to the untouched nipple and I took her into my mouth and pulled. I wrapped my arm around them both holding them in place as I fed on her. When her body shook in climax I came back to my senses.

Getting up from the bed I removed the baby and left the room. Holding her close I walked her into the other room. I had a moment of conscience when it hit me that I was doing this shit to her mother, but that shit didn't last long. I returned to the room where her tits were bare and still leaking and fell on her. There was no other word for it. I pushed my dick into her already wet pussy, latched onto her tit while kneading the other with my callused hand and started to fuck.

I liked the feel of her warm milk leaking all over my hand and was soon moving back and forth between nipples as I fucked into her uncontrollably. No matter how hard I tried it was no use, her pussy fucking sucked me in, and all the mattered was the pleasure. I hated it, hated the hold she had on me after all that she'd done and so I lashed out. "If I could destroy you without hurting her I would." It was a fucked up thing to say to her while I was inside her. She struggled beneath me but all it took was my teeth in her neck to bring her to heel.

I wrapped my hand around her neck and squeezed. "Where the fuck do you think you're going?" I fucked into her harder not giving any care to how deep I was going. One quick look showed there was no blood on my dick so she was fine. I went after her tits next, mauling them with my teeth as her milk sprouted all over the place like a fountain. I lapped that shit up as my cock grew even harder inside her. I felt her quickening around me as she cried out and moved on my dick. I was too far gone to remember that I didn't want her to take any pleasure from me.

She tried holding herself back but it was no use. Before I could stop it, she was cumming on my cock again. I bit into her nipple as I offloaded inside her. "If you're not bred in the next two days it'll be a miracle." I pulled out and pushed my fingers in her to push the cum deeper inside. "Have you resigned yourself to your plight as yet? Are you looking forward to being my handmaiden?" I left before she could answer me, because I really wasn't interested.

***

I took her three more times for the day, each time cumming deeper inside her, giving my seed a better chance to breed her. No matter how I tried not to give her any pleasure she still came on my cock. It was now the end of the night and the baby had just had her last feeding. The others had kept their word and stayed away from the house. I was hard and hurting like I hadn't had her a few short hours ago.

The situation for all that it was fucked made for some erotic visions in my head. That's why I'd hightailed it back here as soon as it was possible to call it a night. "It's time for your bath. I'm going to untie you; it's up to you if you behave or not, just be forewarned, I'm not in the mood for your shit." I untied her and lifted her after her limbs refused to cooperate. I'd started the bath running and since she was already naked, all I had to do was lift her into the water.

I'd climbed in first and lifted her in and sat her on my rod. "Umph." I swallowed the sound as my cock pierced her sore pussy. I figured the water would help ease the sting. I let her rest on my chest for a minute before taking her hips in hand and moving her up and down on my iron hard cock. Her pussy clung to me as she wept from exhaustion. I knew she had to be tired, each time I'd fucked her I'd drawn that shit out for as long as I could, not letting her cum until the very end when she was all but pleading with me to let her get off.

"Fuck me." I murmured the words in her ear and held still to see what she would do. She buried her face in my neck and I felt her body shake before she started riding my cock. She cried the whole time and my heart ached, but because I was beginning to soften towards her so soon, my ire was ignited and I grabbed her hair, pulling her head back. "Cut that shit out, it's only been one day. You deceived me for two fucking years."

"Please Zak, I can't bear anymore, I'm sorry." I shut my ears and my heart off from her words and since it was the only way I could think of to shut her the fuck up, I covered her mouth with mine. That's all it took for her to cum and cum hard, crying out in my mouth, which caused me to jet stream after stream of hot jizz up into her.

She fell like a limp rag against my chest and sap that I am, I bathed her and put her to bed. Tying her down but still lying beside her with my arm thrown around her middle. Offering her comfort because I couldn't help myself.

***

The next morning after the baby had been bathed and fed I took her outside for the first time because I was sure if I didn't Ty would come looking for her. He'd already been acting like he was going through withdrawals or some shit the night before when I wouldn't let him come see her. I wasn't ashamed of what I was doing I just didn't want anyone seeing Vanessa like that or even knowing of her humiliation, that was between us.

The women fell on the baby like she was the first one in creation. Ty was not happy that he had to share but Zakira made her choices known, she clung to me and refused to go to anyone else except Ty and that was only after he bribed her. "Where's Vanessa, how's she doing?" I looked at Gaby ready to snap her head off, but then I realized it was just an innocent question and one she had every right to ask.

"She's fine she was asleep when we left. Connor where are we on the run anything?" I changed the subject before any of the other nosy fucks could stick their noses in. "No we were gonna head on over there as soon as breakfast is over." I just nodded my head and took the baby back from Ty. "I'll meet you guys over there I already ate." I'd made breakfast for me, and Vanessa after I'd emptied myself in her again first thing this morning. I'd like to believe I was still working on my breeding program but I knew no man got that hard that often for a woman, unless there was some serious emotional attachment involved.

Zakira looked around at her new surroundings pointing to things and asking her daddy a million questions; at least I think that's what she was doing. Without the strain of whatever the fuck was going on between her mother and I weighing me down, it was fun and relaxing to be out and about with my daughter. I was really beginning to feel like a dad, enjoying the way she already seemed to trust me, the way she held onto me. I knew she could walk a little, I'd seen her toddling across the living room floor earlier when she was trying to get away from me when it was time to get dressed, cutest thing I'd ever seen.

We'd almost had a little mishap when she toddled towards the bedroom where her mother was tied up. I don't know why I thought it was different for her to see her that way when she was nursing, for some reason I had gotten it into my head that she didn't notice it then, but I didn't want her seeing her like that otherwise. Daddy did not want to be explaining that shit at some later time in life.

I set her down in the old man's office and closed the door so she couldn't pull a runner as I went to the computer. We had three hits on a variation of the account number. Could be nothing, could be something. "Whoa check this out." The others weren't too far behind me and came to look over my shoulder. "That's a lot of fucking money is it theirs?" Lo bit into an apple as his eyes scanned the screen and all the zeroes in each account.

"That's what I'm about to find out. No baby don't put that in your mouth." I didn't mean to scream at her but it came out that way. Her lip trembled and her eyes filled up with tears. "No-no-no baby." I was out the chair and kneeling on the floor in front of her with my arms around her. "I'm sorry baby daddy didn't mean to yell." She sobbed into my chest and clung to me while I looked around at the others for help.

Ty the fuck looked like he wanted to throat punch me, like I wasn't feeling bad enough about myself already. She sniffled and stopped but I felt like an asshole for a long time after. The others did everything they could to cheer her up after I sat with her on my lap and she was soon over it, but I was left with a hole in my gut. I found myself wanting to call her mother and ask if she'd ever had to deal with this shit and how she did it.

"Cheer up bro, that's the first of many." Connor clapped me on the shoulder as he ran his hand over the baby's hair. "I hope the fuck not." That shit was heart breaking. I could see it now, she was gonna run circles around my ass. I found myself wanting her mother to be there to see that too and squashed the thought. What the fuck was wrong with me today anyway? From the moment I woke up, my mind has been on this one track. Like something unseen was forcing me to look deeper.

I'd awakened with the scent of her in my nose and a raging need to be inside her. I was halfway into fucking when I realized the I wasn't thinking about breeding her, my only interest was in the pleasure that I derived from her body. Maybe it was the way her body answered mine without hesitation, or the way she just gave in without a fight.

Yes she was tied down to my bed, but there were other ways for her to fight me and she hadn't. It looks like she had found a way to defeat me after all; her compliance shamed me. Still I couldn't give in that easily, it was my stupid pride I know, but I just couldn't let go that easily. She'd wronged me, even she admitted it, so why should I feel guilty for wanting to exact vengeance?

***

VANESSA

I think Zak might be wearing down, at least I hope he is. I know he thinks that this is what he wants, but I've had a lot of time to think while I've been lying here for the last day and a half, and I know that in the end it will only destroy him. I know this because I know that already he loves our little girl, and I know him. One day he's gonna look back at this and hate himself.

I wanted to hate him for it, wanted to fight him every step of the way, but I realized that that wasn't the way. The truth is that we were both to blame, maybe me more than him, but we both played a part. And when it was all said and done, I still loved him, and if I could say that after the last few days well then. But I had to find a way to get through to him before his hate consumed him. Our little girl needed her daddy and I needed him, if he'll have me.

This morning I had felt the difference in his touch. He'd caught himself eventually, but for those first few minutes he'd been my old Zak. He was still in there somewhere. As long as I knew that, there was hope. I hoped he did get me pregnant, it would mean being here with him a little longer. I was desperate enough to settle for even that. I just had to find a way to get him to trust me enough to untie me. I'm sure he knew he couldn't keep me here like this for much longer, that it was just his hurt and anger fueling this behavior, but Zak danced to the beat of his own drum and he'd give it the old college try until something else came along.

I grew tired from the heat and my limbs hurt a little from inaction, I should probably tell him, but I was afraid that my complaining might send him off on another one of his rants. The last thing I wanted to remind him of was how long I'd kept his daughter away from him. I fell asleep with his name on my lips and an apology in my heart. Poor Zak, it looks like every time I come into his life all I do is destroy it in some way.

Chapter xiii

ZAK

She was asleep when I finally made it
back. It pissed me off that I'd spent the
whole time I was away thinking about her
here waiting for me. It seemed whether I
wanted it or not her pussy had a hold on me.
I didn't want to think about her, didn't want
to second-guess myself about what the fuck
I was doing. But as time went on I found
myself questioning my actions. When it got
to be too much, I made my excuses and
came back because I couldn't fucking stay
away, and I hated her even more for it.

The baby had taken a bottle of
formula for the first time, but I couldn't
even find any comfort in that. The book said
her mother's milk is what was best for her,
and I wanted only the best for my little
angel. I'd put her down for her nap, using
that as my excuse for coming back here so
soon. We were finally getting somewhere.
The string I'd tugged on had started
unraveling and so far we'd found four other
accounts. Quinn was busy moving cash
around right now, which I was sure was

going to anger these fucks and make them come after us.

We'd already done all the we could to ensure that the place was safe, and like I'd said it was time we went on the offensive. Taking their money was only the first strike, if we kept hitting at them, in time we'd expose the fucks hopefully. With the amount of money we'd moved today there was no doubt they were gonna feel that shit, it was left to be seen what form of action they were gonna take in retaliation.

Lo had already contacted the chief with our new findings and for the first time we'd shared the name of the family with him, something he said the old man had not gotten around to sharing with him, but something he claimed not to be too surprised about. He'd made some of the same accusations the old man had made in his files, about this shit going back to Vietnam.

We'd run as far as we could on that for today, and now it was time to switch gears again for the next few hours before we had to get back to work. I stood looking down at her, at all that beauty that had once belonged to me, that still fucking belonged to me. She had circles under her eyes and there were tear tracks running down her cheeks. Her breasts, my new fascination, rose and fell beneath the sheet and my dick flexed and grew with the memory of the pleasure to be had from them. She was a little sticky from before but I wanted her nice and clean for what I had in mind. I'm not fond of tasting my own jizz.

I got a wet cloth and cleaned her up while she came slowly awake. Her eyes flew to mine, as I unzipped and shed my pants. She looked away from me but I didn't care. I wasn't interested in her enjoyment, even though I knew she would. Instead of climbing between her legs and fucking my way to orgasm like I'd planned, I decided to fuck with her.

She wanted to pretend she didn't enjoy my touch, we'll just see about that shit. I knew what she expected, knew what she needed to feed her hate and justification, but there was no justification for what she'd done.

I laid flat on the bed between her thighs. Her eyes flew down to where I was. "What are you doing? No Zak." I licked her first, one deep long stroke with my tongue, ignoring her pleas. I know why she was doing that shit, she wanted to pretend she didn't feel, wanted to keep this part of herself away from me. Too bad for her I wasn't about to let that shit happen. I worked one finger into her, then two, as I went after her clit.

She juiced up real nice even though I could feel her trying to tense up to hold off her orgasm. When it hit her, I let her ride it out on my tongue, before climbing up over her with my dick hanging over her mouth. "Open." She gave me a look that would peel paint and refused to budge. That was fine by me I wasn't interested in her making it too easy for me anyway.

"I said open your fucking mouth." She flinched at my harsh tone but I still had to squeeze her jaw to get her to obey. As soon as her mouth opened a little I forced the tip of my cock inside. "You bite me, you'll be the first woman in history to choke on a dick."

That got her attention, and I teased my cockhead across her lips, painting them with pre-cum. Pretty soon I was fucking her face until the shit was running down the sides of her face. When she started making choking sounds I pulled out, got between her legs and fucked into her. "Don't do this Zak please it's not what you want."

"Shut the fuck up." I was pissed that she was right. Why couldn't she let me enjoy my mad? Why did she have to make me fucking feel when I didn't want to? "Move with me." I both hated and reveled in her compliance. Her pussy pulled at me milking me like she was enjoying what I was doing to her. "Untie me Zak, I want to hold you." Seriously, what the fuck was she trying to do to me? what game was she playing now?

I lifted up and away so that I could look into her eyes and what I saw there almost weakened me. I closed my eyes against the emotion. No, don't fall for that shit she'd only gut you again, she's fucking poison. She moved her body like she wanted me, like she wanted this, fucking with my head. "I want you to cum inside me Zak, give me your son."

"Fuck-fuck-fuck." I came in a never-ending stream of hot thick cum deep in her belly. My body jerked with the force of the climax that took everything out of me. I flopped down beside her with an arm over my eyes. "Don't try to play me Vanessa, it won't work this time. I've fallen for your lies for the last time."

"It's not lies Zak, I love you."
"You have a fucked up way of showing it." I rolled out of bed because she was getting to me.

***

I had to get back but she stayed on my mind. Before this shit had transpired, I'd been well on my way to reclaiming her. I'd pushed aside a whole lot of shit from our past, came to terms with most, and now I felt like we were back to square one. The others weren't back as yet, so I pulled the baby book I'd brought with me and started to read. I went to the section about nursing and was glad I did, because I learned something. Although a nursing mother could get pregnant, it was much easier to breed her if she wasn't breastfeeding the baby.

How can I get Zakira off the tit without harming her? Okay Zak you've lost your mind now. I had to bring myself back from my thoughts because that was fucked even for me. I wasn't as angry anymore, not like I had been yesterday and that was strange. I thought for sure I'd stay mad at her ass for a lifetime, but Ty was right, and so were the others. She'd given me a kid, she could've done so much differently, and one of the things she could've done different was not have my kid.

She'd had her when she wasn't sure that she'd ever see me again. She'd given up a career, one that I knew she felt strongly about, so she could have my kid. Even after giving birth she could've signed up again, women do it all the time. But she'd chosen to stay home and raise my child. I didn't even know what she was doing for a living but that was easily rectified. I had the means at my fingertips to find out all I needed to know about her.

**

Two hours later I sat in stunned silence. "What the fuck have you done Zak?" I flew out of the chair and left the mansion. I fled past my brothers who were on their way back. "Where's the fire dude?" I ignored Dev as I heard Lo telling them to stand down. No doubt the rest of them thought I was going to do her bodily harm.

I hit the door running and didn't even stop to check on the baby but went straight to her. She was asleep again, no doubt tired from my overuse of her body. I felt like scum, like the lowest form of life. I untied her arms gently and tried to work some life back into them by massaging them. "Zak?" Her voice was a drowsy whisper that tore at my heart. What have I don't to you baby?

I finished untying her as she came fully awake. I knew from the look of fear in her eyes that she thought I was sending her away. "No Zak…"

"Shh." I pulled her into my arms with my heart racing out of my chest. "I'm sorry, I'm so sorry why didn't you tell me?" She was a little confused at first until I explained. "You almost died, why the fuck didn't you tell me that shit?"

"I don't understand how do you know about that?"
"Does it matter? You were in an enemy camp for three months and you don't say shit about that to me why?"
"I didn't want you to blame yourself." Her words cut into me like sharp knives, making me feel worse.

"You didn't…are you fucking insane?" For the second time that day I found myself yelling at someone I loved without meaning to. "You let me do this shit to you after what you'd been through?" I felt the bile rise in my throat, I must've given her fucking nightmares and she never said a fucking word because she didn't want to make me feel bad.

"The report said you weren't hurt, tell me the truth, did he touch you?" I would tear the fucking Middle East to shreds to find the fuck if he had. As it stands, there's nothing that can prevent me going after the bastard and cutting his heart out.

"No. He wanted to I think, but when he discovered I was pregnant he was pissed. The girl that was watching over me, her English wasn't that good, but I gathered that his plan was to get word back to you that he'd raped me and gotten me with child. After he found out I was already pregnant the plan changed. He was going to kill me and the baby and send that news to you instead."

My body went cold with self-hate. What kind of animal was I? How could I have done such a thing? I let her go and slid off the bed. "I'll let you go as soon as it's safe for you and the baby to leave. Please if it's possible forgive me. All I ask is that you tell her about me." I turned to leave the room my heart at my fucking feet. If I could kick my ass I would do it in a heartbeat. I've never despised anyone as much as I did myself in that moment.

I stopped short when I felt her little arms come around my waist. "Please don't make me leave Zak, we belong here with you."

"How can you say that after what the fuck I did? You should hate my guts, how can you not? I do." I needed to get away from her, needed to go somewhere and lick my wounds. She was offering me paradise but I didn't deserve it. I'd taken something so beautiful so precious and destroyed it, and after all she'd endured.

"I don't want you to stay here, you deserve a lot better than me." I tried pulling away from her but she held on tight. I closed my eyes in despair at all that I was going to lose once again, and all because of my own doing. As long as I live I'll never forget what I'd done to her. "Don't make me have your baby on my own again Zak, it was so hard last time. Besides, you don't want some other man raising your kids do you?"

I pulled her around and jacked her up before I could stop myself. "You see? Look at me I can't help myself. Even knowing what you endured because of me I was about to choke the shit out of you for mere words." "First of all, what happened was not because of you, it was because of one madman's obsession. And I like it when you get crazy."

She kissed me. Actually got up on her toes and kissed my lips. I pulled her in tighter not trusting that this was real, that she was willing to forgive me.

I held onto her the way I'd always wanted to, like I would never let her go. "Can I have you?" I needed to touch her with care. Needed to show her what she meant to me without the anger and animosity between us. She was the one who took my hand and led me to the bed. She was the one who laid back and spread her legs, drawing me down to her. "Just come inside me Zak, I want to feel you." I wanted to give her so much more.

I made my way down her body and nuzzled her between her thighs, licking the crease before letting my tongue play between her folds. Her taste was sweet on my tongue as I sent my tongue deeper while my nose pressed into her slick clit. She started to move as I tongue fucked her, trying to draw her essence out greedily. I made love to her pussy the way I used to in the beginning, when there was nothing but love between us. Her fingers in my hair led me on, to eat her deeper as my fingers dug into her ass, holding her in place.

When she came on my tongue and her pussy juice ran down my chin, I slid up her body and entered her softly.
It was by far the most sensuous experience of my life. The way she clasped me to her, the way her body opened and accepted mine. There were no hurried movements, just soft touches and fires rekindled. "I've never loved anything as much as I love you, never will Red, my Red." We moved together, slowly at first, until it got to be too much and I couldn't hold back. "Cum with me baby." I teased her ass as I fucked into her, bringing her to the edge. When she started to tighten around me I went for her tit, sucking the milk that was getting ready to spout into my mouth.

The taste of her sweet milk ramped up my lust and our sweet loving soon turned into a hard fuck that left her screaming and gushing around my dick, her pussy milked my cock pretty much the same way my mouth was pulling on her tit. I slammed into her cervix and released a volley of seed inside her until I went blind, deaf and dumb. "That's the one. I just bred you for sure." We were both breathing uncontrollably as I kept moving inside her, never wanting it to end. I slipped out of her when she'd sucked the last bit of sperm from my cock.

Our daughter chose that moment to wake up in the next room and I watched as my woman went to get our child. She came back into the room and sat on the bed to feed the baby while I watched. I couldn't resist leaning over and taking her other tit into my mouth and sucking. I had sense enough to leave some for the baby, though I could've stayed there all night.

"I'll be right back baby, there's something I need to take care of. I love you." I kissed her over the baby's head before I left my two girls in the safety of our home and sent out a call to my brothers. I had held the rage in check, but it was loose now. I'll have to deal with my own fuck up another time, right now I wanted the blood of the fucker who'd taken her on my hands.

They met me in the middle of the yard between our houses. "Do you know where she was the first few months of her pregnancy?" I didn't give them any lead up, just jumped right into the story. The shit that I'd read was still churning in my gut looking for an escape. I wanted to rage and fuck something up, but there was nothing but my own ass for being so fucking stupid. Why hadn't I checked up on her? Why had I let her walk away that day? My own fucked up pride had almost cost me everything.

"Desert Fox had her, he fucking took her convoy, killed everyone and took her back to his fucking camp in the desert."

"What the fuck are you saying, that's got to be the same time we were running him to ground."

"Yes it is, he took her because of me." And that shit burned a hole in my gut.

"How did he know about that?"

"Fuck if I know, but that motherfucker is mine." I turned to walk away, my mind already on what moves I had to make to get to the desert. I know someone had to tip him off, how else would he know that she was mine?

None of that mattered now though, all that mattered was wiping this fuck off the face of the earth. If he'd raped her... I stopped to gag on my own bile as my brothers came after me.

"Zak, wait a minute. You're not going after him alone use your damn head brother. We have the mission coming up let's wait on command. On top of that you've got a woman and a kid to take care of now, and the way shit is going around here, I won't be surprised if there's another one on the way. Because I'm sure you two haven't been watching movies in your damn house for the past few days. Let's secure this place, get

this shit squared away that we're dealing
with here, and then we go into the desert."

He was right, I couldn't go traipsing
off to the desert now with danger at our
door, I had to stay here and protect them, it
was all that mattered now.
"I'll think about waiting but whenever we
go, he's mine to take out understood?" They
all agreed before asking me what I knew
about her capture. I repeated everything I'd
read in the sealed report and what she'd told
me herself. It hurt like a son of a bitch that
she'd been in my enemy's hands and I
hadn't known, hadn't been there to protect
her. And then I'd fucking tied her to my bed
to do the same thing he'd planned to do.

I'll spend the rest of my life making
that shit up to her, as for him. A cold rage
crept into my soul, one day soon I was going
to face this fucker, I don't know how, but I
was going to make that shit happen. And
when I do, I'm going to cut his fucking head
off for putting his hands on what's mine. I
went back home to them and found them in
the tub together splashing and laughing. I
stood in the doorway watching them with a
lump in my throat until she looked up and
saw me. It was hard to believe that the smile
that broke out across her face was for me.
"Look sweetie, daddy's home."

"Da-da." Fuck me.

Chapter xiv

TYLER

"Where is she?" Everyone was gathered at the kitchen table at Zak's place, everyone but Victoria Lynn. I knew without being told that she wasn't in the house, I always know. "She had to head back into town, something about work." I hid my disappointment by taking my niece from her mother's arms and burying my face in her tummy to blow raspberries. That giggle was fast becoming my favorite sound in the world. I sat down as the food was being passed around and hated the fact that my appetite was almost gone.

I knew it was because she wasn't here. I'd grown accustomed to having her near these last few days, even though I made a point of ignoring her. Lately though, I've been wondering if maybe I could take a chance. Being around the baby had kind of softened me up a little, given me ideas of what could be if I only let go enough. There were other things to take into consideration though, like the fact that she made me feel deeply, which was a dangerous thing for her.

What if I caved and somewhere down the line she decided she wasn't ready for forever? No I couldn't take the chance. It was best if I stuck to one -night stands and short- lived flings.

Victoria Lynn wasn't made for that she was the happily ever after type. But what if she gets tired of waiting for you and marry someone else? Zakira seemed attuned to my inner turmoil and her little arms came around my neck and she kissed my cheek before resting her head on my chest.

I closed my eyes and just enjoyed the innocent love. When I opened them again my whole family was watching. The damn women had tears in their eyes. "What the fuck?" My brothers were all shaking their heads at me with stupid looks on their faces. "You are toast brother."
"Shut the fuck up Zak." That just made them all laugh even louder as I left the house with baby Zak on my hip.

***

ZAK

I stroked the last of my seed into her before pulling out and flipping us over. Our hearts beat like drums in our chests as we tried to calm down. I used my fingers to plug her up and keep my seed from flowing back out of her. We tongued each other's mouths swapping spit. It felt good to lie with her like this, with no animosity between us. "I'm sorry I hurt you baby." I've been saying the same thing to her for the past couple of days and will say it for as long as it takes to get this feeling off my heart.

In the past two days I've done everything I could to make it up to her. I'd braved the outside to go get her a ring so she could show off with her sisters, only now Lo and Con were mad at me because their women had reinforcements with their wedding shit. I was willing to do anything I had to to make her happy, and if that meant getting them to and from their dress fittings, I'd Shanghai Ty and Cord into going with me as security.

It fucked with me that I'd put her through that shit, and probably will for the rest of my life, but she was right, denying my daughter a father, or her a husband wasn't the answer. Instead I spent the moments that I wasn't ensuring their safety making sure she knew how much she was loved.

"How soon before we can find out if he's in there?" I ran my hand over her tummy and my dick thumped against her thigh. It didn't matter if I'd planted one in her already or not; trying was half the fun. "There're tests that can tell right now, do you wanna get one of those?" I rolled her over onto her back and slipped back into her. Always, talk of breeding her always got me going. "We'll go later."

We fucked for the better part of the night, reaffirming the bond that we'd almost lost. "I love you Red, more than fucking words can say. I'm sorry I made it hard for you, never again." She tried soothing me but it was no use. I'll always feel the sting of not being there for Zakira's beginning. That little piece of me will always be missing, but I had so much more to look forward to. I tried not to dwell on what could've happened to her when she was in the clutches of a madman, only fueling my hate for him with each day that passed for what he tried to do to my family.

I'd already started hunting that fucker, regardless of what Lo said. If command didn't come through soon I was going after that fuck on my own. "Da-da-da." Shit, my little con artist had figured out that she could get anything out of me by calling my name and she's been milking it for the past few days. Her mother had gotten over her pique that my name was the first the baby had called and not hers, even though she'd been the one to raise her for the first year of her life.

Ty the ass spent every waking moment trying to get her to say his name with no luck. "Daddy's coming princess." I kissed my woman and rolled out of bed to go get my other girl.

THE END

***

You may find the author here

https://www.facebook.com/MrsJordan Silver

My author page

http://www.amazon.com/- /e/B00C65VXJY